RAVELLING

RAVELLING

Estelle Birdy

THE LILLIPUT PRESS
DUBLIN

First published 2024 by
THE LILLIPUT PRESS

62–63 Sitric Road, Arbour Hill
Dublin 7, Ireland
www.lilliputpress.ie

Paperback ISBN 978 184351 8648

Quotation from 'You Tell Us What to Do' by Faiz Ahmed Faiz,
translated by Agha Shahid Ali, from the collection *The Rebel's
Silhouette*, 1991, by permission of University of Massachusetts Press.

10 9 8 7 6 5 4 3 2 1

The Lilliput Press gratefully acknowledges the financial support of the
Arts Council/An Chomhairle Ealaíon.

Set in 11pt on 14pt Minion Pro by Compuscript
Printed in Sweden by ScandBook

For Dublin and her Dubs, including my own lovely four.

Autumn

1
DEANO

Normal funeral. All guilt and umbrellas. Lashing, bit cold for early September.

Deano lanks against the church wall, waiting. Gives the chin to the women sharing brollies just inside the railings. Sadie from the flats shop, with the big orange head on her, Rita from the dry-cleaners, groomed within an inch of her life, Doreen from the Tenters Residents Association, who has managed, for once, to leave that weepy-eyed bichon frise out of her arms. The mental trio turns at the sight of Hamza and Benit coming through the gate to line up beside Deano. Bout time.

A string of frayed yellow-and-white bunting – some novena or saint's bones tour – flaps over their heads, dripping massive raindrops that roll down the back of Deano's still-peeling neck. Stings like fuck. There's no point in him even trying that tanning craic: the freckles are never gonna join up. The aul ones mutter to each other, looking over at himself and the lads. Hamza, rubbing that full black beard of his, grins and mumbles something about Allah in the women's direction. Benit digs his hands deep into his jeans and whispers:

– If you go full Allahu Akbar on them like that time on the bus, I'm leaving, yeah? Why we standing in the rain? Let's go in.

– Nah, we'll wait out here for the boys. And those aul ones will be more worried about you than me, gangsta-man.

– Yeah, did you have to wear that do-rag, Benit? Deano says.

– Yeah I did have to wear the do-rag, Benit says, hopping from one foot to the other. Black. For the funeral. Gotta keep the hair right, fam. It's raining like. 'Mon, can we not go in?

– Nah, just stay here. See them aul ones? They know the story. You stand outside till other people come.

– It's Baltic. There's people inside already. I can see them.

– Fuck's sake Benit would you ever quit whinging? Deano says. Boys said meet outside. They're on their way.

– But it's raining, fam!

– Sherrup faggot, Hamza says, and Deano smiles just a little.

The aul ones hear that alright. Muttering, shaking their heads and gathering closer, their backs and umbrellas forming a shield.

– There were loads at my grandad's funeral, Benit says. Pouring out the door they were. Had to get speakers put up outside. Mobbed, cos of his anti-drugs stuff, back in the day.

– Your famous white grandad, Hamza says. No one's coming to this one at all. Jack's just another dead junkie. He was trying, you know? Coming to mosque and all.

– Like the mosque was what Jack needed, Deano says.

– People were helping him like. He came on a hike up the mountains with us. Those aul ones are just here for the gossip. Probably didn't even know him.

– Come on, leave them be, Benit says. Look, here's the boys now.

4

Down the street, Oisín – blond and tanned – is chatting away with roundy Karlo, fish-belly white and always smiling. Even today.

– Sup, Benit says.

– Alright?

– Going full Kendrick with the do-rag, Benit? Oisín says.

– Am a real nigga, not a wannabe.

– Would you ever quit, Benit? Oisín says, looking over at the women.

– Nigga's gonna speak if a nigga's gonna speak. See you're doing your bit to raise the bar there, as usual, Karl. Nice.

– Yeah, d'yeh like it, Benit? I've me Givinchy under the jacket, Karl says. Bitta respect for the man in the box, know what I mean? See me new Louboutins?

He turns his feet from side to side, showing off the rubbery spikes on the tops of his shoes.

– Yeah, the homeless lad'll appreciate you wearing a five-hundred-quid top to his funeral, Oisín says.

Hamza frowns.

– You really spend five hundred quid on that top, man? Seriously?

– Nah, only three. Sale price.

– You're working in Penneys, and you're spending everything you get on fucking labels?

– Yeah, and I look fresh, Karl says, flipping up his collar.

– In fairness, he does. Respect, Benit says, fist-bumping Karl.

The rain eases a bit, as two black limos glide up to the gates. The huddle perks up. Rita and Sadie suddenly look all mournful, blessing themselves like they're on the telly. Sadie drops her chins to her chest but keeps her eyes fixed on the limos. Everyone's getting edgy before the driver of the first one gets out and opens the back door. One stick-thin, black-stockinged leg comes out, then another.

– Those are some heels, Oisín says.

The driver offers his arm and a leather-gloved hand grabs it. It's not that cold like. A big black hat with a veil appears. Straightening herself as the driver holds an umbrella over her, the woman lifts the veil. Fly shades. She pops a foot-long cigarette holder into her mouth and waggles it up and down between scarlet lips. The driver, looking confused, pats his pockets.

– Fucking hell, boys, Karl whispers. This is the best.

– His mam, is it? Benit says.

– Nah, Sandra's his mam, says Oisín. The big one. Lives down the road.

– No, Hamza says. Sandra's his foster mum.

– Who else would it be in anyway? Has to be his ma, says Karl, patting himself.

Jaze, he loves that jacket.

– Can we've a bitta respect for Jack, boys? That's why we're here, Deano says.

He heads over to the limo, pulls out the Zippo June got him for the birthday, and lights the woman's smoke. Check her out.

– You his mam? he asks.

– I am, yes, she says, smiling broadly.

Those lips look like they could explode any second and she's fooling no one with that fake posh accent. Yeh can't trust a Dub who doesn't wanna be a Dub, as Deano's da used to say.

All the flats know about Jack's real mam. The parties in the flat with the kids left out on the green, nothing but a Formica table and a soaking armchair for shelter. The batterings, the social workers and the constant garda visits. This yoke with the fancy hat didn't even have the excuse of being a junkie like Deano's ma.

Jack told them his ma didn't have a pot to piss in over there in Birmingham. That's why she could never help him out or give him a place to stay off the street, he said.

So who the fuck was paying for all of this gear?

A young one gets out of the second car, pulling at the bottom of her black elasticky dress. No hat, about their age, nice pair of tits, serious arse, ironed scarlet hair. She looks over at the lads and the waterworks start. Jack's mam teeters away, puts her arm around her. The young one shrugs her off. The aul one hisses something into the girl's ear, then spits onto a wad of kitchen towel, fished out of the sequinned handbag dangling from her wrist, and makes to scrub the girl's face. She lashes out, slapping the woman's hand away.

– Me make-up, Mam!

She looks the business, this girl. Orange, obviously. Tarantula eyelashes, and her face is a bit patchy after the kitchen towel and spit. But still.

Deano strolls back to the lads, glowering.

– Not to be trusted, he says out of the corner of his mouth. The aul one especially. The younger one but …

– Sister? Karl asks.

– Come on, boys, let's go in, Hamza says, smirking at Benit. Why we standing out here? Sure it's lashing.

*

Inside, the guest of honour is already there, lying in a wicker coffin on a trolley near the altar. There's a table with a framed photo of Jack, smiling and looking a lot fuller in the face than Deano remembers. A wreath of blood-red roses lies at the foot of the trolley.

The old priest had notions, was dead proud of the fact that he got some Polish artist who did gruesome paintings of life under the commies to do the stations of the cross that line the walls. One of the green electric candles that light the paintings is flickering on and off, making Jesus falling for the third time look like a scene from *Insidious*.

– Fuck, they've Jack like a basket a chips in Zaytoon, Deano whispers into Oisín's ear. There'll be marks and all on his neck, don't wanna see that. Go up near the middle there.

– The coffin's not open, for fuck's sake, Deano.

– I'm going up the front, Hamza says.

– That's for family, Deano says.

– We *are* his family, Hamza says.

– There's Sandra up there at the front, and the pair outside, Deano says. They're family. We're going middle.

– I'm not sitting beside no feds, fam, Benit says.

Community Garda Gerry and Sergeant Dwyer are staring into their laps, arms folded. Gerry's all about building bridges. Dwyer's a traditionalist, thinks a few digs out the back of Kevin Street is all these young fellas need. They're already being given a wide berth by the rest of the small crowd: a few scrubbed-up homeless lads from around Camden Street, a clatter of women from the flats, and Sadie & Co.

Garda Gerry has been popping up round every bleedin corner, over the past few weeks, with his Mullingar chuck-lehead, talking like a turkey, trying to have the craic. He's an embarrassment.

– Ah yeah, hadn't seen them, definitely go further up than *them*, Deano says, pushing past the others to lead them up to a pew a few rows behind Sandra and her younger foster kids.

Hamza turns to grin at the guards, who stare back, stony-faced.

– There's always guards at funerals, Deano says.

Hamza laughs.

– No there's not, you mad rat. Just the funerals *you* go to.

Right enough, there'd been swarms of guards at Deano's da's funeral. Along with most of the flats. Shot in the street in front of Deano. They'd been walking home from hurling. His da wasn't even caught up in anything.

The click of heels on the tiled floor and the noisy sniffling draws everyone's attention to the mother and daughter, as they

8

carry in a plastic-flowered 'SON' wreath. The mother plops it on top of the roses. Pressing it down with the pointed toe of her shoe for good measure. Loadsa flapping and sighing and the pair take their seats in the first pew, across from Sandra and the kids.

The undertaker, a lanky grey man, silently appears at the end of the lads' pew, crouching down beside Deano.

– Excuse me, are you friends or family?

– Neither, says Hamza, leaning across.

– We're friends, Deano says, digging Hamza in the ribs.

– The family, Marian and Candy, have asked us to ask you young men to help carry the coffin after the service.

– No problem, mate, Deano says. Give us a shout when you need us.

– Candy? Hamza says, when the undertaker's out of ear-shot. Fucking Candy?

The priest starts proceedings.

– One of yours Benit, Hamza says, biting his lip. Can't understand a word he's saying.

– Says the Paki. Sounds Nigerian, not one of ours, fam.

The priest raises his voice a bit and pulls the microphone closer, as the sniffling from the first pew turns to sobbing.

– I had the privilege of meeting Jack on several occasions in recent times. He was a young man with a big heart. But life took its toll, as for so many, and he was no longer able to cope. This is a time to pull closer …

The wailing grows louder, bouncing off the walls, drowning out the poor priest. Sadie's crowd sit taller in their seats, lamenting not having come further up the church, probably. Outta nowhere, at the front, Candy's up out of her seat.

– Don't leave me, Jack!

She lashes herself over the coffin, sobbing.

– What the fuck? Karl says, under his breath.

The priest pauses for a second, takes a couple of steps forward, thinks better of it, and retreats back to his mic. He's mumbling something about the community of God but no one's listening now. All eyes on the girl. The mother stands up, shrieks and clutches her chest. For the love of fuck. Candy, thrown by the competition, by the looks of it, hitches her dress up even further and paces up and down alongside the coffin, like a cat about to drop kittens. The mam gets louder, shriller.

– That stained glass won't last much longer if this keeps up, Hamza says.

The young one stops and starts fumbling with one of the coffin's leather straps, struggling with the buckle. And just like that, she throws the leg over, giving everyone an unmissable flash of white knicker.

One of her hold-ups snags on the wicker basket. It tilts and slides a little to the right. The mam stops her screeching. For a bit, the creak of the coffin, the rattle of the metal trolley and the thud of heavy platform shoe on stone – as she hops about with one leg caught on the wicker – make this kinda music beat that echoes all over. And then she does it. She twists and turns and she's suddenly lying face-down on top of the coffin. The priest looks frozen to the spot. There's gasps and screams. The trolley shakes. The coffin slides a bit more, then does a nearly ninety-degree spin and starts to wobble, Candy clinging to it.

The lads shoot out of their seats. Benit launches himself at the base of the trolley, gripping the legs. Deano and Hamza grab the girl's arms. Others slide the coffin back into place, just as the breathless undertakers arrive. Without so much as a glance in the direction of the mother and daughter, the grey men tighten the coffin straps.

– Sit down and don't fucken budge, Deano says, through clenched teeth, into Candy's face.

One's as bad as the other. The mother glares at the daughter, dry-eyed.

Sandra, catching Deano's eye, mouths, 'Thank you', and gets back to fidgeting with her soggy tissue. Her kids gawk at the two women across the aisle, then whisper amongst themselves.

The priest, still looking stunned, half-smiles at Benit when he says, brushing himself down:

– Right, you get on with it there, Father.

The two Guards sit back down and Gerry, catching Deano's glance as he gets back to his pew, gives him a *good-man-there-now* garda blink. Back in their seats, the five of them look straight ahead. Jaysus. What can yeh say?

The priest fiddles with the mic and backtracks.

– I met Jack on many occasions in recent times. A young man with a big heart. Life broke him.

The air is heavy with the smell of burning wax and some kind of perfume that'd make you puke. At communion time, the lads stay where they are. A woman on the balcony starts singing 'In the Arms of the Angel' in an opera voice and someone beside Deano sniffles. Deano doesn't look but Karl's shifting about like he needs a shite, and then he coughs. Benit starts whispering to Hamza again:

– Your folks know you're here?

– No.

– They think you're in school? School'll be looking for a note. You gonna tell your folks you were in a church, fam?

– We're Pakis, not aliens like. We're okay with churches. And, you know, going to our mates' funerals. What are you on about anyway, I've had to sit here through all of your communion trainings and shit?

– Forgot you were here.

– Nice. Yeah, and the funerals.

Yep, all the funerals.

– There's loads of non-Muslims in Pakistan anyway.

– No way fam. You're not all Muslamics?

– There's about twenty billion non-Muslamics lurking in Punjab. Christians, they get everywhere.

– Boys, keep it down, yeah? Deano says.

– Like the rest of this crowd? Hamza says, eyebrows raised. But he shuts up.

The priest, looking shook, struggles through the rest, waving the big gold incense thing a bit too fast, making Deano sneeze. Outside, they lift Jack onto the back of a horse-drawn hearse. The black horses stand quiet, as Karl, Oisín and Hamza rub their muzzles, murmuring, running their fingers through the bridle plumes. They're real horsey people, bought a pony between them when they were fourteen. Deano loved that, sitting around the stables, out the back of Thomas Street. The lads mucking about. Karl has a way with horses – in the blood. Chose them a good one up in Smithfield. Sold her on to the lads with the carriages up at Guinness's.

At the burial, the priest announces that the family wants to welcome all the mourners to Sheedy's for something to eat afterwards.

– Jesus, Sheedy's! Who's on for getting shivved before we can get the sambos into us? Oisín says. We all in so?

Not one of them has ever actually been *into* Sheedy's. They've just heard all the stories, and everyone knows the kind of scald that smokes outside the kip. Karl's cousin had the shit kicked out of him in there by Wino Nestor. That was the month after the cousin got out of the Joy for the second time, after robbing a picture out of a house in Ballsbridge. Deano heard they were cleaning the walls in Sheedy's for weeks after. Had to paint the place. Only the really bad bits but.

*

It's early afternoon when they get to the pub on Cork Street. Apart from the guards, looks like everyone from the church is here. Even the priest's made it. Sitting alone at the bar, head in hands, nursing a whiskey. Sadie and her crowd, with the women from the flats and Sandra (minus the kids), have formed a big group in one corner. Oisín's mental next-door neighbour, Pearl, is stuck in another corner, looking like someone stood her up against a radiator and she melted. So, this is where she disappears to every morning. A row of small stools, propped against each other at jaunty angles, forms a barrier to one of the mezzanine areas. A scrawled sign stuck to the handrail announces 'Resurved Funarel'.

– I'm bursting for a piss, Oisín says.

– Follow yer nose there for the jacks, Deano says.

On his way, Oisín nearly face-plants when his foot gets caught in the pulled threads, like mantraps, that are all over the scratchy mustard-and-red carpet. Jack's mam, hatless now, jet-black hair scraped into a bun that leaves her eyes slitty, makes a beeline for them as she comes out from what smells like the pub's kitchen.

– Boys! Men! she says with a wink. They're making us up baskets of chips and chicken nuggets first. There's punch on the way. Well, sangria really. Keep the summer going, I always say. You'd like that, wouldn't yiz? We're going to lay everything out up there, we've got girls coming in to serve, and we're just going to keep it coming, all day and all night. Give Jack a great send-off.

She dabs her eyes with a Santy-covered paper napkin.

No one says a word.

– I'm Marian, she says, offering her hand, the chips in her sparkling nail-polish showing the grime underneath.

They each give their names and no more. Then stand looking at her again.

– So, how did you all know Jack? she asks.

Fucker doesn't give a shite.

– Met him when he was begging on Camden Street. We're in Colmcille's. We'd see him at lunchtime, Deano says.

– We'd go for lunch with him sometimes, Hamza says, playing nice.

– You're all still at school? I can't believe that, and the size of yiz, she says, smiling. Leaving Cert, I suppose, with you being so *big*?

– Yeah, Deano says, not giving her an inch.

– So, it's a big year for you boys, then? Very important.

– Yeah, we'll take it very seriously.

She bristles, then pastes the smile back on her face.

– Well men, eat when the food comes and drink up, she says, waving her hand towards the mezzanine as she glides back towards the kitchen, reaching up to give Oisín's shoulder a quick squeeze as he passes.

– Where's Candy, I wonder? Benit says.

– Probably back there in the kitchen, Karl says.

– Would yeh? Oisín asks.

– Fuck off, no! Deano says. The state of her. Would have, obviously. But she's fucken tapped.

– I would. She's still a ride, Oisín says. Looper or not.

– Peng ting, Benit says, eyes closed, nodding.

– Peng ting! She's fucking manky, Deano says. She was just riding her brother's coffin for fuck's sake! You don't even get with white girls, Benit. What are yeh on about?

– Still recognize a sweet one, fam, no matter how devoted I am to the sisters, Benit says, blowing a kiss into the air. Bunda too, innit?

– Oh yeah? Deano says. I'll be watching you and Christina, from now on.

– That's rotten fam, Benit says, shaking his head. You know Christina's the queen, fam. And also my sister.

– And also a dyke, Karl says, helpfully.

– Yeah, cos only dykes don't fuck their brothers right, Karl? Oisín says.

– She's his white sister though, she's not even related to him, Hamza says. Not really. If they wanted to get it on, there's nothing stopping them.

– I only said that Candy's a peng ting and youse are all about riding sisters. Paedos.

– And I only said that Candy's fucken grim for riding her brother's coffin. In front of a whole church-load a people. Simples.

– Would *you* though, Karl? And you a man of style and taste, Benit says.

– Nah.

– See? Cos she's a coffin-shagging weirdo, says Deano.

– Something like that, yeah, Karl says, his face going pink.

– Yeah look, we get a drink while we're waiting for this sangria gear?

The Shake'n'Vac scattered earlier – for the funeral, you know yourself – only barely masks the bang of stale drink, piss and puke, but it's enough to set off Deano's sneezing again as they head to the bar.

– No drink for me. Mum'll smell it off me the minute I get home, Hamza says. I'll just have a 7up please.

The massive barman tuts, rolls his eyes and slides the 7up along the bar. Fishing his ID out of his inside pocket, Deano studies the hulk's thick arms, the sweat patches on his white shirt, and what looks like a blob of mayo on the loosened black tie that hangs over his belly. That fella'd fold yeh.

About to order, something at the back of the cavernous pub catches his eye: light on the oily, greying locks maybe. Up a few steps, in the plush area, Wino Nestor has an unobscured view of the front door. He's nicely settled, with a few of his crew, a pint of blackcurrant in front of each of them. Wino sits back, folding his arms, staring down at Deano. Fuck this.

– Lads, I've no money on me, Deano says. Gonna head back to the gaff and get some. Some green at home too. I'll bring it back.

– But we just got here, Karl says.

He follows Deano's gaze.

– Oh.

– Who's that? Hamza says. Oh. Ah no, here, you're not leaving because of him. No fucking way. It's our mate's funeral. He doesn't own the place.

– I'll be back. I've money at June's. Just gonna get it, Deano says.

– Guess who's not coming back, Hamza shouts after him as he bolts out the door.

*

Like a bleedin miracle, when he steps outside Sheedy's door, the rain has dried up, the sun's out. Starting to sweat, he stalks down the street, towards the flats. No fucken way, no fucken way, is he sitting trapped in there with Wino. And him smirking his greasy head off. The same way he did at Deano's da's funeral. Shaking Deano's hand outside. Sorry for your trouble. Yeah, yeh are, yeh cunt. Sorry for me trouble.

Passing the building site, where the Donnelly Centre used to be, someone shouts.

– Alright Deano?

Callum, left school after his Junior Cert, has his own motor an all now.

– Yeah, grand. Just at a funeral. Yeh know Jack, the fella from Camden Street?

– Yeah, no. Who?

– Doesn't matter. Homeless, he was. Me and the boys knew him. Killed himself.

– Ah fuck, sorry, yeah. Heard about him, I think, Callum says, pulling an invisible noose around his neck, his tongue lolling out the side of his mouth.

– That's it, yeah. You still working the sites then? Good money? What's this yiz're building?

– Student accommodation. Fancy shit like. Yeah, it's deadly so it is, the money. Still living with me ma. But I've got the Civic and a bird from Sandycove. Smokin, she is.

– Sandycove me hole. Dún Laoghaire is it? Does she actually know yeh? White stick, has she?

– Fuck off, Deano. You're the one still going into that kip every day. Me, I've got it made. Deadly bird. Wads a cash. Going Crete in a couple of weeks. Send yeh a postcard.

– Whatever. I'm heading. Watch yeh don't get that *Sandycove* one up the pole. You'll have to get rid of yer Civic then, get one of them people carriers, Deano says, walking away.

– Not a hope, Deano, she won't let me ride her, Callum shouts after him.

Zero chance of Callum ever being with a young one he's not riding. Everyone knows he's got two others pregnant already. Went to England, both of them. At least the Sandycove one'll be able to get it done here now.

On the avenue, he passes under the eye of the Garda CCTV pole that towers over the entrance to the flats. Snitchy and Titch – what age are they, no more than fifteen – are leaning against the outside of the closed butcher's, hands tucked into their tracksuits, feeling their balls. Deano tried that for about a month when he was that age, staunching around, hands in his cacks. Oisín asked him what the fuck was wrong with him going around like a prick, mauling his cock. So Deano quit doing it.

A few ten-year-olds on bikes and scooters are hovering around – the real distributors. As soon as Deano turns the corner of his block, out of sight of the CCTV pole, Snitchy is up his arse.

– Are yeh looking, Deano?

– Nah Snitchy, I'm grand.

– I can get yeh anything, Deano. K, Mandy, whatever.

Deano stands and takes Snitchy in. Deano's strictly a naturals man these days: green, hash, mushrooms the odd time, nothing heavy. Pills now and again, but he's mostly given that up. White man's food, as Benit says. And here's Snitchy, all five foot of him, offering him Dublin's best. And Snitchy'll get clipped in some filthy jacks of some scabby pub when he's of no use or when he scopes the wrong bird or when he breaks up the wrong fight, like Deano's da. And no one will give a shite, except Snitchy's ma.

– Nah thanks, Snitchy. I'm grand, seriously.

17

Snitchy drops to a whisper and winks:

– Any other gear? Have some Canada Goose coming in.

Deano shakes his head, laughing.

– I've a couple a knives. Nothing that'll get yeh in any trouble, know what I mean?

– I'm grand, Snitchy.

– OK Deano. Yeh know where I am, yeah? Yeh have me number?

– Yeah, I have yer number.

*

Deano climbs the stairs to the flat. It's the only one not boarded up on this landing. They reckon they're regenerating the flats. They've been reckoning that ever since Deano can remember. Most of the other blocks are knocked this ages, but nothing's ever been built.

June used to say she was born and raised in these flats and she wanted her kids to grow up round here but they've been waiting so long she's had to give in. She'll look at other areas now, as long as she gets a house and a garden; she's done her time in the flats and most of the decent people are gone already. Like her full-time job it is, getting herself moved up the list, hassling the Corpo. She's down there every day nearly, talking to social workers and housing officers and whoever'll listen. Says she's ready to move out as soon as they offer her something proper.

Andrea, one of the twins born premature, has fucked-up lungs. The damp in the flat is killing her. June won't move to a private place but. They'd lose their place on the list, and there's no way she's ending up with some HAP landlord fucking her over. Says her da would turn in his grave if she gave up on Corpo housing. Reckons they might have a house down in Crumlin. There's no way Deano's moving to Crumlin but. Fucking savage they are down there. He's told her he'll stay in a friend's gaff till after the Leaving, if he has to. Oisín's ma offered and Karl's, but there's no way he's kipping in Karl's with that cousin of his fucking around, getting the place raided. So Karl's is out but maybe Oisín's. Anyway, he's not going Crumlin. No fucken way.

He lets himself into the flat. The familiar stink of bleach nearly knocks the head off him. June never quits with it, worse than anyone else in the flats, permanently at war with the black mould.

– Ah, hiya Deano, June says.

Ach, she should be collecting some of the kids at this hour.

– I'm not really back, Deano says, disappointed that he's not going to have the place to himself.

– You left all your bedding on the sofa, this morning Deano. Put it away, will yeh?

– Yeah sorry. I was in a rush.

– Do it now love. So we can use the sofa this evening, yeah?

He pulls the sheet off, bundles up the duvet and pillow and shoves it all in the box in the bedroom, where all five of June and Robbie's kids sleep.

– The kids are at sports day, she says, while she runs a duster round the door jamb. I ran into yer mam today, Deano. She was asking after you.

Deano freezes.

– She looks better, Deano. Says she's trying to get on some course.

Deano blinks and blinks and blinks and keeps his eyes fixed on June's face and doesn't panic, doesn't panic at all.

– Ah, hun, I'm just telling you. She does look a good bit better than the last time I saw her. Birmingham, that's where she was. Cleared out of it to get sorted, she says. She's maybe getting herself together?

He hasn't met his mam in the three years since he'd been taken off her, when she couldn't even get it together to get them a hostel for the night and June, his da's sister, had taken him in.

– Where'd you meet her? Was it round here? he says, quietly, looking at the floor.

– No, down in Rathmines. I was walking back to the bus stop, and she just came round the corner.

Rathmines! That close.

– She living there now?

– Dunno. I didn't want to bombard her with too many questions, Deano. She was friendly. Not angry with me, like before.

Every time it's on the news that a woman's body's been found in a house or a flat or a bog hole in the mountains, Deano's waiting for the knock at the door to tell him he needs to go and identify her. He doesn't know which he's spent more time thinking about or which'd be worse: her being dead and him having to hear what happened to her, or her being alive, living round here, and him having to see her scamming and stroking and being wasted as fuck, with not a tooth in her head.

– Deano, you alright? Should I not have said? She looks better. People *can* get better. Looks like she might be on methadone. The moon face, yeh know? She wasn't always like this, Deano.

– Was she talking right?

June looks a bit sketch.

– A bit slurred, maybe? But she was all there. Better than I've seen her in years. She gave me her mobile number.

– I don't want it.

– I'm not saying you want it. Just that I have it. You alright, love? You're pale.

– Yeah, I'm grand. Can I go into the kids' room for a lie-down? I wanna go back to the funeral. Me belly's hurting but. Just need a lie-down.

– The afters? Where is it?

– Sheedy's.

– Ach Sheedy's, Deano! You shouldn't be round there. There's all kinds in there. Are the rest of the fellas there? Is Oisín there?

– Yeah. Be grand, June. It's a funeral. Jack's ma, the real one, has it organized.

– Jesus Deano! Jack's ma's there! That's about the size of it. If you go back, make sure you stick with the lads and come home early, right? Or I'll be round for you. And don't think I won't. I'll reef you out of it, do you hear me? Karl there, with what happened the cousin?

Deano feels his body get heavy. He needs to get horizontal, quick.

– Yeah look, I'll have a lie-down. I'll just go back for a while, right?

– I don't want you drinking. I know you're eighteen, but still. Not round there. Wino and his people drink in it. We don't want to be around that lot. You don't know who you're talking to round there.

June doesn't even drink, herself. Says it causes too much hassle. Robbie, her fella, drinks the odd time. Nothing serious.

Deano crawls onto the Spider-Man-covered bed. His belly hurts, and his throat's still aching, and Jack's dead and everything's gone to shite.

*

When Deano gets back, there's six or seven red-faced men and a couple of complete yackballs blocking the footpath outside Sheedy's. They get the measure of him, once they see him under the lights, and clear a pathway. Deano's happy, relaxed even. Half a joint of Gracie's best and he's flying. He shoves open the door and gets blasted by a wave of Celine Dion. The place is heaving. He pushes through the crowd, scanning over everyone's heads. Shoals of crushed plastic cups, oozing the last of their dark pink liquid, are gathering along the skirting boards. Two young ones – not bad, not bad at all – try to squeeze through to the food area, one of them holding up a foil tray with a mountain of cocktail sausages and the other carrying a platter of limp, yellowy vol-au-vents. People grab fistfuls of sausages and look dubiously at the vol-au-vents as they pass.

– I wouldn't mind giving you the sausage, love, a heavily pregnant fella says to one of the young ones.

– Any tickles? another shouts into the blondie one's face and goes to poke her exposed armpit.

In the food area, the white paper tablecloths are soggy and torn. Jim Harrison, one of Wino's heavies, is resting his fat arse onto the pink-stained corner of the food table. Legs akimbo, sniffing and rubbing his nose, he flashes a Joker grin at the young one in the red dress who's wobbling between his feet.

– C'mere to me, pet, Jim says, as he pulls the girl tight against his belly. Turn round there a minute and I see what yer like from behind.

His mates let out a whoop as he flips the girl and thrusts himself against her arse, his tongue sticking out of the corner of his mouth. Where the fuck are the boys?

He finally finds Hamza, looking well settled into the snug beside an aul fella. He seems seriously mellow, and signals to Deano that he's been puffing on an invisible pipe.

He pulls up a stool and squeezes into the corner beside Hamza, who's now grinning up at the ceiling. He starts laughing and puts his phone down on the table for Deano to see him texting his mam. Pointless, since it's all in jabber-jabber.

– Staying in Oisín's tonight to go over maths, Hamza explains.

Ah, sure. Deano cops how much of a jocker Hamza's in when, still laughing, he grabs a fistful of each of his own cheeks. To see can he spread the smile to his hands, he says.

– Smiling hands. Deadly, Deano says as he shoots a glance at the aul fella.

– What's goin on? Is it a party or what? the old man says, eyes still fixed on the door of the snug.

– A funeral, Deano says.

– Whose funeral? I didn't hear.

– Name was Jack Larkin, Hamza says, straightening himself.

– Jack Larkin, Jack Larkin. No brother of yours with a name like that. I say, no brother of yours, wha?

He cackles, sticking out his tongue, revealing few teeth.

– No brother of yours.

It's hard to know what to do in these situations, at the best of times. He's old, so Hamza's never going to tell him to fuck off. Deano'd normally say something but Hamza'll only be pissed off at him hassling an aul fella. And Hamza's just so happy-looking. The man's, like, crazy old. And he has three empty pint glasses in front of him and a half-full one in his hand. The stained glass and wooden walls of the snug move closer. Deano's feeling that blunt a bit more now.

– No, he wasn't my brother, Hamza says. He was my friend.

– Is that right? What age was he?

– Twenty only.

– Twenty? That's a holy terror.

Now Hamza looks not so happy. And Deano definitely isn't happy. Jack under all that soil. The door of the snug gets pulled open by a wiry barman, who's joined the big lumpy one from earlier. He gives Hamza the once over but barely glances at Deano.

– You alright here, Marty? the barman says. Same again?

– I will, yeah.

– You? the barman says to Hamza, in a way that says he has no time for Hamza's nonsense, whatever that nonsense might be, now or in the future.

– No, I'm okay, thanks, Hamza says.

– Deano? the barman says.

No point even thinking about why he knows his name.

– Nah, I'm grand, thanks.

The barman, lips pursed, picks up the glasses and leaves.

– Whoever heard of that? Refusing a pint? And none in front of you. Easy knowing you're no Irishman. I say, easy knowing you're no Irishman, the aul fella says to Hamza.

– I've no money.

– Cavan, is that where yer from? he says, finding himself very funny again.

Benit and Oisín tumble through the door of the snug, arms around each other.

– Jaysus, more of them. Youse are no brothers of the dead fella either, are yiz?

Benit and Oisín look at each other, then back at the Marty fella.

– What? they say, in unison.

– Sit down here a minute, the aul fella says. Shove up there you, yeh mad face-holding fella. Where are youse lads from?

– Carman's Hall, Benit slurs.

Deano feels dreamy again, it's coming in waves. Happy, sad, happy, sad. Suppose with the tan, Oisín does look a bit foreign.

– Carman's Hall! the aul fella says. Would you ever get away ourrah that, you're as black as me boot. Where are you *really* from?

– You mean where's my family really from? Congo, is that what you're looking for? Benit says, smiling.

– Born in Congo, made in the Liberties, Hamza says, delighted with himself.

The aul fella puts down his pint and looks into the distance, twiddling his thumbs. Is he going to lose the cool altogether? The lads side-eye each other. The aul fella clears his throat.

– I, eh, I spent a bit of time beyond in Congo meself. Long time ago now, long time. The best of people there. The worst of things done to them.

He lifts his pint to his lips, a slight shake in his hand.

– No way! Benit says. What were you there for?

– Jadotville, son. Jadotville. Have you heard tell of that place?

– Nah. In Congo?

– It is. Likasi, it's called now.

24

– That's in the other Congo.

– Ah, you're Brazzaville so? Congo-Brazzaville. That's the place. I went back there. After Jadotville. Cyprus too.

– Cyprus isn't in Congo, Benit says.

– No, you're not wrong there, son, it's not. Yiz had a hard aul time of it over there in Congo. Both parts. Still not great, I believe.

– It's better now, where I'm from, Benit says. I've been in Ireland a long time.

– Bet you saw things none of these lads in here'll ever have to see, son.

Benit sticks out his bottom lip and frowns.

– Yiz never had it easy from the time of that bastard Belgian, did yiz? Not right what was done to your people, son. D'yiz want a pint? Come on, he says, pulling at the pocket of his trousers.

– Nah, you're alright, Benit says, searching the faces of the others for some clue for what to do.

– Won't hear of it, the aul fella says, dragging out bundles of crumpled notes. Yiz'll share a pint with an aul soldier. Marty's the name.

Deano sees the water pooling in the crags underneath his eyes, as he rubs his nose with the back of his hand.

– Yes, we'll all have a pint, thank you, Hamza says.

*

This isn't so bad. No one's forgetting Jack like. Really they're not. And them vol-au-vents with the curryish shit in them were actually alright. Deano stumbles on the way to the juke-box yoke. Those fucken mantraps! He drops down onto his hunkers. He's gonna get this sorted for once and for all. What if some aul one got caught in this? He pulls and drags at the nylon threads but they just won't break. This is a job for Benit and his bag of tools. Wherever he is.

A gap opens up in the legs surrounding him and there he is, still in his lair. Thought he was long gone. How could he miss him? Wino, giving him the stare, and him crouched on the floor.

He beckons him up. What are you supposed to do? No panic. He gets up – fuck the aul ones, they've survived this long sure – and walks over to the table. He's towering above them. All the big men.

– Everything alright, Dean? Wino says.

– Yeah.

– Family alright? How's June and the kids? Doing well?

Nice. Bring up June. Wino's just that kind of a fella. Rat-faced, perma-tanned, the faded scar on his face where someone had cut him an extra-wide smile years before slightly hidden by his chin-length, oily hair. Is it a dye job? Probably not. He'd have to be getting locks of grey streaked through it in the hairdressers and even the fruitiest barbers wouldn't do that for yeh.

– They're fine, thanks.

Wino's eyes glitter.

– Good, good. That's what I like to hear. Terrible about that young Larkin fella, wasn't it? Least I could do, give him a good send-off. Go back a long way, meself and Marian. Business wise. Hear you were a friend of his. Shame, the way he went. That young one was awful upset in the church.

There's a bit of a glint in his eye as he scans the room.

– Go and have some punch there, Dean, there's more nose-bag on the way. Saw you ran off earlier. Glad to see you're back. Still at the – what's this your sport is?

Deano clamps his jaw shut. Wino bangs the side of his head with the heel of his hand, like he's trying to knock the word out of his brain.

– Hurling.

The two thicks on either side of Wino smirk. One of them makes a clicking sound with his tongue.

– Go on, Dean. Help yourself.

That's him dismissed. Walking down the steps, Wino shouts after him,

– I'll be seeing you, Dean.

*

There's a massive sing-song going on, people ring-a-rosying as the light declines, and Deano camos himself, hunkered down in the corner. Play a bit of Tetris on the phone, take the mind off. Snivelling cunt, Wino. Benit and Candy are sitting on low stools in front of him, hiding him from view. Karl, rubbing his belly, plate in hand, says:

– That's it boys. Time for me supper and he heads off back up onto the mezzanine.

That'll be the fourth refill that Deano's seen him get.

– Is that your real name? Benit says. Candy?

– Well, yeah but I changed it, like. Me mam gave me a stupid name. So I changed it to a normal one.

– Candy?

– Yeah.

– What was your other name?

– Pocahontas.

Jaysus. Deano pauses the game, looks up at the pair.

Benit stares at her, poker-faced. Then they both erupt. Benit's laughing so much, he's in danger of falling off his stool. It's not that funny. They start into some convo about books and shite. Benit's bullshitting for Ireland. Desperate for his hole. She's smart though. Mental, but smart. Says she was doing three A-Levels before she came back. Then Jack happened.

– So, me and Mam came home for a wedding thing and then I was just in Dublin and then I met Jack in the Green and we just got chatting. He recognized me from photos. I'd no idea. Didn't even know he was homeless, like. And we hadn't seen each other since I was a baby. I didn't even know him, you know?

– Yeah, he said, Benit says.

– Did he say much about me? Candy says.

– No.

– I loved him, you know? Proper. He was lovely, special, you know? she says.

Yeah, Benit does know. And so does Deano. And more than you, Missus. Silent tears are running down her cheeks. Fuck it, maybe she is really upset.

Benit puts his arm around her.

Deano catches Wino moving through the crowd still up on the mezzanine, glad-handing a few of the aul ones like a politician at Croke Park. He turns, throwing serious shade Benit's way. Benit, oblivious, pulls Candy closer. That's a mistake, by the look on Wino's face. Deano sinks lower and gets back to his game. Sheedy's was a bad idea.

*

The place quietens down when the coke-heads storm out to their waiting taxis – ready to shout their shite opinions into the faces of the barmen and punters in the clubs in town. Deano says he wants to head off. Benit, who's out for the count, facedown on a pile of coats, gets dragged up by Deano and Karl, who apologize to the last of the women for the drool on their jackets. They search everywhere. Message him. Call him even. No sign of Hamza.

– Must have gone home earlier, Oisín says.

– Yeah, he wasn't too bad, must be planning to go to school in the morning, after all, Deano says.

Rambling down the street, Benit yawns loudly and they stop at a lamppost. A pair of runners swings on the wire overhead.

– What did he say to you, Deano? Oisín says.

– Who?

– You know who. Wino. When you were up at his table talking to him. What'd he say?

– Haven't a clue what yer on about, Deano says, staggering against the stone wall of the health board offices. Boys, I'm heading in here for a kip.

He drifts across the Weaver Park grass towards the playground, heading for the kids' crawl-through pipes. Himself and Benit kipped in there one night last summer. One each. Just couldn't make it home.

– Deano come on, your gaff's just there, Oisín shouts after him, but Deano just waves him off.

– Ah look, Deano, must be love! Benit says.

Deano stops and turns around.

– Story? he says, as he walks back towards them.

In the laneway opposite, Deano can just about make out a couple facing each other holding hands. Big deal. He's sleeping in the pipes. Tight and safe.

– No way I can go to school tomorrow, man, Benit says, pushing his do-rag back into position. Not after that.

– Lightweight, Karl says.

The couple in the lane breaks apart.

– That's Candy! Karl says, as the girl comes out into the light on Cork Street.

– Someone got lucky tonight, Oisín says. Right, see yiz whenever, I'm heading.

The fella comes out of the laneway's shadows, hands in pockets.

– Ah, hiya lads, he says. OK, so can I stay at yours, Oisín?

They stare at him, open-mouthed, as he strides past them towards Oisín's.

– You are fucking joking, fam! Benit shouts after him.

Hamza turns to face them.

– What? he says, shrugging.

2
KARL

On the Luas, Karl shifts out of the way of the woman with the buggy. Small and dark, linen dress, loafers. Brown Thomas, for sure. Balancing her iPhone and one of them bamboo coffee cups over her kid's head, she looks Karl up and down and thinks better of saying thanks.

His mam's voice's in his head, banging on about having to leave his job in Penneys now that he's in Leaving Cert, drowning out Kanye on the headphones. Would he have these AirPods if he wasn't working? No. Would he have these VaporMaxes? No. Would he have been able to buy her the birthday nails voucher for that swank gaff in Donnybrook? No. There's no chance, *no chance*, he's giving up this job. And it's not like he's going to do amazing in his Leaving in anyway.

He shoots Deano a message.

Story. U going out after?

If he's hurling, Deano won't get back to him till lunchtime, but. At the earliest. Since the funeral and maybe Wino talking to him, Deano's started this kinda snakey shite that Karl can't quite work out. Wouldn't even come out to help last night when Karl was giving the brothers a dig-out, collecting for the flats bonfire. Karl and Deano are a bit old to be at it for themselves anymore, but Deano'd never normally pass up the chance to help the flats out – even not his own flats – with a bit of collecting, carrying tyres over his shoulders, steering shopping trolleys full of crates. And Karl could've done with Deano's long legs when he was trying to get back out over the warehouse wall with the pallets for Frankie and Jackie. Something's not right with Deano but he's telling Karl nothing.

*

He gets into the shop, dumps his bag in his locker and heads to the kitchen. It's good when it's quiet like this. The world is just beginning to wake up and you're the only one there to see it.

The lads keep on at him that he needs to lay off the fries and get back to the hurling but seriously, who can say no to the full Irish before work? And he hasn't actually played since primary school. Apart from the egg, he's taken to grilling everything. Healthier. Doesn't taste right but. This used to be his and Hamza's thing, the brekkie in the morning. Then Hamo got the Brown Thomas job over the Christmas and that was it. Says it's closer to home than trekking out to Dundrum but everyone knows it's because he wants to hang out with the yuppies, studying them, as he says. Not that it's all bad being out here without the boys. Sometimes, some things are kinda better without them.

Suddenly, his eyes are covered by hands that smell of strawberries. Tanya.

– Guess who? she says.

– Some Clonskeagh skank? he says, trying to sound bored.

– How's my favourite chipmunk? I swear you'll be the youngest heart-attack victim in the world with those breakfasts.

Tanya's tanned. Like real tan, from the sun, in Spain. Not Salou, but. The family has a villa near Barcelona. So, she'll be going for a little top-up at the mid-term, and the family pops over sometimes just for the weekend. Yeh know yerself. Then it'll be into winter and skiing. She comes back with a tan from that too. It's usually really sunny on the slopes, she says. The snow reflects the light. Karl never got a tan in Dublin during the big snow last year. That's all Karl knows about tans and snow.

She called him on the second day of that big snow and brought over her snowboard and gave all the lads a shot of it in the Phoenix Park. Best day ever. The boys think he spends all his money on clothes. Not all. Some goes to the Credit Union – into the secret holiday fund. Karl's going snowboarding for real. Maybe even skiing.

Tanya's last working weekend next week. She fought with her parents to stay at it, but she has grinds starting on Saturdays and it isn't like she needs the money in anyway. She wanted to get into Harvey Nicks, of course, or even House of Fraser but they were full up. She's happy enough now though. Penneys is pretty cool. All modern behind the scenes, it is.

She slides into the seat beside him. He grins at her, chewing hard on a gristly rasher.

– Gonna miss me?

– Get over yourself, chipmunk, she says, swiping a sausage and taking a bite.

Karl grimaces. She knows full well that messing with the brekkie proper pisses him off.

– I'd better eat the rest of that, hadn't I? Unhygienic for you otherwise, she says smiling, reaching for the sausage again.

He blocks her hand.

– Touch my sausage and I swear, I'll bleedin batter yeh, he says, his mouth still full of rasher.

She pulls her hand back, wipes her shellacked fingers slowly on a paper napkin and arches one perfectly shaped eyebrow.

– I wouldn't dare touch *your* sausage, Karl.

– Ah yeah? I wouldn't give yeh the chance, yeh minger.

She rolls her eyes.

– Aww, I love it when you do your skanger talk, Karlo. Do it again.

He cranks it up, enjoying himself now.

– You callin me common?

She laughs and sticks her feet up on the side of his chair, then puts a serious head on.

– Know the way I'm leaving here next week?

– Yup.

– Well …

Damien bursts through the door. Damo, the type of fella who wouldn't go north of Lansdowne Road without a Garda escort. Except for that one time when he was a kid and his *old mon* brought him to a corporate box in Croker for the England–Ireland rugby match. The atmo was electric mon. The Bollinger was flewing. Damien couldn't have been more than six or something – Karl looked it up – 2007.

– Hello, hello. Ready for another day, are we? Damien chirps like a thick-necked canary.

Damien has the entourage in tow. All the new ones, following him around everywhere he goes. Karl overheard him telling his groupies that his job title was 'Customer Service Moving into Management'. Bit weird for a spa who only works Saturdays, but this lot are lapping it up. He'd have got a slap long ago if he'd started his crap round Karl's way, straight up. That's the problem with the likes of Damien, but. They've never got a slap, nor even the threat of a slap, and they never will get a slap, and that's the end of it.

Damien's told everyone his da is some big shot law fella or government fella or some shite like that. His da made him get a summer job, told him it'd be good for him, and now he's still here at weekends. Damien's kind'd normally be out playing rugby or whatever it is they do, but poor little Damien here has to hang out, tidying up the men's sportswear. The supervisors keep finding him sloping around the bras, but. Been thrown out of lingerie at least three times, Karl's heard.

– Hey, Ton! Looking gorge, Damien says.

– Hi Damien, she sighs.

– Doing anything I wouldn't do this weekend? he says, resting his hands on her shoulders.

He's fucking seventeen like. Acting like a fifty-year-old paedo. Karl pretends he can't see Damien, finishes up the breakfast, staring straight ahead, crunching down on the crackly bit of egg, thinking of his ma. She makes the eggs soft and smooth. Karl can never manage it. Like feckin rubber, they are.

*

The morning passes quickly, busy from the start. Which is good. The day'll fly and he wants to get out with the boys. Deano mostly. A woman crashes his daydream – asks him for the khaki capris in size ten. Ambitious, with those hips. Tells her that whatever they have is already out on the floor but then, looking at her disappointed face, says:

– Ah, no, maybe. I'll go check in the stockroom for you.

He bounces along the hallway, checking his phone, opening IRQaeda group chat.

Deano:
Later P4F smoke, round Hamzas gaff, his ma in Pakiland

Hamza:
No way. Going mosque.

Deano:
Fuck off ya snake. Saturday no mosque. U smashing candy?

Hamza:
Nah, going mosque. No Candy.

Benit:
Ye right know u hittin dat she got jungle fever.

Hamza:
Am brown. Not black, nigga.

Benit:
Black enuf for candys jungle fever

Deano:
Some snake, leaving the boys for randy candy

Hamza:
Not with Candy. Leave her alone.

Deano:
Yup u hittin dat

Hamza:
Shut the fuck up.

This'll go on and on. Hamza's been denying it since the funeral, but Benit's sure he saw them out in Blanch together, when Benit was out playing basketball with the black lads. And some of Karl's Girls (as the group of fourteen- and fifteen-year-old flats girls call themselves) swore they saw Hamza down in Ringsend last week, with some young one with scarlet red hair. But when they shouted over to him, Hamza looked away, like he didn't know Karl's Girls (which Hamza definitely does). So maybe it wasn't Hamza after all. Karl doesn't get it. Not that he would. But none of the boys can. *Candy*, like?

He pushes open the outer door of the stock area. And that's when he hears them, inside in the room.

– No fucking way, you can't invite that pov. He'll probably bring a gang of those scummers with him. Remember the time they met him outside here? Jesus, Ton. United Colours of Knackeragua. Cop on.

– You're such an asshole, Damien.

– I'm warning you. I mean Karl's OK, but you don't know what you'll be getting if you ask him. Well, you *do* know what you'll be getting. Scurvy or something.

– Just shut up, Damien.

– But you know I'm right. You know what I mean, Ton.

And then there's silence. Karl waits for Tanya to say something else. Anything. But there's nothing only the sound of the pair of them mooching around the stockroom. Karl's face heats up and it's like he has a massive stone in his belly. He turns and walks back to capri woman.

– Really sorry, no more size tens, he says. But we're getting an order in next Wednesday, if you wanna check back in.

Fuck it, she looks proper sad, and the capris are pretty good in the khaki.

– The fit's a bit different on the capris. Have you tried a twelve? Or an eight? Try them on, sure, he says, before turning away, his face still burning.

*

Out for lunch, he sits alone, poking at his noodles, thinking about Tanya and the party and the silence from the stockroom. There's Halloween – him and the boys have the bonfire sesh planned. And then, there's Hamza's eighteenth. So Tanya's gaff will probably clash with one or the other, in anyway.

On the afternoon tea break, he walks in to find Tanya and one of the girls from downstairs, trying on clothes.

– I don't think so. The blazer's too much. Deffo no jacket. And I think the pink is better, Tanya says, pursing her lips.

– Really? It's not just that you want to look better than me and you don't want me getting off with anyone? the other girl says, laughing.

Karl can tell she's only half-laughing but.

– What? Tanya says, kinda annoyed.

In fairness, Tanya's not the type of a one to do that kinda shit. Although …

Karl stares at his phone, ignoring the two girls. Messages from the boys, Deano and Benit are up for the kebab and the rest. Oisín going to his da's. And Hamza's not that keen. But they'll grind him down. Unless he really *is* getting his hole off Candy. Chief Karl's Girl, Amy, is on a buzz.

Amy:
You come mine. All the grlz comin. New PLL's 2 watch. Mam sez u stay over. Dominos?

He feels the pull of a marathon sesh of *Pretty Little Liars* in Amy's gaff. Him and the girls, jammies, Domino's, toasting marshmallows on the gas. Whatsup! Amy's ma never has a problem with Karl staying. The boys'll roast him but, if he pulls a Hamza. They'll start on about being a weirdo, hanging out with kid girls and *Pretty Little Liars* and *The Vampire Diaries*. And why is it that Amy's ma is OK with him staying and all. Like when Amy opened her big gob and told the lads that Karl had been round hers for a sleepover with the girls, when he'd told them he'd been in the scratcher, puking his ring and he couldn't go out with them.

Why she had to blab, he'll never know – probably sucking up to Deano or Hamza. Amy likes Hamza. Told him that he looked Spanish and then was fake-surprised when Hamza said he was Pakistani. Funny, cos in first year Hamza *had* pretended he was Spanish when everyone knew he was Pakistani. Hamza laughs about it now but he still says that no one *really* wants to be Pakistani when they're thirteen and in Ireland. Says he's happy enough now being Pakistani – Punjabi first – but Karl saw Hamza's smile when Amy said he looked Spanish.

Anyway, Karl knew what they meant, the boys, roasting him that time about the girls and PLL. Benit and Hamza asked him straight out, in fairness. Said they knew. Said he had to be. And Karl point-blank denied it. They'd have been weird with him otherwise. That was the end of it. That was last year.

– Right, Karl's here. Let's see what he thinks. Tell her, Karl. Blue dress or the pink flowy one? With or without that *jacket*? Tanya says, grimacing.

Karl tips his chair onto its back legs.

– Hold up the blue one again.

Rolling her eyes, the young one holds the rose chiffon skater dress under her chin. Karl squints up his eyes.

– Right. Now, stick on the jacket, he says.

A white blazer, gold chain detail. Karl's seen it. Came in last week. It's a mess.

The girl shrugs it onto her shoulders.

– No way! Karl says, averting his eyes. Take that yoke off you! And hold up the blue dress. Where's this yiz're going?

– Dunno, probs Tramline or somewhere, the girl says.

Jesus Christ almighty! It's that prosto bodycon one-shoul-dered midi in baby blue, from Boohoo. Amy got it in the post last week too.

– Okay, the pink's best. No heels. Wear them Converse you had on last week, the green ones, bare-look tights, hair in a high shaggy pony. Denim jacket. That yoke you've there makes you look like an aul one going to a wedding, yeah?

Tanya laughs and gives the girl, now standing with her mouth open, an I-told-you-so look.

– You are so good, Karlo! Tanya says.

– Yeah, I'm great, amn't I, Tanya?

Tanya frowns a little, peering at him.

– You alright, Karl?

– Yeah, just dandy. Know what I mean, Ton? he says, as he gets up and walks out.

*

He drops home to change his clothes. Has another sorta row with his ma over when he's quitting that damn job and heads out to meet the boys. On the way down the stairs, the guards have a young fella up against a wall. Ach, poor feckin Titch.

– Youse can't do that. He's not eighteen, Karl shouts.

– You mind your own fucking business and head on there with yourself, the taller of the guards says, releasing his grip on Titch's throat.

– He's a kid, I told yiz. Garda brutality, that is.

Raging-guard charges towards Karl.

– What have *you* in your bag, hah, smart fella?

Karl turns and legs it down Marrowbone Lane, the guard only half-heartedly running after him. Titch's going to have to look after himself. Half-touched, he is.

Banjaxed after only a bitta running, Karl falls into a lane-way, catching his breath, hands on thighs. The boys are right, gotta get back to the hurling. Clattering and banging from across the street.

Not young lads collecting, a woman. With a shopping trolley loaded with a couple of huge, badly packed sports bags, picture frames and a lamp thrown on top. It's dark but, as she gets closer, there's something about her. Blonde hair dyed offa her head. Holy fuck, it can't be. He steps back into the shadows, in case she sees him. It is her. Looking better than the last time he saw her but that was years ago and she was having that scrap with some fella she was riding. She's struggling now to get the trolley up the rampy bit of the pavement. Deano's gonna go mental if she's back in the area.

*

Deano's already there, sprawled all over a bench. Good, they'll be on their own for a bit. The place is starting to fill up: Muslim families in for the dinner, bunches of country fellas in tracksuits, up from the boxing stadium, a gang of young ones on their way out for the night.

– Another day working for the man? How's Tanya? Deano says. Tanned Tanya, wouldn't mind a bit a that.

– Yeah, she wouldn't look at you, ya strap.

– Dunno about that. Some of these D4 birds like a bit of a real man, yeh know? All them fellas they have round them are gay as fuck. D'yeh see all them *Made-in-Chelsea* fellas? Benders, the lot of them.

– Why were *you* watching *Made in Chelsea*? Karl says.

– Me controller was broken. June was watching it. All these posh rats, staring at each other like they've had a bleedin stroke or something, I swear. There's these girls, right, and they're trying to get with these fellas. The lads are pretending they're all gagging to ride the girls. But they're *definitely* homos. Total fucking benders.

Karl laughs and whispers:

– Maybe keep it down a bit, yeah?

Deano looks around the room.

– What? Why? Not saying there's anything wrong with benders. Sure, I don't give a rat's. I'm only saying those girls won't get a decent ride from some gay-as-fuck posh fuck like that, yeah? No offence, buddy.

– What do you mean, no offence? I'm not posh.

Deano laughs.

– Nah, you're definitely not posh.

Their food arrives. Mixed Doner Meal × 2, naan on the side, paprika chips, 1 × Coke, 1 × Yup yup 7up!

– Here. How come you've so much grass all the time these days? Karl asks. Yer not even working anymore. Where are yeh getting it?

– Confirmation money.

– I'm serious.

– So am I, buddy.

– Yeh spent all yer summer money on yer gaming gear and the holiday with Oisín and his ma. Not getting it from Lynchy in Charlo, are yeh? That yackball's in with Wino now, I heard. I'm not touching it if yeh got it offa him, right?

– No one's buying offa Lynchy, for fuck's sake! You retarded? Them two young fellas from York Street who threw the leptos after Lynchy's gear are still in Beaumont.

– And Philly Pig's ma. She's still in the nuthouse in James's after it. That's what I'm sayin.

– Lynchy's gear, like! D'yeh think I'm a doughnut?

– So where then?

– Cousin of shop Sadie's – she's like fucken seventy or sixty or sum. Selling small-time outta her gaff in Drimnagh. The grandson who normally does it is inside for robbing nappies and rashers outta Tesco's, fucken eejit. I go down on Sundays and roll her six blunts for the week. She takes Saturday night off, goes to the local instead. She's got arthritis or Parkinson's or some shit. Can't roll her own, in anyway. Gracie she's called. She gives me me green for the week. Good stuff. No funny shit.

– They're spraying it with something.

– Not this stuff. It's clean. Got some squidgy too. And a new pipe.

Karl looks at Deano. Could be true. He's heard some aul one's selling alright. But squidgy and a new pipe? For rolling a few joints? And he's been bunking off school loads. More than Karl even. If his ma's back in town, he'll be fucked altogether.

The cooking lads, sweating behind the counter, wave over at Benit strolling in. Holding up two fingers, one of them nods. Benit gives him a thumbs-up and slides into the seat beside Karl.

– Where've you been till now? Deano says. Not like you.

– Yeah, soz, got delayed down at Marty's.

Who the hell's Marty?

– The aul soldier fella? What yeh doing with him? Deano says.

– Bringing him back a book about Congo he lent me. Then he had me cooking with him. Tried to get me to stay for dinner.

Typical Benit making friends with randomers everywhere he goes.

– No sign of Hamza then? Benit says.

– He really with her? says Deano.

– Dunno, Benit says. Says they're just friends.

– Friends with a girl? Like Candy? Hamza going like this fella here? Deano says, gesturing towards Karl. *Vampire Diaries* an all?

– Hamza has loadsa girl friends that he's not riding, says Karl.

– But they're mostly lezzers I think, Benit says. Or queers.

– Lezzers are queers, Karl says.

– Lezzers fuck women. Queers have blue hair and don't fuck anyone, Deano says.

– Like you then, Karl says.

– Is my hair blue? Deano says.

– There's the girls he knows from clever camp, yeah, Benit says. But they're not like Candy. Don't think he's with her tonight, fam. Think he's out with the Arabs.

– With that fucken skankbag, Mohammed? What's he doing with them? Karl says.

– Hamo's a man about town, Karlo, gotta hang with the Muslim Brotherhood sometimes.

– Mohammed and his mates are dicks, Karl says.

At least that was the agreed position last time Mohammed came up in conversation.

– Sure it's not just that they've better threads than you? Deano says.

– I'd say he's getting uck off Candy at the very least, Karl says.

– Candy's sucking off Mohammed?

– No, Karl says. Hamza, and you knew who I was talking about.

Deano and Benit turn to stare at Karl.

– If Hamza's with Candy, course he's getting uck off her, Karlo, Deano says.

Benit shakes his head, changes the subject, rubbing his hands together.

– So what are we on tonight, boys? I got nothing on me.

– Bumbles? Karl says. I can get some from the cousin.

– Bumbles, white man's food, fam.

The range of what's white man's food keeps getting bigger, soon they'll be limited to grass.

– What the fuck, Karl? Who's hitting yokes, when they're just chilling with their homies? Deano says.

– Just sayin, might help everyone be a bit nicer, Karl says, shovelling rice into himself. Can't believe Oisín's missing this, boys.

– At his dad's, innit? Benit says. Man needs a father. *Definitely* does these days with weird spooks appearing to him, fam. Seeing your dead twin at the end of your bed every night is no good for no one.

– Is it Ruairí he's seeing but? Karl asks. Sounds weird to me.

Etem arrives with Benit's grub, slapping Benit on the back.

– How are you, my friends?

– Good bro. You alright? Benit says.

– Yes, yes, can't complain. You all still at this hurling? My son has started. He's very good.

– Yeah, *we're* still at it, Deano says, pointing to himself and Benit. Shitebag here hasn't been in years. Shows, amirite, Etem?

– Karl, my friend, you're a good man, don't listen to them, Etem says, and he puts down an extra tray of rice and three more chips.

43

Ah here!

– Compliments of the house.

– That rice's got my name on it, Deano says.

– For sharing, Etem says, as he walks away. You look after my boy at the hurling.

– Oisín shouldn't be missing this food though, Benit says. Probably eating hummus and carrot sticks all night long with his dad. White people and hummus, story fam?

– No hummus in my gaff! Deano says. Just Oisín and his faggy primary school mates. All their mas make them eat it.

– Yeah, not *your* kinda white people, Benit says. The amount of it Oisín's ma has in the fridge. Like an addiction, fam.

Karl stands up. His head hurts and he suddenly isn't in the mood for whatever they're planning – white people's drugs or brown people's drugs, hummus or no hummus.

– Look boys, I'm in work tomorrow and I'm knackered. Gonna go home.

– What the fuck's wrong with you? Deano says, a bit concerned-looking.

– Nah, nothing. Be grand. Gotta headache, is all. Just don't wanna be up late like. Heading home.

He knows they're watching him through the window as he walks down the street, talking about him. It's starting to rain and he's only brought his light Harrington. Mistake. October, should always have a hood. He messages Amy, telling her he's in and he'll be round with popcorn in ten. His phone beeps.

Tan:
Didn't get the chance to say earlier I'm having a going away gaff. Wanna come? It'll be Halloween weekend or the next.

Karl shakes his head and smiles as he walks towards Amy's flat.

3
OISÍN

Oisín looks up at the sign above the gate: St Killian's Hurling Club. Might as well, since he's come this far. Might as well. Maybe the only way to get Deano to cop himself on. He's been missing so much school, too much, even for him. Being proper sketch. And the last time Oisín knocked into June's flat, Deano was down the landing, talking to that scruff, Snitchy Noble. Deano said he was just talking, but you know. Oisín's even said it to his mom. She said Oisín should try talking to Deano and that maybe he's depressed and maybe the whole thing with Jack and all was just too much for him. Get him and Hamza round for some jambalaya on Friday, she said. But Deano made some excuse. He's tried talking to him online but there's not much opportunity for real talk while you're playing COD. If Deano throws everything away like some dumb fuck, when he's *not* some dumb fuck, Oisín'll kill him. Stupid fucking waster.

There are fellas and young ones already racing all over the acres of playing fields in front of him – adults, kids, poshies, normals, flats. Running round cones, pucking balls at walls. He feels a wobble in his belly, coming back after months away – long for him. Then he sees him, sitting alone on the kerb, like a daddy-longlegs, putting on his boots.

– Ah here, what the fuck? Am I seein things, am I? Deano says. Is it a ghost or wha? An apparition!

– Alright? says Oisín, smirking.

– Please Mammy, save me, it's some kinda zombie or some undead thing.

– Ha, ha, fucking hilarious Deano, any sign of your ma then? Nah didn't think so. Saw her sucking cocks behind the counter in Spar there a few minutes ago so, you know, she won't be down here anytime soon.

– Fuck off.

– Yeah, you fuck off.

Fuck! No ma-slagging with Deano! Just slipped out.

– Thought yeh were dead, it's been so long. Whacker's been asking for yeh. Why haven't yeh been here this years?

– Months. And you saw me the other day at school, when you turned up for an hour.

– Ah man, months is a long time in this game. What have yeh been up to?

– This thing called Going. To. School. Unlike you.

– Ah here, harsh. Had a pain in me belly, Deano says, rubbing his green-and-white-striped jersey.

– What's that you're smoking? Match prep, is it?

Tying his laces, Deano puts the rollie in the corner of his mouth. Popeye-like, he turns to look at Oisín.

– Ah yeah, it's me protein smoke y'know? Just tobacco but. No green at all this morning. Boys hammered into it last night. Another thing yeh missed. Goin Hamza's after, think he has the last of me stuff. Shrooms though. Aww man, I swear.

– I was down at my dad's, I told yiz. Drove me up from Carlow this morning.

– Still ancient, is he? Is he back riding yer ma yet, or wha?

– Yep, still ancient, Oisín says, smiling.

Better get him off the subject of the ancient dad, and his sudden reappearance a few years ago, after Ruairí's accident. The slagging'll be too much.

– A proper smoke beforehand helps you play better anyway, right Deano?

Deano narrows his eyes, holding out his arm, gesturing towards the playing fields.

– Helps the calculation of the physication, know what I mean bro? Seriously but, why *haven't* yeh been here, yeh lazy cunt, letting yer team down. Hurling too rough for yeh these days, is it poshie? Piano or some other fucking gay thing, opera is that what yer at? Hold on, *studying*, is it?

– Hurling's not the same as school, Deano. It's your Leaving, for fuck's sake, Oisín says, kicking the kerb. Only a few more months to go, what are you at? You just lying around playing COD all day?

A voice calls from behind Oisín's back.

– Oi!

Oisín looks back at the red-faced man stomping towards them, seriously intending something.

– Ah here's the gaffer, you're in for it now, Oisín bro.

– What's that I see? Is that a ghost? Hold me back, it's a fucking ghost!

– Alright Whacker? Oisín says, smiling softly, digging his hurl into the ground.

– This is great Oisín, great, great! Are you back with us, Horsebox? Says Whacker, waving a hurl in each hand.

Whacker always seems to be bursting out of his skin, like a grilled tomato. A Dub, born and raised – played senior county – who speaks with a Kilkenny accent. Aspirations, as someone said. Oisín grins. Weird, being called Horsebox stops the feeling in his belly.

– We'll have a good solid team now, with Deano here. Benit's already out there, see him there? Been here since early.

Up and down that field he is. Puckin like a bastard, puckin like a bastard.

Whacker gazes towards the perfect hurling human striding up and down the pitch.

– Wish yiz were all like him. Every training session, every match, he's here. But sure yer here now, Horsebox, and we'll forget all that. I'll want you midfield now. The pair of yiz there like a couple of Ronaldos or that fella off Galway.

Oisín and Deano look at each other and grin.

– Yeah, I look like Ronaldo in anyway, don't I? says Deano, smoothing down his slicked-back waves.

Whacker inspects him.

– You do, it's them freckles and the scaldy red head on yeh.

– *You* can talk about scaldy.

– We're going to win this boys. Yiz're in the big leagues now. Minors is the big leagues. It's like American football, like the Super Bowl.

– Yeah, just like the Super Bowl, Oisín says.

– Can I get sponsorship, Whacker, so? Nike or Adidas, or something?

– Rizla'd be more your thing Deano, Oisín says.

Deano gives Oisín the mock evils.

– No need for them sponsorships, Whacker says. It's for the love of the game boys, the love of the game, Horsebox. Yiz're men now. Men. Warriors. Yiz are like Finn MacCool or Cú Chulainn. Speaking of that Super Bowl, we're getting a trip to Boston sorted for next year. Thinking for Paddy's Day. Play a few games over there. Think about it. I know yiz're for the Leaving but it'll be only five days and sure yiz'll be off for one of them anyway. Have a think.

He starts beating his leg with the two cracked hurls.

– Right, I'm sticking these in the back of the van and youse two get out there to warm up as quick as yiz can, right? This is great, Horsebox, great that yer back, deadly. Get out there, get stuck into them and if yiz're scared, stick a cork up yer Garda patrol and play on, hear me? Stuck in from the start, right?

– Right boss.

Whacker limps away. Deano and Oisín look at each other.

– Seems proper pleased that you're back, *Horsebox*.

Whacker shouts back over his shoulder:

– It's like having the Protestant son back, Horsebox, the Protestant son in the bible.

They turn to watch Whacker dive into the back of his battered white Hiace, eventually just his stubby legs sticking out in mid-air.

– Was in the van last week going to a match, sliding around in the back, you know the way. Know the piles of shite he has back there? Found a copy of *Fifty Shades* and a big thing of Lidl hand cream tucked down behind the seat, Deano says.

– Ah fucking hell. Good man Whacker.

– Shhh. Here he's coming back.

Now with his high-viz on, breathless from the short walk to and from the van, Whacker says:

– Come on boys, it's men yiz are now. Warm up there, like the bastard warriors yiz are. No fairies out there. It's life or death. Gotta do it boys. Yiz have it in yiz. Are yiz men or tricycles?

– Come on, better go Deano, Oisín says, stifling a laugh.

People nod and say things like 'Hello stranger', and 'About time', and 'Where the hell have you been', as they head to the pitches.

– You coming back to school then? Oisín says.

– You coming back to hurling?

– I'm here, amn't I?

– Yeah, for how long but?

– School? You dope.

– Ah here, fuck off, I'm not a fucken dope.

– Stop acting like it then.

Benit cut his drills short to run over.

– Hear you're back. Is he *really* back?

– Fucksake boys, can anyone see me here? Invisible like you on a dark night, am I, Benit? Yeah I'm back. Why did none of yiz tell me I was so missed?

Benit flashes his biggest smile at Oisín.

– We did. Dream team's back together, fam. We'll be like the Fíanna now, innit?

– Ah come on, what's up with this Fíanna thing? Oisín says. Have yiz all been on something? Deano's got an excuse, shrooms last night, but the rest of yiz.

Benit stands back and examines Deano.

– What's up? Shrooms last night?

– Ah yeah, yeh left early, bro. Had a few. Hamza arrived with them.

– You had a match this morning and you were on a shrooms sesh? Benit says. Typical. Benit likes things clean around hurling. No messing about before a match.

– You know he plays better when he's had a little help, Oisín says.

– Yeh were smoking yerself, Benit, yeh mad rat, Deano says.

– One blunt and I left early. Priorities, fam.

Benit straightens up his do-rag – specially printed with the team logo – and pulls his helmet back on.

– Whatever. This nigga's gonna play ball. See you on the field, my bros. You two better be ready fo ma nigga-passes or ah have yo white asses. Now that's poetry.

He salutes them and walks away.

– So, coming to school on Monday or what?

Deano stops walking, turns to face Oisín.

– Yeh know wha?

Oisín chews the side of his mouth, ready.

– What?

– We'll see how this here game goes and how yeh behave yerself out there, passing to me an all, and then …

– Yeah?

– Well Poshie, even though it's the biggest fucken paedo hole in the world, I'll consider it.

*

Monday morning and there's no sign of him. Oisín's pissed off. Deano swore last night, when they were on playing, that he'd be in.

Here's Karl, an hour late, doesn't have his project with him. Madge, the accountancy teacher living on raw nerves, pulls a face and starts mouthing about the disrespect.

– Ha ha! Karlo's gaff was raided last night, someone says.

There's a murmuring and more laughing.

– Oi, would youse ever shut the fuck up? Oisín shouts.

Madge tells them all to pipe down and keeps a special hysterical eyebrow-raise especially for Oisín. She turns back to Karl and asks:

– Is that true? Is that why you don't have the project in, Karl?

Karl shuffles a little bit to the side, then nods.

– Okay, come to me after class, we'll see what we can do to help you get this into me before the end of the week, alright? She whispers on the down-low.

Karl's jeered down to his seat.

– Again, Karlo? Again? Yer ma shifting gear outta yer kitchen?

Fuck sake. The cousin again. If Karl's mom'd just say no, stop him kipping there. Dick. Hardcore, coke and shit, something to do with Wino Nestor's lot *and* the Northsiders. Asking for trouble. Bringing all that heat down on Karl's folks.

He's family, Karl's mom says. But Karl's folks aren't like that. His da's the coolest man ever. Brought them down to China-town once, after they won their group in the hurling. Parnell Street. You can't beat a spice bag or a 3-in-1, well you can, but this was the real deal. All soupy greens and weird fish. He'd

51

done a bit of travelling in the East, Karl's da told them, just before he started jabbering away to the waitress in Cantonese, ordering all sorts for them. They all just sat there with their mouths open. Apart from Karl, of course. A Traveller who'd actually travelled – Oisín couldn't believe it. He'd been having a bit of a ramble over China way and decided to stay for a few years because he got good work.

Not teaching English or anything boring like that. Nah, Karl's da was a stunt man in kung fu movies, getting lashed off buildings and stuff. And that's why his hip bes at him in the winter and he can't stand for too long, he said. He was always the dopey foreigner getting the shite kicked out of him. Benit asked him had he ever met Jackie Chan, and he said, yeah sure isn't Karl's little brother named after him. Best time of his life, he told them, apart from when Karl's ma had the lads. Nothing could replace having your own family, he said.

Oisín takes a good look at Karl. Wrecked, big dark hollows under his eyes.

– Seriously, Karl? Oisín says, as Karl finally slumps into the seat behind him.

Karl grins.

– Nah, marathon Fortnite bro, yeah? Karl whispers.

Karl still playing with kids. Oisín can't stop laughing. And then he remembers, Karl's Playstation's been broken for weeks.

*

He messages Deano at break. They're getting their first PE session in weeks. Deano messages that his belly's hurting him again. So no, he's not coming in, not even for PE.

Finnegan, the new PE teacher, decides they're playing football. Doesn't suit Oisín but isn't the worst Finnegan has dreamed up. That was fucking hockey. With fucking plastic hockey sticks. The powers-that-be suspended PE because of the Bring Harry Back Campaign. Harry O'Loan, the last PE teacher – Jujitsu champ, played senior hurling for Cork – is on a career break. The lads got T-shirts made up with Harry's face on them, and Oisín himself was in deep shit over the Bring Harry Back graffiti on the South Corridor. Hamza wanted to do a dirty protest – that's what any decent Irishman would do – but Oisín said the toilets in Colmcilles's had so much shite on the walls already that no one would notice.

The match's going fine until Alvar, the slimy Brazilian, starts his usual screeching. He's roaring and bitching at everyone, mostly his own side. Oisín pings a long ball to Benit, who takes a good touch and bangs it in, top bins. Alvar's snapping, screaming at the lot of them, like he's some kinda fucking Suárez. Everyone on Oisín's side starts laughing at him.

– Relax bro, it's only a game, Benit says.

That only makes him worse. Raging, Alvar gets the ball from the restart and turns on the Brazilian sauce, pacing down the wing. Karl, who's pretty handy with a ball himself, wakes up and makes a run towards the box, calling for the ball. With a sweet one-two, he sets Alvar up for a screamer. One all.

Alvar's mid-celebration, running his hand through his man-bun length hair, when Hamza staunches up to him and boxes him square in the face. He crumples in a blood, snot and tears-covered ball, crying out in Portuguese.

– What the fuck's wrong with you, Hamza? Karl says, putting his arm around Alvar, who pushes him off. You weren't even on the ball.

Hamza's eyes are huge and red as he stands over Alvar, clenching and unclenching his fists. Finnegan comes running over, in his just-out-of-the-wrapper, bright green tracksuit.

– What in good heavens is going on here? Hamza?

Hamza looks like he might give Finnegan a dig next. Even just for the 'good heavens'. Everyone gathers around.

– Well, Hamza? Finnegan screeches.

Benit gets Hamza by the shoulders.

– What did he do to you, Hamo?

53

Hamza shakes his head. Obviously though, Alvar said something or did something. Oisín helps Alvar off the ground.

– Oisín, could you please help Alvar down to the staffroom? And you!

Finnegan's squealing now, getting so high-pitched that soon only the dogs'll be able to hear him, and pointing his finger into Hamza's face.

– Principal's office, now.

It's not the first time Hamza's been in a knock but he normally has some kind of reason for it and he's done nothing serious since probably, third year? Then he'd been sent to some anger-management counsellor and he's been grand since. They had him on those pills for his ADHD (the biggest load of cock) but he gave them up shortly after because they were driving him mental, and started selling them to the rich kids in The Lutheran School. They love a bit of speed over there. His two younger cousins got themselves diagnosed the same way but they never bothered taking the tablets at all. Just went straight into the family business with Hamza.

Oisín strolls along beside Alvar. It's just weird. Hamza's not completely mental. And although he's still denying that he's at anything with Candy, Oisín would have thought that getting his hole – which he definitely is – would have calmed him down.

– Wait, I'll get you some jacks roll.

Jacks roll? He hasn't seen jacks roll in the piss-and-shit-spattered toilets here in his whole six years. He holds his own shite till he gets home or till he gets into Boojum at lunchtime.

– Here look, take my jumper, Oisín says, balling it up and pushing it into Alvar's hands. Why'd he punch you?

– You tell me. Just a crazy Arab. All I said was get out of my way. I don't understand. Crazy fucking Arab.

Oisín stifles the urge to straighten Alvar out about Pakistanis not being Arabs. In the circumstances, like, it mightn't be fair.

– That's just weird though. Anyway, you need to get cleaned up.

*

Hamza's pacing up and down, pulling at his beard, while Oisín sits on the low wall beside the canal. It's warm in the sun but cool enough here under the trees.

– The fuckers! Hamza says. The suspension would have been fine but Finnegan pushed it and said I'd two suspensions already. But I haven't! They took that one back because of the ADHD and shit.

– Calm down. Do you have any smoke? You need to chill.

– But no, it wasn't enough for that Finnegan cunt. Wants her to bring it to the board. Wants me expelled.

– What? They can't expel you for giving someone a dig one time.

– He made her get out my file with all the other shit in it from before. I've done nothing for years, only those couple of scraps.

It always takes a while for Hamza to calm himself. Oisín thinks about putting his headphones back on, listening to The Weeknd. Hamza'd hardly notice.

– That Finnegan cunt! Hamza says.

– Jesus, chill will yeh? She won't bring it to the board.

– She *said* she was going to have a meeting. That Finnegan cunt is dead.

– Jesus fucking Christ, Hamo, you broke a fella's nose for no reason. You back on those pills?

– What? No!

– Then why? What'd he say to you?

– Nothing. I'm not saying.

– So he did say something! Did you tell Finnegan and Miss Reynolds?

– Not a snitch.

Hamza stands still again.

– You're not to say it. He did say something. Called Karl a faggot.

– Just like, 'come on faggot', or what?

– You don't fucking call a gay person a faggot, Oisín! Ever. The fucking cunt.

– Yeah, no. Obviously. Yeah, you're right. But we don't know that Karl is gay though. Like, he says he isn't.

– He's got Ariana fucking Grande as his profile picture, bro!

– Yeah, I know. I know. Yeah, you're right. And after that shit with his gaff being raided again as well.

Behind Hamza's back, on the other side of the canal, a blue X5 pulls into the cul de sac. Oisín watches as it creeps along, turning slowly at the bottom, by the derelict warehouse and parking up, facing the water.

– You listening to me? I don't want to be talking about Karl with the teachers. If Finnegan keeps this up, I'll be in deep shit for the Leaving.

Oisín can make out four or five heads in the X5 as a battered white Avensis pulls into the lane.

– Yeah, I'm listening. Look, it'll blow over. Just take the suspension.

– But I shouldn't have to even take that. Alvar's the dick here. Always going on about gays and faggots and *paneleiros*.

The Avensis pulls up close alongside the first car.

– Fuck's sake, you say faggot all the time yourself, Hamza. So do I. So does everyone. Like you with your poetry, people'd say you're a faggot. Not me, other people.

– Yeah, but it's not gay or faggot as in the actual gays. My cousin's gay and he says it … if something's gay, it's just gay. If someone's being a faggot, they're being a faggot. Finnegan's being a faggot like, but Alvar's got a problem with actual gays. That's a scumbag right there.

The fellas in the cars are talking to each other, through their rolled-down windows. Oisín can't make out their faces.

– Yeah, I know all that. Look, just calm down. It'll all be over in a couple of days. You shouldn't have given him a dig in school. Should have waited till after.

Hamza frowns and looks at him from underneath his eyebrows.

– You being a philosopher? You seeing Ruairí or whatever that thing is again? he says.

Oisín, looking past him, only half listening. Someone gets out of the X5. One of Wino's snow-hoovers who was mauling every young one he could get his hands on that night in Sheedy's. He goes to the Toyota, opens the back door, and an unmistakeable ginger unfolds himself out of the car, holding a hurl. Words are being exchanged. Deano, his head hanging, towers over the man. Wino's man reaches up and claps Deano on the back, as he's walking away. Deano strolls back down the laneway, whacking the weeds on either side with his hurl. He picks up speed and starts jogging as he reaches the bridge. And then he's gone.

– I'm going to fucking kill that Finnegan cunt, firebomb his car.

Oisín throws his schoolbag over his shoulder and zips up his jacket.

– No you're not. Just shut the fuck up, Hamza, fucking faggot.

4
BENIT

Benit yawns, stretches. Wank or a bit more sleep? Choices. It's not easy, not easy at all. Someone's rattling about downstairs already. This, the noisiest house in the world. No matter how hard they try, no matter how many complaints from the neighbours, they still can't keep it down. He lies back, sinks into the pillows, listening to the breathing sounds coming through the curtain that separates his side of the room from the little brothers'. Roman snores like a digger yoke, Alex snores like a cat crying, a whiny, whistling sound. Something about his nose. Mama says the weather doesn't suit him because he's got so much Africa in him, being much darker than Roman. Not as dark as Benit though, obviously. And he's got no hassle with allergies or anything. He rubs his nose. Chance'd be a fine thing. *Never* gets sick. Not a single day missed from school or work ever. A gift and a curse. Anyway, the wank's still an option as long as he keeps it subtle.

He's tried getting up earlier and earlier to get some time, even a few minutes maybe, on his own. Wank or not, it'd be nice to listen to some tunes, mill into the porridge, bust out some moves round the kitchen with no one watching or listening. But no, never happens. Someone will be up, crashing around.

He stretches again, massages his left calf, then pauses to delicately run his fingers round the deep scar that ties him back to Congo, its edges still rough after all these years. Just that one bullet, the rest of his little body had been protected by his father's. It's aching again. Maybe the weather. Maybe a sign.

He pulls the special bag from under the bed. Navy canvas with brown leather straps, colourful prints of birds on the lining. Fabric, smooth and silky. Like something that someone who has a butler would have. Of course, Mama bought it. Special like. Not for school. He carefully swaps his kit back into his school bag. Black, torn, nylon, lots of pockets. Normal. After the guards took bird bag #1 off him, he had to put up with Mohammed flashing his cash, offering to pay to replace it. Hamza lent him money out of his credit union and nearly got the shoe because of it. Gotta be careful with the bird bag.

Taking the pink kit bag – some free sample make-up thing – he lays out his essentials. First, the fake Swiss Army knife, bought from Snitchy in the flats. At least he thinks it's fake. Never know with Snitchy. Benit's a regular window shopper in that place that sells cigars, knives, hip flasks and whiskey. He's checked the knives out in their slowly-spinning, well-lit glass cases, over the years. His one, the Snitchy one, looks the exact same as the real ones.

Next, the corkscrew – no telling when a lady might need a bottle opened. He's been checking out wine blogs, Jamie Goode's a king! Owen and Mama sometimes have a bottle of Jacob's Creek and, since he's turned eighteen, he gets a glass too the odd time. On his Christmas job in the kitchens in The

Davenport he downed the dregs of a few glasses, and you *could* taste the difference. Christina gets a half glass too if it's white, with fizzy water in it. What a joke. Can't remember the number of times he's carried Christina out of gaffs and parks and wherever else she's been having the sesh. Thanks a million bro, she says.

Condoms, three – yeh never know. Since he got the high fade, there's been a lot of interest from the cuties. A *lot* of interest. Good for carrying water too – 200 litres or something. You don't want to end up like Bear, having to squeeze a cake of elephant shite to sup the juice out of it.

Next, swabs – unsterile but still in the packet. Check the Sellotape seal. Dirt in a wound, last thing you want. Do the checks. Every time.

Bandages × 3, one for a sling, one small gauze, one elastic – sprains. He had to replenish stock last week after Whacker raided it, when the magic GAA water hadn't worked on some young fella's gashed shin and they needed to bring in the big medical guns – that's Benit – cos the club's first aid tin was found to contain (same as every other time it's been looked in): three safety pins, an elastic band and two balled-up wrappers off something called Fredent. Whacker fired the wrappers the feck out of it this time though.

A tiny bottle of red dirt from his grandmother's compound in Kigali. And the most precious, the most essential essential, a small cracked photo of a smiling group of men, dressed to the nines. Only the middle fella, beaming, towering over the others, in the pale blue suit and trilby hat, really interests him. His mother's photo is big and in his wallet. So he sees her every time he spends money.

Alcohol swabs – always good for cleaning things before you go at them. He can't recall ever using them himself but he's given a few to the junkies, just in case they'd use them and he's swabbed Oisín's and Karl's bacne before he popped them with a needle.

Everything checked off, he sticks it all back in the make-up bag, zips it, and throws it and few books into the school bag. These the books he needs for today? Sure, probably.

It's Mama downstairs. He knows the signs. She's the only one who sets the table for everyone. Must be on an early shift.

When he gets down to the kitchen, she's making eggs, saucepan on the go, whisking. Weird.

– Going fancy?

– I got those muffins you like. Eggs Benedict for you, to celebrate.

He rubs his hair with one hand, has a quick feel of his balls underneath his tracksuits, with the other.

– Get your hand out of there, boy. Manners. Have some respect.

He hadn't meant to. Force of habit – when you're confused and things have gone a bit tilted, check in with the balls first. Plus he's half-asleep. He's been careful since she'd warned him about *sexual* behaviour in the *family* home. Not that he'd ever done any sexual behaviour, as far as he knows, but hey. Apparently, it was time for a chat. Owen had given him the speech about behaving round Christina and the little ones, now that he was growing into a man. Nothing on display. And such. No more wandering round the house in his jocks (hadn't done that since he was eleven), and such. Looking at the ground, offering him a non-alcoholic beer. And such. Those little pink spots appearing on his face. Poor Owen. Such a nerd. And such.

Benit and Christina had a great laugh about that after – Owen, being *her* dad, having the man-to-man with Benit. Christina sitting up on the windowsill behind his bed, blowing smoke rings out the window. Christina doesn't give a shit whether he's only in his jocks or fully clothed. She's bro. His white bro. That's all. And he's bro to her. Always have been. Always will be.

– Yeah, OK. Sorry. What's the celebration? he says, looking away from his mother, fiddling with the packets of rice and pasta stacked up on the counter by the sink.

– Your marks, of course boy!

He fumbles around in his head for what she might be talking about. Has she lost her mind? Confused him with some of the other kids in the house? He takes another look at her, smiling, whisking like a maniac. Eggs Benedict before school, with all the trouble she takes over the sauce, has to mean something big.

Class tests? Negative. Hurling? Negative. He's done nothing that warrants this. *Did* he do a test that he's just forgotten? She'd only be keen on the science subjects anyway, so no.

– Oh yeah, OK. Thanks, he says, a little too rushed, playing for time.

She turns to look at him. Her Coombe uniform ironed to death and smelling of lavender.

– I met Oisín and Deano yesterday on my way home. You obviously wanted to surprise me. Modest boy. They were talking about some parties you're going to …

– Just Hamza's …

– And some girl's party? Hmmm?

Tanya's! Why the hell are the other pair mouthing to his mum about gaffs? She turns back to the pot, smiling that OG smile.

– So, I say to them, no, he is not going to all these parties. My boy has to study and he is not filling his head with parties and girls.

Here she goes. In that weird world of her own. Not a clue. He's eighteen, for fuck's sake – my boy! If they were still back home he'd be married. Or long dead. Or both.

– But they said, no, Fenella, haven't you heard? Benit, *my* Benit, got an A in Biology and an A in Physics.

He turns away to straighten his face. Dickheads. They know what she's like.

– I knew it, knew it all along. You were always a doctor. Finally, it's happening for you! I couldn't be more proud, Benit!

She drops the whisk, turns to him, reaches up and grabs his face.

– You should have faith. Your mama always knew. So, we're celebrating. I got smoked salmon too. Sit down, eat. My son, the doctor. You got lost for a while, I admit, but now you're back on the path. *Your* path. The doctor's path.

In fairness, she's given the doctor talk a rest for the past while. Hasn't really mentioned it since it became obvious that Benit and the academic stuff didn't really go. Always decent marks in French, of course, but that's about it. The parent-teacher meeting in third year was awkward but it was the Junior Cert results that wrecked her dreams altogether. Previously, in Fenella World, it'd been all Doctor Benit this and Doctor Benit that. Going all dreamy, talking about Nobel Prizes. Doctor's sets, a staple for Christmas and birthdays – plastic stethoscopes and small white coats with ripped-off arms all over the gaff. Never actually *playing* Operation – training, she called it. Himself and Christina operating on each other in the sitting room. Only Christina had the skills to steady-handedly remove the tiny balls of soap he'd rolled and stuffed up his nose to see how many he could fit up there, before anyone else discovered what he'd done. Would've been nee-naw time if she hadn't. Like the time he hid the telly remote on Christina so she told Fenella and Owen that he'd swallowed Domestos. No matter what he did, they wouldn't listen to him. Stomach pumping's sore.

*

He leaves the run – a belly full of Benedict don't work. He takes it slow, veers off down by the canal so he can walk by the water. A cat-sized rat sits on a tree root that's burst through the mildly tarmacked path. His mate's mooching around in the red and golden leaves, gnawing at an already-smooth chicken carcass. Rats can't sense you coming at them when the air's dead and thick. He stops and waits for them to finish, everyone needs to eat.

One of those eco-friendly green bin bags floats down past him, something round bulging inside. Looks flesh-coloured. No, orange. It's orange. Moving in the slow flow on its way to the sea. Too far out in the middle to get a hold of. He doesn't want to say, even in his head, what he thinks it might be. He'll only feel stupid when it turns out to be nothing. Eyes fixed on the bag, he slides into a curry chip puddle. Dummy rats sticking with the nothing-on-it chicken carcass when there's a full curry chip right here. Dopes. Don't see the gift in front of their faces. Always be on the lookout for the curry chip.

The bag glides closer to the bank. Wrestling through the hogweed, he gets a soggy foothold, grabs a stick and reaches out, almost catching the bag on the twig. A moorhen flaps up and out of his way but the heron stands still where it is, blade bill pointing down at the water.

– Sorry fam, gonna wreck yer buzz.

Back up on the bank, he keeps pace with the bag now waltzing along with a Club Orange bottle and the lumps of sliced pan that Purply-Headed Anorak Fella lashes everywhere. On the path, in the grass, in the water. Always far too much for the mallards, out in force this morning but passing no remarks. No sign of his bro grey crow. Bad omen with that yoke in the bag. If the grey crow arrives and talks to him, the day'll go grand.

Johnny Two-Cans is already sitting near the far steps at the bridge, rucksack, two Druid's. One opened, ready on the wall beside him.

– Haven't seen you this ages, Benit.

Benit smiles, keeping half an eye on the bag.

– Bit early for you, Johnny. You getting fit?

– Nice morning, mild. Get out and appreciate the day, my friend, appreciate the day, Johnny says, as he takes a glug.

– Yeah, Benit says, distracted. See that bag floating along there? Just wanna check what's in it.

Casual like. Curious. Why wouldn't he wanna see? People aren't curious enough, that's the problem. Don't relax and observe. Ask questions, talk to people. Don't even know when they're missing out. Shutting themselves off from people and things. Good people and things, maybe. Just cos they don't look right or they're afraid of them. Why wouldn't he want to know what's in it?

Johnny squints around Benit to see what he's on about. His sight's completely fucked since his jam-jar glasses got robbed in the hostel. Chances are whoever reefed them got the spins every time they looked through them; Benit tried them on one time and they messed up the whole world.

– It's over here, Benit says, taking Johnny by the elbow. Put down the can for a minute, will yeh? It's a two-man job.

Benit scouts around and hands a second stick to Johnny, who edges closer to the water. They work together with the branches like pincers for the best part of five minutes, but the bag's too heavy, the branches too bendy, and they can't get a proper hold of it. It floats on down the canal towards a pair of above-it-all swans who separate and glide around it. The bag, caught in their wake, is pulled out into the middle of the canal.

– A balloon, I'd say, Benit, he says, breathless from effort. That's all that's in there. Can't see it too well but it looks to be the shape of a balloon.

– Too heavy to be just a balloon, Johnny.

– Other rubbish too. Not a baby in it, in anyway.

Benit lurches and clears his throat.

– Where you staying these days, Johnny? he asks.

Johnny always looks decent. Scrubbed. Clean in his habits, as he says himself. The love of the two cans his only problem, as far as Benit and the lads can see, but his hands look a bit grimy this morning.

– Baggot Street Bridge, got a nice tent. Couple a mates alongside me. Look out for each other.

– No more hostel?

– No Sirree Bobbee, too much hassle. Junkies, God love them, not their fault, banging up beside yeh and puking and God knows what else. Me glasses were nearly the last straw. Then they took me little wash bag with me pictures, yeh know? Me kids an all. Probably slung them as soon as they got outside. Searched all the bins around. Couldn't find anything. Tent's grand. Me own front door.

Johnny's like Jack was – always looking on the bright side. Until Jack didn't. There's always a bright side though. Always. Nearly always. Benit looks at Johnny, now delicately sipping the cider, like this might be the only one he'll have today.

– How are the rest of the lads?

– All grand. Apart from Deano's not going school much.

– Don't blame him. And you? Studying hard, gonna go to college?

– Not sure *uni* is for me, yeh know.

– Well, I know a few lads, lemme know and I'll put in a word for yeh, bit of a job.

Sure, Johnny's probably got contacts in all the best places. Phone never stops ringing down in the tent.

– That's decent of yeh, Johnny, thanks.

– How's the blondie fella? Yiz all still at the hurling?

– Yeah, just the three of us now. Oisín's grand. Hassling Deano about the school thing. Thinks he's doing something he shouldn't.

– And is he?

– Doubt it. He's not thick.

– Not thick at all, Johnny says, slipping his hand into the bag, swapping empty for full. Heard about yizzer mate. Jack. Think the peelers got him?

– What? No, he hung himself.

– Yeah, heard he was in the cop-shop just before but.

66

He stalls, clears his throat, offers Benit the Amber Leaf pouch.
– Probably just a rumour.
– I gotta go school, Johnny.
He wasn't gonna have a smoke, but fuck it. He heads in under the bridge.

*

On the way out of the jacks he barrels into Filipino Cesar.
– Where were you? Me and Kev waited for you at the lights, jogging on the spot like two dicks.
– Eggs Benedict, Benit says, relaxing his face. Eyelashes swishy.
– Hold on, Cesar says, spinning Benit round to look at him as two second years staunch past them, making arrangements to have a knock in the Cabbage Garden after.
– You're wasted. What are you *doing*?
– Ah nothing fam, Benit says, putting his arm around Cesar and bouncing an invisible-but-definitely-there ball.
– When we shooting hoops with your mates again?
They fall in the classroom door. Hamza, sitting on a desk, turns around, frowns and then starts smiling. Gotcha. He knows. He knows.
– Dumbass Benit. Why're you getting wasted before school? says Cesar The Role Model, smiling. Wanna be a real Dub? A loser? Like Deano? Gobbling your coddle?
– Ah fuck off ya Chink, youse eat dogs, Benit says.
Hamza's biting his lip, looking ready to piss himself.
– What the fuck are *you* talking about, Benit, you're from Congo, you eat people! someone says.
Voices echo, laughing. Whoops and cheers. Was it Hamza who said it? It was, was it? He stares as hard as he can at Hamza, searching for a comeback, but Hamza says:
– Nah, bro, wasn't me, and he swivels his eyes, cartoony, towards big Russian, Actually-Will-Be-a-Doctor Vlad.

67

Vlad smiles softly, balancing on his chair's back legs, holding himself with his ruler trapped under the edge of the desk.

– Bit paranoid are yeh, Benit? Hamza says. It was Vlad, I swear. Amirite Vlad? Wouldn't let him away with that dissing, bro.

Vlad just smiles, looking off into the distance.

Benit tries to muster something smart to say. Congo, eating people. Russians, what? Slowly, slowly, it's coming. Face smiley. Face serious. Face smiley. Face serious. Russians, poison. Russians, vodka. Vlad, chicken fillet rolls … He's got it. Wait for it, wait for it. Yes!

– What the hell are *you* talking about Vlad? Youse eat snow!

The place erupts. Little Roland, repping Ghana, bangs his forehead over and over on the table, then rises up, clasping his hands behind his head.

– Man, Benit. Shut. The. Fuck. Up. Worst slag ever. Letting all of Africa down, man. Get in the bin.

Benit slumps into his seat. Seems something went wrong there but he's not sure what.

5
HAMZA

'You Tell Us What to Do'
Faiz Ahmed Faiz

When we launched life
on the river of grief,
how vital were our arms, how ruby our blood.
With a few strokes, it seemed,
we would cross all pain,
we would soon disembark.
That didn't happen.

Was it worth it? The trip to Tallaght? Depends on how bad it gets once he gets back to the flat. It got a bit cheeky in the cinema, right enough. He can still smell her on his fingers. *Definitely* worth it, however bad it gets.

How is it even possible that The Aunties were in Tallaght? What kind of djinn took them out there the one time he was out there too? Lucky break that Candy was in the jacks when they landed on top of him, but fuck, it was close. There's risk – fun risk, get-the-heart-pumping risk – and then there's risk risk – unnecessary, get-your-life-ruined risk. He didn't flinch (at least he's pretty sure he didn't) as Candy walked back from the toilets, straight past him and the clucking Aunties, head held high. Oh yes, that girl has mad back. Not a chance The Aunties would have put them together. Candy, the scarlet hair gleaming in the spotlights, stood looking in the window of Shoe Zone while they Punjabied at him about the importance of education. Should he *be* here? Shouldn't he be studying? Don't waste his gifts, a smart boy like him needs to start thinking about a wife, good wives aren't to be found in Tallaght shopping centre. Or anywhere in Tallaght, as a matter of much-cackled-over fact. He still didn't flinch even as he wondered had Candy, still looking at the shoes, got the gist of any of it. It pays to have practised an Auntie face in the mirror for years.

People, most of them munching, skirted around the Auntie and Hamza cluster. What is it with The Square? All of them eating as they're walking round the shops. You don't get it anywhere else. Custard Creams, like. Packets of them. Not something you'd get in the Merrion Centre. Even in the Ilac it'd be rare. He'd wandered through the Merrion a few times, while the family was visiting the uncle in St Vincent's Hospital. On holidays from Birmingham, on his way to their flat, the uncle had barely made it out of the ferry terminal before asking directions off the wrong scumbags and ending up smashed to bits, lacking his suitcase, with a serious concussion and a whole new set of Paki and, weirdly, black person racial slurs to inform the English branch of the family about. The feds found the suitcase in a laneway with most of his stuff still there, scattered around. Apart from his trainers and the food gifts he'd brought over. Naturally enough. Food and shoes, that's what the yitnas like. Come the revolution, that's what the Dubs will be going for, Foot Locker and Marks and Spencer's Food Hall.

Out in The Square, young fellas, especially the brown ones, shot him sympathetic but still jeering looks as he stood there surrounded by cardi-covered Aunties. Yes, yes, Aunties, he said, of course I'm out here in Tallaght on my own. Just wanted something different, taking a break from studying. Nodding, yes, that's right, The Aunties said, the mind definitely needs rest in order to work at its best. One of them looked doubtful – the smartest one. No one goes to rest their mind in Tallaght, in fairness. There's an exhibition on down the way that I wanted to have a glance at, actually, he said. Oh yes, he's an all-rounder, they understood perfectly. Art, literature, science. *And* business. Such a bright boy! Remember to focus, art afterwards, business first. Always remember that unassailable fact. Each in its place, each in its time. But business, always business first.

Just when he thought the onslaught had burnt itself out, that he'd managed to get away with it and was ready to jog on over to Candy and get the fuck out of this Auntie-packed hellhole, the queen of the Punjabi information-superhighway turned back and, over her shoulder, asked how the work with the ustadh was going. She knew! They knew! All along, they knew where he was supposed to be – learning his prayers online, from the clearly bent madrasa teacher back in Pakistan. Aunties: you need to be on the ball with them one hundred per cent of the time. Assume they know everything. All the time.

The worst bit is he hadn't even wanted to go to Tallaght in the first place. Rathmines was far enough from the gaff like, and no one from the fam or mosque was likely to be at the cinema in the afternoon anyway. But Candy insisted. Nah, The Square's really cool, she said. It's not. It's a quick trip out there, she said. It's not.

Candy'd booked the tickets in advance so they *had* to go to Tallaght. Now, because of Tallaght, he's awaiting his imminent execution when Ami gets back, armed with the info that he's bunked off the praying education that she's been paying for with her cleaning job. Candy decided on Tallaght because *he'd* get in deep shit if *he* was seen with her by any of *his* family. Oh, yes, she was very animated about it. Caring even. Thing is, if he's OK with staying closer to home and risking it, then why isn't she? Plus, he'd have fronted it out with anyone he met. It's not like they hold hands in public or anything thick like that. He'd have covered even if they had seen Candy.

At the top of the stairs he turns the key in the shaky door. Big locks on flimsy doors, that's how it goes here. It's the opposite back in Pakistan. No locks, big doors. Doors that stay open all day and then seal you in at night.

At Abba-Gi's house – if you can even call it a house – that's what it's like. It had started out as just one small house built by Abba-Gi's father sometime after partition. He'd seen pictures – the small house got added to until it was a sort of square-shaped set of interlinked rooms surrounding a chicken- and goat-filled courtyard. With a fountain that leaned to the side and had never seen water, as far as Hamza knew, even though it was beside the well. Abba-Gi had rooms built on top of other rooms with little or no regard for the size or shape of the lower levels. Unlikely that too much consideration was given to foundations. So things seemed to be in a constant state of semi-falling down-ness. As the family expanded and contracted – people went away and others came back – some bits were left to collapse and others built more sturdily and fancily, until the house could be called a mansion, pretty much.

Someone would decide that they'd had enough of Birmingham or London or Paris or wherever and they'd just up sticks and say they were coming back home. Abba-Gi would send a message to the brickmakers and they'd deliver the necessary and then scuttle back to their hovels at the kilns. Red Punjabi earth and brickmakers' blood in every brick of the ancestral home.

Playing ball in the courtyard with his cousins one day, hooting and howling at each other, the adults – uncles, farmworkers, grown-ups – were whispering, huddled together. Hamza found from a young age that it's always a good idea to open your ears wider when you see people making efforts to be unheard. The adults thought they were keeping it on the down-low that day but he'd heard, he'd heard. And he'd heard it over and over in his head every night for the rest of the time they were staying at Abba-Gi's. He'd silent-screamed into his mattress that night but the thoughts wouldn't leave his body. Even now, thinking about it as he struggles with the lock his palms itch. It's like horror procrastination – just as you're about to be slaughtered yourself because you got caught in Tallaght when you should have been becoming an Islamic scholar, you distract yourself with someone else's shit.

The brickmaker and his wife were shoved into a kiln and burnt alive. That's what the whispers in the courtyard were about. Pregnant, she was – her baby roasting away inside her like a suckling pig. She probably refused to suck some kiln-owner's dick or she and the husband owed money. Course they did, brickmakers always owe the kiln owners. From birth to death, as far as Hamza could see.

A lesson learned that day in the courtyard: certain people, by accident of birth or circumstance, must never complain, slack off, look crooked at the boss man, or into the oven they'll go. Brickmaker women get raped in the fields, their daughters given to the kiln owners as payment for one thing or another and Punjab, beautiful, red-earthed Punjab just moves along nicely. Nothing to see here, folks. And everyone forgets. Except Hamza. Hamza never forgets. There are boss men everywhere, ready to roast you alive.

Back in the front room, Abu's at the Venetian blinds, peering down at the street below. The smell of home clings to the walls – cardamom, garam masala and that flowery laundry stuff that Ami gets for Sumera because of her skin.

– What's the salan this evening, Abu? he asks as he looks in the fridge for the first time.

– Dunno, ask your sister, she's in her room. I think it's lamb karahi. You got inside just in time there, son. There's Muslims out there. Don't go back out till they've moved on or they'll drag you to mosque.

Hamza laughs, throws himself down at the scratched-to-shit kitchen table, its green paint almost gone, and stretches his legs out. While Ami's become the greatest Muslim to ever come out of Punjab since she came here, Abu's the worst Muslim the world has ever seen, with a strange but very real aversion to what he calls *real* Muslims. Says he's allergic to them and doesn't want Hamza getting sucked into it. Pretends that he's going to mosque, sometimes dragging Hamza as cover but then sends Hamza off to Oisín's or wherever and slopes off to one of his own mate's houses to get high as the Spire, on something as Pakistani as himself. He'll arrive back smiling like an eejit. Ami will give him a weird look but he'll put his arms around her and say something about all that praying making him happy and she'll pretend to slap his hands away, ignoring the smell – like, she must get the smell – and everything will be okay.

It's Ami, of course, who's insisting on this Quranic instruction. Abu's going along with it because he's got no objection to praying if that's what you're into, he just doesn't want it taking over anyone's life. People need to relax a little more, stop taking all this Allah stuff so seriously here, he tells Hamza when they're on their own. Given Hamza's atheism and the fact that he just likes hitting mosque for the craic sometimes, Islam's probably not going to ruin his life anytime soon. Funnily enough, Abu doesn't seem at all worried that Sumera's gone full Tallyban on it, as Deano says – hijab, prayer mat, the lot.

When Ami gets wind, as she so surely fucking will, of Hamza being out in Tallaght, missing his praying lessons, that shit's gonna be worse than partition, and Sumera, the pure one, is gonna love it. Ami'll get him with the shoe, for a start. She should really have given the shoe up at Hamza's age but she can't – there's too much talent there. Could have bowled for Pakistan, she can put so much spin on it – throw it round corners, hit her target in the dark – a genius of the shoe. When he'd fuck up back in Pakistan, she'd chase him around and around through the cobbled-together rooms and out into the courtyard, chickens scattering, feathers flying. Hamza had always been pretty nimble, good at dodging, but no one on earth could out-run or out-dodge Ami's shoe forever. It was always only a matter of time before you'd feel the cold, then the heat, then the momentary blindness of the thwack on the back of your head. Best not look round to see where she was, just take it like a man on the back of your skull. He'd learned that the busted-nose way. And whatever chance you have in the sprawling house in Jhelum, there's no escaping the shoe in the attic flat on the South Circular Road. And the shoe will only be the start of it.

– Have you taken my charger? Sumera says, glaring at him from the doorway of her room, phone jammed in her hijab.

– No, I've been out all afternoon. Why have you still got that yoke on in the house? Looks like it'll choke you.

Pinned at her throat, she's like a mad aul one on Moore Street with the scarf. She only started wearing it at all because some of her mates started. Now they're all at it. Half the time Sumera's wearing it walking round the flat, even in summer when the attic is stifling.

She pulls a face at him, rolls her eyes.

– I'm going out. Where were you?

– Out.

– Oh yeah? she hisses into his face.

Abu suddenly jumps back, pinning himself against the wall beside the window, like a fella in a cartoon.

– Caught? Hamza asks Abu, ignoring Sumera.

– Don't know, there's a crowd of them down there. They looked up at the window. Don't know if they saw me, Abu says, starting to grin, still plastered against the wall, shoulders bunched.

– Who Abu? What are you talking about? Sumera says, frowning.

– Muslims, Hamza says, delighted.

Sumera scowls at Hamza.

– Oh it's *my* fault? Abu's the one Muslim-scoping but it's my fault?

Sumera won't ever give Abu any hassle. He's now meerkating from a crouched position under the windowsill.

– I'm going out, Sumera says again.

– Well you're safe enough, no one's bothered whether you go mosque or not, Hamza says, smirking.

– They're gone, Abu says. Shukar-eh.

Hamza edges the phone out of his pocket just enough to read the message.

Ronnie:
Need fresh supplies. You around?

– I'm heading to Oisín's, Abu, Hamza says, discovering a hole in his pocket as he shoves the phone back in. Handy access for Candy. All that poetry is paying off, big style. Along with all the talk about Jack. But then, Hamza gets a lot out of the talk about Jack too.

Abu goes to say something to Hamza. You can see by his face that he knows that he should, that Ami would want him to say something, but he's not quite sure what.

– Studying, Hamza calls back over his shoulder.

He heads down the stairs, Sumera scooting after him.

– What are you up to?

– What are *you* up to Sumera? I just be chillin with the homies.

– In Tallaght, is it? she says. She's got her angry eyes in. Fucksake!

– Yeah? Don't believe everything you hear, *Auntie*.

– I know you're up to something. You think I don't know about you, big man about town?

– Fuck off Sumera.

– I'm on to you. I know there's more to this. No one goes Tallaght voluntarily, Sumera says.

– Yeah whatever, see ya, rat, he laughs and ducks down a laneway to double back towards Portobello.

– That's not the way to Oisín's. Got my eye on you, Hamza. Gonna sniff it out, whatever it is, she shouts after him.

He doesn't turn round but roars back:

– Yeah that nose is big enough. Good luck with that.

She hates her big snoot. He's happy enough with his but the nose comment will send Sumera into a spin. Good enough for her.

*

Not a bad guy, Ronnie, as poshies go. Distributes with no fuss, collects the funds, takes his cut, no bother.

Abu's saving for a workbench he saw in the IKEA catalogue, has big plans for DIY when they move out to somewhere stupid like Blanch or Lucan because that's the only place they've a chance of affording. Renting still. But a house this time. In Ami's dreams, at least. She hankers after a garden, says flowers grow so well here. And Adderall sales will help with all that or at least they'll help with the bus fares from the middle of nowheresville to UCD, when Hamza starts there.

Hamza's widened his net, found a few others in the school on Adderall or Ritalin. Most of them happy to pass at least some of it on to him for a few quid. The market cornered, he'd branched out from the tiny Lutheran school to the bigger rugby schools, scaling it up. He's got suppliers in some of the other normal schools. Even had his last girlfriend, the mad Mullingar nerd with the Niall Horan obsession, gathering supplies down there and bringing them on a Saturday to clever camp in DCU.

Poshlads need this gear more than anyone. Half of them are on some kind of shit already – ADHD, autistic, depressed, old-style mental or just with a bit too much personality for their parents' or their teachers' liking. They're hauled off to the doctor. It's the other half who are Hamza's customers – the half that *wants* to be on some shit, wants to have a problem or just wants to pretend they're taking it to focus on exams. Maybe that's not fair, maybe some of them do actually want to concentrate on their exams. Can't see how speed helps but whatever.

The Business – the A 'n' R Business, as Oisín calls it because he thinks that's dead funny – is the reason Hamza gave up hurling and started rugby instead. Hamza needed some way of communicating with the poshies. No better thing than rugby for that.

So yeah, it was just The Business that stopped him going hurling. Not the fact that he shook like an alcky every time he tried to walk up the lane to the club since Ruairí's accident.

Not the memory of the white powder scattered across the road outside the Spar, that thirteen-year-old Hamza, on his way to hurling, mistook for drugs. It wasn't the dark liquid soaking up through the patch of sand that Hamza only understood later that evening, after the call came. Little Hamza had mouthed to all the lads at hurling about the huge drugs bust he'd seen outside Spar and the coke all over the road and the shoot-out he'd barely missed. It was only afterwards that he'd realized he'd never noticed that Oisín and Ruairí weren't at hurling that evening at all, as he, Hamza, made himself the big man in the growing story of the drama he *hadn't* witnessed outside the Spar.

Washing powder. Not drugs.

Ruairí had been sent by his mum for washing powder. She'd asked Oisín to go first but he'd wriggled out of it. And there it was, washing powder, spread all over, stuck in between the stones in the tarmac. They said the van driver screamed like a wounded animal. That's what brought everyone out of the Spar and the houses all around. Ruairí's brain swelled. Took a week for him to actually die.

I just prefer rugby, want to try something new, Hamza told the psychologist or whatever she was. That's right, fam, wanna try something new. And you, Missus, just keep those pills coming.

He's creaming a tidy profit – nothing excessive. Gives the Adderall kids in Colmcille's and his other supply schools a fair price and he and a couple of good lads distribute it to the buyer schools. Practically Fairtrade. Everyone wins. No brick-makers on Hamza's watch. And when full Marxism is implemented, there'll be no need for Adderall at all, never mind selling it to the posh kids. The posh kids will be in Colmcille's or Colmcille's will be for posh kids and they'll all be posh kids or all normal. Or something. That'll be after a while. Hamza's a realist.

It takes cold hard cash to set up full communism. Hence, the upcoming commerce degree – all part of the long-term vision. Get a good posse around you, family first – Ami will definitely be on board. From a long line of socialists, she'll have to be down with Hamza's revolution. He's working on the boys. Oisín gets it but has no urgency – too busy with his guitar and his business ideas for making cash. The others not so much, but they will eventually. Candy's a hundred per cent, from that very first night. Hundred per cent on the communism, hundred per cent on the Punjabi poet – the years in Birmingham, her best mate was called Moazzam. Come to think of it, maybe she has a thing for brown fellas? Doesn't matter. As long as she has a thing for Hamza (and she says she definitely does) who cares?

Blast through the degree, get stuck into the poshies' groups, play rugby, get rich, be with Candy, then bring the house down and the brickmakers in it. Small matter of the family? Think about that later.

Floppy-fringed Ronnie is already sitting cross-legged on one of the stone tables, fending off the swans at Portobello harbour.

– Alright, how's my guy Hamza? he says, and reaches out for an elaborate handshake.

At least Ronnie knows how to do it properly. Goes to that hippy weirdo school. He looks like his mum got hold of him by the legs and ran him along the floor, picking up the odd dust bunny with his face.

– Good, Hamza says. See you're still struggling with that beard there. Looks like you've had face chemo, fam.

– Yeah, we can't all be as successful as you, my man. What age did you start with that yoke on your face?

Hamza strokes his beard. Yep, it's a beauty.

– I came out like this. Nah, twelve. Started when I was in sixth class.

– You joking? Primary school?

– Real man genes, yeh know?

– Where's this you're from again?

– South Circular.

– Yeah, your family or whatever?

– Punjab, Pakistan.

– Yeah, just didn't know whether you were Arab or Spanish or what. Do you know that fella Mohammed?

– I know quite a few Mohammeds, in fairness bro, Hamza says, grinning.

– Ah yeah, course, Ronnie says, going a bit pink. The dodgy one.

– Dawg, I know more than one dodgy Mohammed.

– Shades, big jackets, lotsa snow.

– Ah yeah, I know Mohammed.

– What's his problem?

– Arab.

Ronnie looks down at the ground and half-laughs in that white, afraid-to-get-it-wrong, not-sure-if-this-is-a-joke-and-if-he-should-be-laughing way. Saps. Ach, you've got to have mercy.

– Only messin with you, bro. Yeah, I know him. He's alright, just don't get too entangled with him, know what I mean?

– Got that vibe.

They stroll over to the boardwalk and stand looking down into the dark water.

– Gives you MND, that shit, yeh know? Hamza says, looking at the algae scum gathering round the reeds, beer cans and burger boxes, being whipped up by the stiffening breeze.

– Yeah, my uncle died of it last year. He was super fucked-up at the end.

– Did he eat that shit?

– Not as far as I know. Spirulina, isn't it? Meant to be good for you.

– How the fuck could that be good for you? It's actual pond scum, like. Who looks at that and thinks, yeah, I'll have a bitta that for my dinner? Mindless. Health food shops sell it. You can sell anything to the type of people who'll eat pond scum.

– Don't think my uncle ate it anyway. Ronnie says dragging on his blunt, rocking back and forth on his Nike skate shoes. Wait, maybe. He was into healthy eating and all that. He was a runner. Did marathons.

Hamza cops what Ronnie's wearing for the first time. You've some swag if you can carry off full-on flares.

– You get it from eating bats too. Bats that ate that blue-green algae on fruit. Looked into it when everyone was pouring buckets of water on themselves there a couple of years ago.

– My uncle didn't eat bats either. He was from Stillorgan, Ronnie says, passing the blunt.

– Tastes like chicken, they say. Fruit bat. They only eat fruit, Hamza says holding the smoke in.

– Clue's in the name, amirite? Ronnie says.

– Yeah. I'd rather eat a bat that's been free, flying around, eating mangoes and shit, than a chicken that's been stuck in a cage being fed its own shit.

– Me too, bro, me too. I'm a vegetarian. I ate a burger last week though, I was starving. Where would you get a fruit bat though? Do you eat them in Pakistan?

– Fuck off, no! Chinks eat bats. Friend of mine, he's Chinese, he's eaten bat, he says. Says he liked it.

– Chinesers, yeah.

– They eat everything. Insects, dogs.

– Oh wait, Ronnie says, sure bat soup. Yeah, bat soup.

– Bird's nest soup.

– Imagine. Imagine that, man, eating a whole bird's nest. In a soup. Had shroom tea the other night with a bunch of the lads. Golden Teachers. Got them from Mohammed, *that* Mohammed, and he charged us a fucking fortune. But it's all good.

– How much did you pay?

– Two hundred. Enough for four of us.

Fucking hell, like. That's Mohammed for you. Scamming the nice white boys. If these pretty southsiders are stupid enough to pay ... He'd scam his own mum, Mohammed. Maybe he wouldn't. Maybe that's not fair. Hard to tell.

– You paid it.

– Nah, one of my mates did. Got a loada money for his eighteenth. His dad's a judge. Anyway, speaking of. Here.

He slips Hamza the cash and takes the pills. Four swans sail slowly towards the boardwalk, breaking through the reflected glow of the lights on Portobello Bridge, as Ronnie takes out his pouch to roll a plain rollie.

– Love a smoke after a smoke, man.

– Going skateboarding now? Hamza says.

– Yeah, I'll certainly jump on that board, man. What if that algae is actually a super intelligent life form, sent here to eliminate the human race?

– Could be but it'll only eliminate the dicks who'd pay good money for pond scum and nut butter in shops called Green Fungus or something. Going Weaver?

– Have you tasted nut butter? It's class. Nah, not Weaver. No, no, no. Might hang around here. Few mates of mine got the shit kicked out of them and their bikes wrecked in Weaver last week. Middle of the afternoon. A few of us managed to run into this aul one's house across the street. She just opened the door, let us in and then shut it in the skangers' faces.

– Why'd they attack you? Just for?

– No idea. We're just there, doing our thing in the bowl. A few of the lads from Dún Laoghaire had come in.

– What age were the straps that attacked you? Kids?

– Yeah, mixed, but kids mostly. Couple of mad lads with chains. Few girls too.

– They're nearly the worst. You can't give them a dig either.

– You never know when they've a blade. Like little kids. One of them was throwing nunchucks around. You wanna have seen it. He was about six. Like *The Hunger Games*, man.

– Anyone call the guards?

– Dunno. Not much point, I reckon. They didn't arrive before I got out, that's all I know. She let us out the back into the lane after she made us tea and Mikados – love Mikados, never have them in our house – and told us how to wind our way outta there.

– Anyone hurt?

– Yeah, course. A couple of the lads got a smack of the chains. There's still blood in the bowl. The aul one phoned someone she kept calling Jimmy Joe. Her son, by the sounds of it. Man, it was mental. A load of cars pulled up. Real nice wheels. This big fat fucker in a white tracksuit got out and had words and the skangers scattered.

Ronnie bends to stub out his rollie and holds it in his hand. While he's crouched, looking out over the water:

– What's this I hear about you and that Candy girl?

– Who? No idea what you're talking about. Who's Candy? Hamza says.

– Just something I heard. That she's with some guy who sounded like you. Lotta lads wouldn't mind getting with her. Heard a lot about Candy. Nothing bad like.

Ronnie side-eyes Hamza then stands up, hands stuffed in pockets.

– So, whatever. Surprised you don't know her man. You know everyone. Lucky guy though, whoever he is.

– Candy. Sounds like she's on the pole, Hamza says walking away.

*

Deal done, he heads for a wander to use up some time. You never know with Sumera. So he shoots a text to Oisín to cover if anyone asks.

He puts his fingers to his nose. Fuck! The smell of Candy's gone. Oh no, no, there it is, just a little hint of her along with the grass. Could there be a finer scent? Nope. Must suggest that to Ois. He'd love it. Grass Gee. Gee Grass? Ois will know.

*In the stillness of each wave we found invisible
currents.
The boatmen, too, were unskilled,
their oars untested.
Investigate the matter as you will,
blame whomever, as much as you want,
but the river hasn't changed,
the raft is still the same.
Now you suggest what's to be done,
you tell us how to come ashore.*

Candy said after the Auntie attack that maybe they should cool it for a while. Whatever cool it means. Yeah, what does that mean? In Hamza's experience that's the brush-off but then she asked him to recite the poem again to her on the Luas back. Which was hard to do with some tool bent double with a big string of spit swinging from his mouth, roaring at a Chinese woman down the back about his kids being taken off him, and Hamza staring into the snout of a piebald pony that two young fellas were taking into town.

He mumbled the poem to her anyway. 'I love it,' she said, dropping her head onto his shoulder. 'Do it in Urdu,' she whispered. Come on, not here, Hamza said. 'What the fuck are you on about, Hamza?' one of the horsey fellas asked him – Colmcille's, second years. Hamza didn't bother asking them why they'd the pony on the Luas but they told him anyway. Bringing it to the DSPCA, they said. Rescued it. The DSPCA's in the mountains, Hamza told them, you're going in the wrong direction. Getting him onto the back of the brother's pickup, the pair of them said, acting hard but still looking for Hamza's approval, him being a well-known horsey type.

When they got closer to Fatima though, Candy's head wasn't on his shoulder anymore and she stood up, beside the door, away from him. And when they hopped off she floated away from him in the crowd. He had to go back and find her and she shuffled from foot to foot like she couldn't wait to get away. I need to pee, she said, gotta go. She went to the toilet just before they left Tallaght.

Killing time until, hopefully, Ami's finally in bed, he turns onto St Alban's Road – red-bricked but not as posh as Raymond Street, some dingier-looking houses, but the same kind of mix of people. Management types and inherited money working on developing some artsy eccentricities. And some actual mildly successful artsy types who bought before anyone thought that houses in Dublin should cost more than Pakistan's GDP. An actress who won an Oscar (did she actually win?) for some film with lots of shawls, red hair and shouting into the wind and who now just does films about being raped by a seagull or some such; an artist who uses his own spunk to 'paint' splash pictures that he names after his children. They're all part of the plan, the posh street people – all wannabe lefties. Very right-on, no racists here on this street. No black or brown people either. They make their kids wear helmets walking to school.

*

Daylight's seeping under the blind. Too bright to be early. She's moving about in the kitchen. Abu's talking, sounds like into the phone. If he stays in here long enough, they might all forget about him and go about their business. Now Ami's on the phone. He can't quite catch what she's saying but she's getting animated. Sing-songy. Making arrangements, probably. Getting out and about. He rolls over onto his belly. Time for a wank if they all head out. He pulls the phone off the locker. Still nothing from Candy. Opens PornHub. Steps coming towards his room – closes PornHub – but hopefully heading for the bathroom instead. No, she's gone back into her and Abu's room. Shouting. Now she's walking back out. Bathroom this time. No, back into the kitchen, *alhamdulillah*. No. He flicks the phone off altogether, under the pillow. Facedown. Eyes closed. He's so fast asleep it isn't right.

The door slams open, hitting the thin partition wall, shaking the walnut-effect wardrobe so much that the little glittery hanging flag picture of Mecca tacked to the side of it clatters to the floor. Sleep breathing. Don't give in. She won't deliberately wake him. How long is she going to stay there? He's asleep. Deep, deep sleep. The TV is on with music blaring. It changes to talking. News probably. Urdu anyway. Sounds of dishes being rattled and still the door's open.

He sleep-slurps and turns his face enough that he can see a little of the doorway. He won't open his eye but he could, he just might be able to ease up the lid enough to peek through his lashes. No, not yet. Wait, breathe. A sleep-groan and he turns fully onto his side. No, no, I won't wake yet. I've been working too hard. Has she gone? No sounds of her feet but maybe. His bladder is starting to ache but he's outlasted her before, he can do it again. Fuck! He's actually bursting ...

If Ami is still standing there, she's soundless. How can a woman be so soundless? He's got to go for it. He rolls onto his back and groans, yawns and then rolls quickly back onto his side, flicking his eyes open as he goes, so she won't catch it. Eyes squeezed shut, like they'll never open again. His heart rate's up. She'll see that, he knows it. His breathing's changed.

She's standing there, waiting. Silhouetted in the doorway. Armed. The shoe.

6
BENIT

Some creep of an aul boy's walking round with a group of young fellas, Snitchy and yer man, whatshisname, from second year, and others, younger even. Dodgy. Looking into windows, scoping cars.

He follows them down the lane out the back of Oisín's house and slides on by them, huddled over doing bumps on Sadie's garden wall. They're kids like.

Snitchy turns round with a frosted nostril. Wiping his nose on his sleeve, he says:

– Ah, howya Benit. How're yeh getting on with the knife?

– You okay there, Snitchy? Benit says, death-staring the man, who starts squaring up to him like a nube.

A grown adult, older than his folks. Scumbag.

– Yeah, doing good man, doing good. Yeh need anything, yeh check me out yeah? Bitta sniff, yeah?

– Yeah whatever, Benit says, as he walks on down the lane towards Marty's.

When he arrives at the door of the old folks' flats, he rings the bell for number nineteen.

A voice crackles on the intercom.

– Ah, Benit, the main man. Hold on, I'm nearly ready.

He arrives out in a pair of bright blue canvas trousers, a short-sleeved check shirt and the ever-present bodywarmer, pushing an aul one's tartan shopping trolley. Doesn't need a walking frame, see? All that soldiering has him straight as a pole. He's just a bit unsteady sometimes, is all. No, he doesn't want Benit to get the bits and pieces *for* him, he wants Benit to go *with* him up to the shops and stalls, then down to Lidl for a few bits. Can't beat the spuds in the greengrocers on Meath Street. Floury as hell.

He needs saffron, he says.

– Most expensive spice in the world. I say, the most expensive, Benit.

– You sure you're going to get the most expensive spice in the world on Meath Street?

He stands back, aghast, with a where-else-would-you-get-saffron face.

– You've an awful lot to learn about Dublin. This is the Liberties son.

– I know, Benit says. I live here.

Here comes the speech about people always taking refuge here, and the old handwritten cookbook found in a drawer in a family dresser in a house with a half-door off Francis Street. A cookbook written by a great-great-auntie who was a Protestant, would you believe? A Protestant and not even rich. Well, what ingredients *weren't* called for in that book's recipes, aren't even worth mentioning.

– And do you know where you'd be guaranteed to get them? Dried, they'd probably be, not fresh now. Meath Street! See all these Chinamen coming in now opening shops? And the Ruskies? We used to have all that stuff coming into Dublin, once upon a time. Then the place went to rack and ruin, all the food was going out not coming in and then De Valera – the thundering fuck – ah don't start me …

Dev's nearly the only man who makes Marty swear.

On Meath Street, women stand around, howyaing each other. Girls in well-stretched leggings, causing a draft with the eyelashes, scan Benit. Some half-sniggering. He knows they'll be looking at his arse once he's passed. They won't see much with this dropped-back puffa. He slows down a bit. Give them something to look at. Sweet ones, a couple of them. They need to get louder, man. Louder. Bit of character. One of them throws up the set and he grins. Gotta love the Dub girls.

Benit and Marty cross over, passing no remarks on the slow traffic, ease through the bulgy wall of men outside The Lark Inn asking Marty how he's getting on, and head for the plant and toilet roll stall near the Russian shop at the top of the street. Might as well make use of a big fella like Benit, while he has him. Needs stuff for the window boxes but doesn't want to give all his sponds to Lidl. Benit catches aul ones giving Marty the glad eye before slipping down the narrow pathway to the hidden grotto at the back of the church – the boys' best place for a sneaky, fresh air, looked-down-on-by-the-Virgin-Mary smoke, or a meet. He hasn't been in ages. Must say to the boys to go back down, see what's occurring.

Loaded up with petunias, cyclamen, violas, jacks roll, shallots, a sink tidy, six scrubby sponges, a big packet of only-slightly-out-of-date Mikados, a heap of other veggies, twelve chicken pieces for the freezer, the saffron (also out of date) in Schwarz jars (three for a fiver), a ten-kilo of Dublin Queens and a pink water pistol to keep that feck of a ginger tom off his pots, they head back down the street.

– What you doing with all that saffron?

– Sure, there's only a few tiny bits in it, Benit, look, he says holding one up. I got a recipe on the Jamie Oliver app. On the pig's back I am now.

And he is. The daughter, who lives in Belgium, got him a phone with big writing. Since he discovered Jamie, he can't be stopped. The portions are too big so he gives some to the neighbours – they're all old, not fit to make a decent Stroganoff.

Back on Cork Street, a Lexus pulls up ahead – tinted rear windows.

– That's one of them wrong fellas, slow down, Marty says. We don't want to be caught near them in their fancy cars. Not a good spot, out here in the open.

The car just sits there. Marty makes a fuss of scuffling around in his trolley, looking for something. Benit sticks his hands into his tracksuits pockets and waits. He can't help smiling as Marty ducks down behind the trolley handle, like it'll shield him from some unknown danger.

Out of the back of the car comes a scarlet head, looking flustered.

– That'll be one of his lady friends. Working girls. Don't stare at her now, Marty mutters.

She pauses for a moment, straightening herself and her eyes meet Benit's. There's a flicker of recognition, the start of a smile at the corner of her mouth but then she makes her face solid, turns back to speak to someone inside the car, slams the door shut and walks towards Benit and Marty. Expressionless. Busy. The car stays where it is, engine purring. Benit doesn't have a thing for cars. Like, some of them look decent, but would you spend that much on a piece of metal? The Lexus slowly pulls off but gets stuck at the pedestrian crossing. Candy looks over her shoulder, fixing something that isn't there on her jacket, turns back and grins at Benit.

– How are you Benit? she says, showing her lovely teeth, nearly equal to Benit's own. Marty stands to attention.

– Hello love, he says, smiling and winking at Benit.

– Eh, this is Candy, this is Marty, Benit says.

It costs nothing to be courteous, my boy.

This feels a bit weird. He hasn't actually *seen* Candy since the night of Jack's funeral. Plenty of talk about her though. Hamza's missing in action far too often. Saying he's at mosque when he's definitely not at mosque. Unless, of course, he's suddenly become the most Muslamic fella in Dublin. Unlikely. Hamza finally admitted that he's seeing her only last week, and only to Benit. She's hot, proper sexy in a strange way. And nice. She's just nice. At least she seemed nice at the funeral. Well, after. Tablets, her mother had given her before the church. That's what had her acting up, the coffin and all that.

Candy asks Marty about his shopping. Talks about the saffron. Tells him about her friends' cooking in Birmingham. Marty, leaning on his shopping trolley, is suddenly bolt upright again, looking past Benit. Candy, catching Marty's look, sets off down the street away from them, with a quick:

– See ya Benit.

The car has done a 360 in the middle of Cork Street and slowly creeps along the pavement, pulling up beside Marty and Benit. Ah, *so* not in the mood for this shenanigans.

That touched fella from Marylands, with his miniature pony on a lead, chooses this particular moment to land beside them, grinning.

– Hello, hello, hello, he says. Twins, are yiz twins?

– Yes, twins, that's right, Marty says. Go on about your horsey business there, Tom.

– Born and bred just there, born and bred, Tom says, nodding enthusiastically as he scuttles on.

– Yeah, yeah, good man there, Marty calls after him.

The rear window glides down, shocking smooth. Wino, sitting in the back, phone to his ear, says nothing, just stares at Benit, who starts to laugh, holding his gaze. God's gift, they think they are, butty little fuckers, with greasy hair.

He pulls off his shades. Must be dead sunny in the back there. Pricks like this, big men when they've guns. Big men when they've their hardmen standing in front of them.

Benit widens his grin, in case dickwad didn't get the message, then shifts over to stand in between Marty and the car, folding his arms. Wino just stares back, the droopy corner of his mouth twitching, as the Lexus moves off.

– You wanna watch him. Don't be getting entangled. Know his kind, so I do. You get them everywhere. A wrong un, as me mother used to say. Did I tell you me mother was English? English, she was, from Manchester.

– Nah, you never mentioned, Marty.

Only a million times. Candy's disappeared off the street altogether. Nowhere to be seen.

– Now, he's the kind of a fella who thinks he's better than everyone, yeh know, Benit? Fancy car, all the trimmings. I do see him in action, round here, in Sheedy's. A bully boy. You don't want to be shaping up to his kind. Keep yer powder dry. Bide yer time. All kings fall. Let his own ate him.

*

– Nah, I'm not into that shit. It's just not my ting, fam, Benit says, settling himself into a seat beside Deano.

The others just don't get it. They love hours and hours sitting glued to a screen, shouting and roasting each other. Deano and Oisín swear it helps their reaction times – fast twitches – keeps them sharp at the hurling. Maybe something in that but all those brown people getting fucked up in the dust by hardman Americans doesn't do it for Benit. And then there was the incident with the chickens, Oisín blasting them out of it for no reason and laughing at Benit when he objected. What craic is there in shooting someone's chickens, like? No thanks, fam. No thanks.

– Will we go park then? Have a knockabout.

Deano pulls off the headphones.

– Yeh were only training a couple of hours ago. Yer like a machine, bro. Nah, I wanna do this. Gonna get good. Doing a

93

tournament next weekend. If that fella from Ashbourne can do it, I can. Whacked a kid from Cork out of it last night.

– A kid?

– Yeah, eleven or something, Deano says, laughing.

– You're eighteen and you're proud of destroying a little kid? Good job, fam.

– He was pretty good like. Fuck off.

So, tomorrow night then, we going that Tanya's gaff, right? Go bonfire first? Oisín and Karl wanna go. His brothers' have skin in the game. The Frankie youngfella's got something special lined up.

– Nah, not into the bonfire, Deano says. Be the usual yackballs, don't wanna go. We even invited to this Tanya's gaff, in anyway?

– Karl says yeah. Wall-to-wall cuties. Christina's going too.

– The lovely Christina, she still being a dyke?

– Says she's bi.

– They all say that though, don't they?

Deano loves the bonfire. Never misses it. Only stopped collecting himself this year. Plus he'd have a go at that Tanya anytime. And Christina, if she wasn't Benit's stepsister.

– Why you not into going?

Rubbing his chin, where some half-arsed hairs are straggling down. The beard thing's just never going to work for him.

– Do you want a knockabout or not? Deano says, grabbing the hurl from the end of the sofa. I've me last of Gracie's in the tin there, come on, have a bit of a shmoke on the way.

– Saw Candy just there. With Marty.

– You doing his shopping again? Wait, Candy with Marty? The aul fella?

– She wasn't *with* Marty! Just ran into her on the street. Met her like.

– Met her or *met* her, Deano says, grinning. Don't tell me the Candinator has struck again?

– Jesus Christ, fam. She's with one of me best mates. Bros before hoes innit.

– *Is* she? Ha! So that creep *has* been banging her?

Fuck! And again, fuck!

– Ah wow, yeh weren't supposed to say! Ha, ha, what's it with you and secrets, Benit? Everyone tells yeh shit but yeh just can't keep it in, can yeh, buddy?

He rubs the top of Benit's head.

– That fade's fresh. What's occurring with the Candster in anyway?

– Nothin, just said hi, is all.

*

They all agree that whatever about Tanya's gaff, Hamza's party next month is gonna blow the posh bird's gaff out of the water, no messin. He's rented an Airbnb and the owner knows it's for a party, unlike the last time, when they ended up freezing their bollocks off on the quays at two in the morning after the Kendrick gig, on a school night.

But Karl's not happy, not happy at all, with Deano's tracksuits.

– It's Puma, that's a label, yeah? Fuck off.

And there's some bullshit out of Deano about not getting all fancied up for some rich bitch's gaff. He's actually wearing a jumper. In fairness, even for Deano, that's rough.

– Yeh don't look too stylish man, has to be said, Oisín says.

– Take it or leave it, your choice, says Deano, looking at Karl. Don't even wanna go to this yoke. Happy to head back up to the flat. Benit's wearing fucken tracksuits too.

– Full camo Nike on Stormzy here is not the same thing, Oisín says. Amirite Karlo?

Mobs gather round the base of the three-storey mountain of pallets and boxes and tyres and bikes and a smashed-up car and sofas and shopping trolleys. Mostly pallets though, this year – quality.

– Jesus, never saw so many before, Oisín says. All the flats coming over all nostalgic.

– Last one before they knock the rest, Karl says.

– Ah, you feeling all sad now, Deano? Oisín says.

Looks like half the Tenters is here too – keeping to themselves. They'll be glad to see the back of the place probably. Less break-ins, less cars scratched, less windows smashed, less hassle. Doreen's left the dog at home. Terrified he is. Nearly couldn't leave him, but she had to be here for this last one. Left the telly on loud for him. Loves Corrie, he does.

Benit waves to Marty who's sidling up to some aul ones beside the rusted, unemployed washing line poles. Karl's brothers and their mates are still adding bits at the bottom and lashing bin bags full of clothes up as high as they can, as the Men Who Light the Bonfire light the bonfire and whatsup, we're off! Cheers and woos at the first loud explosion inside the mountain. Bangers and fireworks rip through the air. Men have words with young fellas about setting them off beside aul ones and aul ones act grateful. Wino steps out of the shadows, smiling, then sours and lets a kid know he's scoping him as the kid sneaks up behind Sadie, Doreen and Rita, standing beside the lads. Sadie's mouth puckers but she respect-nods over at Wino. Thick smoke billows from the tyres, blacking Wino out.

– Quit staring at him Benit, Oisín says. Ignore the prick, amirite, Deano?

No answer, Deano's moved way back up against the wall of the block, out of the light.

– What the fuck's wrong with you? Oisín says, as Hamza finally rocks up, in a fouler.

No point in asking him when he's like this. Why bother?

– Nothing. Where's Deano?

Benit throws his head towards Deano lurking in the dark.

– Too hot for him here?

– Spose so.

– Alright then, since yiz asked ...

– Eh, yeah, we didn't, Oisín says.

– Candy's not coming, Hamza says, tight-mouthed.

Oisín gives Benit a questioning look. Benit responds with a shake of his head.

– So yeh are with her? Karl says.

– Course I'm with her. What the fuck?

– Okay.

– Yeah, okay! She's meant to be coming here, then out to Tanya's gaff with us.

– But she's not coming now. So, you're not with her anymore, Karl says.

– What the fuck? I *am* with her! Karl, what the fuck would you know?

– Harsh, Benit says. Cutie stands you up though, gotta cut loose, fam.

– She didn't stand me up, dickhead.

– Don't see her here, Oisín says.

– She's gonna be out at Tanya's.

– How the fuck would Candinsky be out in Tanya's? This is the same Candy, right? Oisín says.

Like there's another Candy in town?

– They're in the Institute together.

They all turn away from the flames and the crackling. The banging is ringing in Benit's ears. Oisín pulls Hamza by the arm, back towards where Deano's standing.

– The Institute? Oisín says, laughing. Candy?

– You taking the piss, fam?

Oisín reefs the buds out of Deano's ears.

– Hear this?

– Not anymore, no. Thanks bud.

– Loverboy here, *is* riding Candy, like he's actually with her, says Candy's going to this gaff tonight *and,* get this, Candy's in the Institute.

Deano frowns, searches Hamza's face and sticks his buds back in, glancing in Wino's direction.

– Ah here, that's some fucked up shit, Hamza. Fuck off, yeah.

– The Institute, really? She a dealer or something? Karl says.

– She has to go there to catch up, if she wants to do the Leaving this year like. Only place she can do it intensively.

– Only place she can pay hundreds of thousands to go to. How's her skanger mam paying for that?

– I don't know, Karlo, maybe her mother works like? Hamza says.

– None of them have fees that high, yeh pack of tools. Maybe ten grand or something. Anyway, why would you be bringing Candy here? What if your family was around?

Hamza's family's *never* gonna be at the bonfire. Hamza looks at Oisín weird.

– Well, whoever. Someone could tell them. Deep shit with Ami then.

– Look around, who here's gonna tell the fam about Candy?

The car explodes behind them. Wino flashes in and out of view through the flames, heading their way, flanked by his heavies, eyes fixed on Deano and Hamza, who turn without looking at him and walk away towards the avenue.

– Youse coming or not? Deano shouts back over his shoulder.

Nah, no need to mention Wino. No need to freak anyone out. Benit looks back, Wino and his fellas have stopped, glaring at their backs as they walk down the road. Benit winks at him and, laughing, turns and follows the others.

*

– What are you on tonight? Deano asks, as they pass big pillar number two million.

– Malibu and milk, Oisín says. In the flask. Chilled.

Benit's got the special-offer pinot from Tesco – recommended in *The Irish Times*, found the magazine on a bus. There'll be glasses at this gaff, he's pretty sure.

– This is the one, Karl says, as they arrive at a house that looks like a town hall, the only one they've seen so far that doesn't have its gangsta crib gates bolted.

A 182 dark green Benz is humming beneath a giant, overhanging copper beech that hasn't quite lost its leaves, and has masses of twinkly lights threaded through it. Nice tree. Big wide lump of a car. How the baldy aul fella with the turned-up collar and the pink jumper knotted round his shoulders got it through the gateway is anyone's guess. His leathery face phone-glows as he pretends he's not looking at them walking in. Hamza gives the bonnet a light drum of his fingers as he passes by. That gets yer man's attention. He rubs his meaty chin, watching. Two girls, nice asses, are laughing and chatting to some big square lad at the door, who stands aside, letting them pass. Why do the worst of the Breffnis always try to act common but then give it away with the chinos? Benit noticed this even before Karlo pointed it out.

The white gravel crackles as yer man moves a bit down the driveway and stops again. A second Sponge Bob, taller, arrives in the doorway. Benit knows this one from somewhere.

– Damien's da in the Merc back there, Karl says.

– Ah that dickwad, Oisín says. That'd be right, did yiz see the neck on him? Just like Damo.

– Ah here, you *sure* we're invited to this yoke? Deano says out of the side of his mouth.

– Yeah? Not a chance, mate, Sponge Bob 2 says, loud enough for the people in the back to hear, as Karl and Oisín get to the door.

– Get outta the way, Damo, we're invited, Karl says, nice and calm like.

The car's still sitting at the gate, yer man probably watching in the mirror.

– You are in your shite. No way that lot are invited.

– Not your gaff, mate, where's Tanya? Karl says, leaning to look behind Damien.

Karl pulls out his phone, starts tapping. Looks rammed inside. There's hella cuties sitting on the widest stairs ever. Like a hotel. A boutique one, Jamie Goode would love it for the hallway alone. Benit loves it for the wall-to-wall girls. Oh yes!

Hamza sighs and makes a big deal of getting on his phone too. Benit'd try Christina but he's no credit. Getting in here is beginning to look dodge.

– Damien, come on, you know I'm invited pal.

– No way mate, Damien says. You, maybe, and …

He pauses, looking at Oisín.

– But those tracksuit-wearing fuckers can shimmy right on out of here.

Benit roars laughing. Worse than 'you eat snow' even! He sits down on one of the big rocks at the side of the driveway, beside Deano, who's cracking open a can of Tennent's. Benit pulls out the Swiss Army knife and the bit of hash that he got from the Tallaght basketball lads, shouts over to the pair at the door:

– Me sister's inside, fam. Gonna get outta the way?

– Yeah, his sister's in there and we're all invited, spunk-monkey, outta the way, Hamza says, stroking the beard, keeping it chill.

– *You* calling *me* a monkey, big man? Damo says, sneering. I guarantee, *his* sister is not in there. I think we might have noticed, and he turns with his eyebrow arched to look at short-arse Sponge Bob, who laughs like a donkey.

You've really gotta wonder how the collar-up lads end up with gaffs like this, when you hear them laughing like that. Fuck them, fam. Like seriously, fuck them. Hamza looks like he's about to do one of his flying kicks – his leg is shaking. Always a bad sign. Benit doesn't have any need for this. None at all. How good's this gaff gonna be, anyway? Not worth the hassle. He pares off a little hash, nibbles the crumbs, slicing into them with his front teeth as fast and fine as the lads on Masterchef chop their onions and garlic. Should have made a couple of edibles. There's a yelp from the doorway:

– He's got a fucking knife!

Benit jumps up. A knife? Everyone at the door is looking his way. What the fuck, seriously?

– Yer mate's a dope, Damo. Quit messin, lemme in, Karl says.

– Is he rolling a J? Damo says.

– Nah, he's fucken rollin yer ma, Oisín says, coming over all Dub.

Benit folds the blade back into the knife, puts it and the tin away, and slowly buckles up the rucksack.

– I'm outta here, boys. Too much hassle.

– I'm with yeh, Deano says.

– 'Mon Karlo, these dicks aren't worth it.

– Messaged Tanya there, Damo, she's not gonna be impressed, Karl says.

– She won't be impressed with you bringing your scumbag mates to her gaff, Damien says, and the other dick brays again.

Must be deadly to be so funny.

– Come on Karl, slapneck's gonna slapneck, Deano calls back.

Hamza and Oisín make their way down the drive.

– See you had yer hate eyes in there Hamo, good lad, Oisín says.

He squeezes between the pillar and the car, then hops up and rolls across the bonnet. Finishes by throwing up the set at the driver, still sitting there with his phone.

– Come the fuck on, Karl, Hamza shouts back.

Karl's dragging footsteps on the gravel follow them.

They ramble down the road, all of them laughing, bar Karl.

– That was a *nice* car, Hamza says.

– Bit blocky for my liking, Oisín says, passing a blunt to Deano. See the R8 down by the school? That's mine. Hear Whacker's Boston gig might actually happen this time?

– No way, Hamza says. He'll never get it together. You can't go anyway, with the Leaving.

– Why not, it's only for five days?

– Yeah, why couldn't he? His aul fella'll pay for it.

– Fuck you, Deano, Oisín says.

– 'Mon, Karlo, yeah? Deano shouts back.

– I'm heading back.

– Back where? Deano says, turning to look at Karl glowing orange under the streetlight.

– The party, the gaff.

– You're takin the piss, Karl, Oisín says.

– I was invited, I'm going back, Karl says, looking at the ground, a bit breathless.

– They're just after not letting you in! Deano says. Did you miss that bit, buddy? Come on, let's split.

Benit goes over to Karl, sticks his arm around his shoulders. There's a bit of a shake in him, like he's shivering. Karl's bro like, even if he is a gaylord. Benit lets his arm slip up into more of a headlock than a hug, just to be clear.

– Come on Karlo, we'll go park. We've enough for a sesh.

– Don't wanna go park, it's Baltic. They didn't let *youse* in, he says, shrugging Benit off. It's youse.

– We'll go Hamza's then, Benit says, desperate.

What the fuck is going on here?

– No we fucking won't, Hamza says. Hamza'll go Hamza's, because Hamza's fucking pissed off. My girl's in there! Are you fucking serious, Karl?

Benit grabs Karl by the shoulders, turns him, leans down to look into his eyes, saying:

– Messing, yeah?

But he's not messing. Not messing at all. Karl wriggles away, won't look any of them in the eye, and starts jogging straight back towards the big house. Benit, stunned, watches the red soles disappear up the hill.

– You faggot! You fucking, fucking, pikey faggot! Hamza roars after Karl, his voice bouncing off all the high garden walls.

This is some kind of dream, yeah? Has to be.

– Come on, leave it Hamza, let's just go, Benit says.

They duck down a laneway, land out on a main road. Deano sticks his arm out for a taxi, says he's paying.

Winter

7
DEANO

He jumps through breath clouds down a flight of stairs. Not gonna slow up till he's well clear of the flat or he'll be in danger of just turning right back around, settling in for the day, telling June the pain in his belly's killing him. He's not going in just cos of the rest of them laying on the pressure but. He's going in cos fuck the lot of them, he'll hit the mean streets of Dub-a-lin town when he feels like it, on his terms. He's no one's bitch. The trip to see the play in town'll shorten the day, might even be a bitta craic and he can duck out any time he wants, in anyway. No pressure.

It's fucken freezing, doesn't matter, just keep on keeping on, going with the flow, on the down-low.

He ducks into Sadie's.

– And I says to him, I says, mark my words you, till you get something done about it, that drippy yoke won't be seeing sight nor light of my Mary Lou, Doreen says, leaning on the counter, jabbing her finger at Sadie and Rita.

Sadie straightens up, coughs at the sight of Deano, but Doreen doesn't quit, oh no. Deano stands as far back as he can in the narrow shop, practically still in the doorway, and gets *real* interested in all the jacks rolls and Kimberleys and tea bags and all the other things on the shelves behind the counter – which is all the things that the flats shop sells. Nothing's ever getting robbed outta here cos no one can get at anything without going through Sadie. And that's not something anyone with any sense would try. Sadie does a bit of a signal towards Deano, trying again to get Doreen to pipe down.

– I says to him, I says, you, yeh gunner-eyed fuck, are a dirty aul bastard and I know you've been at yer away games again.

– Has he the clap? says Sadie. Ah here!

Rita, coming over all compassionate for the fella and his drippy yoke says:

– Ah now, yeh don't know that it's away games at all. There's lot of them that, yeh know, *dribble*. It's just urine. It's their age.

She turns away from the other two pulling her purply-pink mouth down at the corners like a big sad and pretty disgusted clown.

Copping Deano, she gives Doreen a dig in the sides. Doreen straightens up, dog squashed in her arms. Poor thing dressed in a hot pink ballet skirt and a tiny waistcoat with a flower in the buttonhole. It's all rucked up so the flower's sticking into its little face. Jaysus, you'd have to feel sorry for it.

– Ah hiya Deano love, didn't see yeh there, Doreen says, as she lifts the dog up and gives it an open-mouthed kiss on the snout.

Fucksake. The dog turns to look at Deano, its runny eyes pleading, fucking help me, please.

– Now, what can I do for yeh, Deano love? Sadie says.

He steps up to the counter.

– Packet a Rizlas there please, Sadie.

– The big ones, yeah? I'll take yeh down this end, and she makes him go to the far corner of the counter.

As he's passing her the money she holds his hand in hers just a bit too long. Soft and squishy, big for a woman's. She'd level yeh with a clatter.

– Haven't seen you this long while, Deano. Not in the uniform in anyway.

– Missed me, did yeh, Sadie?

– You do be zipping around normally, she says, staring at him.

Awkward. Course she knows something. Knows everything, Sadie does. Or pretends she does, like all the aul ones. Even when they don't know shit. There's a shine off her oranginess today. Shimmery in the folds. Not that she has that many wrinkles even. Puffed out with the fat. Something to be said for that.

– Yeh know, your daddy'd want yeh going to school, don't yeh?

The feeling rises in his belly. She's speaking quietly now, pretending she's checking the newspapers under the counter.

– The anniversary's coming round again soon, isn't it? Your da's.

Next week. Jaze Sadie, didn't know you cared so much.

– Yeah.

Don't flinch. Alls they want is fucken cryin and howlin outta yeh.

Sadie pauses the fake paper sifting but doesn't look up. He fiddles with the packet of chewing gum he's found in his pocket turning it round and round, outlasting her.

– A packet of the big Rizlas, yeh said.

– That's it, yeah.

Behind him, someone's lumbering over the taped-up lino. Doreen and Rita stiffen a little and Doreen's upper lip starts to do a bit of an Elvis. Her dog joins in with a low rumbly growl. Ballet dog's gonna do damage.

– She's afraid of men, Doreen announces, apologetically, helpfully.

Deano doesn't look, but he knows it's a big lump of a man, reeking of some scabby cologne, breathing heavy. Sadie stands up, glances quickly at whoever it is, nods just enough to acknowledge him and starts fumbling in the till.

As she passes the change to Deano, she grabs his hand again.

– No good reason for all that, with your da. *No* good reason. You mind yourself and get to school, pet. Yeah?

She says it loudly, like she's on stage.

– Yeah, he says, pulling his hand back.

Deano's back prickles – yer man's on top of him. Yeah, it's not the biggest place in the world but come the fuck on dude. He turns and bumps into a belly. Jim Harrison, in full white Adidas. Who knew they made tracksuits in that size? Fuck it in anyway.

– Sorry, yeah, he says. Thanks Sadie.

He sticks the head down, paces out of the shop. He pulls out the chewing gums – gone soft, wouldn't yeh know – and falters, maybe heading back up to the flat might be the better option?

Jim Harrison comes charging out after him. Panting again, tongue hanging out, *The Sun* tucked under his arm. Grim. You'd wonder why a cunt like him buys a newspaper at all now that there aren't any tits in it – the bollix definitely can't read.

– Hold up there young fella.

Deano slows down but doesn't stop, doesn't turn around. And it was all going so fucken well. This is where listening to Oisín gets yeh. Yeh can't say no to these slapnecks but yeh can't diss them either. Should have stuck in the headphones, the second he left the shop. Saves all the hassle. Don't even have to be listening to anything. Stick them in, march on into the day, keep on truckin, be grand. Too late now but.

– Alright, Deano?

He's gotta turn round, give him his due. Bend fucken over.
– Yeah, grand.
– Walk with me, as they say, hah? Jim says, cackling.
Fucken gross.
– A little birdy tells me that you're doing business down in Crumlin.
What the actual fuck? What business is it of theirs where's he's getting his grass?
– An unofficial source, I hear. 'Mirite?
– Gotta head, Jim, on me way to school.
– Ah sure, I'll give yeh a lift, if yeh like.
Oh yeah sure. That'd be great Jim. Like fuck he's getting in that car again. Push some weight, no one's watching yeh, Deano. Doin us a favour, bitta cash in it for yerself. Nothing heavy. Just a bitta business. Course no one's watchin *him*. Deano wouldn't be dealin with the lads who clipped his da, would he? And he got outta the car and said he'd think about it and he thought about it for maybe minus fucken two million seconds and then he managed to avoid these cunts for this long, and now here we fucken are.
– Nah, yer alright, I want the exercise.
The nylon snowman moves up beside him, slick with sweat.
– We were thinking we might have to throw an eye over an operation like that.
Gracie, fucken Gracie! He stops and looks straight at Jim, heart racing and it's all he can do not to stretch the fat bollix.
– That right?
– Them aul ones are always having falls, aren't they? My aul one fell down the stairs, broke her neck. Terrible thing, seeing her go like that.
Jim's ma, looks like a ballsack, lives on the ground floor in Kevin Street flats and was at Jack's do, living it large, supping the sangria. And Jim here knows that Deano knows that.
– Yeah.

– Sure I can't drop yeh down the road, Deano? It's no bother pal, he says, opening the car door.

– Nah, yer alright. Be grand.

Fucken paedo cunt. That's it, no way he's going back to the flat. He's fucken going in.

*

– Give him a break is alls I'm sayin, yeah?

– Ah come on, Deano, leavin us out there in Poshville like that. Hamo's right.

– Of course I'm right, you just don't do it. Sly bastard.

– Ah give up, Karl's not sly.

– It was a dick move, Oisín says. Pass us the salt there.

Right enough, a dick move, but Karlo's got to have his reasons. Karlo's never really a dick. Maybe he just wanted to hang out with Tanya. Maybe he's well in there. Who knows? Could be, him being all stylish an all. Could be she likes the ghetto boys.

– Some a them posh girls go for the bad boys. Traveller an all. Tanya probably thinks he's exotic.

– Yeah, look, probably a girl ting, Benit says. Sly move but girl ting. Gotta cut the man some slack.

– He's gay, Hamza says.

– Ah, not again, Oisín says.

– Just sayin, can't be a girl ting. No slack-cutting. He needs to be told. Don't care if he's scuttling home for lunch to avoid us. Needs to take his roasting like a man.

Hamza pulls out his phone – contraband in the lunchroom.

– Storm Adrian, what the hell. No one's going to take Storm Adrian seriously. Why do they call them these non-threatening names?

– Is it a big one? Deano asks. I heard nuttin.

– Nah, it's not even coming here, Benit says. Don't mind Panicky Paula here.

– Love to hear some *threatening* storm names there, Hamza, Oisín says.

– Call it Mohammed, watch everyone duck, Hamza fires back.

– We're not at fucking M yet, dumbass, Oisín says, flicking a piece of coleslaw at Hamza.

– Abdul Aziz then, the whole country'll hit the bunkers.

Hamza shoves his phone back in his pocket as one of the lunch women – a new one – pounces on Anto from fifth year who's flashing his new Galaxy round the place.

– Gimme dat phun, she bellows.

Nigerian.

– Get fucked, Anto says, without even turning to look at her and he grins at his mates round the table.

Big Momma makes a grab for it.

– Get yer fucken hands offa me yah fucken hoor, Anto says, standing up, chest out, slamming his chair back so it hits off the wall.

She lashes him a smack across the face. Class! A space clears and a *woah* rises around the cramped room. Deano sinks down in his seat. Hamza and Oisín are holding their sides laughing. This is what yeh live for. Having none of it, this one – she grabs Anto's arm and tries to shake the phone out of his hand.

– What the fuck are yeh doin, yeh mad bitch? Get the fuck offa me, Anto squeals, and he makes backhand contact with her shelfy tits.

Could fit a row of books on them. Never hit a woman in the tits but. Might be time to break his strict non-intervention policy. Deano bends one leg up, easing himself into maybe standing when the time is right. In fairness, yer one's probably got this covered. He eyes the others. Benit and Oisín look like they may be stirring. Hamza turns back and takes a bite of his burrito. The other lunch women run from behind the counter but yer one's not for giving up. Eyes wide, she does a No Face on it, puffs herself up to twice her size.

– Fuck man, she's gonna blow, Oisín says behind his hand.

She's chatting shit that no one can understand and no one knows whether to laugh or let a roar at her. Some of the fifth years start baying when she twists Anto's arm behind his back. He's a bit of a dick, Anto, but this is probably going a bit far. He's trying to flip round to punch at her, but she gets him by the back of the neck and he can't move. She's hissing now as he wriggles like a lizard. Gotta admire a strong woman. Imagine riding that. Probably smother yeh. You'd go out happy but.

The other women try to coax her off him and two teachers appear in the room – must be some kind of a secret alarm under the counter – knocking fellas outta the way. She ignores their softly muttered orders to let go of him and instead marches Anto through the double doors, still holding firm, with the pair of teachers trotting behind.

They turn back to the table.

– Well, *she* won't be back, Oisín says. Did no one tell her the rules?

– Could be straight off the banana boat, Hamza says. Just being pure African.

– Ho, yeah, if I spoke to my mum like that, watch out bruv, Benit says, shaking his head.

– You'd get the shoe treatment, Hamo, Oisín says.

– No doubt about it, bro. That's why I'm such a well-rounded individual. Threat of the shoe.

– Mams here should do a bit more shoe-throwing, solve a lot of problems, Oisín says, full-mouthed. Pretty fucked up though, taking his phone and, yeh know, getting him in an arm lock. Can't be doing that shit.

– Bad shout getting a woman in the tits but, Deano says.

Hamza rolls up the burrito paper, carefully wipes his hands on the paper napkin and says:

– It's a conundrum boys. Do we support the efforts of the probably underpaid immigrant worker of colour, or the underage *compañero* from a difficult social background whom she was trying to relieve of his property? Much to think about.

Hamza rubs his beard. Always at this craic these days.

– You gay bro, are yeh? Deano says.

– He's an extreme leftist, Oisín says. That's what some sham called him the other day on Insta, 'mirite? He'll be out selling papers for some of those baldy People Before Profit women, once he turns eighteen. Full Trot by Christmas.

*

Passing by long-term empty classrooms, they head back for maths before they hit town for the Macbeth matinee. Oisín runs a ruler over the bumpy broken paint, where chunks of plaster are missing all along the corridor.

– I can't fucking wait to be out of this kip, I swear, Oisín says.

– But yer always going on at me? Deano says.

No one understood why Oisín landed in Colmcille's. Said he wanted to go with all of the lads from hurling, rather than with his mates from his faggy school – the one with the kids on scooters with cellos on their backs. His mam doesn't agree with fee-paying schools in anyway, she says. You'd think she'd be raking it in with that café. Apple pie and cream is €4.50 in the place sure. And since his aul fella's been back on the scene, after Ruairí went, there's gotta be some cash floating around the place.

Hamza's shiteing on, some bollocks about the gig economy, as they're milling through the crowd of shams coming down the dirty wet stairs. Not paying attention, Hamza bumps off Baba Nestor, Wino's thick-as-shit nephew; a mouthy, short-arsed tool who thinks he's a hardman, with a group of fanboys too scared to ever tell the dipshit to just shut the fuck up.

– Watch where yer goin pal, yeah?

Hamza stops, frowns at him shakes his head and, laughing, says:

– Yeah, that's right, bud, you keep chilling, patting Baba on the shoulder.

But Baba loses the head, throws Hamza's hand off him.

– Don't touch me yeh fucken Paki.

– What the fuck did you call him? Deano says.

– Deano, come on, he hears Oisín say.

– Ah here, what are yeh going to do about it, Paki-lover. Jaze, boys, there's an awful stink a curry round here, wha?

And Baba's fans all laugh on cue. Deano gets him by the throat, slams him into the wall. He can't stop himself.

– I *said*, what did you just call him?

Baba's turning redder. His bug-eyes bulging even more than normal. Aul ones fall downstairs, don't they? And das bleed out on the street in front of yeh.

Hamza and the rest are behind him.

– 'Mon Deano.

Benit's big shovel hand is on his shoulder.

– Let's go bro. Not worth it.

Nice and quiet. What the fuck's he doing? He never does this shit. Always stays outta trouble. He drops Baba. The fanboys do throat-slitting gestures. Deano takes the rest of the stairs in one step.

No one says anything for a while. They get to the classroom, fall into their desks.

– Bad move, bro, Oisín mumbles. You're in deep, touching Baba.

Yeah, yeh think?! Fuck, fuck, fuck, fuck, fuck, a million times fucken fuck those cunts. The Babas and the Winos and the Jimmy Harrisons and their fucken scumbag mots and their fucking scumbag mams and fuck the lot of them. Why the fuck did he fucken come into this kip today? What the fuck was wrong with just staying in, watching YouTube videos, in the scratcher?

Hamza twists round.

– He's just a waste of space like. He's dumb as fuck. Came into Brown Thomas a few weeks ago, bought Gucci. He literally couldn't count the money. Just pulled out a ball of cash and says, Here, is that enough? I say yeah – he was dropping like 600 quid – and he's just throwing money at me. And then I realize, he literally didn't know how the numbers worked, how to count what he had on him. Is that enough? More money. Is that enough? He didn't even know if I was giving him the right change. Be grand. I don't hassle myself over shams like that coming out with that shit. You don't need to either. Be grand, I'm telling yeh.

Yeah, sure. Be grand. That's not what Hamza's face is sayin. Everyone knows it won't be.

*

Might be the only chance in the next while of being in close proximity to girls, living, breathing ones, loadsa them, right beside you. That's what Oisín and the boys said. True dat. He thinks about going back to June's, closing the door, curling up with a sausage roll dripping in hot sauce, forgetting about Baba and Jim Harrison an all. But fuck, he's done enough laying low. And girls …

And it's alright, Macbeth, as these things go. Not a complete waste of time. Good story, could do with a bit less killing, and that Lady Macbeth … Some tulip. What a fucken bitch.

– Marty loves this Shakespeare craic, says Benit. I said, yeh know, a lot of innocent people get killed, and he says, apart from McDuff's kid, how can we know they were innocent? Says there's not many kings or princes innocent.

– Discussing literature with Marty now? says Hamza. Weirdo.

– Yeah, what's weird about that? Always weird if yeh wanna do something different, Karl mutters from behind.

Hamza ignores him or maybe doesn't hear him. Either way, he just walks on. Deano doesn't answer Karl either but. It's not

117

the time. Karl still deserves some shade after the party, but yeah, there's nothing wrong with talking about Shakespeare if that floats yer boat and Hamza's into all this shit himself in anyway.

At the theatre, Hamza heads straight to the jacks and comes out dressed in civvies. Man about town. He slopes in with the rest of them and sinks down low while the teachers sit back a couple of rows with the dodgier ones.

Girls! Yes! Could have been unlucky and had the whole place filled up with lads, but no, there's ones from two different schools. The green uniform ones file into the rows in front of Deano and the rest. The blue uniforms are all over the other side. Culchies, by the sounds of it.

– Cuties incoming, Oisín says behind his hand, as a couple of right sweet ones sit into the seats in front.

Deano's phone buzzes in his pocket.

Rockgod:
I'll take redser. Don't wanna be breeding more gingers you take the blondie one.

The pair sitting right in front of Deano and Oisín are laughing and joking with the rest of their row. Girl-laughing. The blondie one gives Deano the eye. She did, she did, he saw it.

Rockgod:
She no likey the look of u. Soz mate.

Oisín's got it wrong. This one's live. Or maybe not. Man's gotta be realistic. They smell nice in anyway. There's a fatter-looking one down the end. Bitta meat on her. He could go for her maybe. She looks back at him, smiles. Like, that was definitely a smile. Ah, we're in boys! That's his type. Well, *maybe* his type. His type is any of them, in fairness. Take anything at this stage, he would. Nah, not really.

Redser and blondie turn round, looking behind them for their teachers. Yeah. Scoping. That's what yiz are at, yeh lil maggots, lil cuties. Yeh can almost see the top of the blondie one's tits down the front of her school shirt. And yeah, there he is, Mister Flute's on his way to say hello. Oisín pretends to stare at his phone. It's Oisín they're looking at. Always Oisín they're looking at. Gets tens. These two are tens. Nah, the redser's probably a nine. They've both got stupid accents. Hamza leans forward.

– Where are you guys from?

Oh they'll like that. Always with the direct approach, Hamza. And 'guys'! Smooth bastard. Karl and Benit are having a laugh with the meaty one down the end of the row.

Giving Hamza the aul we-don't-really-give-a-fuck-about-even-answering look, Redser and Blondie say together:

– Vilmount Lane.

Ah, the anorexic factory. No wonder they're so skinny. The chubby one's obviously an outlier. Oisín got with one of the Vilmount girls one time. A sack of bones she was.

Everyone, apart from the Colmcille's boys, goes quiet when the emergency exits announcement starts. The lights go down. Fucking Baba Nestor. What was he thinking?

The actors do their bit. Pretty shite to be honest, apart from the Banquo lad who's cool and does it in a Dub accent, which sounds pretty good and makes a lot more sense than all that fah-fah talking. At least you can understand him.

*

It's all over once everyone's dead and then there's a discussion about the whole thing. The actors stay on stage and the mic gets passed around to anyone in the audience with something to say. Meaty talks about Lady Macbeth, giving it loads with themes and feminism. They always start this shit, the girls. Mind you, Meaty can talk.

Hamza stands up and says that Lady Macbeth's a pussy. If she wanted shit done, why didn't she just do it herself? Ms Foster looks like she's gonna gobble a monster cock and tells Hamza that that's very disrespectful to all the performers and that he must apologize right this minute and that there will be consequences. Course he won't stop but. Asks if they wanted a discussion or if they wanted to tell them what to think. Because that's not a discussion and that's not what Hamza's here for. He's got that glint in his eye. Getting a rise. Oisín's delighted, slapping his thighs, laughing. Loves this English stuff, especially when Hamza starts.

Maybe apologizing to Baba'll be enough? Not a chance. Not a fucking chance. Maybe taking a beating from Baba in a fake knock will be enough. Maybe, maybe, maybe. Not in the mood for a beat-down. What a fucken spa! Why the fuck did he do it? Alls yeh gotta do is keep yer mouth shut. There's nuttin else for it. He'll just stay in, once he gets back to the flat. Stay in. Stay safe. Fucken move down the country. Cork even. Nah, not Cork.

Oisín finally, lazily, half puts his hand in the air, to get stuck into Hamza's aggro but then David the autist starts. He's got the mic. For the love of all that's good and holy, as Karlo's mam says, David's got the mic. He does his usual pausing, getting it straight in his head, has a go, like he's revving her up. Here we go. And nah! He stalls. Could be here for-fucken-ever.

– I'd just like to say, I'd just like to say, I'd just like to say …

Funny thing, David can quote every word of this yoke, straight through, if he's let. There's some sniggers from the green uniforms in front. Fucksake! Dave'll have something proper to say when he's got warmed up like.

– Yes, David, Ms Foster says, coaxing him along but getting edgy.

Push him too far and David'll lose his shit.

– On the, on the, on the question of Lady Macbeth …

More sniggering. Especially from Redser and Blondie. There's a sharp *Shhh* from the end of the row in front. Either Meaty or the teacher. Deano turns round to look at David, who's started the fucken hand fluttering. Jaysus!

– I have to, I have to, I have to ...

Redser and Blondie lean in, heads together. David's gulping air. Deano wishes he could just stick his hands over his ears like David does when he needs a bitta peace. Fuck it, fucken skanks. He leans forward, elbows on the girls' seatbacks, inserts his head between their two heads, and says, loudly:

– He's aw-fucken-tistic. Bitta respect, yeah? Shut the *fuck* up. And he sits back in his seat.

The blue uniforms' teacher turns round, gives a little smile and the whole front row goes silent. The pair in front, the worst of them, sink down as low as they can. Proper. Fucken. Order.

– Go on David, bro, say what yeh were saying, Oisín calls back.

*

– You sure yer alright? Benit says before he leaves him outside the Spar.

– Yeah, just don't wanna go.

– But yeh always want to go hurling.

– Just knackered, Deano says.

– Fair enough. Just relax man, yeah? This evening, just stay in. Don't be thinking about it, fam.

In Spar, they've no sausage rolls left and June'll have the dinner ready in anyway. But he can't resist the scraps of chicken tenders and yer one sticks them in a bap with cajun sauce and charges him half price only and he nearly fucken cries, he really does. And then it's back home and it'll be grand. Be grand!

A message from Hamza, reading his mind.

Hamo:
Be grand. Will I call round?

121

Now, this is a big deal. Hamza should be studying tonight. Never comes out on a Monday. If he's suggesting calling round to Deano's, Deano's in proper deep shit. So yeah, this won't be grand. This is fucked. Enjoy the bap, it might be your last is what that text is saying. June'll give out yards about him eating before dinner but he'll say, believe me, June, *not* a problem. And then he'll eat his dinner and he just won't go out. Ever again.

A dog, tied outside the offy, tries to make friends. He drops to his knees beside him – a big dopey Golden Retriever. The dog is all over him, tries to put his snout into the bag with the chicken tenders in it. Even the fucken mutt just wants something from yeh. Deano gives in, opens up the bag and drops a couple of bits onto the ground for him. The dog tries to lick his face.

Deano turns the corner, brushing blondie hairs off his front and he runs right into her – what the actual fuck? A slimmed-down, hippied-up version, but yeah, it's her. Mam.

8
KARL

Karl slumps to the floor in Oisín's room and pulls out the little sketch pad his da got him – with art paper, the proper kind, checked with the fella in the art shop an all. Pure quality, his da said. And he's not wrong. It's bumpy even, that's how you know. He flicks to the last page he was working on. Another Marie Antoinette-type. She could do with a few more tiny curls in that hairdo.

Hamza hits the door off Karl's legs as he comes in.

– What the fuck is that about? Black? Hamza says, staring at the half-painted wall behind the bed.

– Just thought it'd be cool to paint it black, Oisín says.

Karl hasn't said a word about it. And he's not going to. Oisín did mention it to Karl before he actually put paint to wall. Just in passing. Cos, yeh know, Karl knows about colours and shit. Dunno, black, on your walls, when you're seeing dead people or imaginary people or whatever. His own mam and his nanny are plagued by dead people, ringing at the door to tell them someone else had died. They only mention the doorbell ringing *after* they've already been told that the person has died, but. This bit's difficult, getting tiny little ships or like a chandelier or something drawn into the little woman's hair.

– What are you at there, Karl? Your tongue's sticking out again. What you think of this black shit? Hamza says.

He pulls his concentrating tongue in. Always been a thing when Hamza's getting angsty about something else, he starts on Karl.

– Looks like you're going full emo, Oisín. 1980s shit or sum. Benit knows what I'm talking about. Clichéd.

Hamza looks at Benit, who eyebrow-shrugs.

– Still seeing ghosts? Hamza says.

– Yeah, he is, Karl mumbles.

– I'm right here, yeh know.

– When did he last have a visitation? Hamza asks Benit.

– Dunno, last night maybe? Recent like.

– Same as before?

– Think so.

– Fuckwits, stop talking about me, Oisín says.

Oisín was shaky the morning Karl first went back to hurling training. Not sleeping well, he said. But sure who hasn't seen some kinda ghost or something? And the black can be painted over.

– It's a djinn, Hamza says.

– Why would some foreigner ghost thing come visiting Oisín? Karl says. A púca more like. Local.

– Cop the fuck on, Karl. Djinns are everywhere, Hamza says.

– Whatever bro, Oisín says. What's the story with the Airbnb? Sure they're OK renting it for a party?

– Yeah, it's a djinn. You need to talk to some people who know about this shit, fam. A couple of my uncles get rid of them for people, Hamza says.

– At the mosque, is it? Oisín says.

– Don't go mosque, Ois, Benit says. They'll have you with a tea towel on your head. Jihadi by Christmas. Live with the púca-djinn. It's better man.

– The Airbnb? Oisín says.

– Right, fuck you infidels. Yeah, all cool with the Airbnb.

Surprised he didn't keep going till he got Oisín agreeing to a Muslamic exorcism. Party's the only thing that'd distract him.

Oisín's mam calls from downstairs, asking if they want dinner. Sometimes she goes a bit mad with the vegan shit. Hamza gives Oisín the look.

– What's the dinner? Oisín shouts down to her.

– Coddle.

She has funny notions about coddle as well.

Oisín asks the question with his eyebrows. Hamza and Benit nod.

– Yeah, they'll have it.

Proper order. No need to ask Karl.

– Maybe I'm just mental. So what?

– Fair play, Ois, Karl says.

– Can't be Ruairí if it looks like you look now, Benit says.

– It'll have a message for you, Hamza says. But I'm telling you, you don't wanna wait until it starts talking to you. You're in deep shit then.

Hhmmm. This *does* sound like sense. You don't want things talking to you or at you, if Egg Malone two doors down on their floor is anything to go by. Wrecked the gaff on the orders of the Child Jesus of Prague and Pat Kenny. Oisín's sensitive an all, into his music. But Karl's seen plenty of proper mental and it doesn't look like this.

– Could be a succubus, Oisín says. Fucking *love* a succubus.

– If it had tried to fuck you, bro, you'd have told us. Anyway, it looks like you. You're pretty but you don't wanna fuck yourself, Hamza says.

Benit visibly brightens.

– I'd love if a, like, really hot one came and *forced* me to ride her all night long.

– I think they ride you, that's the point, Oisín says. And you're not into it. Like, you don't want to do it.

– They're probably ugly, Hamza says.

– Of course, they're dogs. Otherwise, you wouldn't have to be forced, would you? Oisín says.

Oisín's back strumming. Not listening. Karl's always thought that was cool. The way he can just zone out and let it go. Pity more people aren't that way.

The doorbell rings and the sounds of Deano taking off his shoes and coursing he'll have the coddle Helen, drift up the stairs.

– Looking full in here, boys, Deano says as he pops his head round the door.

Deano's been laying *really* low. Always some excuse for staying inside. Sore belly, no time, whatever. Oisín, delighted to see Deano, puts the guitar aside.

– Come on, we'll go sitting room.

But Deano edges into the bedroom, gawping.

– What the fuck, bro? he says, looking at the black wall.

– I like it, Karl says.

– I'm kinda thinking it's cool too, Benit says. Whole lot done, be like a man cave, bro.

Helen calls and they bundle down the stairs. She's heated up a lasagne to go along with the coddle. She's a woman who really believes in the power of a freezer. One in the shed, one in the utility room, and that's on top of the freezer bit in the fridge. The platter with the cucumber and carrots and the bowl of hummus is already in the middle of the table.

– I thought we'd just have this as a starter because we've to make things stretch a bit.

She pours herself a glass of red wine, asks them all do they want a drop. Benit looks tempted, asks her what it is, but refuses anyway. She likes her wine. On more than one occasion, they've come in and found her conked out on the sofa, with an empty bottle tipped over on the carpet and another one half gone, her lips all black and the *Late Late* blaring about some kid with a gammy leg or sum. Oisín says he knows that she's a pisshead, but she's still the best. She's sound an all, but Karl's glad his ma is never in that state.

Hands grab bits of carrot and everyone's double-dipping like bastards. Oisín turns the radio up.

– Some slut, that Ariana one, Deano says, a scum of hummus forming on his lips.

Karl catches Oisín's eye-pop. Fucken hell. Hamza's beaming as he keeps on scoffing. Maybe she won't have heard. What the hell is Deano thinking? No one says a word. Then Benit coughs and says:

– That's really nice hummus, Helen. Did you make it yourself?

Deano stops chewing and silently asks, what the fuck's going on? And Karl says:

– Are those new blinds, Helen?

– They are, Karl. I got them last week. Gruff had the other ones chewed to bits.

Maybe she didn't hear. No one wants the full on feminazi routine when you're trying to eat coddle.

– And in answer to your question, Benit, yes I made the hummus. Left over from the shop though.

She brings over the huge coddle pot, asks Hamza and Oisín to clear the platter and their small plates off the table, and settles into her seat.

– So …

Here it comes. Deano's chin is on his collar bones.

– Deano, I know we've had the slut chat before. Promiscuous boys are heroes, promiscuous girls are sluts because all girls can get men to have sex with them anytime they want, but it's very hard for you lads to do the same. Something like that?

– Straight facts, innit, Benit says quietly.

– But Deano, I also remember that I did ask that that word never be used at my table again, am I right?

That's it? That's all she's got for him?

– Sorry, just slipped out, Deano says, grinning at the rest of them.

She always lets Deano off lightly.

– Did Oisin tell you about the new group I'm in? she says, sliding the sliced bread off the board into a basket.

Ah, Jesus Christ, no way! Not another one of her groups. Last time Karl'd heard her going on about one of her groups, she'd ended up giving a lecture on the benefits of wanking while she whipped up scrambled eggs and smoked salmon for them.

She'd been to an orgasmic yoga workshop that morning, she told them. Karl thought the morning wouldn't be a good time for things like that but what would he know? It turned out to be just a load of people, total strangers, lying beside each other on yoga mats with blankets thrown over them, wanking while the facilitators blared out 'Born Slippy' so loud that the wooden floor was vibrating underneath them. And Karl used to love that song. She just lay still and shut her eyes, pretending to relax until it was all over. Kinda like Karl did as she was telling them this and spooning their eggs and salmon onto their plates. You want to have got the smell coming from the aul fella beside her, she said.

Then she went off on one about how having healthy conversations about masturbation (or self-love as the people at the orgasmic yoga thing had called it) would solve a lot of problems. There should be more masturbation, not less. In privacy, though. No one else wants to see any of you touching your pennies. He remembers the bit about the pennies most vividly. He'd never heard cocks called pennies before or since, but that's Oisín's ma for you. Even Hamza's felt sorry for Oisín sometimes. Oisín says he doesn't mind and that him and his ma just have very open conversation.

– Weaving, she says, as she dishes out the perverted coddle.

Deano's looking at the tomatoes and herbs floating in his bowl. Hamza laughs.

– Problem, Deano?

– Nah, just looking. Thanks for the dinner, Helen. It's not coddle, but, like, it's great, thanks.

– I browned the sausages too. And there's beans in there. Pintos.

– I see that, yeah. Thanks.

Karl prefers the browned sausages but he'd never say that to his own ma.

– Hold on, hold on, don't eat any more. I want to take a picture of it for Peggy next door.

Helen set up a Facebook page called Coddle Wars, where she puts up pictures of what she calls coddle. And she made them all like the page.

– She'll be ripping about this one. I've turmeric in it. Just a little bit. Small bit of cinnamon too.

– That's maybe a step too far now, Karl says.

– You should listen to him, Ma. He had coddle in his bobos, Oisín says.

– The point of coddle is that it's cheap and cheerful and you put in whatever you've left at the end of the week, the day before payday.

– You shouldn't brown the sausages and you shouldn't cook it in the oven, Deano says.

– Does June tell you that? Bet she does. Brilliant. I'll drop these pictures in the Facebook group. Start a row.

Aul ones and their Facebook groups. Must be mental in there when they get going.

– Anyway, my new real-life group, The Liberties Weavers we're called. A thousand years of weaving in the area. Here I'll show you, she says, and she heads out into the hallway.

– Here, Karl, you'll be really interested in this.

She places a piece of woolly, prickly fabric, all bright pinks and greens into his hands. It's beautiful.
  – Isn't it lovely? Wove that myself, she says. Do you want it, Karl? I'll be doing more.
  – Why's he getting our weaving and I get none! Oisín shouts from the table.
  – Because Karl appreciates nice things.

*

It's late. Karl could do with getting into the scratcher after all the coddle but nah, they insist on a knockabout on the street. Get yer fitness up, if youse two want any chance of coming back. He gets enough of that guff from his da. The brothers go down to the hurling, Frankie's pretty good an all. But his da says he looks like an eejit, coaching when he can't even keep his own eldest at it.

They're only getting warmed up, their breath wafting around them, when Hamo's gotta go meet Mohammed. Karl doesn't have a lotta time for Mohammed – son of a pair a doctors, private school out the way, dripping in cash. Pretends like he's from a tower block in Tottenham or sum, Oisín says. The day Benit had his bag and the cans in it robbed by a pair of guards outside Longitude and they threatened to shoot him and Hamza if Hamza didn't give up arguing, Mohammed was the big man, pulling out a clip stuffed with wads of cash, giving it to Benit to buy a new one. Him and his posse, swaggering round town, covering the southside schools in snow. Although they're not into it that much themselves.

Oisín starts on Hamo about leaving the knockabout to hang with a dick like Mo. Hamza's leaning on the hurl, laughing at Oisín, saying it's better than hanging with a djinn, when a crowd of flats girls come round the corner, high-heeled runners, arms linked, high ponies swinging. They see Karl and the lads but pretend they don't. And they start singing:

130

– We are Teresa's girls, we wear our hair in curls …

The flats song. Apart from Tanya, these are the best type of girls in the world. No question.

– Just seems a bit weird, like. Always going on about saving the world, then hanging out with Mo and the Arabs. Dealing coke, all fucken labels and bling, Oisín says, lowering his voice.

The girls' song's getting faster and faster, louder and louder.

– We never ever drink, that's what our parents think …

They stop further up the street, start fixing the hair, looking at themselves in the windows of the houses on Ebenezer Terrace.

– Getting pretty worked up about some fella you hardly know, bro, Hamza says, still grinning.

He's probably meeting Candy in anyway.

Outbreak of aggro. One of the girls screams at another one. The rest of them take sides, divvying themselves up.

– You said that about Charlene, not me. Yeh fucken lying bitch.

The lads are all watching them now, but Karl picks up the sliotar and starts whacking it against a gable wall. Gotta give girls their space when they're scrapping. They'll hardly yop each other out of it. They're screeching now, right up in each other's faces, waving their arms about.

– Someone's gonna get hurt here, Oisín says. Should I go over and break it up?

– You nuts? Deano says.

Suddenly the girls turn together to look at them, standing, watching from the corner.

– Fuck are youse looking at? the smaller one screams down the street. Have I got a fucken telly on me head or wha'?

Her enemy bursts out laughing and they link arms, gather their ladies and strut on up the road, ankles twisting from side to side, towards the flats.

9
DEANO

He pauses at the corner. Approaching from the side, as if he could just change his mind at any moment and not bother knocking on the reinforced door.

As if he could just wander round to Oisín's instead and they could have a laugh and he could have a go on the guitar, finally. Get the courage up to just have a go. And Helen might make some scran. And if she's upstairs, they might go out the back and have an cheeky smoke, sitting at the garden table, the bamboo hissing in the wind. Like it's whispering. That'd be whopper.

As if he could just not bother going where he's told to go. As if picking up packages or envelopes or whatever is optional, just something Deano can take or leave. Nah, yer alright there, Jim or Wino or whichever scumbag, can't be arsed this evening, I've to scratch me nads and smoke a bong, go hunting for girls and polish me ornaments. Sorry bout dat, I'll catch yeh again, maybe.

He comes out of the shadows and stalks across the mud- and hole-covered yard, setting off the security lights that make the night brighter than the dazzliest summer's day. The plumbers' and the builders' supplies places on either side are in darkness. Overnighting workmen's vans and a couple of giant skips take up half the space in the yard. He twists his ankle as he drops into a pothole. Fucksake, this is all he needs, them laughing, watching him stumble on the CCTV.

He raps the door and waits. Green wood on the front, reinforced with metal on the back. A million locks to be pulled back before it clangs open.

Quick in-out job. The fella inside, always someone different, will let him into the tiny porchy hallway, hand him what he's there for. Deano'll slip it inside his jacket and head off to wherever. Never far, in anyway. No big deal. He'd had to go out to the edge of Tallaght the other evening but that was grand, took Titch's bike. Or the bike Titch's been using.

No big deal. Like really it's not. OK, so this is only the fourth time, but it's been no hassle. Whatever he owes for clattering that Baba prick will be done with soon. Has to be.

They said, that night they caught him rapid cutting through the Bailey Gibson site, that they were asking nice and polite like, and that after what happened with the nephew they didn't have to be polite, but they liked Deano and they felt sorry for him with his da an all. So, nothing heavy, just deliveries. Good boy, Deano, we'll look after yeh. Few quid in yer pocket for the Christmas, am I fright or am I fright? Jim said. Cos that's really funny like. Great man for the words is Jim. And the jokes. In his white tracksuits, grinning with those little bits of spit at the corners of his mouth. Heard yer ma is back about the place. Looking well, I heard. And a nice big wink, the cunt. That's Jim, all concern. Yeah, it's all grand. All just fucken grand.

Unless, of course, he gets lifted and there's thousands' worth of sniff in the jiffy bag. And that's it, curtains. Off up the Joy to join all the tapped fuckers. And what would Oisín or his da think of that? What would Jack say? Always banging on about staying away from that shit and from the likes of Wino. Never get entangled with them, he said. But Jack's dead and his da's dead and half the place is dead and what does it matter? And what the fuck is taking this lad so long to answer the fucken door?

He thumps hard this time and the lock-sliding begins, chains pulled, bolts slid. It opens just enough for him to slip inside. The bluey light flickers in the hallway. A huge lad in Robocop gear is standing behind the door. This is new. It's normally scurrying yitnas who don't look you in the eye, or the kind that do look you in the eye to let you know how much they fucken despise you. This lad looks down and straight into Deano's eyes.

– Good evening.

Latvuanian or sum. He could kill you with a tap of that head-sized fist, but the flattened nose is in the middle of a big soft baby face. A cross between Shrek and Justin Bieber.

– Come in, wait here, the Latvuanian says, as he's tapping a code into the keypad at the first inner door.

A long corridor leads down to another coded door but the Latvuanian makes it clear that Deano's to stay in this first bit while he goes on into the inner sanctum. Through the glass panel Deano can see it looks a bit less nasty through there. There's a side table, a lamp, fake flowers in a vase. A line of four boxes sits along one side of the hallway, at Deano's feet. The musty smell in here's gonna set off his sneezing any second now. There's a browny-green patch up high on the opposite wall. Damp is a living thing.

He shoves his hands deep into his pockets and stands away from the wall and its condensation. If this takes much longer he'll stink of the place too. The box closest to him has been cut open, the flaps sitting up. He can't quite see what's inside. Checking out the cameras, he sticks his foot on the edge and drops to mess with his shoelace, flipping the box open. Plastic lids on purple plastic bottles. Lube. Bottle after bottle. The other boxes have the same tags on them. Four boxes. Of lube.

– You come in. You need to wait, the Latvuanian says, poking his head round the door.

Fucking fuck!

– Aww, I don't think so, bud. I'm just here to collect …

– Orders are you come.

The way they say yer life flashes in front of your eyes. Not true. There's only white or black. A flash of blank screen. A feeling like yer gonna spritz yer jocks. And yeh hear, for some reason – as you follow a giant Latvuanian down the hall because you've got no choice – yeh hear Whacker saying, stick a cork up yer Garda Patrol and keep running. But yeh can't run. Yeh have to make out that you've no problem with this craic at all. Confident, look at me stalk down here, chest out.

The Latvuanian leads him down another narrow hallway to the left and pushes open one of the glossy peach-painted doors.

– Is okay. Is no problem for you, I think. Just need wait for boss man, boss.

So, the hardman routine wasn't fooling Igor here. Eastern Europeans, wide to everything.

– Yeah, yeah, I know. No worries, Deano says, casual like as he moves into the officey room.

Cream leather sofa on one side, desk with three chairs on the other but they're all on top of each other because one side of the room is so close to the other side of the room. No windows other than some high-up ones that lead onto the windowless hall and the rooms on either side. Airless. Recently magnoliaed. A tiny little room like a toilet or a coffin.

– You sit.

– Alright.

The Latvuanian gives him an almost smile as he closes the flimsy door and the room's walls rattle. It's a funny thing being trapped in a little room, waiting, when yeh can't tell anyone where yeh are and yeh might never see anyone yeh know ever again and yer arse is wobbling and yeh want to cry or fucken wreck the gaff. A very funny thing. The phone buzzes over and over in his pocket. He scratches his nose. Them feckin cold sores. You're run down, June says. It's the Leaving, June says. Take them vitamins I got yeh, Deano. June'd be round here like a shot if he texted her. Like a shot. Oisín too. Only down the road, both of them.

It's probably like this most times, with lads like him. They probably don't even know what they're supposed to have done. Maybe they've some idea. He's done fuck all, that's all he knows. But shure, you've only to look crooked at the wrong prick and that's the end of yeh. Don't get entangled with them boys, Jack said. And here we are with the boxes of johnnies this time stacked up beside the fake leather sofa.

Footsteps, words. The door is opened by the Latvuanian, and Ratty McFuck, his half-greased-back long hair falling over his face on one side, ambles in, coat on, ready for the off.

– Dean, Dean, heard you were in the building, thought I'd come and say hello. No, sit down, sit down, relax.

Cunt.

– Here's the little something for you, good lad, Wino says, pulling a small Jiffy bag from his pocket and a smoke from behind the greasy ear.

– Mind if I smoke?

Yeah, yeah, I do, you fucken piece of shredwank with yer fucken big …

– Nah, go ahead.

He sticks his tongue out, grinning, and rubs the fag over and back a couple of times on his bottom lip like a ponce.

– Nothing exotic, Dean. Just wanted to see how you're getting on. With things.

What? What are you supposed to say? What? Grand, yeh cuntcha, just grand. I'm here to pick up yer shit, and take it to wherever you and yer arsehole mates want it taken because of yer fat fuck nephew.

– What's the problem? Gone mute, Dean? Quiet's good, don't get me wrong. I like quiet. Too much jibber jabber, know what I mean?

– I'm grand.

– Being treated well?

He's not being treated any way. Knocks on the door, gets the package …

– Yeah, no bother.

Wino stands up, moves around the desk, dropping the Jiffy bag on it, pulls open a drawer, takes out an ashtray and sits back down.

– How's June?

– She's fine.

– Leaving Cert this year, am I right? Tough one that.

Deano nods.

– Still playing the hurling, yeah? Good game. Never got into it meself. Too violent for my liking. More of a football man, me. Played for St Jude's.

No chance.

– I did, yeah. Quite handy with the ball, he says, looking off, dreamily.

There'll be a point to this sometime. A giant of a spider appears from nowhere, high up on the wall behind Wino, and scurries – you can kinda hear its feet tapping – over to check its web. But no! He's about to meet another huge fella coming from the opposite direction.

– Do yeh think the Dubs will do it again next year? Hard to see anyone beating them. Played county, meself, yeh know? Minors. Well, I started. But …

The spiders are heading straight for each other, crawling along the edge of the window frame. One of them pauses and rears up. Wiggles two of his legs in the air. The other fella stops. To watch probably. Or laugh? Deano could laugh now.

Is it true, St Jude's? Minors? Not likely. The slimy fuck. No one would even *want* to play with him.

– Long time ago. Injury.

Spiders are nearly there. Nearly meeting.

– Smashed the boot into the shin. Deliberate. No doubt about it. You could hear the crack everywhere. Passed out even.

The two hairy lads pause and then both of them rear up on the back legs and wave the couple of front ones at each other, like girl slapping, except not really making any contact at all. Fuck like. The size of them and this is all a spider knock is.

– The bone came out. Sticking out, it was. Smashed. Kinda grey, lots of the red stuff.

He suddenly turns round, looking for what Deano's looking at. Fuck it, in anyway. He can't see them from his short-arsed angle. Wino turns back.

– Ever play football yerself, Dean? Different game altogether, but yeh know, a sportsman is a sportsman.

What the fuck is this? The spiders lay down their legs and one climbs over the other and they both go on about their business.

– I've played a few times. Down in Sandymount.

– Ah, Sandymount, is it? Aspirations. I didn't say notions, see that? Wino says, stubbing the fag out and smiling, like a human almost. Yeh are *doing* the Leaving, yeah? Important thing, education.

And he half-laughs.

– Didn't get much of it meself.

Say something. Say something.

– No?

Up he jumps, lets out a puff, brushes something off his coat and picks up the Jiffy bag again.

– But sure there's more than one way to get educated, am I right, Dean?

Deano stands too, pulls his sweat-stuck jeans off his balls. Wino reaches over the envelope and then whips it back.

– Plans after the Leaving, have yeh?

– Not really.

– Is it college?

– Nah, I dunno, Deano says, looking at the lump of fairly fresh pink Hubba Bubba stuck to the hairy carpet.

– Yeh know, I'm all for education, me. But Sandymount and Trinity College, fancy schools and that, that's not for the likes of us. You and me. I've family at them places. They'll let yeh in alright, but you'll never be one of them. And they won't let you forget it. Don't get involved with them. Stay with yer own. You'll understand when you find yourself with a family of your own.

Wino slicks back his hair. Yeah, the voice of experience, with no kids. He reaches out with the Jiffy bag again, Deano goes to take it and he half whips it back again.

– The likes of us, Dean, we make our own, yeah? Because those cunts won't ever give us our fair share. We've gotta take it, yeah?

He's leaning in close now and Deano feels like he should crouch a bit.

– Take it, yeah?

And this time he actually hands over the envelope.

– Go on, get outta here. I've things to do.

He slaps Deano on the back as he's walking out the door.

– Fierce cold out there tonight.

– Yeah.

– But you're sweating away there. June and the kids doing well in anyway?

For fucksake!

– Yeah, grand.

He walks behind him. The Latvuanian, does the code on the other side and holds open the door.

– Piotr, see this young man out. That's a good lad there. Am I right, Dean-Oh? he says, laughing as he walks away.

– Stopped pissing cats, Piotr mumbles, looking at the drying ground as he cracks the heavy main door.

And he's out. He's out. And he's breathing and he knows he's breathing because he can hear himself panting, and he starts to lean over but thinks better of it. CCTV.

He stumbles a bit as he starts to cross the yard. A car pulls up in the shadows by the gate. Deano goes wide to stay close to the far wall, away from the revealing glare of the security lights. He ducks in at a corner.

The car idles and then drives on. Decided against it, did yeh?

A girl in a fur-lined hoody comes through the gate, looking at her phone, thumbs flying. She leaps over the still waterlogged potholes in her Uggs and slides her dropped hood back up over her scarlet hair as she gets to the door. She scans the place, doesn't ring the bell or knock, doesn't see him and then gets back to her phone. Mad about something. She's pacing up and down, annoyed, when the door clangs open and a woman, fucking Marian, sticks her head and arm out. The girl grabs what she's holding out, turns on her heel and marches away, twirling the bunch of keys on her finger. Deano sinks further into the shadows. She's out the gate and away.

What the fuck's she doing at a gaff like that?

Once Candy's out of sight, Deano rushes back towards the gate.

He's down at Weaver Park before he knows it. The skaters are standing on the edge, looking down into the bowl, frowns on foreheads, rollies between lips, considering whether it's dry enough yet. Small kids trying to smash up the castle in the playground. Deano sags down onto the small wall, pulls out a blunt he made earlier.

– You alright, man? one of the skaters, a fella with a shitty beard and flares, says.

– Yeah, be grand, Deano says, forcing a smile that doesn't quite make it.

He takes a drag and holds it out, offering it to the skater lads and one girl. The fella who asked him comes closer and lifts it from his fingers.

– Yeh don't look too good, man. Sure you're okay? You a friend of Hamza's, yeah?

– Yeah.

– And Oisín. I know Oisín as well.

It's coming. He thought he was imagining it but no. He turns,

– Sorry …

And pukes into the shrubs behind them.

10
OISÍN

Oisín's cheeks are burning and he's only been waiting five minutes for her. He just doesn't get how she manages to sit in this office all day with sun glaring in and no air. A rock crystal lamp, the same as the ones his mom insists he turns on every evening to clear the energies, spreads soft orange light through the incense smoke. She swishes in, folders clutched to her chest, a multicoloured splash.

– So sorry about that Oisín. There was a situation with the second years but you have my full attention now. How have you been since last week?

She takes her crystals off the shelf and arranges them in an arrow shape, pointing at him, on the low table between them. He doesn't want her full attention, thanks very much, but he knows he's going to get it.

– Hi Miss Hutchings. I'm grand.

– Now, tiger's eye. Would you like to hold it while we speak?

In the name of fuck! He looks out over the roofs towards the mountains. Imagine being out in Massey Woods on a day like this. Tramping through the mud. He'd jump in the stream, throw himself off the rope swing. Anywhere but here.

– No thanks, Miss. I'm good for tiger's eye.

She pops the tiger's eye back into position in the shiny stone arrow on the table. Balls of fluff float up into the air off the pink throw around her shoulders as she flops into her seat.

– So, how did we get on during the week? Did you try out the heart-space meditation we did?

Did he fuck! Big red heart overflowing, bursting, in fact. Becoming too big for your heart space, widening out into the room. Becoming one big heart. Right up his street.

– Yeah, I gave it a go.

– And? she says, leaning forward, all hopeful eyebrows.

Ach, she's alright, Miss Hutchings.

– Yeah, yeah, it was alright.

She nods, fingers to lips, steepling. Then releases back into the armchair – that bouncy wooden IKEA one that everyone has – with a concerned but confident single eyebrow lift.

– How're things at home?

She's always intent on making out that there's a problem between him and his mom or that the aul fella situation is about to overwhelm him. He's an aul fella, married to some other aul one, and he's his dad. Get over it, Missus. He has. Throwing his head back, he stares at the luminous star-covered ceiling. What the? Hope to Christ she isn't dragging young fellas in here to her cavern at night.

– I've those stars on my ceiling, Miss.

– Oh do you? I love them, Oisín. Do you love them?

If she's coming on to him, he's outta here.

– They only light up in the dark, Miss.

A little furrow appears in her brow and her face squelches in a bit.

– I know, I know, but still so lovely. They remind me of nights in West Cork, you know, clear skies, oh, magical.

They're plastic. Made in China. He's seen the sky at night in West Cork.

– Yeah, me too.

– So, home?

– All grand.

– Good, good. And the work, the study?

She's down to her baby voice whisper. Wonder does she even notice she's doing that. The study. A little cough and she gets serious, squirms like she's screwing an arse lightbulb into the seat. Digging in for the long haul.

– All going fine. Going better anyway.

He smiles at her. She's only doing her job, his mom says. She's a genuine person, she says. A bit mental but heart in the right place. They've been chatting in the café. Brings her kid (now that was a surprise because, would yeh?) along for half a brownie and an elderflower cordial every Saturday. Telling his mom that he could do great things, very academic, needs a bit of direction, but the music, his eyes light up when he talks about the music. She leans forward and repositions the stones. He catches a glimpse of her cleavage, lacy white bra. Well, there you go, you really can get a semi for just about anything.

– Have you had any thoughts on your CAO choices?

Fuck this! No, no he hasn't. The fucking pressure! It's this, this kind of shit that has him here in the first place. Your whole life decided by putting numbers in boxes. And then you get in a box. And you're a number.

– What about the engineering? Those tests showed you had an aptitude.

– Yeah engineering, I'm still thinking about it.

– How about the sleep?

– Yeah, no problem there.

– And the other thing? she says, hopefully.

He should never have said a word. She keeps going back to this. Loves it, she does.

– Ah, that's all grand, Miss. Think I was just dreaming. You know yourself.

And he shrugs. Too many times, fuck it. Like a big eejit.

He, it, sat at the end of his bed, woke him four or five times last night. Sitting there smiling at him. Try waking up suddenly, sitting up, opening your eyes and seeing, in the shadowy dark, your room just as it really is, with a person just sitting there, watching you. You'd get a fright, right? You'd jump. Your heart would race. No matter who it is. Your twin, just like you, a mirror image of you. Come on, how can it be Ruairí? says the djinn expert. Who else is it? Smiling, kind, the same as him. But try opening your eyes night after night – because it's every night now – to find a person watching. Not that this didn't happen before. They both saw them sometimes, him and Ruairí, shadowy giants in the dark. Not often, although Mom told them about their sleepwalking when they were little and their stories of chatting with the old lady at the end of the bed, but neither of them remembered that, and they thought that maybe she was making it up to make them sound special. Embellishing, at least. And they were never lit up, in full colour, like Ruairí or the djinn or whatever the fuck he is. It is.

– Sure? You haven't seen anything strange at night since?

– No, nothing, he says, stretches his arms up above his head and fakes a yawn.

– Well look, do you want to use what's left of the time to do a relaxation, meditation?

Relief, just go with it. Keep her happy.

– Yeah, sure.

– You sit back there now. Would you like a blankie? Blanket?

Good save, Miss. Not.

– No, I'm grand thanks, he says as he settles back and closes his eyes. Humour her.

– I'll chant om, she says. You know the drill, you can chant out loud with me, don't feel embarrassed.

– Hhmmm.

– Or you can mentally intone it.

She's getting sing-songy now. Yeah, mentally intone. That's what he'll do. Mentally intone.

– Ah-Oh-Mmmm, she starts, sounding a bit like a didgeridoo.

Just lie back and ignore her. Brings him back, it's the sound of the past, Mom hunkered down in the narrow space between their two baby beds. Eyes getting heavy, jealous of the kids allowed to stay out on the street later because it's still bright, it's still daytime. Mom, reaching across to hold hands, and when she's done omming and has crept out, closing the door softly.

In the distance, whispering:

– Oisín, Oisín? We need to wake up gently, now.

He sits up suddenly, then stretches, making a meal of it. She's cleared the stones off the table and she's swishing round the room.

– I nearly drifted off there, Miss.

She smiles.

– Same time next week?

– I don't know, I have study and …

– Same time next week, Oisín?

– Yes, Miss. See you next week.

*

He considers himself in the mirror at the top of the stairs. The hair's coming along well now. Planning to have it long by the time of the Leaving, it's growing outwards in thick creamy blond ringlets. And he knows it's cool, he knows. Girls ask to touch it when he's out. Course, girls, white girls only, sometimes ask to touch Benit's hair too when he's going full fro but that's a different thing. His mom calls up the stairs:

146

– Are you sure you don't want some of this pizza, pet? Your favourite, with chorizo.

He's told her already that he's getting food with the boys at the gaff before the others arrive.

– I don't want you drinking on an empty stomach. Will you walk Gruff before you go?

– What the fuck? You're a Nazi, he shouts down at her.

He puts on the shirt she bought him 'as an early Christmas present' in one of her vintage shops in town. Covered in foxes' heads, it's gonna go down a treat with the ladies at the gaff. They like that kind of thing, the cuties. Little bit different, but not whack-job different like a cowboy outfit or a kilt. Planning to get lucky. Wearing his lucky socks. Extra splash of the Sauvage but not too much. Nothing worse than too much. There are three bedrooms in the place, he checked it out earlier, met up with Hamo and the fella who's renting the place – a chunky no-neck who couldn't put his arms by his sides, was already growing an upper back hump, gym tits bursting out of his shirt, trousers too short and tight round the bollocks and shoes too long for his feet. Mom's mentioned, more than once, that you should never trust a man who wears shoes that are far too long for his feet. Some truth in that. He checks out his own white Converse now in the mirror. Normal, nothing flashy, size ten feet, size ten shoes. No need for shoe-bragging here.

The agent had congratulated them on paying that bit extra for the place. He has other identical apartments in the building – right down to the face cloths in the many toilets and the prints of fat babies sitting in the middle of sunflowers on the walls. What were they paying extra for? The view. And what view was he talking about, cos Oisín couldn't see it. The view of the outside, yeah, the *outside* of the Aviva. When Oisín let a 'Fuck off, no way!' burst out of him, the agent fella nearly splattered with indignation. 'We're a rugby nation, you know!' Fair enough. It made Oisín wonder could you get people to pay top dollar for a stay in a shitty gaff if they had a view of the outside of a five-star hotel.

Pleasant enough afterwards, your man, even though he was clearly annoyed with Oisín for not understanding the ways of the world. He winked at them when he was leaving and said, 'You two have a great time, guys,' in a really weird way and Hamza came and put his arm round Oisín's shoulder.

Hamza explained it when Slapneck was out of earshot. He'd emailed to make an enquiry about the apartment because he and his partner (that'd be Oisín) were going to have a bit of a bash and secretly, he, Hamza, was going to pop a certain question.

'There'll be no problem because they don't want to offend the gays and they trust the gays to not fuck shit up. With good reason, because the gays just don't fuck shit up.'

Fair enough. 'Think of all the gays and even lezzers living round your way, what do their houses look like?' Hamza said. Oisín had remarked on this before. They all keep their houses and gardens nice and their hair well-cut. Oisín'd even said that he wanted to move into the house with the pair on the corner. You can see them through the window, Carl and Louis, reading, their Scottie with his little protective booties, their lamps and their throws, art on their dark blue walls.

What he can't get over is the agent believing that he'd ride Hamza and that they'd be getting married, at their age. The gays play the field. They'd be riding all around them. Hamza pointed out the beard, more mature, but still. And the gays don't have jihadi beards. And there's no chance that Oisín would ride Hamza. That's the main point. If he was on the turn, Brad Pitt is probably the only one he'd consider letting in the back door. Even then, he's not reciprocating. Doesn't want Brad Pitt's shite on his cock any more than he wants Hamza's. Actually, he'd prefer Hamza's. Better the devil ... Letting agents obviously aren't very observant people.

– You going to walk Gruff or not? his mom calls up again.

He'll walk the dog, of course.

– You're so fucken lazy, why can't you walk him? he says, grabbing the lead from the hook in the alarm cupboard.

– Why do you have to talk to me like that? she says with zero conviction.

– You're the one who sent me to Colmcille's. What did you expect?

She keeps a straight face but her eyes are laughing.

– You'll mind yourself tonight, won't you? Your dad's coming up tomorrow afternoon, so ...

He sighs.

– Yeah and I told you I'd be back.

– Just reminding ...

– Stop talking, Mom. I know, you've told me. I'll be back.

The smell of the pizza makes his belly talk up. He has a look in the fridge, grabs a full chorizo and bites off the top while he sticks the lead on Gruff.

He takes him on a circuit out onto the South Circular. Passing Spar, two young Roma girls in their long skirts, roses stuck in their shiny black hair trailing down past their arses, put their scarves around their head as it starts to drizzle. They're half-heartedly asking the odd person for money. Rounding off the end of the begging day. A Muslim man, one of Hamza's dad's mates, he thinks, comes round the corner and starts shaking his head. Gruff hunkers down for one of his epic shits.

The Muslim man lifts the chin to Oisín but he's more focused on the begging women. He's frowning, not happy, starts berating them in Arabic as he passes Oisín. It sounds harsh at the best of times but this fella's definitely pissed off. Maybe he's just mental, having a rant. The women first look at each other, then at Oisín who gives them a half shrug. How's he supposed to know? The man's bearing down on them now. He switches to English.

– Shame, shame on you. Muslim women begging. Go home!

The women look at each other, open-mouthed, and start giggling, nervously.

– But we're not Muslims, one of them says, almost apologizing.

But your man's not listening. He's gesticulating and furiously shaking his head as he stalks on down the road. He shouts back:

– Shame!

That's them told. Gruff has shuffled to another spot and is grunting. The pair of women look at Oisín, gawping. One of them starts to laugh and ends up bent double, hands between her knees.

Oisín smiles at them. The laughy one's very pretty. You couldn't get with a Roma girl though. You'd only end up having to marry her, with her whole family, a hundred of them, bailing into your house, and her brothers battering you if you put a foot wrong. Hardy men.

– Think it's the scarves, maybe, he says, patting his own head.

Gruff finally finishes, leaving a sparkly log on the cobblelocked patch outside the door of Spar, and a piece of tinsel hanging out of his arse. That's what you get when you take the deccies out of the attic in November.

*

– He is a pikey though, Hamza says, dragging one of the modular sofas into a corner. More room for dancing.

– But there's no need to call him that, Oisín says. This pizza tastes a bit weird, doesn't it?

– You need to cop on, fucking SJW.

– Pass the garlic sauce there, Benit says. Is there hot sauce in this gaff?

– They don't give you food when you rent a gaff, Benit, Hamza says. And where's your contribution to the rent and the gear?

– Ah, I'll Rev you in a few, fam. Relax.

Hamza stops what he'd doing.

– Just give me your share, Benit and I'll relax, yeah?

Has there ever been a time when this didn't happen with the pair of them? And this'll only get worse when the rest of the brown lads arrive. Everything's just right though, the weather: not wet, the apartment: cool as fuck, the boys: looking fresh. The pizza: not so much but maybe he's just got a funny taste in his mouth. Epic, this is gonna be. Epic. And girls. Swamped with cuties, they'll be.

– I've a few ready-rolled for yiz, Deano says, as he carries another pizza out of the kitchen. What's the story with these tiny kitchens, man? Size of the gaff.

– Google's got a big restaurant. Keeps them at work. Quinoa and mung beans and all, Oisín says. Don't need a kitchen.

– What? Is your ma cooking for Google now?

– What the fuck is the taste off this pizza?

– The hash, Karl says, coming back to the table, wiping his hands on a fluffy white bath towel. This gaff's massive. See these towels? Quality.

– See, Karl doesn't give a shit about me calling him a pikey. Hamza says, back dragging furniture around.

But Karl's getting those pink dots on his cheeks as he pulls a slice off the pepperoni pizza, careful not to drip anything on his fancy blue shirt.

– Leave him alone, Hamza, Oisín says.

– Doing nothing to him. Am I, Karlo?

Hamza still hasn't forgiven him for Tanya's party.

– Let it go, Hamo, Deano says.

– Let what go?

– You know. It's not just the hash, Karl. It's the sauce. There's something up with the sauce, Oisín says.

– You coming up on one? Benit says.

– No, just the few crumbles of hash on the pizza.

– Pizza's whopper, Deano says. Anyone who says different's fucked up.

Right, time to let them have it. This is a good one.

– I was thinking …

– Here we go, another grand scheme, Deano says.

This is his best yet. This one will hunt, as Hamza has taken to saying for some reason. What the fuck does that even mean?

– I was thinking: lil rope ladders for the Romanian kids to get out of the clothes banks.

– Won't work. Urban myth, Hamza says.

– Where have you been, Hamza? Deano says. Florin in fourth year's little sister was stuck in the one beside the library. The lads who collect the clothes arrived the next morning and out she ran, squawking. Legged it. Happened more than once.

– Yeah? Did Florin tell you that? Benit asks.

– Nah, who was it? Snitchy, I think.

– Right, Snitchy, Benit says.

– Snitchy knows these things, bro. Finger on the pulse. Ear to the ground, yeah? Deano says in Snitchy's voice. He's coming tonight, right?

– Yeah, Hamza sighs. 'Mon, we need to get the place cleaned up.

Shitebags ignoring him.

– See, the Romanians come to the door asking do you want to give them your clothes and jewellery and net curtains in good condition. And you say, no thanks but would *you* like to buy this tiny rope ladder for your kid to climb out of the clothes bank?

– Soon as you give them the idea, they'll start making the ladders themselves. Limited in its ability to maintain profits. And Romanians aren't sticking their kids in bins overnight anyway.

He picks up a cloth, throws it to Benit, and tells him to shine up the chrome legs of the table.

They've got marks on them, apparently. If Hamza's getting this tetchy already, he'll need something decent in him quick or he'll spend the night minding the table legs and putting coasters under cans and glasses. That kind of thing is normally Benit's job. He's already left paper cup towers on either side of the kitchen doorway and he's scattered piles of the paper napkins, that Oisín's mom persuaded him to bring, on shelves and counters and on the multi-coloured table nests dotted around the step-down loungey area. Like a lot of sneezing is expected.

– Hamza's right. Cute fuckers, the Roomanians. Resourceful, Deano says. They'll make them ladders outta yer ma's net curtains. Youse wanna watch them Romas coming over here, stealing yizzer way of life, Karlo. Anyway, we right, boys?

Deano opens up his little French tin and places five blunts on the now greasy glass-topped table.

– Open them up now, Karl says. You're shit at rolling. I'll do it.

Nothing wrong with the blunts, but let Karl at it. It's his way back in. Karl thinks no one can roll like him.

– What are you, Karl? Fucking fifteen? Hamza says.

– This is no ordinary gaff. We are kings, Benit says, grinning, as he lies down and starts roly-polying over and back on the rug.

Hamza's rummaging in the cupboard in the long hallway.

– There's a ping pong table in here, he shouts in. Give us a hand someone.

There's a little rush in Oisín's belly as he walks out into the hall. Nothing to be too bothered about. Still, a bit weird. There was only a tiny bit of the hash that Deano gave him on the pizza, couldn't be that. And there it is again.

They hawk the folded-up table out, dragging it past and over a Christmas tree with all its decorations on, four fully-inflated Swiss exercise balls, a Dyson, three stacked boxes of wine glasses – best they stay where they are – walking poles and a selection of racquets for something or other.

– Table tennis, I'm the OG, niggas. Let's do dis ting, Benit says, as he's tightening up the legs on the table.

– Bagsy first game, me and Deano. We've unfinished business from the summer.

They're basically even, Oisín thinks, but Deano swears he's a game up. They smashed the campsite record for longest rally and the longest time spent on the table. On the last day, they even got up early and refused to go to the beach, staying playing instead. They stopped to eat and piss but if no one was around, they took a slash in the bushes beside the tables. That's how high the stakes are here.

– Oh you're going down, bro, Deano says, picking up a half-covered bat.

Another rush. Could be poisoning.

– Feeling a bit weird. Maybe that pizza was actually dodgy, Karl says, patting his belly.

It's shrunk a bit lately, since he's been getting back to hurling a bit. He's taken to going for a run, a jog, more like, a couple of times a week too, he says. Looking a bit stocky.

– You shedding the pounds tryna get with Tanya, Karlo? She coming, yeah? Oisín says, spinning the bat in his hand.

Oisín wouldn't mind a bit of that. No one would. She's the definition of a ten. And decent as well. Karl's ignoring him or not listening.

– Karlo, he's asking if Tanya's fair game. We'd all give that a go, Deano says as he serves.

– Fuck off the both of yiz.

– No fair, buddy. Yer not smashing that, yeh can't ban the rest of us. Seen the way she looks at me, only gagging for a bitta this, Deano says.

Deano's great but there's a fair gap between himself and Tanya.

– If anyone's hopping on Tanya, it'll be me, Oisín says. Or Karlo, obviously.

Karl's not doing anything to anyone. If he'd just stand aside, Oisín could get right in there. Course, there'll be plenty of other cuties later. Been a bit too long since he's seen any action, if he doesn't get somewhere tonight …

– My balls are gonna burst, I swear, if I don't get with some young one, Deano says.

Benit's on the sofa, eyes closed.

– Feeling strange, fam. Wanna see if I've anything for a dodgy belly.

– Seeing anything yet? Hamza says, grinning.

What the fuck?

– What you on about, fam? Benit says.

– Little treat for the boys. Mustafa in the pizza place, passed him a few mushrooms to put in the tomato sauce.

Deano drops his bat. Benit stops rummaging and Karl keeps on waving his hand in front of his face.

– You spiked us? You fucker.

– You're welcome, Hamza says, folding his arms over his chest and laughing. It's only a few, you're not gonna get much visuals. Enjoy.

And he will enjoy. He's already enjoying and now he's gonna demolish Deano. He's battering him but the balls get slower and the serves get messier and it just doesn't seem so important to bury Deano's ping pong dreams anymore. The bat feels light, so amazingly light it leaves a tail of green in the air when he moves it over and back.

– Seeing that trail? Deano says, happy now.

– Oh yes siree. A flare.

– Green.

– Yup.

– Thanks Hamo.

Hamza goes over to Karl, grabs his head and knuckles it. Forgiven.

Brown fellas arrive in dribs and drabs. Deece lads mostly. And Mohammed. Posse in tow – fellas with their Moncler jackets hanging at their elbows, fellas with gold chains that weren't bought in Argos, fellas with their CKs fully on show.

– Why does Hamo have anything to do with him? Oisín side-mouths to Karl, as they're clearing the last of the pizza off the table.

– Don't ask me but that parka in hot orange is rank. Don't care what skin tone yeh have. Fucken vulgar.

'Vulgar', he didn't lick that off the landing in School Street. Mohammed and gang take over the best corner of the sofa, legs as far apart as possible. Got big balls does Mo. The shit-talk from girls about manspreading pisses Oisín off because, in fairness, the jewels need some room. If he had a neat little pocket, like girls do, he wouldn't need to spread either. But Mohammed and crew are taking it to the extreme. There's enough room on that sofa, with all the bits of it, for at least thirty people but twelve of them have it covered straight away. Even Mo can't piss him off now though.

*

– Yeah, yeah, I do. I do want to have kids. That'd be the best thing ever. Have a wife and kids and my own house and do something for money that I like, Oisín says to Russian Vlad.

Five languages, doesn't make a single mistake ever in any of them, as far as Oisín's ever heard.

– Yes, yeah. We won't start a family yet, my girlfriend and I. Study first, in the Netherlands. Live together. Family later. It's all good.

He passes the pipe back to Oisín who sinks back into the sofa. Marshmallow soft but still firm underneath, like a five-star hotel bed.

– Supportive, he shouts, smiling at Vlad.

– Yes, Vlad says. I like it very much. Have you had much drugs?

He's always like this. Serious, clever, and then he comes out with something that makes everyone piss themselves but never cracks a smile himself. The corners of his mouth quiver a little but no full smile.

– Not much. Yet.

– Good job, Vlad says, as he raises his litre-bottle of vodka. I brought food. Left it in the kitchen, if you'd like some.

– Not black bread?

– No, just dumplings. You drinking?

Oisín pulls the ancient but unopened bottles of crème de menthe and blue curaçao out of the shopping bag sitting at his feet.

– On this tonight, maybe later. Gonna mix it up. Feeling good right now, nice pizza.

– This spells disaster or ecstasy. Let's hope, Vlad says.

Karl dances over to them. A happy boy. Still no sign of Tanya but he's buzzing.

– What you two talking about?

– Having a family, Oisín says. Nice woman, have a house, mind my family. Boys and girls, I'd like.

Karl looks at him like he's got two heads. And maybe he has. Karl starts laughing.

– A family and a wife? That's the gayest shit ever, Karl says, and he springs back up. Gotta dance. These feet just can't stop moving boys.

– Did he just say that having a wife and kids is gay? Vlad asks.

Hamza drops beside him on the next section of squashy sofa.

– We're talking about family. Oisín wants five kids. How about you? Vlad says.

– Ah, what the fuck are you on about bro? Hamza says, looking at Oisín.

– I think it'll be great. That's what I want.

His arse bones are dancing into the squash but nothing else is moving. Apart from the walls. The walls roll and bubble occasionally. All good. Hamza's got a bit of a halo.

– Do you see my arse bones? Am I moving?

– This is a party and you two are here bullshitting about kids?

– My arse is dancing but not the rest of me. Mad. Yeah, I want loads of kids. I mean it'll be up to her …

Hamza laughs.

– Your imaginary girlfriend?

– Don't see no girls here. No Candy either. You promised girls. The best we've got so far is Titch there.

Titch, with his new long do, turns around in the middle of passing out pills to some of the fifth years.

– Someone looking for me? Youse need antin there? Titch says, the big smile spreading on his face.

He can't help himself, Titch. He's like an even smilier version of Karl. A big eejit trying to be a hardman. Same as Snitchy, only less hardman, more eejit. Dunno what age he is even. Fifteen? Sixteen? Snitchy's settling himself in at the head of the table, laying out a silk bandana.

– Got this great squidgy an am providing samples to the chosen few, Snitchy says, as he pulls out a knife and starts paring.

– Holy shit, Snitchy, what the fuck's going on with that knife, Oisín says. Blinged up to fuck.

It's sparkling like diamonds in his hand.

– Who'd you rob that off?

– Didn't rob it off anyone. Made it for me ma.

– It's a Swiss Army knife, Oisín says. You didn't make it, Snitchy.

Snitchy's not fazed.

– I made it that way for her. For her birthday. Swarovski crystals. Took them off some shoes I found. Look.

He holds it up.

– I dug out the little holes, glued in the diamonds. See? It's a heart and an M for Mam.

– It's not gay when it's for yer ma, Titch pipes up.

Snitchy nods in agreement at him.

– Said to mind it for her, Snitchy says. Doesn't like knives, she said.

Oisín lets out a wail:

– Where's the girls?

Snitchy holds out a closed fist to him.

– Here, take this, have a nibble. That'll cure yeh, Snitchy says.

He takes it and chews a little off the corner even though he already has the little cube that Deano gave him earlier out of his shirt pocket. Not often that Snitchy's giving out freebies.

Two of the skater lads fall over the planter full of ice and water and cans. The colouredy drinks might be nice to have a sip of. Grabbing the bottles, he heads into the kitchen and takes a cup from Benit's tower. Two lads he doesn't recognize, one white, one brown, bit older, are wearing the faces off each other pressed into the corner of the worktops. Well now.

– Can I get past you there, just wanna see what's in the cupboards.

A nice glacé cherry would be just the thing. The pair don't let go of each other or even acknowledge Oisín, but shift a bit to the right so he can get at the cupboard and wine fridge that's full of Tyskie and what looks like a tub of hair gel. Cupboard's only got salt, pepper, olive oil and a box of Barry's. Hamza reaches across him and grabs the teabags. The snogging fellas are holding each other's faces, nose to nose and grinning their heads off. Nice. Oisín scooches them up a bit more and finds a cocktail shaker, lashes in the crème and curaçao – the colours together, man! Whopper. And then looks for some kind of mixer. Too sticky otherwise.

He steps out into the big room. Yusuf from fifth year bounces past on a space hopper, tries to take the steps, loses control and pitches into the ping pong table. Vlad and Benit are spitting ping pong balls at the gaping mouth of one of Mohammed's posse, a small fella who must be sweltering in that jumper – it's got Versace in big writing across the front, now *that's* vulgar. Deano's got Karl on the floor, both of them with ping pong bats in hand.

– Tap out and I've won.

– Nah, fuck off, you didn't, Karl laughs.

– Chicken wing, wanna chicken wing, Karlo? Deano says, flipping him over.

The intercom keeps buzzing. The front door opening and closing behind him. The cocktail shaker!

– Need a mixer here! he shouts over the noise.

Hamza grabs the shaker from behind and pours something steaming into the mix. Tea? Tea. Nodding along with the music, he plonks the lid back on the shaker, waves it around in the air, throws his head back and glugs a load of it.

– Tastes like a My Little Pony, he says, passing it to Oisín who has a look in at the purply-brown liquid, before knocking it back.

– Nice.

– That Deliveroo guy was called Elvis, Hamza says.

– Which?

– Which Elvis?

– No, which Deliveroo fella?

– Mohammed just got Deliveroo, I brought it up.

– Is he hungry?

– Mohammed?

– Nah bro, Elvis.

– Nah, he just delivered it, the food. Eddie Rocket's.

– Eddie Rocket's and Elvis. That rock 'n' roll vibe? That's like a message. Someone's trying to tell us something.

– Who? Hamza says.

Yusuf space-hops in between them and on out into the hallway towards the bedrooms. Didn't know they made space hoppers in blue. Mohammed only plays rap. Why does he only play rap? You need variety. Oisín's gonna provide that variety. He pulls out his phone.

– Was it real Elvis? Oisín says.

– Real enough. He was on a bike.

– Dead?

– No.

– That'd be fucken class if dead Elvis showed up with chicken tenders.

– He's Brazilian.

– From Tennessee.

– Live Elvis, Deliveroo Elvis, Brazilian.

– Maybe he moved.

– He did, he was just downstairs. In Dublin, Hamza says.

– That was a magazine. My mom wrote for it sometimes.

– I know. You told me before.

– I saw him in Dún Laoghaire once, Oisín says.

– Dead Elvis?

– Nah, Oisín says. Another Elvis. At the festival. At the pier. In all the gear. He was good.

– Deliveroo gear?

– Elvis gear. White suit, rhinestones.

His face hurts, he's smiling so much. His belly is laughing even if he isn't really. Or is he? He is. They both are.

– You sure that wasn't dead Elvis?

– Maybe. Sure the one outside was really Elvis?

– Yes, really. I saw the delivery slip with his name on. I asked him and he said yes, that's his real name. He could be dead Elvis now though. Never know. He could've been killed on the road after.

– Fuck, do you think us talking like this could've made him dead Elvis? Another dead Elvis? Oisín laughs. Go out, see if he's okay.

– He's gone by now. If we did it and he's dead, we've to keep quiet about it. This talk here never happened, yeah?

Out of the corner of his eye, Oisín sees a flash of blond hair as someone ducks into one of the bedrooms. He stares down the hall. The blond head bobs back out, smiling back at him. Fuck. He rubs his eyes.

– Speaking of dead, hold this, he says, and passes the shaker to Hamza.

– We can't do that with just the power of our minds. We can't kill Deliveroo Elvis. Just not possible, Hamza shouts after him.

– Just be a second, Oisín says, as he runs towards the bedroom.

He reaches his hand into the blackness of the room, looking for the switch. Nobody. Two single beds, duvet a bit creased on both where bodies have obviously been. He steps into the room, reefs open the wardrobe, even pulls open the drawers. No one. He jumps, heart thumping, as he turns to leave and catches his reflection in the mirror on the back of the drawer. There he is. There he is now. There's a crash so loud that it drowns out the music. Back in the room, Hamza's still in the same spot, at the top of the steps. Now along with a load of other fellas watching four, no, five of Mohammed's crowd, and Karl underneath them all, rolling around in a heap on top of the now-flattened ping pong table. The music starts up again.

– Django, Hamza says.

– Don't think we should let them fight to the death. Dublin 4 and all, Oisín grins.

– Best place for Mandingo fighting.

– Karl's gonna get smashed up there.

– Nah, judo. He's loving it, look.

True enough, through all the cheers and roaring, Karl's getting the better of them. Or at least he's not dying.

– Wait, do you think Elvis brought this with him? Mandingo fighting. From the same place as him.

– Brazil?

– No, Tennessee. The South.

– Fuck, you're right, Hamza says, open-mouthed.

– Everything is becoming everything else all the time, Oisín says.

– Yep. Everything, Hamza says and they share a smile, a smile in the air, a smile that everyone could smile if they tuned in.

– I saw Ruairí just there. In one of the bedrooms. He's not there though.

– I saw him too, Hamza says.

– Did you really? Oisín asks, excited, happy.

– Nah, bro. Just wanted to make you feel better.

*

The fox heads on his shirt move around a little but then settle back into position. Mohammed's up again supervising the decks. The lad that's DJing doesn't need Mo's help, but Mo insisted on having the decks brought down and he paid for them, so the poor DJ lad just has to put up with it. Decent of Mo to fork out for the decks and he's probably paying the DJ fella. Music's good and getting louder. You can hear and feel every bit in the floor, the tiniest sounds, the littlest clicks. Massive.

Conversations. Lads playing body Jenga, piling up limp fellas and then pulling them out of the pile. Someone's gonna suffocate. The Fear. Fuck. How will they explain that to the guards? How? No one's dead. No one's dead. Are you too high, bro? Nothing's wrong. I'm grand. Never better. Karl's talking clothes with Mohammed. Hamza's collecting food at the door. There's a flash of scarlet hair. She's here. Hamza beaming. Hamza with his arm around her. Candy smiling. Mohammed already knows Candy. Candy doesn't like Mo but Candy smiles anyway. Jack's on the sofa. Wait, Jack's on the sofa?

No, he's gone. I saw him too. No, no, I did, Deano says. I saw him for sure. He was here a minute ago. Deano has a wet face now. I don't trust him, that's all, Hamza says. Or is it Deano? No, Hamza. Who? Karl. I like him, don't get me wrong, bro. Benit says you're all good. All good people. People of the good people. We are kings. Mansa Musa. We are all Mansa Musa. Benit's in the middle of the glass table, swimming, flying on his belly. Mansa Musa could fly, fam. He could fly. Benit's stepsister. There's a cutie. Along with her girlfriend in a biker jacket. Older. Too old. This is it. Two dykes and a taken. I saw Ruairí. It's okay, bro, one of the skaters says. It's just the mushrooms. Who's Ruairí? His brother, one of the fellas who was wearing the face off the other fella in the kitchen says. How does he know? How? It's okay, pet. Hamza told me about it. Night-time. Don't worry, it's just a djinn.

*

He's tired, that's all. The music's quieter, or maybe further away? He heads out onto the long narrow balcony. The bland buildings down at the river are twinkling now. The blackness of the mountains is calling to him. Two more brown lads are lying feet-to-feet, staring up at the now clear sky. You can't see any real stars but the thump of The Weeknd is making stars in his belly. Exploding. His smile smiles the widest it's ever smiled. The two feet lads are smiling too. One of them holds up a massive carrot and bends his knees to wriggle closer to the other fella to pass it on.

– Gonna get your cooties but hey, I love ya.

– Don't say it, bro, just feel it.

Oisín's smile gets wider. Pure indica in that last blunt. Starts slow, but when you're coming up … Like acid. His belly lurches like he's on a rollercoaster. Fun, almost. Or is that the pizza.

– Pizza. Pizza's the best, he calls over the feet boys.

– Nah, bro, spice bag, one of them says.

– Spice bag, yeah, but pizza. What about pizza? It's so round.

– Sometimes a shape. Another shape.

– Fair enough, yeah. Sometimes a shape, Oisín says, scooting his arse along the boards a bit closer to them.

The two lads are narrowing their eyes, staring up. He does the same. The thump gets louder, vibrating under him.

– The Weeknd's playing in me arse, boys.

– Cool story, bro.

– If you do this, the squintiest fella says, you can see all the stars past the orange. They're just behind there. You just have to find them, fam.

And he's right. He's right. Oisín's eyelids are heavy. They close altogether and refuse to open.

If you do this, close them, you can see everything.

– Everything's becoming everything, Oisín says. I'll explain in a minute.

– No need, one of the fellas says. I know, fam. Watch this.

Up he hops on the edge of the balcony rail, arms outstretched. He's taller than Benit and possibly even Deano. With the straight-up hair, he's probably a foot taller than Oisín. Smoke between his lips, smiling the kid-in-the-know smile, he's a perfect human.

– Parkour, I like it, Oisín says.

The fella drops beside him, high fives, passes the smoke.

– *Mais ouais.*

Nights, nights should always be like this. Cool on your face. Lads, kings, in tune with the universe. Music thumping in your gut, in your arse. Dublin, best place in the world. Best place in the universe. The fella's back up, running along the rail in the opposite direction now. He sticks out his leg, arms waving to counterbalance. Over he goes. Fuck! Fuck! And grabs the rail on the other side, flips up and over and he's back, laughing and they're laughing together, all three and Dublin and the Aviva sparkle in the starlight.

– Kings, Oisín says.

– Kings, the two boys nod together.

*

He's shivering a proper shiver. His eyes spring open. The music's faint. He looks down the wooden planks but the feet fellas are gone. Casting off the bathroom rug that someone's thrown over him, he pulls himself up to standing with the door handle. His watch is gone. The watch his dad gave him. Dad's coming tomorrow. Inside, the big sitting room part has Mohammed showing his squad something on his phone. He looks up at Oisín and throws up a set. Ah, fuck off, Mohammed. He gives him a thumbs up. Never mess with that prick.

In the opposite corner, some weirdos – probably Hamza's clever-camp mates by the look of the jam jar glasses and the blue hair – are huddled round some game. Backgammon or chess or something. He's half-tempted. Chess. He hasn't played in …

– Oh, I love this shong, a girl's voice squeals from the middle of the crowd sitting round one end of the dining table.

Christina. The girlfriend – the butch one who never speaks unless she's talking about music, is engaged in some heavy conversation with Deano. And cunts, she likes to talk about cunts, the fanny kind. No one else wants to join in but there she goes, cunt this, cunt that, and punk this, grime that. NCAD. They're all about the gees there. Painting them, sculpting them. If Oisín called a girl's snatch a cunt, he'd be roasted. She's alright. They've all the chats about music. He scans the room. That's it? That's it? Still?

'Total Eclipse of the Heart'. Who plays that shit? Hamza's stretched at one end of the corner sofa with Candy's head in his lap, both of them out for the count. He needs a piss. What the fuck time is it? Two brown lads, maybe the feet fellas, can't see their faces properly because they're squished into each other's shoulders, are hug dancing in the middle of the floor. To this.

There's someone else in green jeans curled up under the sink in the main bathroom. Karl's lying in the jacuzzi bath, no water but the motor's running. His arms hanging over the side, an open can of Dutch Gold is lodged in his gaping fly, a cock and balls drawn on his left cheek. Funny because Karl said he was only drinking Stella in bottles from now on, if he was drinking beer at all. It's French, Karl pointed out. Whatever that has to do with anything. Karl's alive anyway, eyes slightly open and he's breathing. A smile on his face.

Oisín steps over the under-sink fella's feet, undoes his fly with a shaking hand, and holy shit, it's a painful and slow unloading. He needs a drink maybe, turns and looks at Karl's can. Nah, maybe not.

Finally done, Jesus, he heads down the hallway – the parquet crunchy and crackling under his feet – to the first of the bedrooms. Must be some cuties. Four fellas are stretched across one of the single beds, like slices of bacon. A pair of Nikes sticks out from underneath the heap of coats on the other single bed. Keith from fifth year. He recognizes the hole that one of Keith's mates put in the side of his shoe at a knock in the Cabbage Gardens. Pulled a knife and everyone thought that things had taken an unwarranted turn for the worst, but your man just pulled off Keith's shoe and stabbed it, screwing it in for maximum damage. They were Keith's Christmas Day shoes.

The other two bedrooms are full too – all fellas, stretched, happy. Filipino Cesar and twenty-four-year-old Nero the Bangladeshi from the other sixth-year class – are standing, smiling, supping Cokes in the hallway. Fuck this. He heads back to the table. A load of black lads are up pogoing to 'Fuck tha Police' with Deano (who wouldn't even know that song if it wasn't for Oisín) in the middle. One of the black lads slides to the floor, pipe in hand and calls out for a light as the rest of them just keep bouncing around them.

Deano gives up and comes over to the table.

– Is that my watch?

– Yeah, it was falling off yeh. You kept opening it up. Gonna fall through the slats on the balcony, yeah? Deano says. Mo gave yeh a blanket yoke. Here ya go, bro. Alright now?

– What the fuck time is it? How long was I out there?

– Dunno, ages, Deano says.

– Fucking three o'clock? Oisín says.

A bag of pills sits between them, stuck on some goo on the table.

– Who's starting on bumbles at this hour? Oisín says.

– Who said I'm only starting? Want? Deano says.

– Nah, whose are they?

– Mine, Deano says. Go ahead but, take what yeh want, a present for yiz all.

Neither of them touch them. Karl staggers in and rebalances himself, Dutch Gold in one hand and Oisín's bottle of crème de menthe in the other, against the jamb of what would be the kitchen door if it had a door. He smiles at them all like a man who's found the perfect place to piss but Oisín's pretty sure he can't even see them.

– Alright Karl?

Karl weaves over towards the glass door but gets his foot caught on the leg of the sofa, waking Hamza and Candy with a hefty splash of Dutch Gold.

– Could be worse, could have been Oisín's green stuff all over yiz, Deano says.

– Where'd you get the cash for all that? Oisín asks Deano. The pills and the hash.

Snitchy, at the end of the table, perks up. He's taken a stretch, no longer the skinny baby he was, legs spread wide, he's taking up as much space as possible.

– Hear you've joined the firm, Deano, Snitchy says as he lifts up his bottle. Man it's good to make a living, amirite, Deano, am I?

This is a new Snitchy. He's always been a weasely fucker. Grand, but weasely. He's got new gear, fancy jacket, Boss hat, thinks he's a king.

– What's he shiteing on about? Oisín says, leaning closer to Deano.

Snitchy moves and pulls up a chair closer to their end of the table.

– Didn't mean to speak outta turn boys, he says, sniffing and flicking his nose with his thumb. Only heard that Deano here's been helping out a bit. One of the boys, know what I'm sayin?

Oisín fixes Deano with a stare. Karl does big strides across the floor.

– Alright, Karlo? Deano says, trying to distract. Them crocodiles gonna get yeh?

Oisín fumbles for the cube of hash, pulls it out and nibbles at it. Something's not right.

– Here, you gave me this, Deano. And all them pills, Oisín says.

– A generous man, Snitchy says. Always a generous man, Deano.

– Fuck off, Snitchy, Oisín says.

Snitchy looks actually hurt.

– That's not nice, bro, he says as he gets up and moves back down to where Titch, his right-hand man, is sitting.

Oisín realizes the talk around the table has stopped. People are looking at the floor. The lads are still dancing though, and some of Mohammed's crew are on the sniff at one of the coffee tables.

– Whatsup, Hamza says, stretching and yawning.

– Why was Candy so late getting here? Deano says.

– Work, she got a job in The Bistro. She got here ages ago.

– Ah yeah? Cool, Deano says, half-laughing.

Oisín's not taking his eyes off him. He says:

– What's Snitchy on about?

– How would I know what Snitchy's on about? Snitchy's retarded.

– I'm right here, boys, right here, Snitchy says.

Titch laughs. Snitchy tells him he's a pox and boxes him on the shoulder.

– What's the laughing about, Deano, Hamza says.

What laughing? What's he laughing about? Warm liquid pours down the back of Oisín's thighs. He jumps up and feels nothing there, his jeans are dry. Residuals.

– What the fuck's wrong with you? Deano says.

– Like I pissed myself. Out through the back of my legs.

Hamza moves closer to them, pulling up a nest table to sit on. Candy's off the sofa, staring at a picture on the wall.

– Seriously, why were you laughing, Deano? Hamza asks again. Have you something to say?

– Laughing? Who's laughing?

The jeans definitely aren't wet. There's nothing on the chair.

– When I said Candy's working in The Bistro. What's funny?

– Nah, bro, just think that's nice for her is all. Good that she has a *job*.

Candy's pulling at Hamza's arm.

– What's going on, Deano? Is that right what Snitchy's saying? Pushing weight?

– What are you on about, fuck off, Oisín.

– You don't have the money for all this gear, this isn't Gracie's few joints. Snitchy, what was that you were saying?

– Calm the fuck down, Oisín, Deano says, shaking his head and swigging from a bottle of Jagermeister.

– Are you selling? Hamza says.

Benit appears behind them.

– What's the story. Relax, yeah? Deano's not selling. Nothing bad anyway. Amirite, yeah? Smalltime.

– Don't give a shite about what. It's who, Benit. Who, Oisín says.

– Wait, are you selling for Wino, bro? That's fucked, Hamza says, rubbing the back of his head.

– Fucking right it's fucked. You're a scumbag dealer. Everyone! Deano's a scumbag dealer, Oisín announces as loudly as he can.

The dancing stops. Mohammed lifts his head, drops his shades onto his face, leans back facing the dining table, arm on the back of the sofa, feet amongst the baggies and credit cards on the coffee table.

– And you're a fucken snobby cunt, Oisín. What the fuck if I am selling green? Where do you get yours? Who gave you the hash, yeah? Wait, you've even sold on jellies! Isn't that the next big plan? Don't all have daddies funding everything for us.

– It's Wino. You said, *you* fucking said, he did your da. You said! What the fuck? That's why you don't have a da at all.

– Is this because of the nephew? Benit says.

He's hand-in-hand with a girl in a tiny green dress. Where the fuck did she come from? What nephew? Now his arms are pissing. Like a flow of warm water from the middle of his biceps. He turns them over and scratches at them till long welts start to rise. Everyone's staring at him. Staring at him. Staring at him. Heart banging his ribs. It's like he's sweating outside his body. His body's outside his body. Deano's really working for Wino. The nephew, of course!

– You alright there, fam? Benit says, putting a hand on Oisín's shoulder.

He looks around at the rest of them at the table.

– What's wrong with him? Benit asks.

– What's wrong with me?! Oisín says.

– I think he's eaten too much hash, that's all, Candy says. You OK, Oisín?

He turns to look at her. She's smiling. Nice.

– Do you wanna get some air? she says. Come over by the window.

Nice. Calm. She's maybe right. Deano's smirking, looking at the ground, his legs stretched to trip.

– Working for Wino, man? That's just thick. What the fuck? Hamza says.

– First, I'm not selling nuttin. Second, what the fuck business is it a yours? Third, you're a dick snob hypocrite. Fourth, you're fucking selling yourself, Hamza ...

– Come on, it's not the same, Hamza says.

– No, it's not the fucking same. He's a specialist. You're a scumbag, Oisín says.

– Fifth, *lots* of people work for Wino, yeah? Isn't that right, Candy? Deano says.

– What the fuck are you talking about? Hamza says.

– Just sayin, Deano shrugs.

– He-ar, leave Deano alone, yeah? Karl says, leaning against the big yucca tree.

It topples under his weight and they both fall in a heap, pouring soil and beer onto the glossy tiles.

What the fuck's Deano saying? Is it this fox shirt? Poison on the inside? In that film, *Tudors* or something, poisoned dresses. Oisín looks down the front of his shirt. Nothing there. Nothing at all. He wants to tear it off. Why not? Pulls at the buttons, drags his shirt off, and fires it in behind the sofa. Safer there. Bareskinned, he does feel better.

Candy's pulling Hamza's arm now. Coaxing him back to the sofa but he's all up in Deano's face.

– I'm not fucking selling, Deano spits at Hamza. Fucken Snitchy by name, yeah? You stupid cunt.

Snitchy stands up.

– Ah here. Now, I'm gonna leave but, before I do, has anyone got a smoke for a bump? Can't say fairer than that? Smoke for a bump?

A chorus:

– Fuck off, Snitchy!

– Where does your grass come from, Oisín, where? Yeh posh cunt, Deano says.

Now, Deano's standing over him. His voice is echoing. The music's back on, Sia's been shot down but she won't crawl.

– Leave him alone, Deano. He's just had too much, he hears Candy saying in the distance.

– How's yer *job* going, Candy? In *The Bistro*? Deano says, in a voice Oisín's never heard before.

Nasty. Spiteful. Not Deano. What the fuck is going on? The intercom goes and he jumps. The two fellas are back on their own, shuffling in the middle of the room. Is it the guards. It's the guards! Snitchy's gone out the door. Deano sweeps his stash off the table. Mohammed's up, shades on, heading for the door, entourage, tucking T-shirts in, pulling trousers up, dragging jackets on. Everyone's moving. Everything's moving. All action, all the time. Oisín can't. He can't. Fucking can't. He's stuck. There's glue on the chair. This feeling is never gonna end. He'll be like this forever. He looks for someone. Who's he looking for? Who? She finds him. She's whispering.

– It's OK. Look at me. Just look at me. It's OK. I know this. Yeah. I know this. It's gonna pass, Candy says.

He stares into her eyes.

– Like you're never gonna feel normal again? Do you think you're gonna die, yeah? she says.

He nods and nods and nods. He nods so much his neck hurts.

– You're not though. We're gonna breathe. You and me, yeah?

And she's nodding and her eyes are wide and she's an angel. Her scarlet halo all around her. And she's holding his hand. Everyone's looking at him again. Are they?

– It's her! Karl's voice breaks through.

– Who? someone says.

– Tanya.

Candy's holding his hand tight and she's telling him to breathe. Just breathe. Tanya has a box, a present wrapped. And everyone asks what the hell is that? And she says it's for Hamza, is it not his birthday? Hamza's saying, what the fuck are you trying to say? to Deano. And Deano's sneering. And Oisín's voice pours out of him, saying yeah, and what the fuck are you doing selling for Wino? And his breathing's helping but when it stops, when he looks away from Candy's eyes, the banging starts in his chest again and his arms piss. Hamza's calling Deano names and then he shoves Karl out of the way and calls him a pikey faggot. Tanya's got her arms round Karl.

And then Hamza's yopping Deano out of it.

*

It's bright. There's warmth on his face. Sunshine or a lamp. A tap is dripping somewhere. His shoulder aches and something's digging into his left cheek. No way he's opening his eyes. Digs and shouting. Karl smashing a bottle. Opening his left eye, he sees blurry green. If he's dead then it's not too bad. Hair in his eyes – his own. He moves and rolls onto his back, making a cracking sound. The yucca's leaves, his pillow. He rubs his stinging cheek and black crumbs of dried blood come away on his fingertips. Yucca blades.

Rolling back onto his front, he lifts himself to all fours. It'll be alright in the morning, Candy said.

His shirt's back on and he's shivering but no one's staring at him and his heart seems normal. Lumps of dried tissue cling to the ceiling above him. The kitchen doorway has Karl in it, curled in a ball, Tanya's beside him, using Karl's jacket as a pillow and her own fluffy pink coat as a blanket.

He gets to his feet. Mohammed's in the far corner of the sitting room, his eyes like saucers. He's messing with the decks, packing them up, holding some cans to his ear, bending his knees to unheard sounds. Mo, the morning after. No! The Arabs are strewn around the sofa, silent now, staring into space.

Someone's moving and rustling about down the hallway. Oisín struggles towards the jacks. Hamza comes out of the bathroom, black plastic bag in hand, stuffing crushed cans and cider bottles into it as he goes.

– Lemme take a slash and I'll help yeh, Oisín says.

Hamza grunts, headphones in.

After his piss, he checks the bedrooms, looking for Deano. Everyone's gone.

Hamza says:

– They ran. Fuckers! As soon as I took out the bags.

Hamza goes over and taps Karl with his foot.

– Get up and help, you. We've only an hour before the fella gets here.

Karl stirs and Tanya stretches herself out like she's had the best night's sleep. All blonde hair and expensively straight teeth. Hamza says nothing to the Arabs. Just picks up around them.

– Does anyone want some Danishes or some pain au chocolats? Tanya calls from the hallway, where she's fixing her hair in front of the mirror. Lotts & Co do some great pastries. Coffees anyone?

– I'd eat a pain au chocolat, Karl says. I'll come with you.

– We're trying to fucking clean up, Karl, yeah? Hamza says.

Karl ignores him, gets his coat and leaves with Tanya.

– I'll have a pain au, if yiz are getting them, Oisín shouts out the door as they're stepping into the lift.

Mohammed walks through the sitting room, clicking his fingers. The Arabs jump to attention. Some finish gathering up the decks into a holdall, others get everyone's jackets. Mohammed still has the orange parka hanging off him. Dick.

The Arabs saunter out the door in a line, ahead of Mohammed, who pauses to fist-bump Hamza. Oisín just keeps on cleaning. Mo sticks his head outside the door, mumbling orders. Then ducks back in.

– Am helpin fam, he shouts.

Ah here! Oisín watches him from under his hair flop. Mohammed, nodding his way around the sitting room, bin bag in one hand, rapping with the other. Glasses on, pods in, arse hanging out. Oisín scrubs at the walls with one of the fluffy towels. Mohammed's moonwalking in spurts, picking up some cans or wrappers, leaving others. Suddenly, he looks at his phone, drops the bag at Hamza's feet and legs it for the door, stopping to tell Hamza that Zeb says he's Rev'd him that money for the shisha already, Revolut must be broken. The posse, the lot of them are still in the hall.

– No sign of Deano then, Oisín says, when it's just the two of them.

– No.

– You battered him, right?

– Wrong, Hamza says, as he sweeps one of the many piles of crisps, broken glass and chip wrappers that Oisín has left dotted around the floor into a dustpan.

– You hit him though, right?

– Gave him a slap, yeah.

– Why?

– Don't wanna talk about him, Oisín, right.

– Cos he's selling?

Hamza fumbles a headphone into one ear.

– What was all that about Candy and a job?

Hamza's struggling with the second headphone.

– Bro, what was he saying about Candy?

– Dunno what that cunt was saying, right? And you can fucking stay away from Candy too, creep.

The other headphone is in. He demonstrates that he's turning the music up loud and starts whistling a tune. No point talking to him when he's like this. It's fuzzy but he's pretty sure he wasn't creeping on Candy. He'd never pull shit like that. Bros before hoes.

– Is there a hoover for the bedrooms?

Oisín stands in front of him. Up close, Hamza looks like a sack of shit. No sleep at all. Blood balls for eyes.

– You look like dirt.

Hamza pulls the headphones out. A tinny, hissy, grating rhythm fills the space between them.

– He was shiteing on something about Candy. Dunno what. And you were all fucking over her, Hamza says.

– No, I wasn't, you dick.

– Yeah you were, holding her fucking hands, fucking, oh Candy, I'm not well, oh Candy, look into my eyes, oh Candy, suck my dick.

– Fuck you, I'd never fucking say that.

– That's the way you were acting.

– I was out of it. Must have been the hash. OD'd, that's all.

– You can't OD. You were perving all over her.

– Candy was just being sound. You battered Deano. What the fuck you do that for? Over him selling, was it? Where's he anyway?

– Don't give a fuck, fam. He's a loser. And you're a creep. Move on.

The floor's still a little warm but the empty room is definitely starting to chill.

Oisín throws down the black bag.

– You can finish yourself, cunthook. Fucking yopping your friend out of it over nothing. You're the loser creep.

He grabs his coat and stalks towards the front door.

– You and your skank girlfriend. At least she's not a bullshitter.

– Yeah go fuck yourself, Oisín, Don't wanna even know you. Or him. Hear me? Don't come near me, yeah? Hamza roars down the hallway after Oisín storms out.

11
DEANO

It's one of those cool-as-fuck, but actually just manky, places. He has a peek through the barely see-through window. Bits of gramophones lying about the place. Piles of records, but they're covered in dust. A rusty typewriter. No proper windowsill, just rough block with abandoned webs sweeping majestically from the corners, dotted with the embalmed corpses of half the creepers of Dublin. Even the spiders can't be arsed coming back for their lunch. June'd have a fit.

He pushes open the door. Big long table in the middle with benches so you've to sit with a load of beardy randomers who talk about black lives mattering, sex work and feminism – no thanks.

A girl with bright orange hair and a mopey face leans her head on a brittle wrist and pokes at the phone next to her coffee cup. None of the girls in here are smiling – the world's no laughing matter. He'd give any of them a whirl but none of them'd even look his way. No wait, that one with the granddad coat is eyeing him and no, she's decided against.

He passes around and through islands of people with lattes and wine and quiches, and chickpeas dropping onto the painted, uneven concrete floor. Holly is tacked to the walls here and there, and up high above the front windows, a massive Happy Holidays sign made out of lollipop sticks, by the looks of it, hangs at a funny angle.

She's not here yet, and he can't keep wandering around like a gobshite with everyone looking at him. He heads into the other room. It's massive but there's no seats free in here either, except at a low brass table with little leather pouffes around it. He stalks down and sits on one, his knees up round his ears. Fucking cringe.

There's Oisín's mad next-door neighbour over in the corner. She lifts her eyes from her *Irish Times*, recognizes him and waves. Or beckons? Fuck, no! He gives her the eyebrow hello and nothing more. He'll never forget the time she called himself and Oisín in to 'rescue a plastic bag out of her tree'. Fuck, the relief when they got out into her back garden and found there actually *was* a Tesco bag flapping around in the upper branches. Deano climbed up a bit after Oisín, just to not be on the ground beside her. The sons of Tuireann in the Garden of Hesperides, she said, over and over, clapping her hands – they looked it up later. She said she'd have to reward them for their heroism, gave them a cup of tea and a fig roll. Then reefed up her top and flashed her tits so quick that they weren't totally sure that it had happened until they checked with each other outside after. She just kept on nattering as if nothing had happened. Huge brown nipples. The fig rolls were stale too.

There's no way of knowing who's staff and who's not. People are clattering around, carrying plates and drinks but then sitting down and eating at tables.

– Deano, a small voice says behind him.

He strains to turn around he's so low down, and his arse is stuck to the pouffe. He bounces up, fixes the stuck tracksuits. They stand and look at each other. They dodge each other as she goes to sit, to try to get past him, to pull off her coat. They both laugh, because that's what you're supposed to do when this happens but his laugh hurts his throat. She doesn't try to hug him or touch him in any way and thank fuck for that.

She fumbles to get the coat off again once she's sitting on a pouffe. She's changed the image altogether. Gone are the sovs and the tight dresses. A kinda hippy skirt, dangly earrings, different. The last time he saw her, before the time near the offy a few weeks ago, she hadn't seen him at all. Walking along with Oisín and Karl, yeh wanna have heard the roaring coming from round the laneway. There's always someone roaring in the laneway but as they got closer he realized it was *her* voice, thick with something, gear or cough bottles or drink or all three probably. And he, the fella, whoever he was, roaring and crying and holding his head like a dope, when Deano saw him first.

And then up he got, the fella – wearing Snickers, so he had a job – and roared, 'Does he fuck yeh up the arse, does he?'

Echoing, bouncing off every wall in the Tenters. And then he shouts it again. In case someone in Donegal hadn't heard. He, Deano, was frozen. He should've moved, just left but no, something held him on the spot.

And she went to walk away and screamed back at him, 'You're the scumbag. Riding an eighteen-year-old. Yeh brought this on yerself, yer nuttin but a pervert.'

And the fella howled and crumpled to the ground, balled up, rolling around like a crazy egg among the dog shite and takeaway wrappers. He looked like he needed the hospital, hooting and screaming at the sky:

'How could you do this to me?!'

Standing there at the end of the lane, Deano, Oisín and Karl. It was sunny. Deano had his uniform jumper off, tied round his head. His whole head itched. She looked straight at Deano with her scaldy eyes and her scabby mouth but she never saw him. Deano'd never seen a man cry like that, like an animal, before or since.

And Karl said, 'Will we go chipper?', and steered them off towards Mario's.

No one said a word after. Like it'd never happened.

Deano saw yer man the following Monday, walking along with an eight-year-old in a communion dress, coming from school. Beaming, she was, the little girl. They love that, the little girls, wearing the dress to school after the communion. He was beaming too, the arse-fucking fella, chatting to the mammies with their own young ones in the white dresses.

That was ages ago. Today her hair is brown, not that greeny-blonde it used to be. She's a good bit wider too.

– I'm on a programme, Deano. Getting me act together. I need to apologize to you.

Fuck this. This is not the shit he expected. Not that he expected any of this. Why'd he answer her message? Why'd he even let June give her his number? Gotta get out of here.

– Need to go to the jacks.

– Okay, she says, looking at the ground and wringing her hands. Will you be coming back?

He puts his coat back down on the pouffey thing after pretending to look in the pockets for something.

– Yeah, sure. Why wouldn't I be? he mumbles.

She mini-shrugs. Her eyes look wet.

He finds the bathroom down a tunnel where he has to dodge over boxes and sacks of rice. He locks himself in a cubicle and sits down on the closed toilet lid. The toilets are actually grand. Smelling of eucalyptus or something. He likes these kinds of jacks with the sink inside the cubicle and the walls to the floor and ceiling. No one's looking at you. You could do anything in here. Ride, wank, scream. Standing, he puts his forehead to the door. It's cool and it slows his thinking a little. What the fuck's he doing here? Even June'd been wary of him meeting up with her, asking was it not a bit soon, was he sure, did he want her to come and sit somewhere else in the café, just in case.

Can he afford to lose the jacket? She won't even be able to see him leave. He could slip out the side door, risk the jacket, call the café later, ask them to keep it for him. But what if she takes it? That'd be like her, robbing. Fuck it. Doesn't matter. June's right. It's too soon. Not his problem, in anyway. It's hers, his ma's. She's not a real ma. He's not letting anyone down. He needs to concentrate on the Leaving, get back on track. Live a good life. Make the money for Boston. Quit smoking. Quit bunking off. He can do it. Doesn't have time for this shit. For her shit.

He walks back down the tunnel, the hum of the café crowd getting louder. His mouth feels like an old sock. Should have asked for some of that minty water everyone had on their tables before he decided to leg it. Quick exit now, slip past the crates, in behind the piano and out. He punches open the door from the jacks and strides towards the exit, eyes down. No problem with this, no problem at all. He reaches for the handle, almost there.

– Deano?

She's moved to a table beside the door, holding his jacket, putting it round the back of a red-painted chair. She rubs the collar and when she goes to sit down, she catches his eye. Caught rapid! She smiles and shows him the better table and then the smile melts from her face. He watches her realize. He continues walking, pulls back the chair and sits down, stiff-backed, without looking at her – he can't.

– Is there menus or what in this gaff? he says.

He peers at the cracks on his hands, the bruises, the missing chunks from hurling. No menu appears and she says nothing but he knows she's there, silently watching him. When he gives up and looks up, she's craning her neck, shifting in her seat, looking about the place.

No, there's no menus. Course there's no menus. Shure, why would there be menus? You've to go up and look at the board on the wall with squiggles at all different angles, in different coloured chalk. So now Deano's standing leaning from one side to the other, beside her, straining to see bits of the board past the people behind at the counter. Everyone in the place can see that he's with *her*.

He gives up.

– D'yiz have any burgers?

A Spanishy young one looks up, a big smile spreading across her face, and says, in a total Dub accent:

– We only have what's on the board, waving her dripping ladle towards the back wall. You can have the broad bean patty, it's delicious.

Doubt it, in fairness, but she's acting sympathetic, trying to be nice. And he stands up taller. Hopes she's getting his good side. Budges up a bit, away from *her*.

– Only vegetarian left, Deano, she adds, and does a sorry face. Howya Mrs Cusack.

What the fuck? His ma a regular in here or sum? Chatting shit about him to the workers?

– That's cool, he says, sticking his hands in his pockets and making like he's really concentrating on this fucken board full of fucken beans and flowers. The best kebabs in Dublin are only over the road, the best spice bag, just at the corner but he's here, in this place, with her.

The waitress says to sit down and she'll come to the table, maybe she can find something he'd like. Knew she had the hots!

Back at the table, he picks at a crusty glob of something yellow on the table's edge, gets his long blackened thumbnail to it. Might as well clip it now. He's not gonna be playing Oisín's guitar any time soon. The snobby cunt. He chews at the corner of it, trying to peel it off, and gets crumbs of yellow, sweet and smelly in his mouth. Can't just gob it out on the floor.

– You okay, Deano? she says, half-reaching towards him.

Is he okay? Maybe he is. Maybe this is all okay. Maybe sitting here with yer junkie ma on a Saturday afternoon's totally grand. Maybe this is what life's about. Yeh go out and yeh end up with someone's old yellow sauce under yer fingernail and in yer gob and that's about the size of it. Yer friends don't give a shite about yeh and all yeh want is a peaceful life. No hassle. No bullshit. Bitta quiet in the head. Is that too much to fucken ask for? He could just swallow it. What's the harm gonna be?

– D'yeh need a tissue? she whispers, starting to fumble in her bag.

He gulps.

– Nah, I'm grand thanks.

Sometimes you've got to just swallow it down. Deal with the results after.

– Well, I've found something for you. Brie and parma ham with rich pesto spread on our signature pea and beetroot bread with a crisp side salad, the Spanishy one says.

This has all gone too fucken far. The graffiti outside Benit's gaff – *This is what I feared all along* – flashes in his brain. Jack had put that there a bit before he died. But he wasn't talking about bread. As far as Deano knows.

– Can I've the car boot salad and a skinny latte please, love? his ma says, flashing her new teeth.

– Of course you can, Mrs Cusack.

The girl is giving him such a big smile now.

– The pea and beetroot bread thing with the cheese please, he says.

He has to. This brown girl has sorted it out specially for him. It's only manners.

– And can I get chips with that? Fries, I mean?

She leans in closer to them both, hands on the table. They're so tiny, like little doll's hands. He can see down her top a bit. She's coffee-coloured all over.

– I can give you our *delicious* parsnip chips?

She's getting a bit cheeky with it. Is it because she thinks parsnip chips are a treat or because she knows they're not?

– Nah, yer alright thanks, I'll stick with the sandwich. D'yiz have hot sauce?

The girl shakes her head, but then says she'll see what she can do.

His mam is watching him, smiling, as the girl winks at Deano – definitely a wink. As she turns away he sees the back of her head. Bald! Shaved totally. She's all long bits – normal – at the front and then this freak show at the back.

– D'ya not recognize her? Dharma. She knew me when she saw me. Remember when you stuck that 99 into the back of her head? The poor pet. I was raging with you.

He spins around in his seat. Dharma, little half-Indian Dharma who lived two doors down until her ma quit her messin, got a big job and a deece fella and moved to Naas or somewhere? No way. Is that baldy patch because of him and the 99?

Her hippy ma had arrived home up the pole, after travelling in India. Dharma Dorcha, that's what some grown-up called her when she was only little.

– Here you go Deano, she says in a sing-song, and carefully arranges the plate in front of him. Her eyes are really black. She's brown but he remembers her browner.

The side salad's a two-centimetre-long piece of lettuce and a half a cherry tomato, but guess what, there's a shitload of the pea and beetroot bread. Concentrate on the food, swallow it down, don't look too much at her. Get this mistake over with. The ham's not bad, as it happens. Bit stringy and not a patch on the stuff June boils up, but at least it's meat.

– Talkin to June, yiz are goin to Robbie's mam's for the Christmas, I hear, she says.

This is what it's all about. Trying to get an invite for Christmas. Not a chance. He glares at her. Let her know he knows what she's at. She'd walk on the back of anyone's neck. She holds his stare and quietly says:

– I'll be with some people offa me programme. Need to stick with people who're clean. Christmas is the worst time, yeh know?

Fucken right it is. Fucken right. When yer wallowing in yer B&B and being dragged to the Vincent de Paul for free packages and the Christmas dinner with every yitna and scumbag in Dublin. One Christmas is all June allowed that to go on for. Put her foot down. That was the last straw. Deano was moving into June's.

– It's too soon, Deano. I shouldn't have come today …

You're the one who wanted it, yeh mad fuck.

– I've got to look after meself …

Oh yeah, you. That's what's important.

– But I hafta think of you as well. Yer not ready to hear me. Sometimes people aren't ready to hear and yeh shouldn't push them. Wait until they're ready to hear. Have yeh heard of *The Power of Now*, Deano? It's a book that …

The power of now is drowned out by the sound of someone attacking a piano. Deano looks behind him and sees a lad in a Hawaiian shirt pounding away on the keys, And now the fella starts warbling. Deano can't understand what he's saying. People turn and force smiles. He has a glance at her. She's got a grin painted on and she's trying to nod in time but there *is* no actual time. Hawaii is just throwing shapes and howling away. People are shuffling, gatherings bags, going up to pay. He catches her eye again. There's a flicker, then she bursts out laughing.

– Will we head? she says. I think we've heard enough.

Dharma's at the till while he's sticking on his jacket. She looks over and smiles that smile again, and gives him a big high wave that she turns into a thumbs up, like she used to do anytime she managed to get a rare goal past him or any of the other lads out under the washing lines. And he's still here with *her*.

– See ya, Mrs Cusack! she calls over the heads of the queued up customers.

Mrs Cusack. For fucksake.

*

At least she didn't try hugging him. She looked like she might there for a moment outside, but he musta made it obvious that that wasn't gonna happen. Ever. Maybe that'll be the last of it. Probably be back on the gear before Christmas. He walks the long way round so he doesn't have to pass Oisín's. Stupid, cos he's probably in his da's in anyway or out shopping or sum. Might as well just go home to the gaff. Nah, go shop, Wine Gums. He needs the green ones. Clear his head.

Big crowds on Donore Avenue, queueing outside the community centre, milling around in Father Danny's rose garden outside the side doors. There's tables set up, lads from the drugs team are handing out plastic bags and boxes of varying sizes. Aul ones and young ones and in-between ones carry their hauls away, or stop to mooch through, pulling out boxes of cornflakes, tins of marrowfats, twelve-packs of Tayto, boxes of Erin cup-a-soups. Some stand around, chatting to the team, sipping from steaming paper cups.

Everyone's in the mood for the Christmas now. June's got all the stuff in, hiding the Santy stuff in the back of Sadie's. She's making the dessert and, of course, the ham, for bringing over to Robbie's mam's gaff in Walkinstown. They're all invited. Twenty-two altogether. He doesn't have to sit with the young ones in the sitting room anymore and he can have a few beers. Half of them'll fall asleep after dinner and Deano'll head back to the gaff early. It gets so hot in the house with all that crowd and all that cooking. Worth it though, Robbie's mam does a great turkey with all the trimmings, sausage meat stuffing. A combo of all your favourite things.

Past the centre, on the tarmac outside the boxing club, there's another queue, a snaking line that leads all the way back to the door of Sadie's shop. Trestle tables all in a row. A chill truck is parked up behind them. He veers closer to see what's happening. Jim Harrison drops like a stone out of the back of the truck and shouts at someone in the crowd:

– About fifty.

Doreen and Rita are being squashed and bumped in the queue and Wino arrives out into the middle of the melee, signals with his hand to move back to give them space and returns back to the head of the tables, picks up a turkey and hands it over to the aul fella at the top of his queue and scribbles something on the sheet in front of him as the aul fella scuttles off. Wino's laughing and glad-handing and having the craic with the aul ones. Deano pauses for a second just to watch. He knows he's seen him, but Wino doesn't acknowledge him at all. That's the way.

He ducks into Sadie's.

– What's going on? he asks her.

Sadie folds her arms across her chest, sinks her head low into her neck, raises her eyebrows, purses her lips but says nothing.

Deano shrugs.

– Just asking, is all. They're dishin out turkeys. Are they selling them or giving them away?

Sadie stays quiet but he can see she's in pain trying to hold it in.

– Package a Wine Gums, please.

She hands him his change. She can't keep it bottled up any longer.

– Nothing's ever for free with them boys. Ask Tom the butcher.

Tom's next door to Sadie's, whatever she's on about. He's not in the mood to get into this right now. Doesn't wanna know. He stands at the door, watching the queue shrink.

– Here, Deano. Do you want a selection box? And will you give these to June for the kids? Sadie says.

Who doesn't want a selection box? She piles them up and struggles to find a bag big enough for them all.

– Remember that, Deano. Nothing's for free.

– Not even the selection boxes, Sadie?

She looks offended then laughs.

– Nothing's for free with the likes of *Mr Nestor* there. Steer clear of all of them, Deano. And mark my words, every one of them eejits out there, grabbing their turkeys, will pay a bigger price than they'd ever pay in Dunnes Stores or Tom's.

She backs in behind the counter again. She's said too much.

– I see Doreen and Rita in the queue there, he says.

– Yeah, well, I seen them too. I seen them too.

*

Three days till Christmas and everyone's giving him the cold shoulder. Or maybe the other way around. But what does it matter? He didn't have to sell the stupid Christmas trees for Whacker. His Boston fund's coming along fine. He has enough money to get presents for all the kids and June tomorrow. He doesn't need anything else. It's getting milder. It's shit at Christmas when it's warm on the day itself. Alright for the Christmas swim but yeh feel better if it's freezing. Oisín's probably still doing it this year, without him. Fuck him in anyway. He's heading Thomas Street direction, might as well knock into Karlo now. Just drop in. That's what mates do.

There's a new young fella begging outside the Centra. Deano stops and pulls out what he has, a tenner and some coppers. The young fella doesn't even bother with the change-for-a-hostel routine. Just smiles and says howya.

– Not that cold. But will yeh get in for the night? Deano asks.

– Ah, should do. See how it goes.

– What're yeh doing for the Christmas?

– Dunno, what're *you* doing? the young fella says.

Cheeky. Whatever.

– Just going to family, bud, Deano says.

– Me sister's in Wexford. Getting the bus down tomorrow.

Deano hands him the tenner and walks off with a Happy Christmas mumbled over his shoulder.

– Thanks bud, the young fella shouts after him.

He ducks down a side street, just to go where he doesn't normally and heading straight for him is Hamza, who spots him right away and now it's too late to turn back. Hamza's smiling in anyway. That could mean anything but.

– Good, you can help us out, Hamza says, like they'd been talking only yesterday. Gotta get back to the flat. Whole family's gone to London.

Another sick or dead auntie or uncle, no doubt. Hamza has more relations than anyone else ever and most of them are dead or dying or wrecked in some way. Most of them aren't even actual relations either.

– So what's the problem?

– You can scout for us, Hamza says.

– For who?

– Me and Candy. She's on her way over. Hold on, I'll message her to stay where she is. You can go ahead of us and keep an eye out.

– For Aunties?

– For whoever, here, take my keys and open the door for her, if everything's okay.

– Okay.

Deano turns around and walks ahead of Hamza. No sign of anyone of note anywhere along the South Circular. There's a queue outside the fancy butchers but obviously no Aunties in it. This is all he needs, pimping for Candy. He gets to the gate and still nothing. Pulls his hoodie up and opens the door.

A girl in gym gear comes jogging along the railings, looks around her and turns in. The red hair's gone! Just plain brown now, but she's unmistakable. She passes by him and up the stairs with only a quick Hiya. Deano stands guard at the door, smokes the end of a blunt until Hamza arrives.

– Come on up.

– Nah, better not. I'm no gooseberry, bro.

– It's grand, looks better if you're around, walking in with us.

He trundles up the stairs after him. Candy's sitting on the top step, hugging her knees. Dunno what she's got to worry about. Hamza puts on the kettle as soon as they get in. The place smells like it always does, fucken delicious. But, for once, there's no grub on the stove. Hamza pulls open the fridge and hauls out a giant pot.

– Ami left you stocked up, Deano says. Who's dead this time?

– No one, wedding.

– And they left you at Christmas?

– Uncle sent the fares. I said keep my share. Gotta study.

Hamza grins.

Truth is he probably will be studying. Only enough, though. Like he says, Goldilocks study. Enough points, along with his fake ADHD mentaller points, to get what he needs for the masterplan. Candy goes over to the front window and peers down, nervously.

– Would you get away from the window, Hamza says. First thing they'll do if they arrive is look up at the window.

If he's caught with Candy here, he'll be on the first plane to Karachi and be married within a month. To his cousin. They sit and have tea while the curry heats. He can see it, like. He can see why Hamza'd want to smash this but yeh don't want that kind of thing in yer family's flat. She's laughing and chatting away. Her lips are moving but he hasn't a clue what she's saying. Poetry, she's on now, or some shit that makes Deano's eyes glaze over.

The doorbell rings and they all freeze. Hamza runs for the door but Candy grabs hold of him.

– Don't answer it. Just stay quiet.

– I have to answer it. They'll be onto the parents if I don't. I'm supposed to be here studying.

Candy's bricking it but.

– What if it's not your Aunties?

– Who else would it be? Hamza says, leaping down the stairs.

Deano checks out the window. There's at least three of them. Proper Aunties. Hamza's dead. They're all dead, if they get up here.

– There's a few of them. Would yeh not be better off in under one of the beds or sum? Deano says. Wardrobe maybe.

Candy goes over to the pot and stirs it.

– You studying much? Hamo says you don't go in much these days. Were you okay after the party? Hamo was off his head.

Oh yeah, off his head. Battering yer mate is called for just because yer off her head.

– He feels shit about it.

Like fuck he does.

– Did he hurt you? You've no marks.

– I had marks. They've gone now.

Okay, so he hadn't fully connected but that was probably from Benit holding him back. He was trying to, and Deano did have a little bit of a shiner after.

She's ladling the curry into three bowls. Bit too relaxed, she is.

– Do you have a problem with me, Deano?

The sound of Aunties and Hamza chattering bounces up the stairs.

– Hadn't you better hide? Deano says.

– I'll hide if they're coming up. So, do you?

– Dunno what yer on about, Candy.

– Yeah, I think you do. Do you not want me getting with Hamza?

He shrugs. Doesn't give a shite. Why would he?

– None of my business if he …

– If he what?

– Wants to get with you. Nuttin to do with me.

– Yeah but you were acting like it was your business at his party. And now even.

What? What's he done? Nothing. He's barely said two words to her. He walks over and picks up the White Lady on the mantlepiece. Hamza's mam bought it because everyone in Dublin had at least one in their window. They moved into this flat but and it's got no windowsills.

– I've got nothing against yeh. Yer Hamza's mot. Yer grand like. But lookit, he's down there making sure no one knows about yeh. Yeh know like?

– Ah Deano, you're concerned about me? Sweet. Didn't know you cared.

Now she's not even half-smiling. She comes up close to him. She smells good, of flowers or something.

– Look you, I don't know why you think you're so much better than me. You're not better than me, Deano.

– I'm not selling me hole, he mumbles, and I know it's not your fault like …

Fucking hell! How'd he get steered into saying that out loud? All his weight drops into his feet. He should just jump out the window.

– What'd you say?

Her eyes are gone bulgy. Green like a cat's. Not evil-looking, normally. Evil-looking now but.

– I know about it and what yer at. I saw yeh.

– Know what? You *saw* me?

She's raging but she'd better pipe down or every Auntie in Dublin will be on their asses.

She's staring right through him. Calculating. Chewing the corner of her lip. If she turns on the waterworks now and Hamza comes back up, Deano's a dead man. He takes a big step further away from her, his cheeks red and hot.

– It's your business. He's a Muslim but. Not a very good Muslim, but still.

She's looking at the ground now and she's staying very still, apart from her tits, heaving up and down. Fuck, she could throw a lepto or anything. You never know with hoors. He holds out his hands, warding her off.

– No harm, Candy, I'm just saying for both of your sakes. You're a prosto like and he's a Muslim. Like it'd be bad enough even if he wasn't a Muslim but he is …

He can't stop himself now. Like, she's probably ridden half of Dublin already.

– A *prosto*? Do I look like a prosto to you?

There's a right and wrong answer to this one, he's pretty sure. He takes a look at her. In fairness, she doesn't look like a prosto right now. No make-up, he thinks. And the brown hair. And the gym gear. Fuck it, he's waited too long to answer, she's revving up again.

– Well, Deano? Where'd you see me? Who said I was a prosto?

– No one. I saw yeh coming out.

She's calculating again, mapping. This is a bad situation. A very bad situation. Sounds like they're finishing up at the door. Like a gang of turkeys, gobbling away. Candy's face is flying off her, but she says no more and goes back to the cooker, takes the bowls, all three, to the table.

– This'll be going cold, she says, calm all of a sudden.

He's rooted to the spot when she turns away from the cooker to look at him. All the anger's gone now. She looks a bit sad if anything. He can't look at her with those big eyes of hers boring into him.

– And what were *you* doing there, Deano?

So she does know what he's talking about! She puts the wooden spoon back into the pot and walks back closer to him again. Fuck this.

– I'm not judging anyone, just sayin, Candy, yeah?

But her face is kinda melty now. Like she's afraid.

– And I'm not judging you, Deano. Just *saying* that you need to stay away from there. And them. Or maybe it's you who should be staying away from Hamza.

– Ah here, what the fuck? Why would I be staying away from me best mate?

– Because of who you're hanging around with, what you're doing. You shouldn't be near them. Hamza shouldn't be … here, let's just eat this, she says.

He's lost his appetite. The front door slams and the sound of one pair of fast feet echoes in the stairwell.

– Got rid of them, Hamza says, gleefully grabbing his bowl and settling in. You not eating, Deano? Come on, it's great. You still fucked off about me smacking you one? I barely touched you.

– Nah, I'm gonna head off.

– Ah, look, come on. Only messing. I'm sorry, fam.

– Nah, it's alright. I'm heading Karlo's in anyway, he says, backing towards the door. Catch yeh later.

Leave the pair of them to their shitshow. She'll tell him. Or maybe she won't. Course she won't.

He's down the stairs and out the door before Hamza can catch him, if he was after him. Out the gate and across the road, where he recognizes Jim Harrison's X5 parked up on the pavement. What's this fucker doing sitting there in the dark? For once though he doesn't acknowledge Deano, just keeps staring past him, like he's scoping something. Deano looks back across the street. Doesn't see anything but Hamza's gaff.

*

A new year and this one's gonna be great. He can feel it. Over the Christmas. Hardly saw the boys. Fresh start. Out of that hole of a place, into the real world. Away from uniforms and being told what to do and what to think all the time. Anything is possible. Anything could happen. Things can get worse but things can get better too. Joined the gym, gonna get all them gains. Taking care of body and mind, that's the key. He'll get the belly sorted and he'll be on the pig's back, as Da used to say. June's moved up the housing list. Maybe Crumlin's not so bad. Nah, Crumlin's still a shithole but yeh can get the bus out of it and some of the Crumlin lads are alright. This time next year …

– Howya doing Deano, and a happy new year.

This cunt gets everywhere.

– Garda.

Garda Gerry sniffing and snooping, slithering everywhere. Is he even a guard at all or just some touched lad that they let wander around the area pretending? They did that in one of the stations with a fella from York Street flats, let him sit inside with them, at his own desk. He brought his papers with him in a big doctor's bag every day. Started work at nine, finished at five. Gerry's maybe like that, only they've given him a uniform.

– Not a bad day. Think there's a stretch in the evenings already. Maybe that's me being optimistic.

– Or thick, Deano mumbles.

He's blocking his path now. Kids on new bikes are gawping over at him. Chatting to a guard.

– We've a new initiative.

– New initiatives are the best initiatives, Garda.

– You can call me Gerry, Deano. I'm not that gone on the Garda bit.

– Alright Garda, be seeing yeh, Deano says, floating past him under the eye of the all-seeing cameras.

– Deano, I've a couple of questions for yeh, Gerry Garda calls after him.

– Arrest me then. I'll answer yer questions, Garda, Deano shouts back as he stalks off.

The kids on the bikes, whoop and laugh and cheer.

– Come back here, I want a word with you, Gerry Garda shouts.

Fuck! There's no time for this. He's only dragged his arse out of the scratcher, was sitting in his onesie, duvet wrapped around, the kids piled beside him on the sofa, watching *Lord of the Rings*, not fifteen minutes ago. He walks back, head hanging.

– Working with the youths round about here. The drugs team and a load of others, maybe even the old folks will be involved. Sure it'll be a bit of craic anyway. Like a youth club maybe but, yeh know, with street cred.

Because, yeah, he, Deano, is really hankering after a youth club with, yeh know, street cred. Good man, Gerry.

– It's for up to twenty-year-olds, we're thinking. So grand for you. The schools, the GAA, the hurling, all going to be involved. We're gonna have a meeting …

– Yeah, gotta run for me bus.

– Ah well, sure I'll catch you again.

Nah, you won't. The Garda, what is the point of them? They do fuck all for yeh and spend their time harassing yeh, mouthing at yeh or beating the shite outta yeh behind closed doors. That's it. That's their only job. They get bred in some kinda incubation tank down the West. Come out of little furry eggs and grow extra big heads, hands and feet. And then they send them to Dublin when they're all scaldy and overcooked. He reaches for his headphones. Fuck! Left on the side of the couch.

Johnny-Two-Cans is rushing down Cork Street. Wearing some mad jacket with a Rugrat's head taking up most of the front of it. He pauses for a second to shake Deano's hand, wish him happy new year, on his way to some free dinner down in ah, yeh know the place, rucksack on his back, can in hand.

But then up the road comes Oisín, Karl and the dog. Karl's beaming. Oisín isn't. They stop, cos they have to.

– Alright, Johnny, Oisín says. Haven't seen you in ages.

Johnny rubs the back of his head, getting all sketch.

– Yeah, been away a couple of times. Had a couple of court dates missed down the country.

– Ah nah, you weren't at the lamb leg thing again, were you? Oisín says.

Goes into Tesco's, robs a lamb leg, tears the packaging, heads back in later or to another Tesco's with a worn-out receipt and returns it.

– Ah the court dates were from ages ago, yeh know yerself.

– But it never works, Johnny, Karl says.

– Worked grand there last week with a turkey crown in Dunnes. Just down the country, yeh know, I do be on me day trips.

Whacked out of it on the bus, he means. Getting sloppy in Moate or wherever it was he got said he got caught the last time.

– Still at the hurling are yiz? Johnny says.

– Getting back into it, I am, Karl says.

– Not much going on this time of year, Johnny, Oisín says.

Yeah, not much going on. That's right. If he doesn't get to the pick-up soon, there's gonna be trouble. Already late.

– We're all going Boston with the club, Karl says.

Karl's assuming a lot here.

– Boston, is it? Isn't it well for yiz? I've never been. Been to New York, worked there for a while. Had to leave. But that's another story.

He hands his can to Oisín and makes to start rolling his Amber Leaf, settling in to tell the other story.

– Gotta hit the road, Deano says. Nice jacket, Johnny.

– Yeah got it in the special sale in the Simon, classic.

He doesn't look back. He knows they're watching after him, Oisín in anyway. He dives down behind the church, goes the long way round, just in case.

The evening's coming down already, all the doomy cloud.

– I love yeh, that's all, I wanna be with yeh!

A lad at the bus stop, scabs on his face, bellowing into his phone. She must be deaf, his mot.

He buzzes the door and the clanking begins. Less security in Mountjoy. And he's back, the Latvuanian. Inside, he shivers, the soft day outside doesn't transfer in here in the dark.

– Where were you? Did yeh go home over the Christmas? Deano says.

– Yes, home. Baltic in here, not so bad outside, the Latvuanian says. Not pissing cats *and* dogs.

– Well, you'd know about Baltic, Deano says, grinning.

It's nice to be nice, as his nanny always said. The sour and serious Latvuanian face disappears, replaced with an almost smiling one.

– How you know Baltic? he says.

– Eh, is that not where you're from? Sorry like, just thought you're from over that way.

– I *am* from Baltic. You're smart, the Latvuanian says, tapping his temple.

Nah, not smart at all. Not smart enough in anyway. Wouldn't be here talking to you if I was, would I, buddy?

– What kind of Latvuanian are yeh?

– Lithuania, you know this?

Of course Deano knows this. It's stuffy, no air in the passageway.

– Yeah, Vilnius, right?

Now the Latvuanian looks like he might actually fully smile.

– I not Vilnius, I from real Baltic. Palanga, you know?

– Ah here, nah bro, sorry don't know it, Deano says.

– Football, right? This is how all Irish know Lithuania.

Deano's turn to smile.

– Yeah, football. And lads at school, and I'd a sorta girlfriend, Lina's her name, a while back. She was Latvu … Lithuanian.

Bit of a stretch to call her his girlfriend but she's not here, so doesn't matter. The big fella's nodding now, the chunky head on him, and definitely grinning.

– Yes, yes, Lina.

– Bit weird, but okay bro, Deano says.

Lina's only seventeen or sum and this fella's over thirty probably. How does he know Lina who Deano met at a gaff in Pimlico, and who wouldn't even allow him to feel her tits, and who then threw up in a bin straight after what Deano thought had been a decent enough meet? Fuck, could be her da.

– My wife, she is Lina.

Fucken hell, dirty fucken scumbag.

– Alright bro, that's your business, Deano says looking at the floor.

– My Lina. She is back home, Palanga.

Deano sticks his hands in his pockets and leans against the felty-flock wallpaper that's seen better days. Thank fuck for that.

– Ah yeah? She coming here too? Deano says.

Palanga's eyes go all evil.

– No here! My wife *never* come here! he says, leaning down into Deano's face.

– Ah bro, here, no offence like. No need to get aggro. Just thought, yeh know, she might be joining yeh.

Palanga stands back, shaking his head.

– She never, ever, come here. Never, you understand me?

He points like he's trying to jab a hole in the floor and the ceiling and the walls of the building. Ah jaze.

– I didn't mean here in this place. Mean is she coming here? In Ireland, yeah? With you, in Ireland.

Palanga stops, the anger melting out of him. Deano looks down the corridor to the fire door with the lock. He *really* doesn't wanna know. But he does know, he does.

– Ah *here*, yes. In Ireland, yes. Soon. And my boy too. I not work here too long, he says, wagging his finger. I learning English. When is good English, I not work here anymore.

He leans in towards Deano again, this time more friendly like, confiding.

– Is not good place, he whispers, and shakes his head.

– Gotcha, Deano says. Anyway, man, have yeh something for me?

– Yes. I don't have. You come with me, I find out.

He leads him back down the narrow corridor, in through the first and second doors. A dead-eyed black girl, not much clothes, walks towards them and then turns into one of the many doors with numbers he can't read in the dim lamplight. There's noise of men talking, laughing, music somewhere.

– What's your name in anyway, Deano asks.

– Piotr.

Shoulda remembered.

– Deano.

He ushers Deano into the same room as last time but leaves the door open. The sofa's gone and the smell of damp's got worse. There's chewed and broken pens on the table and an ashtray from Sheedy's that's overflowing with lipstick-covered fag butts. A big patch cut out of the carpet reveals a chalky hole underneath. The cleaners haven't been in in a while. No sitting this time, he's not getting trapped again. He leans against the wall, close to the door, closing his eyes. So warm back at the flat, on the sofa, with the duvet.

The thump of music quits and there's a hum of voices in the next room. The quiet's worse than anything else. Plasterboard isn't worth a shite. A woman and a man. Weaselly and raspy, like a starting-up digger. Wino.

They move out to the hall. Right beside the door. They stop, whispering.

– … don't have her calling here again, Marian, yeah? Don't want her around here.

– … only in for a few minutes. Quick cuppa …

– Not paying for that school an all for her to be knocking round here, d'yeh hear me? She's a smart one.

– She knows what she's about, Wino …

Fucking fuck! Lemme die, lemme die right now. Make a noise? Don't make a noise? Just go out, stick your head out, just looking about, nothing wrong here?

Mumbling, mumbling. She's kinda laughing. Deano heads for the door and … they're on the move.

– No … Wino come on, no, I'm working, I've got a lot …

No sign of Marian's posh voice now. The door to the next room opens, the door closes. There's kinda grunting and shuffling and moving. Just moving. Then, more muffled but still audible:

– No, come on …

There's a bang and the whole wall shakes. Fucken headphones. Never forget the headphones.

There's a laugh, both of them laughing. But no one's laughing. Not really.

Deano coughs as loudly as he can.

– Come on, Wino … maybe later … one of the girls …

A yelp, an animal yelp … and grunting.

He chews his lip. Where the fuck is Piotr?

He steps out into the hall. There he is, there he is, down the corridor. Come on fella, come on buddy. Just bring it over here. Piotr raises a hand but then ducks into another room. He can still hear it out in the hall. Grunting and banging. Piotr's on his way again, smiling.

And the rumble starts, rain, rain as heavy as it's ever rained, and now there's no sound, no sound at all except the rain pounding on the flat roof above him. He wraps his arms across his chest and digs his nails into his armpits.

– What you do there, friend? Piotr says.

– Dunno, just waiting, yeh know. Yeh were a long time, Piotr.

– Yes, package will be ready soon. I come to tell you. You wait few more minutes, sit in there.

– I'm alright here. I'll go out with you, wait at the door, Deano says.

– Okay, you don't want sit?

– Sitting all day, bud.

He's back at the door, waiting. Piotr stands, says nothing. Another young one, Roma-looking, is heading their way. Bit of a limp. She hands the small packet that's more tape than paper to Piotr, unsmiling, turns on her heel and limps back up the corridor. Piotr passes it to Deano and starts the process of opening the door.

Out ta fuck! Out ta fuck!

– Wait, Piotr says, blocking Deano with his bear arm. The boss man ...

– Well done Piotr, fuck off now like a good fella, yeah? Wino says, ruffled, hair in his face, out of breath, wiping his hands on a J-cloth.

Wino jerks his head in the direction of the giant Lithuanian's disappearing back.

– They're great at some things, strong, you wouldn't mess with them, them Ukrainians, but they've no manners. Don't know their place. The commies' fault. Everyone's equal, all that shite. Know what I mean, Dean? People need to know their place, right? Otherwise it all goes to shit.

Nothing you can say to that.

– I didn't know you were here, Dean, I'd have given you a cup of tea meself.

And he lets out a laugh like the one from the room.

– You've what you came for, I see.

Deano doesn't trust his voice. He nods. Wino beckons Deano down to his level. Don't get too close. He grips Deano's face with both hands, whispers:

– Bit of advice, man to man, try the older model. Bit dry but very grateful, know what I mean?

Deano pulls back, puts on the blank face. No smile, no frown. Disappears into the back of his own world, leaning against the wall.

– Do you see these boys here?

Wino picks up a newspaper from the table and starts prodding the front of it.

– These Muslims ...

He turns the paper round to show the photo of some fellas raging down a street, burning a flag.

– Fucking animals. Did yeh ever see the way they treat women, these Tallybans? Burkhas an all? They took the crib outta James's hospital because of them. Did you hear that? Look at them raging there. Yeh can't control that. You know what I mean better than most.

Does he? Jesus fucking Christ!

– Fellas outta control like that. Get a rage on them over fuck all. Follow no orders. Stoning girls for going to schools an all.

Wino slicks his hair back.

– You alright, Dean? Look pale. You getting your vitamins? Another word of advice, stay away from fellas who can't mind their tempers. They cost you in the long run.

Tongue between his teeth, Wino finishes what Piotr started and heaves open the door, hiding himself in behind it.

– Put up the hood there, Dean, before you head out. It's raining. *It's raining men, hallelujah, it's raining men*, he rasps as Deano jogs out into the blackness.

*

They're crying and wailing outside again – way more than they used to. June says it's cos of all the building going on, driving them into the only green bits left, out the back of the flats. He heard aul ones, Sadie and the rest, giving out in the shop about their bulbs being dug up. Should be culled, they said. A bloody nuisance, they said. Make a nice coat, they said.

Deano loves them but. No baby ones now, but there will be soon. He pulls himself further up on the sofa, leaning his arms on the windowsill. Two of them are messing about, tumbling around on the roof of Whacker's half-collapsing shed for hurls and shit. Rarely has hurls in it, sometimes has shit.

Whacker's pointed out their white shite and their tracks and the distinctive stink of their piss. Whacker loves the foxes and the birds. Like Deano's da did.

Deano rests his chin on the windowsill. The smallest one crosses a wall and curls up in the darkest corner of the shed roof. If you hadn't watched her land there, you'd never spot her. She just fades into the shadows. A black cat crosses in front of her. She raises her snout out of her tail but does nothing. The cat's used to them, doesn't pass any remarks.

There's a pair of them now, one down low, sounds almost like she's laughing and the other one howling beside her. Not like wolves but, more like babies or seagulls crying. Whacker, pretending he's a culchie, reckons that this is what all the banshees were. Just foxes crying. Says his ma was a country-woman – probably made that up – and that most banshees disappeared after the electric came.

What fucken hour is it? He rubs his face. He'd the best of intentions. Go school in the morning, Young Scientists, back on the straight and narrow. Get that shit, those sounds out of his head. This is the way. Yeh think yer gonna change things, start fresh, blot it all out, but yer caught.

He checks his phone on the coffee table beside the bed – 2:30 am. If this keeps up, he won't be fit to go in in the morning after getting himself psyched for days over it. After all the boys messaging.

He climbs onto the back of the sofa and pulls the curtain up again, the nets scratchy on his back. The night sweats are something else these days, even with the chill in here. There's a tipping point, when yer getting what you need out of it, doing a few deliveries. All okay, everything on the down-low. No one's getting hurt. And then there's the point where things go tits-up. Yeh need to know when yer getting near that point and get out ahead of it. He's getting a few quid, repaying the debt for putting hands on the nephew. Yeh never repay yer debt though. Yeh always owe.

12
KARL

The bus is already looking full when Karl gets there. Finnegan's standing beside it, counting heads.

– Ah Dean, and Mister Karl Quilligan, good of you to grace us.

– No bother, Sir, anytime, Karl says.

Deano raises a hand, gives the peace sign. He's looking ropy but at least he's here. Bombarding him with messages, all the boys, did the trick. An intervention, Oisín said.

Karl climbs on the bus. This isn't going to be so bad. Day out with the nerds. Some of the fifth years are in with a chance. Not Karl's buzz in anyway. Something about growing things with no soil. Where do the roots grow? You need roots in the dirt. Karl's no gardener but he knows that much.

– You need roots, he mutters, as he slides into a seat beside Oisín.

Finnegan's beckoning. Not him he's looking for. Rarely is. Being a good boy, these days. Maturing.

– Mr Cusack, Dean, a word. There's a peculiar smell off you.

A load of roaring and whooping.

– You saying I smell, Sur? Deano says, making a big deal of sniffing his armpits. Smells mighty fine to me. How bout you ... here, check it.

He sticks his armpit close to Finnegan's nose. He's stoned, obviously. But whatever gets you through the night and onto the bingo bus. Or the Young Scientists bus.

– No need for smart-arse stuff, Dean. If you've been on something ... Your eyes are pink.

– He's tired, Sir. All that studying, Karl shouts up.

There's a rising hum of support.

– Well, I *was* sitting down in me seat on the bus but yeh dragged me up here to tell me I stink peculiar.

– I did not say that you stink, Finnegan says.

Definitely not. If there's one thing that you can say about Deano, it's that he's very clean. No matter the battle for the shower with all of June's kids, he's always fresh. When they went on the tour to the Aran Islands, Deano hogged the shower at least twice a day. Some of that'd be wanking but still, clean.

– Look, you haven't been here in a long time, Dean, Finnegan says, lowering his voice.

Karl stands up to find a place for his jacket and bag on the shelf above. He moves a step closer to them. It's a skill, listening in. Famous for it, Karl is. A source of pride, since he was a kid and he'd be sent by the older cousins or Deano or whatever gang around the flats to listen at doors, hang about near groups of men, kicking a ball at a wall.

– If you've turned up intoxicated, we have a problem, Dean.

Deano lifts up his arms, surrendering.

– Look Sur, I swear to you ...

Doing a spit cross on his throat with his finger.

– On me mam's grave ...

Oisín covers his face with his jacket. Karl stifles his own laugh. Benit's standing behind Finnegan and Deano, trying to get down the bus.

– Your mam's alive. I met her yesterday, Finnegan says.

He what? Deano's still smiling, doesn't seem to be passing any remarks. June, Finnegan must mean June.

– I wouldn't disrespect you or this fine institution we call Colmcille's, Deano says, waving towards the rest of the bus. Or the school motto or my family or my ...

– Just sit down, Dean. Any trouble and you're suspended.

Cos that would be Deano's worst nightmare. Deano, grinning and slapping palms on his way down the aisle, slouches into an empty window seat across from Karl and Oisín. Oisín nudges Karl out of the way and slots in beside Deano. Hamza's pretending to be asleep in the seat behind. Fair enough. Pissed off as usual since the party.

– Just wanna give him this music, Oisín says, by way of explanation for dumping Karl.

Droves of people march along the canal. Grown men in suits fly along on hoverboards and electric scooters in the cycle lane. Everyone's rushing somewhere. Women, all in uniform, grey and black skirts, runners, oversize bags that hold high heels. Headphones on all of them, blank faces.

– All of these people are miserable.

Oisín leans across.

– Yeah, miserable ants.

– Ants are happy, Benit says.

Hamza sticks his face between the headrests.

– Until we seize the means of production ...

Thinks this is his way back in. Trying to make them laugh or argue.

– I will, yeah. I'll seize the means of production, gimme a second, Karl says, and then thinks better of grabbing his bollocks.

– If it was real work, they'd be happy. It's work in the service of financial capital. They all know the emperor has no clothes but they're all afraid to say it.

– Fuck off and give it a rest, Karl Marx. We're not even properly awake yet, Oisín says.

– What are yiz saying? Deano says, just starting to liven up a bit.

– Nothing, go back to sleep. Just saying that you're the man most likely to climb the corporate ladder, Hamza says, sneery.

– What the fuck are yeh on about, yeh mad Paki? Deano says, keeping his eyes closed.

They all go quiet. Please God, for once, just stay shut up Hamza. Gotta do it, let Deano off with a bitta messing. Him being here at all is a big enough deal. Karl glances back at Hamza. He looks like he's actually, physically, biting his tongue. Moody bollix.

They're stuck in a jam at the nice end of the canal now, where nice trees and nice statues of poets live. There's even more birds here than at their end. Even birds know that it's quality round here.

Bricks, red bricks, brown bricks, white pillars, shiny doors, more brown bricks, yellow bricks. Big windows, steps up to shiny doors.

The best gaffs are brown brick gaffs – the ones with the fanciest cars outside. Like the ones on the road to the American embassy. Mercs and Lexuses and fancy plants. Massive trees. Intercoms at the gates and you can only see a bit of the house. Girls with well-ironed hair and unpatchy orange legs live here. Fellas with big necks and chunky heads. Brian O'Driscoll lives here. Some decent people probably live here too. Not that Brian O'Driscoll isn't decent. And Amy Huberman's definitely decent. Apart from those Newbridge ads, God love her. Maybe doctors or Lotto-winners or lawyers. This is the land of back gardens where you could charge an entry fee and people would pay it. A land of servants, housekeepers, butlers, even. A bit Downtony, as his ma says. You'd wonder about butlers. Like, who is a butler? You never hear of anyone saying they actually *are* a butler. Maybe there's no butlers out here actually.

There's the place where the young fella was kicked to death years ago, by his posh mates. Karl's ma warned him over and over: stay away from them private school people. And they look down their noses at Colmcille's! No one gets battered in Colmcille's without some kinda reason. His belly rumbles. Never satisfied for long. Especially since he got back into the hurling – a bit.

Finally they're off the bus and into the RDS. The place'd melt your head. There's that kind of musty, kind of metallic smell. Karl shivers. Early. Not many about. Experiments about lighting a lightbulb off snot and getting chimps to recycle and shit are being tweaked and messed with by girls and fellas in drab uniforms.

– If I was doing this ... Oisín says.

– You did do it and yiz lost, Karl says.

– We didn't lose! We got a commendation or something, didn't we, Hamo? Anyway, if I was doing it now, I'd do it on harvesting knicker scum, Oisín says.

– You mean skid marks? Deano says.

– No, girls! Knicker scum. Whatever comes out of them.

– Ah, nah, fam, Benit says. Nah, nah, nah. Stop now, my man. What would you know about what comes out of them? They're not like they are on your phone in real life, you know?

– On my phone? I quit porn ages ago!

They all roar laughing.

– Sure you did, Ois, Karl says. Sure.

– I did. I went to some dark places there, Oisín says, rubbing the back of his head. Dark places ...

– Me hole yer not watching porn, Deano says. That's yer only chance of seeing a woman. And you'd a girl, what is it, four years ago? Eight? Doubt yeh even got anything out of her anyway. D'yeh get yer hole even once? Betcha didn't, neek. Girls yeh get with once in a club don't count.

Being a bit of a bitch there. No need for that.

– Ah here's the expert. When's the last time you got with anyone? Oisín says.

And now Oisín's getting pissed off too. This shit's a pain in the hole.

– Anyway, back to the knicker scum, Oisín says. The healthy stuff, the good stuff. It's probably full of proteins or something. Collagen or some shit. Stick it in as a secret ingredient. Face creams. Serums. Get the Chinese involved. Everyone could be collecting batches.

Hamza side-eyes him.

– Crème de la Mer-type thing, Hamza says.

– Ha?

– Crème de la Mer. Secret recipe, costs over a ton for the smallest jar. We sell it in Brown Thomas. Serum's even more expensive. High-end luxury item. You'd have to get it while it's fresh.

– Think so? Thought maybe scrape it off the knicker-crotch dry. Or everyone who's oozing or harvesting or whatever we'll call it, could have a special little thing, a fanny pad, jam rag-type thing for collecting it.

– We can think about that but, you know, fresh always sounds better than dried. Like that wheatgrass shit, Hamza says.

– And orange juice, Karl says.

– Bits in, Benit says. Love the bits in, fam.

Some of these things look interesting enough. Pie charts and things like that aren't up to much, but the ones with bubbling coloured things and bottles of sand and toothbrushes and toilets, look cool. The RDS is only really good when it's Funderland or an ice rink. Ice-skating's Karl's thing. He's better than them all. Like practise for skiing.

Still dodgy about whether to go Boston or not cos that'll be the end of skiing for another year unless he stops buying new gear altogether. And no, that's not happening. If he says a word about maybe not going Boston, the boys'll roast him. And he's roped into yet another fundraiser for the trip. Some Nordie women's football thing. Whacker's an awful man. Had him working like a slave selling the Christmas trees in Harold's Cross, every chance he could.

– But yeah, might be difficult to do. Where does it come from anyway? Hamza says. Inside them, I mean. Could it be bottled at source?

Oisín's got Hamza on a roll and he's softened up, smiling a bit. That's all you've gotta do with him, distract him with an idea for making money.

Another busload has obviously just arrived. A huge clatter of black-jumpered lads busts past them, talking shite. Hamza gets shouldered and spins round to give them daggers. Keeps a lid on it but.

– Don't they need it for lubrication of the mucous membranes or something? Benit says.

That's Oisín's mother talking. Straight up.

– Yeah, yeah. Like snot. If we could inject them with something so they produced more of it …

– A hot sausage injection like? Deano says.

– Shup you, this idea could really work, Oisín says.

– Yeah? How about I spunk in a jar for yiz and yiz test that, Deano says.

Oisín stares at him, wide-eyed.

– That's it! Two ranges, we'd have no end of supplies for the men's stuff, the cheap option, but then we can do your Crème de la gee stuff at the high end.

– I need scran, Karl says. All this businessy science stuff is making me hungry.

*

There's nothing worse than that lil excuse for a tray of limp dick chips you get at these places. Good job they're actually serving chips and sausages at this hour though.

– Don't feel like I'm out at all if I don't get the sausages.

– Where the fuck's Benit with me roll? Oisín says, turning around in the seat. These feckin plastic seat yokes make your arse slimy after only a few seconds don't they? Where is he?

– Calm down, yeh shoulda got what I got. All this healthy shite slows yeh down, Karl says.

– You could do with some healthy stuff yerself there, Oisín says.

– Thought you'd be going for the granola and yoghurt with the company you're keeping, Karl, Hamza says.

– What does that even mean? Will yeh let up on him? Deano says.

Hamza says nothing but gets up and walks away from the table, leaving his food half-eaten, shaking his head.

Oisín and Deano turn to look after him but Karl just keeps on chewing and says:

– Where's he off to?

– Who knows? Fucking gimp, Deano says.

Benit arrives back with a salad box and Oisín's ham salad roll.

– Salad? Deano says looking out under his eyebrows.

– You OK, Benit? Karl says.

Benit smiles.

– Nothing else vegetarian.

Oisín drops his roll.

– Vegetarian?

– Trying it out for a while. See how it goes. Have yiz watched that video I sent yiz of the factory farms? And the chicks?

– Ah jaze! No, I haven't watched the video, cos I'm not a bender. Sorry Karl, Deano says.

Karl's still munching, smiling at the paper plate in front of him.

– Yeh'll still eat sausies though, right, he says.

– No Karl, he won't eat sausages if he's a fucking veggie, Jesus! Oisín says.

Hamza slumps back into his seat.

– Had a little tantrum there, did yeh? Needed a time out, yeah? Deano says.

Hamza says nothing, folds his arms and takes a look around the gradually filling hall.

This is just acting the bollix.

– Yeh were getting on his back for no reason, Deano starts.

Oisín puts his food down.

– Can we just fucking get on with this shit and stop acting like pussies?

– Here we go, Oisín knows better than everyone, Deano says.

– Come on boys, there's no need to start all this again. I'm heading if yiz start, Benit says.

And that's Benit all over, not picking a side. On the fence. Safest spot.

– You can fuck off an all, Deano says. Fucken yellow as a dandelion under all that black.

– For fuck's sake, you're acting like a dick, Deano, Oisín says.

– What's new? Hamza says. I'm off, laters.

And he walks away, throwing the crumpled napkin on the floor. Oisín bends to pick it up.

– Get fucked Hamza! Deano shouts after him.

– Fam, sit down and stay quiet, Benit says.

This shite is not what Karl wants. No conflict, alright? No need to act like a bunch of bitches. Deano folds his arms across his chest, sits down and stretches his legs out underneath the table.

– Such a big man yeh are, Oisín says. Why'd you even come, Deano? Why didn't you just stay at home? Not as if you'd even understand the stuff here, fucking thick.

– Yeah, Oisín, is that right? Thick, am I?

– Don't tink dis is worth scrappin over, fam, Benit says.

He can feel Deano staring at him but Karl keeps his eyes on the table. No need for this shite at all.

– Why'd yeh fucken beg me to come? Fucken on yer knees yeh were, yeh snobby cunt.

Oisín's on his feet. Squares up to Deano.

– Sit down, Oisín, man, Benit says.

Deano gets slowly to his feet. Posing.

– Ah nah, fuck this, boys, are yiz all on the blob? Quit will yiz, Karl says.

Deano takes a step closer to Oisín.

– You're an asshole, Deano. Why start shit with everyone just because you're fucking up big time? Oisín says.

– Wait, lads, yuppy boy has spoken, Deano says.

– Oisín's not a yuppy, are yeh? Karl says. Cop on, Deano.

– And you can fuck off an all, Karl, yeh fucken loser, Deano says. Crawlin up that Tanya one's snatch.

Karl stuffs the last bit of sausage in his gob, picks up a napkin, wipes his mouth, stands up, has a good look into Deano's eyes and walks away. He's becoming one of *them*. Pushing weight makes you like them. Before yeh know it, yer driving someone else's Beamer, thinking yer a king, stabbing lads because they looked at yeh funny and wearing Gucci mink. Yeh still live in the flats but, and anytime, *anytime*, could be yer last time.

– Going for a piss, Karl says as he heads out into the main hall.

– What the fuck's the point? Fucken losers the lot of yiz, Deano roars. Don't fucken come near me.

Deano staunches past Karl and away towards the front door.

*

Clammy hands. Nothing worse. He scrubs and scrubs at them then splashes cold water on his face and looks in the mirror.

His face is red. Karl hates that pinkness. He'd wear concealer if he could get away with it. Imagine that. Problem solved. Or a mask. One of them Venetian jobs.

Deano's got no call to be speaking to him like that. Never, never has he let Deano down. Apart from Tanya's party. Never. And that wasn't even his fault. It wasn't him who wouldn't let the rest of them in. Damien's fault, the prick. What's Deano thinking? It's not as if Karl hasn't come under pressure to push weight – hazard of living in the flats. But yeh don't. Yeh just don't do it. Head down, stay out of it.

He gets it, course he does. The nephew thing. Yeh don't touch Baba Nestor, that's just it. Dangerous business. But just because yeh have a debt to pay, if that's what it is, doesn't mean yeh have to turn into a right bollix. It's Deano but. Deano's alright. Someone's opening the outer door to the jacks. He scrambles into a cubicle, throws down the lid and sits down.

He's given Whacker the deposit but he definitely doesn't wanna go now. Why would he go now, if this is the way it's gonna be? Oisín being a condescending cunt. Deano being a scumbag. Hamza raving at everyone. Benit … Benit's grand. How can he go Boston now but? That's his skiing money in anyway. Now his da's on for coming too. Delighted he's back at the hurling. He's *not* back at the hurling. He's not. Doesn't even know why he dropped the fifty quid to Whacker. And now what?

The place is rammed when he finally strolls out of the jacks. No sign of any of them when he gets back to the table. Out in the main hall there's all kinds. Floppy-haired lads, chopped-haired lads. Ironed-haired girls, sloppy-haired girls. Too many Dubes and white knee socks. They should complain. There's no way that burgundy sack skirt–white knee-sock combo should be allowed. Fucksake, it's 2019, sick.

Standing at a yoke about ethical fashion or some shit – how is that science? – fronted by a dumpy Chinesey one and a tall redhead, both of them with Cork accents, he spots

Benit's head in the distance. Benit's alright. The *only* one who's alright. He spins to wave at him, catch his attention, and backs into some lad.

– Sorry, he says, straight away.

The fella, much taller, bulging eyes, shoulders him.

– I said sorry, yeah? Karl says.

Like for fucksake, is there something about science that turns everyone into a wanker?

– I said sorry yeah, the scumbag mocks back into his face, like a fucken girl, and shoulders him again.

– What the fuck? Karl says. What's your problem, bud?

But the big lad in the better uniform is getting into his stride now and he takes a swing at Karl's face. An amateur: in School Street flats you learn to see that first punch in slow motion. But an amateur with mates who are loving it, and are suddenly surrounding Karl and saying 'Go on Ferg'. There's bodies all around him. He can't see over to where Benit was, or where any Colmcille's lads are. They're in between stands. The fashion crowd's behind him.

Karl's fucked is what he is. Fucked. He's going down fighting but and he manages to give Ferg a good dig in the belly. Everything goes white as a blow lands on the back of his head. A posh fuck special. Karl crumples. He's kicking and lashing at Ferg, he thinks. Someone gets pushed down on top of him and Karl grabs him in a chokehold. Blows are raining in from all sides. He's on the floor, feet all around.

Someone's dragging him backwards to his feet. He turns and sees Benit as he gets pulled away and back into the heaving mass of bodies.

– Karlo! Benit's voice shouts.

Karl's face is wet. Could be blood, could be tears from the couple of thumps he's taken to the face. Girls shrieking. There's a flash of the Chinesey one with her hands to her face, bawling. Someone jumps on him and he goes down again and catches a kick to the ribs. Out of nowhere:

– No fucken way, no fucken way. Karlo! Away ta fuck, cunts!

And Deano's flying through the air, landing on some lad's back, dragging him to the floor. The rest of the black uniforms swarm on top of them and Deano disappears from view.

Karl's protecting his face with his arms and lashing out blind kicks. He hears Deano again, and he's back, pulling black uniforms off Karl. Deano grabs him and pulls him out of the mosh pit. They stagger against the stand about snail slime being used as a butter substitute.

It's a mass of bodies, Oisín's in there pulling lads off Colmcille lads and shoving them away, Benit's doing Benit, like there's no need for panic, smiling as he reefs two fellas out of it at the same time. And Hamza's there battering some fella, he'll kill him if someone doesn't stop him.

A girl, raging and upset, stomps up, leading the high-vizes and walkie talkies. Teachers – adults in anyway – come running. Surprised they didn't notice the human mountain building up in the centre of the floor before now. The teachers start dragging the Colmcille's boys out of it. Deano's wrangled off by some high-vizes, Finnegan and some other Colmcille's teachers following, grim-faced, behind. Deano manages to wrestle himself out of their grip and runs back, pointing his finger at the black uniforms, the scumbag who started it.

– Don't mess with the Colmcille's boys, yeah?

He catches Karl's eye as they march him off again and winks.

– No one fucks with Karlo! he shouts back. Fuck da po-lice! Fist thrust in the air.

Black uniforms gather. Some of them are led away too. The fella who started it melts away into the crowd. Crafty fuck.

Ms Braxton, the art teacher, is all up in Karl's face.

– Karl, were you involved with this?

What does she think? His uniform's in tatters, hanging off him, his face must be a mess. He can already feel his left eye swelling.

– I'm disappointed if you were, Karl. You're better than that.
Not, are you hurt, Karl? You OK, Karl? No.

She walks away after the other teachers, though. Leaves him alone. The Chinesey one creeps over, looking worse than he feels.

– You alright like? she says.

– Yeah, be grand. You alright? You don't look well, he says, wiping his face with his sleeve.

Yeah, blood. And snot.

– I didn't start that.

– I saw. Want a tissue?

– My da's from Cork too.

– How did you know I'm from Cark?

He laughs. She laughs.

*

There's a fug on the bus, engine idling, doors closed. No air con and the windows are steaming. Oisín's already back and then Deano straggles on last, head hanging. A low cheer goes up for both of them. Deano walks past him, past everyone, to the back of the bus, throws himself down, leans back, eyes closed. The teachers aren't back but the bus driver's obviously been told to act the hard man.

Finnegan gets on. Gives everyone the hard stare, sits down in the front seat. There's a blur rushing down the bus and out. Hamza. He's flying across the car park. Everyone's piling on to see out that side. He runs up to a couple of lads strolling along, hands in pockets outside the hall. They're talking, laughing, looking at their feet. And then one's on the ground. Flattened. A moment later Hamza's back at the bus.

– That was him right, Karlo?

– Think so, yeah.

– You, *Hamza*! Back up here beside me, Finnegan shouts.

Spring

13
OISÍN

– Can you not get this fella to see sense here? Whacker says to Oisín, who's pulling off his sock for the third time.

There's fucken something stuck in it. Prickling his foot.

– He's tricking around with fools. Dangerous fools, Whacker says.

Deano's sitting on the only bit of a bench there is in the concrete shed they call the changing rooms. No one's been bothered to empty the overflowing rain basins and buckets but by the stink off them, it's fairly clear that more than one person couldn't be arsed walking the few extra feet to the actual toilet they had newly put in over Christmas.

– Away off to fuck wit yeh, yeh gobshite, I'll be out to yeh in a minute, Whacker shouts suddenly, as a red-faced kid comes to the door.

– But I've to leave me gear in here …

– Did I fucken tell yeh? Did I? Away to fuck wit yeh, he says again, turning a deeper red, foam gathering at the corners of his mouth.

– I can't leave it out here, it's lashing and I've to change me shoes.

– Away ta fuck! Whacker and Oisín roar at him, as Oisín jumps up and pushes the kid away from the door.

Whacker's on one, whatever it is. Always best to get it over with.

– Good man, Oisín. We've a bit of business here, don't we? I say, a bit a business. I've been hearing things, Oisín. About this fella here. Things I don't like to hear.

Whacker's pacing up and down now, shaking his head, with his hands behind his back. Serious business. Nothing, except cheating – by the other side – gets him this scaldy. And he's never asked Oisín to be a witness other than the time that Drimnagh fella was caught trying to reef Whacker's car radio out with a Stanley knife. Whacker had it superglued in. The poor fella would've been at it all night. Whacker made him eat a chilli selection that he had Oisín run down and get in the Crumlin shopping centre. The young fella only managed three-quarters of an ordinary red one and Whacker threatened him with the rest, including the Scotch Bonnet, if he ever caught him doing the like again. He's on the Dublin Development Squad now, the young fella. Still a mouthy prick though.

– Now I know youse lads do be laughing at me …

– Nah, we don't Whacker, Oisín says.

Deano, elbows on his knees, shoulders slumped, smiles at the floor. Bad move if Whacker's seen it.

– Do you wanna know what I've been hearing, Oisín? I've been hearing that this granola bowl here has been hanging around with a certain person of the family Nestor. And with his fucken lackeys. And moving in circles that we don't want anyone belonging to us moving in. All friendly like. *Fraternisin.*

Ah, now this is a bit much. Deano's not moving in any circles.

– He's not hanging around with them, Whacker! Oisín says. Wino Nestor's an aul fella. Deano's not, Deano's maybe ...

What the hell do you say to describe what you don't even know yourself? What is he doing with Wino? Anything? Nothing?

– I don't care what age that shite-swab is. This fella here is lurking round him. I know he is. I've been told.

Deano says nothing to defend himself. Typical silence. Just backs down.

– By who? Oisín says.

Who's the fucking arsehole blabbing? It's one thing the boys having a go but it's another thing snitching to Whacker. Getting him riled. Giving him a stroke.

– By none of your business, Oisín. But by more than one person. People who know. Now, I don't mind, yiz know I turn a blind eye. Yiz can do whatever yiz like, I know yiz do be on the whacky-backy. And the rest. I know that. D'yiz think I don't? I know it all. I know yiz are always out hunting down Gemma Hussey ...

Deano catches Oisín's eye, looking out from under his eyebrows. This is not the first time Gemma Hussey, whoever the fuck she is, has been mentioned. But Oisín, for one, has never hunted down any girl and he and the boys have definitely never hunted down any girl in a pack. So whatever Whacker's on about here, he needs to reel himself in a bit. Some things are beyond understanding though and Whacker, shinbeating and thumping the water pipe like one of them Shaolin monks, is not to be argued with just now.

– But I won't put up with dumb fuckers. Fools, who go looking for trouble. I won't have anyone looking for their one-way trip to a boghole in feckin Navan or some shitehole. D'yiz see Seamus Canavan out there, do yiz?

Cue the Seamus Canavan story.

– That fella's been with us since he was a kid. Started with …

– All his friends, Oisín says.

– Must've been six or seven of them …

– And they all stopped, Oisín offers, trying to keep the voice unrushed.

If he hears you trying to rush him, that's when he digs in.

– Coming to training over the years …

– But Seamus …

– Kept it up …

– Gave a hundred and ten …

– Per cent. And look at him there now, out there, a fine man, an electrician and what happened the others? Will I tell yiz? Will I? The other five or six of them, what happened them?

You can't do the punchline for him.

– They're dead is what they are. All of them, dead.

Bottom lip over top lip, story told, point made, Whacker stops in front of Deano, sticks his hands on his knees, leans his face right in.

– Are you listening to me? Your aul fella, may God have mercy on his soul …

He pauses to bless himself in a way that Oisín, for all his atheism, is pretty sure is arseways.

– Your aul fella was left bleeding to death out there on that laneway by the likes of Wino Nestor, am I right? Did you forget that I had to stick my fist. This fist …

He holds up what looks like a load of sausage meat inside a shiny skin, in case either of them wouldn't know whose fist he was on about.

– Into his guts to hold them in and try and stop the bleeding. And you standing there gawping. D'yeh remember? Cos I remember, I remember very well.

And he's roaring now but he stands back and wipes snot onto his still-clenched fist and Oisín realizes Whacker's crying, and looks away. Fuck this. This whole thing's going to shit.

– He's not hanging out with him but, Oisín says, more quietly now.

Like he wants Whacker to have a word, whatever he's heard,
he doesn't know but still, Deano's not hanging out with Wino.
Whatever about Deano, he's not that thick to be any kind of
mates with that crowd.

– And you've been seen, Deano. Coming in and out of
that place at the Barn. You know the place I'm talking about,
don't yeh?

– No, Oisín says. What place?

– *You* know the place, don't you, Deano? *Don't* you, Deano?
Deano nods a small nod. What fucking place?

– Deano? Oisín says.

– It's not Ziggy's of the Barn, is it Deano? And let me see, it's
not the Camile takeaway, is it Deano?

If he's going to go through all his favourite establishments in
Dolphin's Barn, they'll be here till next week because Whacker
loves the Barn.

– And it's not the God Is Good, Tilapia shop, is it Deano?
And it's not the fire station, is it? Although a good hosing down
is probably what it needs. Going in and out of the place all the
time, you are.

– Who told you that? Deano says, suddenly interested. Cos
it's not true.

– Lots of people have seen you. But you've been in and
out. Now it's one thing chasing the hairy rasher but it's another
thing altogether going into them places. Them girls don't want
to be at that. Do you think they want to be riding you?

– What the fuck? Who's he riding? Who are you riding?
Oisín says.

Like, this can't be right. He'd know if Deano was riding
someone. It'd be the talk of the place if any of them, well, bar
Hamza, was getting any. Whacker stops pacing in front of a
hanghead Deano.

– Tell him, tell Oisín what you're at!

– I'm not at antin.

– Is that yer payment, is it? Selling shite to poor kids and getting paid in Gemma Hussey.

Fucking hell.

– Ah here, who the fuck is this Gemma? Oisín says, exasperated.

– The holes are bein ridden off them girls. They do be burst open. Is that what yer like now, is it, Deano? They wouldn't look at you, if they weren't getting paid. And that's only the half of it. Yeh'll end up with a green micky. Is that what yeh want, a green micky?

– I'm not fucking riding anyone, Whacker, shut the fuck up.

Never has he heard Deano say anything like that to Whacker.

– Then what are you doing in a knocking shop? Deano? Hah? Hooring around with hoors! Selling drugs. Yer mammy is the way she is because of people like you. Yer a pusher and a ...

Deano jumps up.

– You fuck, leave me ma out of it.

Oisín steps in between them. Whacker's twirling the hurl in his hand.

– I won't leave yer ma out of it. That's what yer at. You're hooring and selling God knows what. What have I always said to yeh? Hah? What did I always say?

He's gonna blow for sure. Veins are popping all over his head.

– I'm not! I never touched any of them. I never even seen them, Deano says.

Ah here, now. This is too much shit to deal with right now. Too much. Oisín sits down on the bench beside Deano but they may as well be in different parts of the world. All the exaggerating he did, he thought, at the back of his mind that no, there was no way that Deano would ever get really in with Wino and the likes. Not really.

– Me arse yeh haven't. Pewther says yer …

– Piotr? Deano says, all interest.

Whacker looks like he's going to shit himself. Oisín has no idea who Piotr is but by the look on Deano's face, Deano knows Piotr well enough.

– How'd you know him? Deano says, slumping back onto the bench and meeting Whacker's eye.

Whacker looks sheepish. He pauses to lick and bite his bottom lip. Not like Whacker to have to pause before answering.

– He's Tommy, Tomaz, or whatever his name is, that young fella's da. He told me he's seen you. And he's not the only one. So yeh can stop yer shitting and shite-ing out of yeh. What are yeh going to do about it?

– I'm not selling either.

– What are the packages about then? Yeah, I know about the packages. Yeh stupid ginger scaldy little fuck! he says and lashes a smack to the back of Deano's head.

– You said those packages had nothing to do with Wino! You said, Deano, Oisín says. You fucking swore.

– They *had* nothing to do with him.

– You said they weren't even drugs. Are you fucking dealing? Are you dealing Mandy? Tell me you're not dealing gear? Fucking tell me. Come on, you're that much of a scumbag? You fucking lied?

Deano starts to slide off the end of the bench where it's missing a leg and he has to brace himself, letting out a big sigh.

– Do youse think I would ever deal gear? After me ma?

– Dunno, Deano, you tell us. Seems you're riding someone called Gemma Hussey and a load of prostos and I didn't know that, Oisín says.

– Not riding anyone and I looked in them envelopes and it was always money. Just money, except one time, maybe some pills were rattling around but that's it. Not even that many pills either. It's nuttin. Take the envelopes from here to there and that's it. I never even seen Wino. Didn't know he was involved even. It's no big deal.

– No big deal, Whacker says, rubbing the top of his head. No big deal the man says. Do I have to fucken suspend yeh? Yeh pup, yeh!

– Suspend me from what? Deano says.

– Training. The team. Everything.

– What are you on about? I'm yer best player. I'm the only one who turns up half the time, Whacker. What do you want me to do?

There's a shake in the voice.

– I want yeh to stop what yer at, yeh thick fuck. That's what I want. You clear away ta fuck, d'yeh hear me? Away home with yeh, I'm sick of the sight of yeh.

– But I'm here for training … yeh can't …

– Go home now and have a big think for yerself about your da bleeding out there on the laneway in front of yeh …

Fuck, that's too much. Deano's crumpled over, arms around his belly, shrinking but Whacker gives Oisín the nod and he follows him towards the door.

– I just wanted to go Boston, that's all, Deano mumbles.

Oisín hears him but walks on out the door. His breath catches in his throat and he starts coughing. The away-ta-fuck kid is sitting on his kit bag outside between two parked cars, banging his hurl on the ground, with his bottom lip stuck out. Whacker ruffles his hair.

– Don't you be worrying there, Horsebox, come and stick yer stuff in me van, I just had a bit of business in there to sort out. How's yer da? Coming up to watch yeh when he gets out? Best player we ever had under-twelves here, yeh know that, yer da? Best player. Maybe we'll get him back into it when he gets out, what d'yeh reckon, Horsebox?

The kid's face lights up even though he's soaked.

– Ma says he'll be getting out in a few weeks and then he'll be coming up definitely, Whacker.

– Good man, Whacker says. You tell him, we need coaches up here. Das like him, right?

*

Bang! His eyes snap open. He's there, at the end of the bed. Smiling. Watching.

Oisín's heart's hammering like he's just run a race. The room, exactly the same as when his head hit the pillow. The laundry basket spilling onto the floor. The book thrown on the pillow beside him. Just a grey caul hazing everything. No colour. Except him, the other one, his blond hair and sallow skin in a spotlight.

He sits and watches and smiles. He'll soften now, becoming smoke, then mist, then gone. And Oisín will be able to move then, drink water, have a piss. His breathing will settle. And he'll sleep.

But no. The other one, always still before, stretches out an arm, something in his hand. Fuck! Oisín hears his own breathing, fluttering, in the distance.

He turns his fist over and smiles even more. Showing, knowing. He slowly opens his hand, lit up, in Technicolor, in the monochrome nightworld.

Oisín starts to shout, roaring for his mother but no sound is coming out. Frozen in the bed. The other one ignores him, smiling. On his outstretched palm a small square swatch of woolly tweedy fabric, so many colours, reds, greens, blues, a perfect square, bar the three tiny frayed threads that he tugs on and pulls loose at one corner. Leaving them trailing over the heel of his hand. And then he starts to fade into the ether, becoming part of the air, the darkness, the shade, the wardrobe, the lamp, the poster. But this time, for the first time, he, Oisín, is able to make a sound and the sound is, No, don't go, and it is loud and echoes around the room and the silent house.

14
BENIT

One of them's normal. You'd suspect, maybe, in the way you might suspect with Karl. The trousers are a bit too tight around the jewels but apart from that, normal. The other lad though, wow. He pony-shows into the room, handlebar moustache, trousers too short, showing off his diamond-pattern socks. Braces. On the trousers, not the sparkling teeth. Mum would like those teeth – almost as good as Benit's own.

They're OK, Hector and River. They talk about percentages. Say that this means maybe five people in the classroom are gay. Benit glances at Karl who's doodling like he could draw his way to New Zealand. At that rate, maybe Benit himself is one of the five? There's Karl and then there's Gaymie – who was Jamie until he left his phone with Grindr open on the side of the bowl in Weaver. He takes in the room – nah, there's no sign of anyone else who's even the smallest bit gay. Dicks? Nah, fam. Nah, nah, nah. He loves his own. Best thing he's ever produced. But, nah.

The two lads give it loads about talking to your mates and how to treat people, trying to talk street. Aul fellas, even the gay ones, should just stick to their own speak. Just silly otherwise.

– So what would be a good way for you to react if Oisín here told you he was gay? Hector asks Karl.

Karl's dying. Oisín turns to look at Karl, all serious.

– Wait, do youse recognize your own kind? Deano says. I never knew that, Sur.

– It's Hector, no need to call me Sir, Dean, Hector says.

– Is that cos yer gay, we don't have to call youse Sur, Sur, Deano says. That's discrimination, right there, Sur. That's like gay-bashing. There's nuttin wrong with bein gay, Sur.

River and Hector smile that heard-it-all-before smile. Pros, not some pair of student teachers from Tipperary and, to be honest, Benit thinks it's a bit funny but he's getting kinda tired of the slagging and the smart-arsing just for the sake of it. It wears you out. Those can't be their real names, though. Suppose if you're going around schools telling everyone you're a bender you wouldn't use your real name. Or maybe you would, if you were proud of it. And why wouldn't you be? Love is love.

– And riding is riding, Benit says, not copping that he's speaking out loud.

Everyone around him falls on their desks laughing. Karl even cracks a smile. He's gonna have to get this under control. Keeps happening, something just blurts out and he hasn't realized he's been actually saying it. When he's running he catches someone's eye and they're laughing and then he realizes that he's been having that convo that he thought was just in his head. Miss Ramsey is trying to kill him with a stare.

– Just saying, he says. No biggie, Miss.

Karl still looks dead embarrassed but he answers River.

– Dunno. Suppose you could say, that's grand, Oisín.

– That all you'd say, Karlo? And me pouring out me gay heart? Oisín says.

– And what would be a bad way, Karl? A bad way to react to Oisín? Hector says.

– Dunno, do a dolphin dive out the window?

The pair turn away to hide the laughing. Same as anyone else, just a bit gay.

He knows he's right, riding is riding.

*

What the fuck is he going to put on his CAO form? How are you supposed to know what you want to do forever when you're eighteen? Benit wants to go hurling, go the gym, fuck as much as he can, hang out with the boys, smoke a bit, have a laugh, make Mama proud. Maybe not in that order.

He sinks back into his seat with his Bovril in the giant B mug that had appeared, without comment, in Marty's cupboard a few months back.

– There's nothing to be afeared about. Just stay calm, watch and wait. Do as you're told. Stay out of trouble, get through it, and in the meantime it'll come to yeh, son.

Marty sets his own Bovril onto the tiny side table and gets up out of the chair.

– Did I ever show you that book about India, old India? Before partition? Them Indians knew all about what was going on here with 1916 and all. Very up on the history. The jewel in the crown me arse. What do I say about them, Benit?

– Our arrogant neighbours.

– There's a bit of a lackage in the British establishment that makes them do that. Something not quite right, he says tapping his temple.

– What do I call it? he says, fumbling at one of the bookshelves. Think it's somewhere here, and he climbs up on his stepladder.

– The common denominator?

– Aha! That's right. That's what it is.

And he launches into the speech.

– Every. Fucking. Time. Wherever there's conflict and people killing other, right now, what's the common denominator?

– The Brits.

– Ex-actly, he says holding up his finger like Jesus or some lairy mullah picking a fight as he turns around one foot on the top step of the ladder and the other lower down, he leans his elbow onto his thigh.

Benit sips the Bovril. Can't believe he never knew about Bovril until he met Marty. You can't blame the Brits for everything though.

– What about Congo? It was others in Congo.

Marty falters and almost falls off the stepladder.

– Are yeh joking me? Are yeh?

He starts to spit.

– Their hands in everything. Everything.

– But the Portuguese …

– You've been reading.

It's true, he has, just on the internet but he won't say that to Marty. Unless it's in a book, it's not worth a shite. And don't get him started on Wikipedia.

– Well, at least I learned yeh something, as the man says, wha? At least I learned yeh something, he says, as he climbs down the stepladder, bookless.

– Now, let me tell you, who d'yeh think Stanley was working for *really*? When the French and that bastard Belgian were carving things up, who d'yeh think was lurking, profiting? Who d'yeh think was behind the slave ships? Who?

Benit smiles and takes another sip of Bovril.

– The Brits, Marty?

– The Brits, is right, is right, is right.

– They did some good things too.

– Yeh won't get a rise outta me, so yeh won't, Benit. They could've done those good things at home and left everyone else alone. They starved the poor fucking Chinks sure, made them all addicts, the fuckers.

He hasn't mentioned the Chinks before.

– Anyway, fill out whatever this form is, apply for whatever you want. You say yeh can change whatever it is after?

– Yeah.

– Well then, you've no problem. And there's more to life than college. I watch the nieces and nephews and all. And some of them, God love them: thicks.

Benit sprays Bovril onto the heavy wooden chest that's Marty's coffee table.

– Yeh can clean that up, Benit. I'm serious, they may be thicks when it comes to book learning, maths with letters. But some of them might be great plumbers or carpenters or feckin street sweepers. But what are they doing? Feckin business studies. There's one of them, me sister's grandson beyond in Galway, and sure that young fella'd chaw the bottom of a door to get outside and his mother has him at some business thing. That fella's as wild as a feckin Hun but d'yeh know who put up me lovely book shelves for me?

– Mam thinks I'm still going medicine.

– And are yeh?

– What do *you* think?

– I think I don't know what you're capable of, Benit, but I'd say it's plenty. Think about what yer good at. D'yeh want another cup?

– I'll get it, Marty.

– Yeh will while yer cleaning up. You need to find what your plenty is, Benit. We need everyone, yeh know? That bastarding cat!

And he's off and shuffling to the window with his water pistol.

*

– Yeah but she's losing her mind over it. Wants me to put down medicine, Benit says.

– Sure, put down medicine then, Oisín says. Put all the medicines and dentistry and laws down, all the big ones.

– And business studies, Karl says, as he passes the pipe. Don't forget business studies.

– Yer da still on about that? Deano says.

– How doesn't he know that you're shite at business? Hamza says.

Unfair, as far as Benit knows, Karl's not totally shite at business. His da's just being sensible making him take business instead of art and Karl only draws them tiny women anyway. You need to be able to draw a bowl of fruit to be proper good at art. Benit leans behind and over the headboard and opens the window even more. If Karl's mam catches even a whiff in here, Karl's a dead man. The last time she thought she smelled something, she grounded Karl for three months and barred the rest of them from his gaff.

– Put down business studies then, Oisín says. Keep your da sweet and even if you don't change it later, you'll never get it. Put your real choices lower down.

– What the fuck? What happens if I do get my first choice?

– In fairness, Karlo … Oisín says.

– Unless you put your first choice down as some PLC course you'll be grand. Put commerce in UCD down, you're safe enough, Hamza says.

Benit thumps him behind Karl's back. Karl doesn't need this hassle.

– I only mean Oisín's right, just put down something you know you've no chance of getting. We all have things like that, Hamza says.

– Don't even know what I want to do in anyway, Karl says.

– Who the fuck knows what they want to do? Oisín says. 'Cept Hamza. And that's cos he's a prick. No one *really* wants to do business studies.

All part of Hamza's strategy. And if it works, things will be better and no one will ever have to sit around choosing courses. Everyone'll just know what they're good at and everyone'll have to take their turn cleaning the public jacks.

– Except there aren't any public jacks to clean …

He's done it again. They all look at him but then get back to passing the pipe. It's just that his mind moves faster – or is it slower? – and in different directions than other brains do. Like a superpower but maybe in reverse.

– A superweakness …

– Benit, sherrup, Oisín says. We're trying to get Karlo sorted here.

He opens his eyes to see they've all crowded around Karl's laptop.

– HPAT, you've to do that too, Oisín says.

– None of us have to do the HPAT, Oisín.

–For authenticity like.

– What? We all applying now? Benit says. I don't have a card on me to pay for it.

– I'll pay for it, youse pay me back, Deano says.

– I've enough for me own, Karlo says.

Awkward. Everyone's scared of Deano's money.

– This is stupid, boys. Can't be doing this.

– Shut up, it's a laugh, Hamza says. Five places we can do it there, one each. You take Trinity, Deano.

Deano walks away from the desk.

– Boys, this is a loada bollocks. Don't even wanna be applying at all.

Oisín turns on him.

– You are fucken filling out this CAO thing or I swear, I will smash you. Oisín says. Few seconds ago you were mouthing about paying the application fee for us all like the big man, and now you're not applying?

– Don't be a, dope, Deano, Hamza says, not looking up from the screen. Mess apply now, change it after.

Deano rubs his nose, rocks back and forth on his toes.

– Trinity and them places, they're not for the likes of us ...

– You better be joking, Hamza says, lips tightening, pausing his fingers on the keys.

– Not you, me. Us, I mean. Me and Karlo, or, not Karlo.

– Swear, if you don't sit down and apply for medicine in Trinity, Deano, Oisín won't have to smash you because I'll put you through that wall.

They all, bar Deano, slowly settle around the laptop. Give him time to save face, to pretend he never said that. Karl goes ahead, Royal College of Surgeons. Hamza next, UCD. Doctor Hamza sounds good and he looks the part with the beard and all. Benit can feel Deano creeping closer behind him. Oisín glances over his shoulder but he's not quite there yet. Oisín goes UCC after an argument with Benit because Benit can't understand what they're saying down there. He's never been, but *The Young Offenders* taught him enough. Deano sinks onto the bed and no one passes any remarks. He's still not ready, so Benit's going NUI Galway.

– Doctor Benit, Fenella'll be so proud, Oisín says, clapping him on the back.

And she would be. She would be. No one even glances at Deano. They all just wait and pretend they're looking at other choices until finally, he says:

– Budge up there, Benit, lemme have a look.

Hamza checks the code, Medicine, Trinity, TR051.

– Sure this is okay, Hamo? Deano says, staring at the keyboard.

There's a quiver in his hands. Benit looks away, slaps Deano's shoulder and says:

– Do it for the boys, so we can all get our white coats, Deano.

– Can't let some dope get the better of me, can I? Deano says and he hits the payment button and it's gone.

15
OISÍN

Not long till Boston. Not long at all. Oisín's hurl whacks the dead heads off daffodils poking through the railings all along his street. A wood pigeon coos the sound of summer at the start of March. Damp from training but the evening's so mild, he doesn't even need his hoodie. They said it's going to be a scorcher again this year. Like they always do. Like the whole of Ireland forgets its own climate when there's one half-warm spring day, and then everyone's in a deep depression when it rains or it's ten degrees in July. Clocks'll go forward in a few weeks and then sure, it practically *is* summer.

Things aren't so bad. Life's kinda good even. If Deano stays on track. Dad's around a bit – swimming with him. Fuck, he's starving.

Rushing around from the laneway at the back of Oisín's house, there's some fucken scald carrying a hammer. One uncontrolled eye halfway down his cheek and the other up on his forehead. No way he's a DIY enthusiast. And another, lardarse, sweating like a bastard, bird shit-coloured hair that looks like it's sellytaped onto his head like a Lego hairdo. Runners, tracksuits. Jaysus, a third, yellow and puffy, taking up the rear with a baseball bat. Oisín pulls his hat further down over his eyes and does the I-can't-see-you walk up to the front door, whacking the daffodils and starting to hum, feeling the stooges give him the once over. The door's open as always but he turns and locks it once he's inside. Mom says if you build a fortress, you're only asking for it to be attacked, but this is maybe not the time for the open-door policy.

He walks straight into the kitchen, past her to the table, throws the hurl in the corner, and pulls up a chair. The big orange ceramic pot, giving off the best of smells, is already on a placemat. Grabbing a baguette and tearing off a strip, he says:

– You wanna've seen the absolute fucking scumbags outside. Wouldn't wanna be whoever they're planning to kick the shit out of. Why's it so dark in here?

She has the lights on only at the cooker, the table's in near darkness.

– How many? his mam says.

– What's in the pot? Better be jambalaya. Yes! How many what?

– Scumbags? How many scumbags?

He starts spooning the rice and chicken into his bowl.

– Salad too, he says. Oh yeah, bring on the summer! Amirite Ma?

– Oisín, for fuck's sake! How fucking many before I fucking leather you!

She's swearing? He does a whiplash turn.

And then he sees him. He'd passed him by altogether, sitting on the leather sofa up against the island, eyes darting all over the place then fixing on Oisín.

What possible set of fucking unbelievable circumstances could have Snitchy sitting on his mom's sofa?

Snitchy gives him a half smile. Standing in the kitchen, at the sink, behind Snitchy, she frowns the frown of doom, watching Oisín like a hawk.

Oisín turns back to his bowl. Takes a forkful of rice. Stares hard at the table. How much to say? What are the odds? The river's been dealt but he doesn't know what his own cards are. Gotta go all-in right now.

– Who's that? he asks, eyes fixed on the food.

– Pearl next door says you know him, she says.

Fuck! What the fuck's dipso Pearl got to do with this? A million and one things this could be. Deano, Hamza, the party, blackmail, Snitchy's off his head, anything, it could be anyfuckingthing.

She waves her arms around to catch his eye and hauls him out into the hall.

– Oisín, what's going on here? she says.

– You're asking *me* that? Who the hell's that lad on the sofa?

– You're saying you don't know him?

She looks dubious.

– I'm just in the door. You're the one who's got some skankbag sitting on the sofa. No, I don't know him. Has he got something to do with the scumbags I saw out the front? They were looking for someone.

– Yeah, they were looking for him, I'm sure. He landed over Pearl's wall. She was in her kitchen and thought it was you messing.

– Pearl's so off her tits she thought that yoke in there was me? Great.

– Shut up Oisín! Pearl says he fell in over the wall and landed on the washing machine.

One of the two broken washing machines that Pearl keeps, with cushions inside for her seven half-feral cats to sleep in. His mom wipes her forehead. Sweating up, not a good sign.

– When he got his breath back a bit, he asked could he stay and hide there, in Pearl's, for a few minutes. Pearl took him in, locked the doors, drew the blinds.

Pearl probably thought God was being good, if she's having one of her episodes. Young fella lands in her lap.

– He's running from some men, he says. They just started chasing him. Then he says to Pearl that he thought he might know the next-doors – us. She sent me a text and sent him over our wall for safety. Do you know him, Oisín? So help me God, if you lie to me!

– I haven't a clue who he is.

She might let it pass.

– Think I've seen him before. He might be in the school, dunno what year. Maybe from the flats.

– He knew your name, knew you lived here.

She's not stupid but he's not giving in now that he's started. Snitchy obviously hasn't said much. So he doesn't need to either.

– Sure, he lives up the road. Why wouldn't he know where I live? I'm The Don, like.

– This is no time for your bullshit, Oisín.

And she storms back into the kitchen, stands at the sink again. Snitchy hasn't budged.

– What's your name? she says.

– Brian.

Jesus, seriously? Brian?

– Brian what?

And then he only goes and gives his real surname and she's off.

– I think I know your ma, she says. Sharon Noble?

Ah, 'ma', she's down with the flats now. Oisín takes a seat at the table, facing her and Snitchy, who's obviously desperate but keeping his face blank. A Snitchy talent Oisín's noticed before. Snitchy with his Garda face on. Now she's asking how his auntie is doing in the new house in Crumlin, and how his nanny's ankle is. Snitchy's face twitches. Can't believe this one, in her nice house in the Tenters knows his ma.

– So why were they chasing you? she says, all casual-like, wiping the worktop.

– Dunno, they just started. Came at me with baseball bats and hammers. Threw a knife at me.

– *Threw* a knife at you? Right, she says, going to the larder cupboard.

– Yeah, here look, Snitchy says, messing with the pockets of his jacket.

Fucking do not pull a knife out in my mom's kitchen! But he does. Oh yeah he does. The love-heart one from Hamza's party, though half the sparkles have fallen off it. And she just raises one eyebrow, pulls a ramekin from the cupboard and says:

– Would you like a pecan, Brian?

He looks up at Oisín. What the fuck?

– No thanks, Missus Oisín.

She folds her arms, gives Oisín the death stare.

– So you *do* know each other.

This is fucked. Why, when your life is looking up again does this kinda shite arrive on your sofa? Bam!

– I was in the hurling years ago. Oisín was in the older age group.

Slick swerve under pressure, impressive.

– They threw that knife at you then, did they? And you just stopped and picked it up? You shouldn't be carrying a knife. What did they think you were doing?

– Well, now I need a knife, don't I?

He and Oisín lock eyes.

– I was just standing talking to me uncle at the car, Snitchy says. Came outta nowhere, they did. Roaring and shouting at me. And they fired the knife at me. And some rocks.

– So, a group of men you don't know came running at you because you were talking to your uncle.

– Yeah, he was just giving me money for me birthday, Snitchy says.

– When's your birthday?

– Tomorrow.

– This is some present you're getting, isn't it? He was just giving you money for your *birthday*?

– Yeah. Dunno what them men wanted. I just ran.

She wipes the worktop to within an inch of its life. Then heads up the stairs. Oisín listens for signs of her creeping back down on the sly but there's nothing.

– What the fuck, Snitchy! Oisín says, as quietly as he can. What the fuck are yeh doing in me gaff? My mam's gaff, like? And that's *your* knife. What the fucking fuck have you been at?

– Me ma's knife, in fairness. I've been at nuttin, Oisín, I swear. I just says that I knew yiz to yer one next door so she'd let me in. Them cunts were on top of me. Had to vault the gate in Tenterfields and cut across the grounds to get here ahead a them. Me and Titch were just there, not even selling, just standing there talking and these fucken looper tallybans came out of nowhere.

– The lads I saw outside weren't Muslims, Snitchy.

– I know. What? Snitchy says, looking confused.

– Did you know them, the fellas chasing yeh? Wait, where's Titch?

– Nah, didn't recognize any of the cunts. Dunno bout Titch. He did a legger back into the flats. I came down this way.

Snitchy's leg is jumping, a milky-white, unhairy knee, with a red and yellow gouge out of it, jutting through the tear in his tracksuits.

– I fucken saw them outside. You're a dead man, hundred per cent.

Snitchy says nothing, just pastes on his blank face again.

– Swear to God Snitchy, if you've brought down some shit on my mam's house.

– Look out the front and see if they're still around, will yeh? Snitchy says.

– Course they're fucking around, you dumb fuck! They're looking for you.

She's on her way back down the stairs.

– Who else's in the house? Snitchy says, like he's some hard-man scoping it out. Yer aul fella here? Hear he's proper old, yeah?

– I wouldn't be fucken starting any slagging if I were you, Snitchy, he hisses, as his mother bursts into the room, mobile in hand.

– Right, you've no phone on you. I've got your mam's number. Here, it's ringing.

She hands him her phone and Snitchy stares at it in his hand like it's some kind of viper.

– Now, please, she says, and strides over to the fridge where she starts sorting the eggs in the rack for the first time ever.

Snitchy doesn't have his phone? Seriously? So he *was* caught on the hop. He doesn't move, just looks at the phone until she grabs it off him and explains who she is to Snitchy's mam, and heads out of the room with the phone once the sobbing starts at Snitchy's mam's end. He and Snitchy look anywhere but at each other as they wait for her to come back from the hallway. She hands the phone to Snitchy and explains the situation in whispers to Oisín – Snitchy can stay here for a bit until his mam can arrange a safe place for him. They'll have to get him there somehow. How the fuck they gonna do that with a fucking crowd of orcs outside the door and his mam's car at the garage getting fixed, he doesn't know. One thing he does know, you don't allow Snitchy and whatever trouble he's into hang around your house for very long.

*

An hour, maybe more, passes, and they stay in their cocoon, waiting for someone pro-Snitchy to call. Oisín's mom goes back up, to watch *Eastenders*, she says. She eventually comes back down and sends Oisín out to have a look about on the streets. He grabs his hurl and heads up the road through a whirlwind of young fellas and kids, riding bikes like they're in a rodeo but checking out every passing civilian. They look him over – definitely not Snitchy – and he strides on towards Deano's flat.

Deano's none too pleased to see him at the door and he frowns at the hurl.

– Snitchy's in the house, Oisín whispers.

– Yeh wha? Deano says, pulling him into the flat.

The rest of them are sitting around watching the telly. June, with a heap of kids attached, doesn't even turn around. Robbie sees him and waves his mug of tea.

– He's got some hardcore fellas after him, I saw them. Like real straps. Didn't recognize them from around. They threw rocks and shit at them.

– Them?

– Titch was with him. They split up when the yitnas started chasing them.

– Oisín, come in love. Do you want a slice a cake there? June says.

The Battenberg's on the table. June's is the only place he's ever got Battenberg.

– Nah, thanks though June. I'm just after me dinner. Actually I will, can I cut it myself?

Battenberg, it's the perfect mix of bad and good. Should be Class A, bound to be doing serious damage.

– Didn't see yer mam at the yoga this evening, Oisín. Tell her not to be slacking off, June says.

Mouth stuffed with pink and yellow, Oisín says:

– Yeah, she's got a bad stomach.

– That's that vegan diet. Have yiz 7up in the house?

Some chance.

– She only lasted two days with that vegan thing, June. She was starving. Can I've another slice?

– Knew it. You go home now and boil up the 7up for her.

Deano pushes him into the bathroom doorway.

– What's the story? Are yeh gonna stay here monching cake all night? What are yiz gonna do? And how did Snitchy get into yer house?

– Fucked if I know what we're gonna do. Those skangers didn't look like they were just out to give him a pasting either. One of them had a hammer. Some of your mate Wino's lads, I'm sure.

Deano scratches at the back of his neck.

– Doubt it and he's not my mate, for fucksake. What's Snitchy done in anyway?

– I don't fucken know. He's shiteing on about his uncle giving him money, saying he wasn't selling. It's Snitchy, you never know what's bullshit. This is the kinda shite you're bringing down on yourself too, yeah?

Deano kicks the door jamb.

– I'm doing nuttin with that fella, d'yeh hear me? Haven't even heard from that lot in a while, he says, rubbing his hair. Hardly Wino in anyway, Snitchy's well in there.

– Well, he's pissed someone off.

– Gotta get back. He's down there with me mam.

– So why the fuck are you *here*? Deano says.

– Came out to scope the area. Had to go somewhere or it'd look bad. The place is crawling with lads on bikes out there. They're flying around all over the place. Snitchy's ma was off her face on the phone. Bawling. No one in Snitchy's fam will take him in.

– Is yer ma gonna throw him out?

– Nah, yeh know what she's like.

– I wouldn't be leaving me ma with Snitchy in the house and a gang of scumbags screaming around the place looking for him, that's alls I know.

– Just wanna know if you know what's going on, or anywhere we can put him.

– I'll get me jacket and me hurl and come down with yeh, Deano says.

– Do you know something about this? Oisín says in a whisper.

Deano goes red and clamps his jaw tight.

– I'm only asking, Oisín says.

– I don't know anything about Snitchy's business. I steer clear. Whacker's orders, yeah?

– Whatever.

– Just going out with Oisín for a bit, Deano calls back and they're out the door before June or Robbie can say anything.

Deano sticks the hurl across the back of his shoulders and starts laughing and talking just a bit too loud.

– So I'm listening to that gaylord music and yeh know what? It's not that bad. I like that Gojira stuff.

– Yeah, it's great, isn't it? Did you listen to the second album? Man …

On the corner of Oisín's street they pass a gang of older lads, astride their bikes, huddled around a mobile phone. They nod at the pair of them and one of them puts the phone to his ear, takes instructions, and they disperse.

– This is fucken mental, Oisín says without moving his lips.

They chat and fake-laugh about music and hurling on the way down, pretend they don't even see the car slowing beside them to give them the once-over. Back inside the house though, Deano's shoulders are up round his ears.

– I'm only here to stop any trouble, Deano whispers in the darkened hallway. I'm not getting involved with anything Snitchy's into.

Oisín noisily opens the kitchen door. She's taken Oisín's seat and is sitting directly in front of Snitchy, still stuck in the corner of the sofa, like he's trying to burrow his way into it to get away from her.

– How's it going Helen? Deano says, like a fella who's just arrived on the off-chance of a feed. Both her eyebrows shoot up when she sees him.

There's not even a flicker of recognition from either Snitchy or Deano but Snitchy's leg's going again.

She stands up, announcing the plan. Snitchy's mam stopped answering her phone altogether. They're gonna take Snitchy, in Pearl's car, to his auntie's flat in Fatima, in the hopes she's in.

They leg it over the back wall into Pearl's and Oisín's mom goes to Pearl's front door. It's a risky business, involving schizo Pearl.

She's whirling around in the kitchen, cooing and singing opera alternately. Her huge circular table that makes it nearly impossible to get around the kitchen is piled high with packets of every kind of cake and biscuit you can imagine. Pearl sings her way to the gilt mirror in her hallway, haphazardly pinning up her masses of red hair.

– Unruly, unruly, unruly, she says as the four of them awkwardly stand around watching her. I know, I know, we have to get a move on. Get this young buck to safety. Where *are* we going dears?

– We're going to take him to Fatima, his auntie's flat, Oisín's mom says.

– Ooh Fatima, Fatima. Let's hoop we doon't have a visitation from Our Lady. That's the lawst thing we need in these dark times.

She grabs Snitchy's chin.

– You, young man, are about to get a second chance. Grab it! Hold it! Never let go! I had a visitation once. Not the Virgin, oh no, the baby Jesus. Now where are my keys?

She literally has the poshest accent anyone's ever heard and it worsens when she's in a high phase. Oisín's never heard the baby Jesus bit before though.

– Maybe I'll drive, Pearl? his mom says.

Thank fuck for that.

– Oh yes, you must, you *must*! But I'll come too, Pearl says as she pulls a green feather boa from around the neck of the red chiffon-nightied shop mannequin, whose head seems to be a coat rack.

– Is it chilly out? I haven't *braved* the elements since lawst week.

She rustles in a huge velvet patchwork bag and the keys emerge.

– Let's go, we warrior band. I'm Gráinne of the Tóraíocht, beloved of Diarmuid. Who are you, Helen?

– I'll be Macha, cursing the sons of Ulster.

Snitchy's completely lost his blank face now and he looks like he's about to run out the door and take his chances with the yitnas out on the street.

And Deano only goes and pipes up:

– I'll be the Diarmuid fella so, Pearl, he says and nudges Oisín with his elbow, sticking his tongue out.

Loves all this legend stuff, Deano. Pearl, fixing a purple velvet hat on her head, says:

– Ooh, I have you under a *geas* already, Diarmuid. I'll have to see to you later, though, we've work to do here.

And she blows him a kiss, winks at him, slings her bag over her arm and heads out the back door to the car parked at the end of her garden.

They fold Snitchy into the back footwell and put a jacket over him, and start off for Fatima. They can see men, in twos and threes, smoking in the shadows up at the flats, turning to scope the car as they pass. Gangs of young fellas are still whizzing around out on Cork Street and over towards Marylands. Something's seriously up. Sadie, Doreen and Rita are having a conference on the corner outside Lidl. Sadie sees them stopped in traffic, and waves them down.

This is all they need.

– What the fuck does she want now, Oisín's mom says between gritted teeth.

Pearl rolls down the window and Oisín sticks his feet up on Snitchy's jacketed back.

– How're yiz all doin, the orange head says in the window. You okay, Deano?

– Eh, yeah, why?

– Just checkin. Ah, nothin, just me being silly. I knocked inta June's and saw yeh weren't there. So, yer grand? Don't mind me, Helen. There's something goin on round the flats is all. I'll see you at the bingo in the morning, Pearl? As long as the young fellas are alright.

They land at Fatima.

– Pork in the shadows there under the tree, away from the light, Pearl instructs.

– Oisín, you and Deano get out first and just make your way up the road there slowly, text me if there's a problem. I dunno, swing your hurl up in the air, if all's clear. You hop out then, Brian, and make a run for your auntie's door. Get away from the car as quick as you can.

Two fucken ninjas, the pair of them in the front.

– Brian, you text me as soon as you're in safe, here's my mobile number, she says as she hands him a scrap of paper. Get out, the pair of you.

Oisín and Deano amble slowly, swinging their hurls, chatting about Gojira again, no way am I choosing engineering, I saw yer one that walks around with the ginger cat in the pram the other day … Keeping an eye on the door of the ground floor flat. No sign of anyone and Oisín swings the hurl up and holds it there, like it's his party trick, balancing it in the palm of his hand.

The car door opens and slams shut behind them and they keep walking until they get to a tree and sit down on the seat at its base. Deano pulls out his tin and starts to roll as Oisín watches Snitchy's chicken walk to the door. Snitchy knocks and knocks. Even at this distance, you can tell that Snitchy's starting to panic.

Outta nowhere a pair of hoodies appear on BMXs that are far too small for them. They've *Scream* masks on. They make for Snitchy at the door. Deano's up and staunching straight for the car, Oisín right behind him. Don't look at the door. Don't look at the door. The car engine starts up but the lights stay off. A Luas hisses its way towards town behind them and a man with his dog crosses their path to the car.

– Not a bad night, the man says.

Deano's at the car and out of the corner of his eye, Oisín can see Snitchy still standing at the door as the two masked kids bolt away into the darkness on the bikes. Oisín dives into the back on top of Deano and they watch as Snitchy takes a ramble in the opposite direction from the car – cool move – and circles back around.

He finally gets back to them and climbs in, silent and white-faced. The car roars off.

Oisín's mom's eyes look huge in the mirror.

– What did they say to you? Oisín says. Did you know them?

There's a line of sweat on Snitchy's upper lip. His eyes are bloodshot and watery.

– They wanted to know my name and where I lived. What was I doing there.

– Yeh told em nuttin, right? Deano says. Didn't tell them yer name.

– I'm not a dope, Snitchy says, stony-faced.

Silence. Then Snitchy says:

– Just bring me to me nanny's.

– But your mam said that you couldn't go there, she's not well, Helen says.

– It's grand. I'll climb over the wall. I know where the key is. I'll get in.

When they get there, there's no one on the quiet street. She kills the lights. He clambers out and scales the wall like a monkey, and he's gone.

No masks appear, no mob, no baseball bats, no hammers.

16
KARL

– I went somewhere last night, Karl says.

His belly's turning over but it's now or never. Deano's in a weird mood. Quiet. Best time to get him.

– Yeah? Where'd yeh go, buddy? We missed yeh. Round in Oisín's just for a bitta scran.

– Celery, carrots and hummus?

– You better believe it. So were yeh with yer *girls*? And can we speed this up a bit?

With the spawgy legs, he always moves faster than Karl, but he's charging everywhere today, like he wants off the street. Edgy, he is.

– Sort of, I was with Tanya.

– Ah, the posh rat, was she asking for me? I'd lump the gee off that.

Yep, he's made that clear many times. But Karl still can't help grinning.

– Yeah, she asked would I make sure that yeh stayed away from her.

Deano stops dead on the street.

– Wait, did she really say that, bro?

His face has fallen. He means it.

– Nah, course not. Don't be a dope. But nah, she didn't ask for yeh.

– Right, right. You were messin. I feel yeh. Where were yiz, in anyway?

Karl's having second thoughts about seeing this through.

– Heard there was some hassle last night at the flats? he says.

– Dunno. Heard nuttin.

He's being sketch again.

– Were yeh in her gaff? he says.

– Went town. Out out.

– Okay? You trying to tell me something, buddy? Deano says, and he stops, eyes popping, jabbing a finger into the ring he's formed with his other hand.

– No wait, I meant ... he says, and he switches from his index finger to his little finger.

– Ah fuck off, no, yeh scumbag, Karl says, happy that Deano even thought it was a possibility.

Deano straightens his face.

– Yeah, I know. Long shot. Thought yeh were in there, buddy. Seriously, I'd hop on that anytime.

– Yeah, you've said.

– So what's the big deal? Yiz were out in town? Any craic? Yeh weren't with her fucken scumbag mates, were yeh? Damo there?

– Nah, just me and her ... We went The Pronto.

– Yeh what? The fucken gay place?!

And Deano starts to laugh. And he's laughing so much, he's holding his sides.

– Oh, he says, waving his hand at Karl as he's doubled over near the bins outside the offy. He falls against the post box.

– Yeh went ... Yeh went ... Wait'll I tell ...

– Fuck off, Deano, I shouldn't have told yeh.

He can see that Deano's trying to get serious but he can't.

– We just went to see what it was like.

– You went out, with tanned Tanya, the best-looking yoke about these parts, and yeh brought her to The *Pronto*? Did yeh get bummed?

– Fuck off, would yeh, yeh thick.

The base of the postbox gets a kick. His bottom lip's starting to shiver. For fuck's sake. He doesn't need the wobbly lip now.

– Just fuck off like, Deano. No need to be a cunt. I was just fucken telling yeh where I was.

Deano straightens up altogether.

– What the fuck, Karlo? I'm just joking. Come on, it's kinda ... I'm just having a laugh. You're telling me yeh were in The Pronto. Did everyone have their cocks out?

– No! What the fuck, Deano?

They nearly did though, that's the thing. Some of them.

– Yeah, look, sorry, buddy. What was it like?

Deano's saying the words but he still wants to laugh.

– It's for gaylords, right? And like, no problem there, Deano says holding his palms up. But why'd yeh take Tanya there.

– She took me. There were loads of girls there in anyway.

– Are yeh sure they were girls? Lezzers?

– I don't know. Just girls. Women. You're being a cunt, Deano.

He picks up the pace again.

– Wait! Tell me Tanya's not a lezzer? I'm gonna kill meself if that Tanya's a lezzer.

And he'd never thought about that. It just wasn't a thing. Tanya's Tanya. That's all.

– It's everyone's business if Tanya's a lezzer. Next you'll be telling me Candy's a lezzer. If Candy's a dyke, like, shit, Deano says.

– Candy's not a dyke! Why did I say this to yeh?

– Cos I'm yer mate, buddy.

– Don't say it to the rest. Can't listen to more of this bullshit. Anyone can go in like, to The Pronto.

– Who wanted to go in the first place, you or Tanya?

He hadn't expected an interrogation. Why the fuck did he even think this was a good idea? No one needed to know. He won't even bother telling him about the fella starting on him, acting the big lad, and Karl offering to settle it with a dance-off, which Karl won.

– So, *are* you a bender? Deano says quietly, almost whispering. Then:

– Bro, Hamza's da ...

Karl follows his gaze across the road outside Griffith Barracks. It is Hamza's da, right enough. Hands stuffed in pockets, long black hair flying behind him, stalking along, jeans hanging off him, grinning his face off. He stops when he meets two men in the full white gear, and pumps their arms up and down so vigorously it looks like he's going to reef them out of their shoulders altogether.

– Salam, he's shouting.

– Off his tits, Deano says, opening the package of Hunky Dorys he's been carrying and passing it to Karl.

– Yep.

Hamza's da lets the other two Muslim lads head on towards the mosque and he heads towards the flat, catches them looking and pauses, rubs his head, half waves and then walks on.

– Hope he's not heading home in that condition.

Hamza's da stops at a tree. It's getting dusky and he's smiling at the ground underneath the streetlight.

– The shadows of the tree, Karl says.

– Yeah, Deano says. He's marvelling.

He doesn't know how many times they've stopped to look at the shadow patterns of the trees on the pavements on the way home or the way out. Marvelling, Karl named it. Deano said it was the gayest thing ever but he was well into it the next time they were stoned and walking by. The shadow trees look like those Japanese paintings, or the Van Gogh one on the cover of the book beside the jacks in Oisín's house.

– Love Hamza's da, Karl says as they move off down the street.

– Yeah, betcha do, buddy. A fine-looking man for his age, Deano says, sticking out his tongue.

Karl jams his foot between Deano's ankles and he stumbles.

– Fuck off, Karl says.

– Yeah, you fuck off.

– Here, have you seen Snitchy about? Been texting him. Heard he has some of that Boss gear. Wanna get a few fresh threads for Boston.

– Nah. I've nuttin to do with fucken Snitchy. Thought you only bought the real deal in anyway?

– It is the real deal. From the ram-raid of the shop in town. Here, tell the rest of them about The Pronto and yer dead.

– Whatever, buddy, yeh big bender.

*

Whacker kept saying, 'I'll look after yiz, don't you worry boys, I'll look after yiz'.

But nobody knew what that meant when you're talking about helping out at an aul ones' football gig. When they were selling the Christmas trees, it meant fifty quid into your pocket at the end of it and all the rest to the Boston fund but this could mean anything. Word has it that Whacker and the rest of the aul fellas have paid the bulk of the Boston trip out of their own pockets and that they, especially Whacker, have to try to claw back a bit. Whacker's trying to keep it cheap – affordable, he always corrects – for most of the lads. Have a little bit of a pot for spends while we're over there. But how this gig is going to make any decent money is anyone's guess.

Ladies football. Like really. And not any ladies either. Aul ones. People's mas. Not Karl's ma, thank fuck, but other people's. It's dirt, ladies football. Total dirt.

Whacker and the rest decided to start this ladies craic locally, *'for seniors'*, he said with a wink. And he didn't mean normal seniors either, like adults. He meant old. Forties. Couldn't be trusted with hurls in their hands at this late stage in life, and them being Dubs mostly didn't help either – what would Dub women know about hurls apart from threatening to burst their kids with them – but they could manage football. So these *senior* ladies started playing down at the club but no one had ever seen them. Until today. So a Ladies Football Extravaganza *and* Strictly Come Dancing is what it said on the poster. A brochure'd been produced. He'd got Karl to do the cover art – eighteenth-century French woman obvs – and Whacker said he'd done a great fucken job, stick a fucking ball into it there would yeh for fuck's sake, Karl, I told yeh it was legend themed, where's Cú fucken Chulainn at all? – and then Whacker and the rest of the men and Oisín's ma had bought or got their friends to buy ads in it. Hamza considered advertising his Ritalin business in it, under another name, until he found out that it cost two hundred quid for a half-page and that no one would be reading it.

A load of the ones from up North start pouring off their coach. Mostly big hair, full faces of make-up, nail art – pretty impressive, in some cases – and is that a whiff of booze? At this hour. This is gonna be a classy operation. They say 'Well, wee mon' to Karl and ask where the changing rooms are.

Shockingly, a kind of tent marquee thing has been set up for them with showers an all. Showers! It might have made a real difference to Karl's commitment to the place if he hadn't had to piss up against the back wall for years, or if there'd been such a thing as a shower even mentioned.

– Would some of these ones be Protestants? Benit asks Whacker, staring as yet another bleached-blonde thing gets out of the bus, chewing gum.

Whacker looks at him weirdly.

– I know that one there looks like she might have a bit of a Proddy head on her Benit, but are yeh thick or what? Them Proddies stay away from this altogether. It'd stop them walking the Queen's Highway or some fucken thing.

– Okay, Benit says, and shakes his head. Not my ting, fam, religion.

Hamza's resurrected his hurling career and is busy over at the goals, huddled with a group of younger lads before they go up to the far training pitch. He high-fives a couple of them before slipping something in his tracksuits and zipping up.

Whacker's warming up by smashing a hurl into his shins and making sure not to wince. It must be years since he's actually seen his shins but if he ever does get to see them, they'll be hardy. Now Hamza's using Benit's penknife – the Snitchy special – to try to open a packet of bunting, but he slices himself.

– Go and get the magic water to pour over it, Benit, Karl says, grinning.

He's missed this. The smell of mud and grass and sweat and boots, and fellas laughing and crying and raging. And the magic water that's just water.

– Get up there and see what they're at, will yeh, Karl? says Whacker. We've a schedule to keep to.

The Dub women are already on one of the training pitches doing star jumps. They've no idea what they're letting themselves in for. They're the mammies of some of the nice kids.

Karl climbs the steps of the coach and catches them down the back, filling up their water bottles with vodka.

– No, no Sandy. Gin only for me. Mark my bottle there hai. I'll boke, so I will, if a drop of vodka passes my lips, I swear.

Sandy, the barwoman, it looks like, glances up at Karl but passes no remarks, keeps on pouring. She even has a funnel. Karl does a little cough and they all turn round. He expects them to hide what they're doing but no.

– It's only a bairn, carry on there, Sandy.

They all cackle.

– Em, looking to start the warm-up in a minute. So, yeh know, bring yizzer bottles with yiz, Karl says.

Can't believe this. Deano and his protein smokes doesn't come close to this lot.

The match kicks off, mams of kids from all over – the Tenters, Crumlin, Rialto, Drimnagh – all lining up, looking sober, against the Nordies, who're looking like they'll reef the tits offa any woman. And then the Dub aul ones don't know what hit them. They're doing all skillage – not much actual skillage, bar one who used to play for Dublin, dunno where she was drafted in from – playing football, keen on the rules. The others seem to know the rules but don't give a bollix about them.

They're eventually beating the shite out of each other. Some of the Nordies are beating the shite out of their own team. There's dragging out of ponytails and stamping on fingers. Karl and the lads are like a relay team over and back to the pitch with the magic water. One of the Dub mams already has a bloody nose by half-time, when the Dubs collapse on the pitch, shell-shocked, and Whacker goes over to give them a pep talk, lashing the hurl into his shins the whole time and going even more crimson. They start to sit up and the Nordies arrive back from the bus, surely refuelled. Whacker tells the ref to fuck off and hands him a fifty, and somehow Whacker's now the ref. Things start to go the Dubs' way. The Nordies lay off a bit after one gets sent off for punching a posh Dub mam in the back of the head. Only after the posh one had elbowed her in the face, bursting her lip but. One woman down, the whole thing rebalances and the Nordies start to behave. No one seems to be keeping score but the best estimate, calculated by Benit and Hamza, is Nordies 4-16 and Dubs 0-18. Miraculously, everyone's happy with that and they all bail into the changing rooms together.

*

The Malt House is already rammed when Karl gets there. Probably the first big crowd it's had since it opened a few months ago, because no one round here wants to go into a place like this. No carpet, just bleached floorboards and big white lamps with light shades made out of bottles. Karl likes it but. It's got that duck-egg blue on the walls and separate hand towels, like facecloths, for each person.

The jacks are unisex, so there's no urinal and the Nordie women club together with the Dubs and refuse to use them. The staff jacks are made available. In fairness, Karl doesn't want to go for a shite next to some women. On the other hand, he woulda liked to see what women get up to in the jacks. Not the fanny stuff, the other stuff.

There's a small stage area with a neon sign that says SHOWTIME over it. Hipsterish. Goes with the craft beers. Karl's tried them when he was out with Tanya. Rotten. He'll try another one here. They refuse to sell Guinness even, so he's going to have to.

The band arrives. They're priests. Priests, like! Where do they find these lads? The holy boys head out to the curtained-off, back-stage area, where Karl and Benit had been ordered to leave wine and crackers spread out nicely on a plate. Makes sense, them being priests.

Whacker comes in all chuffed with himself.

– Great game! Great game, altogether, he says, rubbing his hands together.

It's Whacker speech time.

– This is a new era for the club. We're going from strength to strength. That's what it's about. Going from strength to strength. Bringing the community together. From nippers to the size of you ladies, he says winking at them.

Some of them frown and some of them say 'woo' and one of them wolf-whistles and shouts out, get them off yeh! Whacker, scarlet, wipes his forehead with a curry sauce-covered napkin and licks his lips.

– Now we've our camogie teams and they all do very well but we haven't had football for the mammies before at the club. It's all men at this age and we could do with a bit of eye candy round the place, he says, with his widest smile.

– We're not eye candy, one of the Nordies, who's got a pair of knickers on her head, shouts up at him.

– No, we're not! a Dub one says.

– Oh you are, ladies! You are!

– What the hell? a manly-looking one roars up. We're feminists, we do not subscribe to your patriarchal norms of female beauty.

She's pulled, laughing, back into her seat to the sound of a hundred howler monkeys getting their freak on.

– *Tiocfaidh ár lá, a mhná!* another one them shouts.

You'd think they'd take the compliment. They can't be getting many. The band starts up. Whacker slides up beside him.

– Going well, our Karlo, going well. Watch out now when these boys get going, the women'll be a bit wild, he says, rubbing his hands together.

– Hardly, with the priests.

– What? What priests? Whacker says.

– The ones on stage? Karlo says.

– Yeh what? They're not priests, Whacker says.

– Are they not the telly priest band off the *Late Late*? Karl says.

– No, they just dress like priests.

– Why?

– Sure, how would I know? For the craic, like, Whacker says. Sure the drummer's Jordan Kenny from Drimnagh, the lad who robbed the AIB, 'member? Great centre forward.

And then it's all this eighties shit. 'Uptown Girl' and 'Addicted to Love'. 'Girls Just Wanna Have Fun' has them all up dancing and then they keep demanding it over and over. The priests put the foot down after the fifth rendition and the women aren't happy. They try some 'Final Countdown' and all that but they keep roaring for Cyndi Lauper. But they shut up and do all the actions for 'YMCA', and then drop to the floor for 'Rock the Boat'. Karl's a dab hand at 'YMCA' and 'Rock the Boat' from all the family weddings.

And he suddenly realizes that it's Candy behind him, rowing back and forward, laughing her head off. Now that's unexpected. He looks for Hamza and there he is, holding a pint, laughing and shaking his head when she keeps beckoning him to join in.

– Come on Karlo, she says as he pulls him up from the floor at the end. We'll get a drink. What are yeh having? Don't answer. Shots.

For a crazy person, she's kinda decent. She stands out here. Even without the scarlet hair. Swarthy, she is, as his mam would say. He puts his back against the bar, watching Oisín and Deano arm-wrestling with Benit's thigh as a table.

When he turns back she's got a row of shots, lemon slices and a salt cellar lined up on the soaking wet bar for the two of them. The last time Karl did tequila, he sprayed the walls of the Tivoli and got fucked out on the street. They *sláinte* and throw back the first one. She looks over her shoulder towards the lads, still in the middle of the competition.

– Deano's enjoying himself.

– Suppose.

– Is he like your best mate? Of all of them, I mean.

– That's a bit *serious*, he says and he bites down on the lemon.

– Just asking, yeh know. Hamo talks about him a lot. Just wondering about the dynamic. Is he still bunking off?

What the hell has Hamo been saying to her?

– You some kinda social worker, Candy?

She laughs and throws another one down her throat. He turns back towards the lads. Oisín's on Deano's back using his fingers as horns, the pair of them rushing at Sandy who's flapping her red coat at them, with a crowd cheering them on.

– Would he be into bad shit? Like not just messing about. Bad people.

She can talk. Jaysus Christ, if he'd known this'd be the way, he'd have said no to the tequila. He hadn't noticed how pissed she was.

– What's this about, Candy?

– Wino.

She's direct, he'll give her that. Still, gotta stay sketch. You never know who you're talking to.

– Deano'd never have anything to do with Wino. I know Wino and yer ma are friends an all ...

She's not looking at him now. She stretches her arms out on the bar and looks up at the scenes behind them reflected in the mirror above the fancy bottles of whiskey. Her voice lowers and he has to lean in to hear her above the '*olés*' from the floor.

– Yeah Wino and me mam, she says and she smiles. And Wino and Deano. I asked him to leave him alone, you know? And I think he will. He says he will.

She must've been on them funeral tablets again.

– Jack, you know he was like you, Karl? He told me.

– Maybe ease up on those shots, yeah, Candy?

He scouts for signs of Hamza, catches his eye as he's on matador duty now and nods to him to come over. He's all for minding people when they need it but this too much for him, whatever she's on about. She grabs his arm and straightens herself, smiling at Hamza as he stalks over, grinning.

– He was. You don't let them hassle you about it, yeah, Karl? Don't say anything to Hamo, right? About Deano. I just don't want anyone getting hurt, that's all.

She sounds actually nervous. She looks straight at him, like she wants to say something that he seriously doesn't want to hear.

17
OISÍN

It's misty, not quite foggy, out through the plane window on the approach into Dublin. Patches of Ballymun through the clouds, dropping, dropping, it's way greener than you'd think when you're down on the streets. The lurch in his belly and the ringing in his ears isn't just from the altitude, he's pretty sure.

They'd all got the news at the same time.

Before the flight, Logan airport, hungover and knackered, laughing and messing about the cool shit that happened in Boston. Then phones beeping all over the gaff. And Karl's face pale. Even paler than usual. Whacker went quiet for once.

A head in the canal.

He's dreading switching his phone back on. It wasn't just the horror show hangover that had him on his knees in the jacks back at Logan, sweating his way through the three hour delay. The storm of messages from the lads back home fucked everything up. He said nothing to Deano, but he knows they're both thinking the same thing.

It could be anyone's head, of course. Doesn't *have* to be Snitchy's. Anyone at all. It's not the first bit of a body the canal's ever seen, like. But there'd been no sight nor sound of Snitchy after getting him out of the house. And Benit had ordered a spanner set off him but hadn't heard from Snitchy at all since.

You've gotta be cool about these things. His mom was playing it cool in her one message before they took off – no mention of the head, all about picking him up and when and where. Deano still hasn't really looked him straight in the eye since the messages started. The head wasn't the first bit they'd found it turned out. No, bits of a body in a burning skip. That was first. Mightn't even be the same fella. Mightn't even be a fella sure.

Deano, beside him, lifts and stretches the legs. His eyes are closed but he's not asleep. Wouldn't be a surprise if he'd been awake the whole way through the night. They'd rock-paper-scissored for the window seat. Then thumb-warred, then arm-wrestled. Oisín hadn't won but Deano said he didn't give a shite if Oisín was that much of a pussy that he had to have the window seat.

It's better to be able to at least see the ground or the sea, or whatever, rushing up to meet you, if you're going down. There's nothing worse than being about to die and not having a clue. You'd want to know, Oisín'd want to know.

Ruairí knew. He brought Mom out three separate times to the shed to show her where her birthday present was hidden. She wasn't to look at it until the birthday the following week, but he kept bringing her out to make sure she was sure of where it was. He told Oisín but that wasn't enough. She had to know. Thursday afternoon, that was the last time he showed her where it was, the model Spitfire he'd built for her with her name painted in hot pink and green – her favourite colours – down one side. Right before she sent him out for the washing powder. He'd got very good at the calligraphy and he was just showing off. She spent the birthday in Crumlin hospital with

Ruairí and his huge purple-and-red head. She broke the wing off the plane one night when she rolled over on it on the sofa and Oisín never saw it again after that.

The wheels bounce one, two, three times and everyone claps when they stay on the ground. That's the dangerous time, take-off and landing. The rest of the time, up in the air, you're just bouncing around.

She donated his organs. Ruairí had the best of organs, with all the homemade smoothies and the winter supplements. You didn't give his eyes, tell me you didn't give anyone else his eyes? Oisín had said. What was he on about? What did it matter? Seemed important at the time. That was the difference between them. Everyone thought they were identical, but they weren't. Oisín had his greeny eyes, same as his mom, but Ruairí's were brown. Big moo cow, brown ones. She never answered the question about his eyes. He still doesn't know. Maybe he took the eyes with him for seeing in the dark. Funny, no one's ever asked him, even Hamza with all his questions and his djinning, no one's ever asked what colour the night-time fella's eyes are.

Deano yawns, avoids looking at Oisín.

– Well, another one yeh didn't hijack, thank fuck, Deano says to Hamza across the aisle.

Hamza, flicking through the *Cara* magazine, bares his upper teeth, shakes his head and says:

– Do you think I'm thick? I'm not going down with you lot. You infidels will die without me.

If ever there was a person who would not, under any circumstances, blow up a planeload of people, it's Hamza. It'd be a bad use of resources and it's always bad PR, as he says. No one likes a man who blows up randomers.

He'd gone off into a corner on his own back at the airport in Boston when Candy started messaging him. Sure she was on about the head too. He called her. Oisín knew it was her even though he couldn't hear Hamo way over there. You can always tell when he's talking to her or even thinking about her. Always. 'She's a good one', is all he says about her though. 'She's a good one, Ois.'

*

Standing in the queue for the bus, they're all shivering. It couldn't have been that much warmer in Boston, could it? He texts his mam: OMW. She's staying at home to see him before she heads to the café. Proper order. He's betting on a fry.

The bus ride's a laugh, some of the hurling culchies start the singing again, they never give up, those lads. The whole way into town it goes on and he finds himself joining in – takes his mind off it. Tourists on the bus look thrilled and they cheer and stomp their feet in appreciation. Some of them – Italians maybe, middle-aged, manbags, colourful trousers – even join in with 'The Wild Rover'. No nay nevering and clapping hands above their heads. Probably rugby fans who got a singing education on their last trip over.

By the time they hit town, there's talk of the guards having ID'd the chopped-up fella. They couldn't have, surely? Not that quick. Lads on the bus are saying he's local, from round the area. How they're getting this kind of info, no one knows. By the time they pull up at the Bleeding Horse, the word is that it's two aul fellas, Russians. Sure.

Lifts are offered by Whacker and other coaches and das, but the five of them bail into his mam's car, pulled up on double yellows. It's really good to see her, even if she has those puffy bags under her eyes. A second bottle was had last night.

After they've dropped off Benit, Hamza and Karl, and it's just the three of them left in the car, she says:

– All phones off? Put them out there where I can see them.

Oisín asks why, but Deano, still silent, just takes his out, shows her he's switching it off, and passes it in to Oisín in the front.

– Right, this is likely that young fella that was in the house. I haven't had any contact with the family but it probably is him, she says.

When it's said, when it's out floating in the air, it's even worse than when it was inside and just a thought that you kept pushing down further into your body, away from the front of your head, away from your mouth. It takes a lot of energy to ignore a big thing, but it's not so easy to deal with it out in the open either. This is fucked.

– Do we go to the guards now then? Oisín says.

– No, Deano says, eyes still firmly fixed on the scenery of the south inner city.

He doesn't want to go the guards either, he wants to wash his brain out with Jeyes Fluid but what the fuck are they supposed to do? His mom is going to want to go, of course she is.

– I agree, his mam says. We don't know yet. They'll identify whoever the poor fella is soon enough. Then we'll have a re-think. The most important thing is that you say nothing to no one. Not even the other lads. You haven't told them about the other night, have you?

They normally would've done. Oisín doesn't even know why they haven't. Not as if the others would spill, but still. Himself and Deano hadn't even said anything to each other, even before the head.

– We haven't talked, Deano says. We're not stupid. Mightn't be him in anyway.

Who the fuck else will it be? Fucken poor cunt Snitchy and all his big-man talk and all. Fuck!

– Do you want to come in for some food before you head home, Deano? I've Superquinn sausages and the hummus you like? Or do you want to just get to your bed?

– Thanks, but June's got the fry on too.

She wheels around by the flats. Deano sits and makes no move to get out. Kids in bodywarmers and tracksuits fly past on other people's bikes, women walk empty buggies through the complex – babies left for the few hours at the Mercy Family Centre, best crèche in the world.

– Deano, are you alright? she says, reaching for his arm between the seats.

He sighs the biggest sigh Oisín's ever heard out of him.

– Just tired, just really tired, Deano says, and his voice breaks and he's definitely starting to cry. Oisín hasn't seen or heard Deano crack at all since his dad's funeral.

– I know the pair of you knew him, she says. Don't tell me anything about the poor kid. We can do nothing for him now.

– That's cold, Oisín says.

This is not the way things should be. His mother should not be saying this stuff. None of this is right.

– Oisín! she shouts. Do you fucking realize what we're dealing with here? Do you? Now, we're going to stay quiet and see what happens. The only people that know he was in our house, in *my* fucking house, are us, Pearl and his family. Let's keep it that way until we see what happens. You are the only one who saw those men outside and you need to stay quiet for now.

– Would you be saying that if it was me in the canal, would you? Oisín says.

She speaks through gritted teeth, staring straight over the steering wheel.

– I am trying to make sure that it isn't.

– I'm heading up, Deano mutters.

– Right, go on so, Deano. Let us know if you hear anything and we'll do the same. Come down though, don't text.

Fucking criminal mastermind, all of a sudden.

She turns the car and says:

– We're just going to get home, you have a shower while I'm making the food and then you get to bed.

– Like I can sleep!

– We won't talk about it, Oisín. Leave it till we know more.

Walking in the door, her hand shakes a bit, struggling with the key. Fuck, just close it and keep all this outside. She gives him his phone back but he doesn't switch it back on. Not now, not now. He'd like to throw it in the bin.

Standing in the shower, he blasts the cold onto his back and doesn't shiver, forces himself to not shiver, overcomes the shiver. Take the pain, freeze the pain, breathe. Wim Hof would know how to handle this. Wim Hof handles everything. The shake in her hand, just a millisecond, so slight maybe it was just his knackered eyes playing tricks on him … Her coldness in a crisis gives you confidence. But her hands don't shake.

Ruairí going took it out of her but she eventually got back to normal. There's the wine, that helps, she thinks, but it doesn't really. Other than that, she's like a robot when she needs to be.

His granda told him about when she was six, and the two of them having to crawl down the street and into a shop to get away from the gunfire criss-crossing the street in Armagh, the Brits like. The thundering bastard in the shop told them to mind the display of socks as they fell in the door, his granda said. She didn't cry or even let a murmur out of her the whole way down the street, sometimes on her hunkers, sometimes on her belly, with Granda trying to cover her. Only that shop fool's stern face and the angry glint in his eye after she knocked a couple of the sock hangers off as she rolled under the display, made the tears come. 'Isn't that a holy terror, the fucken socks, would yeh credit it, gossun?'

She's the way she is for a reason. The counselling, weird and all as it is, has taught him that much.

The smell of sausages wafts into the bathroom. You can't beat it, even when he tried being vegetarian that day, he couldn't resist the smell of sausies. There's a knock on the door as his foot hits the bottom step on his way to the kitchen. Another weirdly shaped delivery for the neighbours, no doubt. He pulls the towel off his head – no need to look gay in front of the delivery man.

Deano, eyes hanging out of his head, is leaning against the wall, holding his chest.

– Not Snitchy … In the canal. *Titch.*

18
BENIT

He wakes up crashed on the sofa, never made it up the stairs after wolfing the muamba nsusu she'd left him.

The place is deathly quiet but, for once, he wishes it wasn't. He'd planned to unpack when he got in – likes to be organized in both directions, packing and unpacking – but a crushing knackeredness had come over him, out of nowhere.

The messages came through while he was sleeping: It's Titch. It's Titch. Fuck. That's a surprise. Harmless, smiling, thick as a brick. A kid acting the scumbag, but head in the canal? Nah, fam, nah. There's a thing about cutting off someone's head. It's worse than other things.

He watched a couple of those beheading videos, that journalist, and others. They don't sharpen their knives, that's what it looks like. There's screams and then the screams stop. Vocal cords cut. People like to be facing away from their beheader, if it's a planned thing. ISIS or whoever don't give you a choice. But himself and Oisín had got well into beheading research for a while. Always face the blade. Over before you know it. The way to survive or, if you've no chance of surviving, the way to make things as good as they can be, in any situation, is to plan ahead. Then you're confident, you're ready, and if you don't make it, just before you don't make it, you can relax, you know you've done all you could.

Maybe he was already dead when they hacked it off. Hopefully. He would've screamed if he was alive. Benit shoves that away. He's heard Titch screaming and squealing when he was having a mess knock with Snitchy or whoever.

And where the hell is Snitchy? He sends him another message about those spanners he's supposed to be sourcing for him, doesn't mention Titch. Just a whatsup.

Titch's big smiley head. It's the ultimate disrespect, taking someone's head. All your thoughts and your spirit are cut off from your body. He sits up properly and scratches the crusty drool from his cheek. That's why headless horsemen. They keep coming back looking for their heads. There's bits of your spirit everywhere else but it's mostly in the head.

The front door clicks quietly. Judging from the gentle creep, it's Owen. He closes his eyes, not ready to have the chats, senses him hovering over him, checking him out. Owen tiptoes out to the kitchen. Decent. Ah here, this isn't fair. Benit performs a big yawn and stretches and Owen lands back in, smiling and anxious.

– I didn't mean to wake you, I've the kettle on.

He has a fetish for tea. Leaves half-drunk cups, milk curdling on top, on every available surface. Better than having him on the drink as the women always say. True that.

– Well? How was it? Owen asks, acting furtive.

So Owen knows about Titch, or at least about the head. Why wouldn't he? Benit's brain is slowing down. Like always, when he's exhausted. His eyes are foggy. Owen's blurry around his edges as he moves about picking up hoodies, gathering up his dirty mugs, putting some shape on the place, as he says himself.

– Terrible thing about that young fella. Did yeh know him, Benit? From the flats, me da would've known his family. Not bad people. Did yeh know him?

Owen's staying-calm voice is choking him.

– Nah. He was at school. Think he left a while ago. You'd see him around but I didn't know him.

Owen straightens and heads back out to sort the food. No need to make it worse for him and in fairness, it's not really as if Benit *did* know Titch. Not really. It's mad, Owen's da, Len, was a king, a giant with a big laugh and big belly, even right to the end when he collapsed with a stroke and never really woke up properly. He stood up to the pushers in the '80s. Benit heard all this second-hand, of course, and not from Owen either. Owen's da had set up a rota with other men in the area watching a couple of the Dunne family houses, reporting every movement in and out of the house. The guards didn't have the time or so the story goes. Len, Grandad – 'Sure isn't yer mammy part of the family now, that makes me yer granda, if yeh like, son' – played it all down when he was talking to Benit, but Benit's always kinda known that Len was involved in more than quietly watching houses. There was lashing shams off balconies and giving scumbags a hiding when they wouldn't see reason. Sounded like Congo. Lately, Benit's been thinking about that, Len and his mates. He gets it, you do what you have to do but what about the fellas who're just junkies themselves? Selling's the least worst option for getting the cash. But then, sometimes there's no time for sitting around weighing up the ethics of everything and everyone's actions. Sometimes you've just gotta do shit. And maybe that's half of Owen's problem – Owen's not like Len.

Len was a total hero in the area but he told Benit not to mind whoever was waffling on about those days, that what-ever he did wasn't a big deal. Eight kids he had, he said, and

275

he didn't want a single one of them on the gear. Too many in the grave too young because of it. He only did what any father should do to protect his family and the kids in the area. And then he continued afterwards, long after all the junkies were on methadone, calling community meetings, raging about the young fellas getting bullets in the back of the head, fronting up to the boss men. And no one touched him in all that time. That's a real man.

Owen rattles in with a plate piled high with eggs, rashers and toast.

– I know yeh prefer yer mam's but here yeh go, welcome home.

This grub is the business. Benit looks over at Owen who's settling into the armchair opposite, steaming mug in one hand, slice of buttery toast in the other.

– So, how are yeh really, Benit, with all this with the young fella getting done like that? Bit of a shock, isn't it?

Owen's alright.

*

– What's up with yeh? Is it just all this with Titch? Benit asks and passes the blunt to Oisín who taps it out the bedroom window and finally lets go of his own smoke.

He always holds onto it for so long. All that breathing training his mum gave him. What a hippy.

– Nothing much. The usual pressures, bro. Yeh know yerself. Life, love, the universe, Oisín says taking another wheeze.

His mum's downstairs and how she hasn't got a whiff yet is anyone's guess.

– Gonna change your CAO choices soon, fam?

– Yeah, Benit, I am cos, yeh know, I'm not sure I want to dedicate myself to medical science.

– Fair enough, fam. I'm sticking with mine.

– Well, you were always bound to be a doc, amirite?

– Got it in one. Do you think he was dead before they cut off his head? Benit says.

– Now's not the time, bro. Not while we're smoking.

Oisín pulls himself in off the windowsill and sinks back onto the bed. The black on the walls is kinda cool now that Benit's looking at it. Still, probably not the best idea for Ois. Benit rolls backwards off the bed and onto the sheepskin rug.

– I think I'm gonna take a break from the green. Need to get in touch with myself, Benit says.

– Oh yeah? You not been touching yourself enough, bro?

– My higher self, you know?

– Nah. That's a bit weird. Do you want the end of this? Oisín asks.

– Yeah, one last blast before I find God, fam. Ima find my soul, you know? You need a clear head for that.

– I'm feeling quite close to Jesus right now, bro, Oisín says.

– Where'd you get this stuff? It's blowing the top off my head. Really like …

– Skate park, Elmond gets it. Dunno how. From the States. All these American strains. Ultimate Trainwreck, sativa heavy.

– Ah man, I think I'm getting a … I am … nah it's …

– Yeah.

Benit rolls about on the floor. The carpet's so squishy. New. Oisín's mam got it put down while they were away. The old one was manky with mud marks from boots walked up the stairs even though shoes are banned in the house once you come in the front door. The only white house he's been in where this happens. It's a filthy habit, wearing your outdoor shoes inside.

Oisín's just smiling off into the distance.

– Think I'll take a piss, refresh myself, Oisín says, but doesn't move.

– I know there's something more going on. I feel it now because of this stiff.

– You getting a stiffy for me? You're not my flavour, bro, Oisín says.

– The djinn. You're seeing it since we got back. Know you are.

He knows it, he knows it. He feels it. Oh yes. It's there. The djinn is back. What's that? The spirit world calling. The walls are kinda moving. He's had too much.

– This feels a bit shroomy, Oisín says. Yeah, I'm seeing the djinn since we got back. But no. But yeah.

Oisín's doing that sniffing thing that he does when he's uncomfortable. Like a nervous tick. Like he's been on the bag. Which he never is after he tried it once and it turned him into a wanker. He shouldn't be uncomfortable when he's stoned though. Benit can smell it. There's something more than grass in the air.

– It's Titch. I'm sure there's something wrong with you about Titch. It's OK if you don't wanna say, fam, but I know, I'm feeling it in here.

Tapping his third eye.

– Intuition, baby.

– The thing at night, it changed. He's Ruairí like, as usual. Why haven't you ever asked me what colour his eyes are?

He leaps up and starts pacing, but in a bouncy, happy way, swinging his arms.

– I'm just getting the energy out, bro. He turned round to me, he was standing at the end of the bed last night. He used to always be sitting, but now he stands. And he's lit up and the rest of the room is dark, I can see everything is the same as it was when I went to sleep, but it's all shadowy-grey, like things normally are in the dark, and like, he's illuminated, like he's backlit or you know, the light is in him …

– Like the Buddha.

Oisín stops mid-flow and considers.

– Why would the Buddha be lit up though?

– Dunno, fam, cos he's God, innit? Benit says.

– Nah, he's not. He's just a fella who fucked off on his wife and kid and sat under a tree for ages. And ate all the foodstuffs, by the looks of him. Lazy cunt obviously had people bringing him shit. *Om shanti.*

– *Shanti, shanti.*

– He's smiling, the djinn fella, like he always is, but this time, this time he nods, nods. Just like that, down at his hands, and one of his hands is bunched up, like in a loose fist but with his knuckles up, you know what I mean, like this, and so his nails aren't up …

– I feel you, fam, I feel you, like this, Benit says, and demonstrates.

– That's exactly it, *how* did you know, Benit? How did you know?

Oisín's face must be sore from that grinning because Benit knows his own is. Oisín's got tears in his eyes but they're laughing tears. This stuff is unreal. Rapper grade.

– And he turned his hand over like this, and he did this before, he showed me this before … and there's this thing in the middle of his hand …

– Ah fuck nah, an *eyeball*? Benit says, curling into his shell, covering his head with arms.

– What? No, not an eyeball, what? Nah, it was like a piece of material …

– Shit?

– No, material! Fabric. Well, like woolly, woven stuff. Like coloured. Like that thing Mom gave Karl that time, only smaller. He did this before. Showed me the patch. And it's unravelling at one corner, like a couple of threads have come loose … but this time, wait, this time … he squeezes the threads … he squeezes them together and then he lets go and the patch is all fine. It's fixed, you know? Fixed.

– Is this just a dream? Wait, are you making this up?

Oisín's sitting back doing the Wall Chair pose beside his bookshelf. So many books. Encyclopedias. Who even reads them? Not Oisín. Years and years of Guinness World Records books.

– Do you say Guinnesses Books of Records or Guinness Book of Records, no that's only one, or Guinness Books of Records? That's the one, isn't it? Benit says.

– Like a wool patch but with small blocks of colour in it.

Oisín's looking a bit wild now. Those curls are still at the awkward stage. Like he won't ever have a fro but he's getting woolly.

– You're like a sheep bro, more than a brother.

– The hair? Yeah, but I am a bit of a brother. Like I'm cool. That's how I roll.

– Cursed with a black man's penis, yeah?

– Yeah. I've me flute tucked into me shoe.

– You're not wearing shoes, fam. Helen's rules.

Things are returning to more stable ground. No, there goes the rollercoaster belly again.

– These black walls are maybe not a good thing, fam. They're soaking up your energy. Stealing your vibe.

– I know. I know. But there's depth, you know? Depth in blackness. You know, if you eat lion's mane mushrooms, you don't get dementia? Oisín says.

– Deep colours? Like rich? Benit says. Dark blue bro, that'd be better.

Oisín nods, eyes wild again.

– He was here.

– Who?

– Snitchy.

Ah no! He's seeing Snitchy now.

– Nah man, you're just too stoned is all, Benit says.

– In this house. He was here, just before we went Boston.

This isn't good. Saying these mental things. Snitchy shouldn't be in Oisín's house. Maybe Snitchy's always in Oisín's house. Maybe Benit just doesn't know this. Maybe he's downstairs with Helen right now.

– Is he … is he here now? Benit whispers. Cos I've been texting him and I'm not getting no feedback from him. Like he's missing.

– Yeah, he's missing. He was here. You can't say it to the boys.

– Why not? It's just Snitchy.

– Cos he's missing, Benit. Titch's head's in the canal …

– Nah, it's not. Like, they don't just leave it there …

– Benit, focus, yeah? I'm telling you something. Snitchy was with Titch that night, Titch is in bits, Snitchy's gone. But he was here that night. We had to help him out.

Benit jumps. His heart literally jumps in his chest. It's pounding on his ribcage. What night? He goes to stand up but has to stretch back on the floor again.

– Gonna have to explain, fam. I'm not liking what I'm hearing. Does Helen know? Who knows?

– Yeah, she was here. No one else. Except Deano.

Deano knows. What the hell? This mightn't be happening at all. He closes his eyes and opens them again. This is like that time. What time was it? He jumps again at a bang from downstairs.

– What was that?

– Just Mom closing the back door. You're getting paro. Just stay cool, breathe. You know what to do. He was here and then we got him away and now Helen wants to …

– Why are you calling your mum Helen?

– Not the point. She wants to, you know, keep it quiet. And I get it, I am keeping it quiet. Like, I don't want to be in the canal either but do you say nothing? You're a good egg. What do you think?

– You just told me. And now I know too, Benit says.

Oisín's eyes widen, as far as blood-red eyes can widen in these circumstances. He's a pretty boy but he looks old, like an old man's face is on top of his. This was fun but now, not so much.

– You're feeling worried by this. We need to just stop about this right now and wait and talk about it with the boys.

– No.

– That's you, me and Deano and your mum who know.

– And yer one next door.

Too much. Maybe Oisín is making this up. The one with the feathers and the hats next door like. How does that even happen?

– And Snitchy's mam, of course, forgot about her. And whoever she told.

– What the fuck? Put on some Bob there. We need some Jah.

He rolls onto his back and covers his eyes.

– I've got to think about what you're laying on me here. This is major.

*

This is what you call a proper dilemma. An ethical question. You've got to think carefully.

On the one hand there's Titch, who never, as far as Benit knows, did anything *proper* bad to anyone. Harmless. But now in bits in a plastic bag, but, like Oisín says, he's gone. There's nothing to be done for him. That's just the truth.

Then there's Snitchy, who's probably in bits somewhere too but just hasn't been found yet. But what if he's just stuck somewhere? What if he hasn't been done yet? He could be saved.

Nah, no chance, people don't just disappear without a reason.

Marty hands him the mug of Bovril.

– So this friend …

– Nah, Marty, I'm only saying he's a friend, I'm just asking like a hypothetical thing, you know? He's not a friend. I'm asking for a friend, who has this friend, yeah?

– So this not friend, just a fella, like the fella says, knows about someone who's maybe in a spot of bother and this fella's friend has already definitely been in a spot of bother and maybe the two are related? Have I got that right?

– Sort of, yeah.

Marty gets up and potters over to the bookshelf. He's either lost his train of thought or he thinks he has a reference book for just this situation.

– Where in the name of all that's good and holy is that feck of a thing? Marty mutters, and heads down the hall to the bedroom.

Benit can see how people lose their minds over this kinda thing. He can't get over Oisín's mum though, staying completely quiet on it. Everyone staying quiet. Snitchy's fam included. Why isn't he even being mentioned on the news? Like all the grown-ups are in on it and Snitchy and Titch are just pawns.

– I found it. Now, this, this is yer only man in this current situation, which, if I'm honest, I don't fully understand.

He holds out a bulky, grey book.

– The I Ching. Do whatever it says in that book. Ask it a question. Has to be specific. Throw up the coins …

A fresh hell in every moment.

– Thanks, Marty. I'm kinda asking your advice, what you think this fella should do.

– And I'm telling you that I probably don't want to know the details, and that without them details I can't give you a right answer. But this yoke probably will. Because it's all in there, in your head. In your gut.

Marty sinks back into the green velvet armchair and flips up the footrest. The movement seems to waft the smell of him into the air – lemons, mothballs and, ah no, a hint of piss. He'd noticed a small dark patch on the crotch of Marty's pale-blue canvas trousers the other day, but when he'd said it to Marty, he'd ranted about that feckin cat spraying on his tulips and him spilling his tea on himself trying to grab for the water pistol.

He's obviously not going to give him an answer. So that leaves him in the shitter.

Marty peers at him over the rim of the cup.

– That friend of yours has a problem. He needs to assess who's the bigger enemy, who's going to do the most damage, d'yeh get me, Benit? And there's not just damage to the flesh and bones, a dead man feels no pain, there's damage in here and here.

He points to his head and heart.

– And that kinda damage is harder to fix. That goes on for a lifetime.

19
DEANO

Known to gardaí. Here's what he was wearing. How did he afford these things? No angel. No angel, alright.

The whole place turns out for Titch's funeral. All five of them stand at the back outside. Deano looks up at the clear blue sky. Nearly a day for shorts. Titch was a great man for the shorts. Summer and winter. He had that extra bit of blubber on him, baby fat.

Young fellas, all kinds, Peaky haircuts, tracksuits, Boss and North Face, Colmcille's grey, Jamebo blue. In gangs, ones and twos, mingling with the aul ones, the aul fellas. Flats girls, arms linked, grim faces. For show or for real, they've showed up for Titch.

There could be room inside but their place, the five of them, is out here. Out here with the boys. In the air. Deano lifts his nose high and drags in as much of it as he can.

The guards hang back, uniforms and detectives. Probably a load of them inside. If he never sees the inside of a church again, that'd be dandy by him. Another box, another young fella. No open coffin. He hopes they put Titch back together as well as they could. You've got to put a fella back together, don't yeh? His teeth grind and his jaw hurts. Sadie and the rest were in bits, going in. June was hunched over the sink, shaking, this morning when he caught her. He said nothing. Just backed out. A woman needs her privacy. She'd only be embarrassed.

He glances over at guards standing in the middle of Donore Avenue, arms folded, watching the crowd spilling out the gates and up the street. The thud-thud of the helicopter can be heard in the distance, and it's coming, coming, and it's over Cork Street, and it moves overhead and then hovers somewhere down over Blackpitts, and a hiss rises from the crowd. Hard to judge in this case. Hiss at their ignorance chopping the air over Titch's funeral or just concentrate on the fella in the box, have a bitta respect for him or something.

Nah, this is just too much. He's joined in with this shit before but June says that you've gotta think of what they're facing sometimes, the Garda. That they had to deal with whatever was in that bag floating down the canal and whatever bits of him were in the skip. Deano's seen worse and that didn't make him a cunt. But the line has been crossed. The no-go line. You can't, you just can't. But Titch wasn't even a bad young fella. Even Snitchy wasn't, isn't, that bad. But the line … the hissing is turning into more of a growl. Yeh don't talk to the cunts. What if they're the only thing between you being you and you being a head in the canal but? Oisín and himself haven't said a word about it since the day but these things don't need to be said. He's gone about normal, even went into school. Left early, but still.

Holy fuck, there she is, feckin turban headscarf on her, staring over at him, waiting. He nods. She deserves a nod.

– Three o'clock, don't look. Is that yer ma? Karlo whispers over his shoulder.

– No.

– She's lookin well.

Lookin well. She's wearing a fucken turban.

– Not her.

– Ah yeah, yer right. Yer ma's smaller than that one.

Good man, Karlo. Deano can feel her trying to catch his eye. Begging for him to just look over at her again. He studies the carvings over the door. Oisín's mam told them that the church door is a big vagina. So that was interesting. You'd want a hefty flute on yeh to scutter the fanny off that.

He glances over and suddenly June's beside her, standing looking over at him. She smiles. His ma looks more relaxed. She better not be trying to get her feet under June's table. She adjusts the turban scarf – probably gone full Sinéad O'Connor or something – and her flouncy sleeve slips down and there it is, the watch he got her in Boston. She sees him staring and turns her wrist a couple of times, letting it catch the light.

Days like these, springy, blue-sky days like these always make you think of summer. Give you hope, false hope, mostly, but it always feels like a big summer is on its way.

– Go Lion's Head soon as? Deano says to Oisín, standing at his shoulder.

Oisín tries a yeah, but it gets caught. Deano stares straight ahead. A man needs privacy if he's coming over all pussy. Oisín coughs it out.

– Warm enough to go today.

– Not today.

– Nah, guess not. Yer mam's over there with June.

No point in continuing with this.

– Yeah, so?

– She *is* looking well, Karlo chips in. That get-up suits ...

– Don't need the fashion commentary just now, Karlo, thanks, Deano says.

So what if yer ma rocks up outta the blue? So what if she looks like a fucking Sikh hippy skanger? It's not the worst thing that can happen yeh.

You'd wonder did they hack any bits offa him before he was dead. A bullet in the back of the head, they say, is quick. But time slows down when bad shit is happening. That time he went over the handlebars when Oisín was giving him a cross-bar, sailing through the air – on a day just like this, maybe a bit warmer – and every bit of that full somersault is printed on his brain.

The priest keeps droning on over the speaker. The tiredness creeps over him. His ma now has one of June's kids in her arms and she's talking into her face, smiling, happy. Her eyes dart about, still looking to catch his eye. Are yeh watching me? Are yeh, Deano? See, I'm a proper human again? They're all proper humans. No one better or worse. Maybe some are better, like June or the boys, but everyone has a bitta worse in them and the worse can get bigger depending.

– You alright, fam? Benit says. You look like shit.

Like a shit on a swing, as June said to him that morning.

And then he sees it, in Benit's face. He *knows*. Oisín's been talking and Benit fucking *knows*. And that's it broadcast everywhere, Benit can't keep a lid on anything. And that's them in plastic bags like Titch. Deano turns round to Oisín.

– Yeah? he says, tipping his head towards Benit. Nice one, Oisín.

Oisín blank-faces. This isn't the place for explanations but Oisín'd better have a decent excuse for this. The crowd presses around them. He turns to move on out. He's head and shoulders above most of them but it still feels like he's drowning in Lynx and sweat and smokes and fry-stink. His face heats and he can't breathe. He pushes through and the faces turn to look at him busting through the crowd. Karlo goes to follow, but he hears Hamza say:

– Leave him be. Just needs a moment.

Out into the air at the back, he slumps onto the small wall at the railings. Hands on thighs, he gulps in air.

Whacker and a crew of the lads are shaping up for the guard of honour. Deano refused. There's no way, when yer keeping yer mouth shut about this shit, that yeh can do a guard of honour. Something heavy might drop on you out of the sky. Besides, Titch hadn't been seen at the hurling for years. He did carry a hurl with him, but only for whacking stones at Deliveroo riders. Oisín had words with him round at the skate park, asked him what he was gonna do when one of the Brazilian riders came after him, told him he wouldn't be able to outrun a grown man from the favelas. Titch said that he'd bring him down the flats and that'd be the end of the Brazilian. And in anyway, he mostly only threw stones at Pakis, no offence Hamza, know what I mean? Hamo spat on Titch's shoe and told him to cop the fuck on. Titch told him to mind his own Paki business. Then apologized again. But he stopped pucking stones at the Deliveroo riders, started on buses instead. Titch was a bit of a spa, come to think of it.

He's no idea what he'd say to the guards in anyway. He didn't see the scalds that were looking for Snitchy. Only Oisín saw them. And he'd no idea who they were. At least he *said* he didn't know who they were. Snitchy, MIA. Could be in a hole in a ditch somewhere, up the mountains in a bog hole, could be gone somewhere else. Broke free. The word round Colmcille's was that Snitchy's in Spain, living the dream in some sham's compound. Seems unlikely but.

So what would he say? I was with a fella who might have been with the young fella who was filleted. Not filleted, as Hamza pointed out, just basic butchery, breaking up the carcass. That's all we are in the end. His da, Jack, Titch. Once it's all over, it's all over. You're asking for a world of pain if yeh go to the guards. And then yer dragging Helen into it. Always banging on about fairness and things being the right thing to do but she's keeping herself to herself on this. Ethics me hole. The only one who'll be in deep shit is Oisín. So it's not really up to Deano. Not at all, in fact. He'd be letting down a mate. It's the right thing to do, to say nothing. But now fucken Benit knows, probably everyone in town will know within an hour.

There's a stir in the crowd. They must be finally finishing up. He moves up along the road to meet up with the boys. The exhaustion is hitting him hard now. He can barely keep his eyes open. Must be a funeral thing. The coffin's being carried out. Another basket effort, what the fuck!

People surge out behind it. Titch's mam, in a heap, supported by sisters or cousins or something. Lordy, Titch's da, the oldest junkie in town. So-named, according to June, after he survived being crucified in a garage in Drimnagh. Something to do with Wino again.

And then the man himself appears out, all humble, looking at the ground. Marian and Candy straight after him. Short back and sides plainclothes filter out through the crowd, and Wino turns to a couple of them and holds his hand out. The red-haired one smirks and shakes his hand. You wouldn't know, any of these fellas could be on the take. But then, maybe the ones on the take wouldn't be the ones shaking his hand in public.

– Are you okay, love? Deano? a voice says from behind.

Sadie. Poking her nose in again.

– Be grand, Sadie. No worries.

She comes up close behind him, those huge tits – wonder if they're as orange as the rest of her – pressing into the middle of his back.

– Make this business not your business, she mutters. D'yeh hear me? Seen yer ma over there. She's looking well.

He searches for her and June but they've disappeared into the crowd. Deano flinches as Wino glides past, entourage in tow, ignoring him completely. Thank fuck. Lads like Wino blanking you is the way you want things. Publicly for sure but when you really want them to ignore you is during the hidden-away times. On the stairs, down the back alley, in that scummy gaff.

And thank fuck they've all kept on blanking him since Boston, since Titch. Not a word, not a text, not even a sly meet-up with Jim Harrison. There's either someone else moving their shit for them or they're not moving shit at all at the moment. Makes sense, Wino's crew probably have guards all over them since Titch showed up. But word is that he's not responsible this time. Not directly anyway. Still, nothing goes on without him being in the know.

He leans up against the back gate of one of the nice houses that backs onto the main road that's now filling up with the church's outpourings. The hurling boys line up, the family – mostly women and girls – passes through, clinging to each other.

– His poor mam, a whispered voice says alongside him. Losing your baby is bad enough, but like that …

She's snuck up on him.

– I'm loving the watch, Deano. It keeps great time.

He's not getting involved with her today. He doesn't want any hassle and she's not doing anything wrong, but this is just not the day for it.

– I love it in anyway. I showed it to June. See she has one too.

There's a fucking limit! He spins around to face her, raging.

– Yeah? And wha?

She jumps back against the wall.

– And nothin, it's just nice. She has one but I got one too is all.

Bullshit. Just more bullshit. Oisín and Benit are trying to catch his attention over near the church gate as the crowd starts to move off slowly behind the hearse. There's lads with cameras out trying to look discreet. Even RTÉ are here. He'll wait until they pass near him and he'll move back in step with them and they'll all walk to the graveyard or crematorium or whatever the fuck place yeh need to go to when you're like the offal tray in the butchers.

– Deano, I didn't mean anything by it, I swear. I never had a watch like this.

She did, plenty. And much nicer too. All robbed and passed on. He turns to look at her head-on. She's plastered up against the wall, almost cowering. He always remembered her bigger. She's got a few extra centimetres from the turban yoke but she still seems so tiny now beside him.

She's hard to read. She still has that smooth-faced junkie look. Maybe the features and the muscles and the lines come back after a while. They're right. She does look well. Clean and no scabs is looking well for her.

– Yer da ...

No! No! Enough.

He staunches away in the opposite direction, well away from her.

The crowd shifts and fills in around him. He's backed against the wall. The fat back of Jim Harrison's head, neck rolls with spiderweb wrinkles falling over the collar of a pure white shirt, appears directly in front of him. Close enough that Jim can probably feel Deano's breath. And Wino at his left shoulder. Some other sham at his right.

– You're a well-liked young man, aren't you Dean?

He says nothing, just stares at the back of Jim's neck.

– Good to have friends, am I right? People looking out for you.

Fuck this! He's not dancing to this fuck's tune today. He turns and glares down at him, mouth tight. Wino doesn't look up. Getting quieter.

– You now, you've all kinds of friends, haven't you, Dean? All kinds. Some of them a bit on the dark side.

Deano can feel his temples throbbing. He'd love to just fucking hit the cunt. The fella on his right squashes closer.

– I've to tie me lace here, Wino says, and he signals to Deano to join him as he drops to the floor.

Deano hesitates. Jim half turns to look at him. Deano folds to his hunkers. It's hot down low with a wall of legs around you. He's looking him right in the eyes now, stinking of garlic.

– Some friends of yours have had words on your behalf, Dean. Saying you're to be left to your own devices. I'm supposing now, you know nothing about that. There's been no … *chat* outta you.

It's like his whole body is gonna fall out through his arse.

– I'll be brief, outta respect for the occasion.

Fiddling with the laces of his tan brogues, he stares straight into Deano.

– I wouldn't like it now, if anyone was putting pressure on anyone close to me Deano. Wouldn't like you and your pals getting close to certain people, know what I mean, Deano?

What the fuck's he on about?

– Yeah.

– But when someone's making representations, saying maybe no contact between my people and yourself might benefit both of us, I'm maybe choosing to go along with that. And maybe some of your *friends* might choose to stay away from my people too. Yeh get me?

– Yeah.

– Good lad.

He stands up and Jim and the others part the crowd for him and he melts away. Deano stares for what seems like the longest time ever, above everyone's heads at the hearse trying to pull out through the gates.

Oisín messages him, asking if he's coming or what, and he tells him he'll float over after them. Just needs a breather for a bit. He closes his eyes, feels the sun on his lids. Then June's in front of him.

– You alright, love? You look pale. How's the belly?

– Be grand. No bother, he says, and he manages a smile.

She moves in closer, gripping the youngest's hand.

– She's here for you, yeh know? She's thinking of you and what this must be like for you, yeh know? She loves her watch in anyway.

She starts to smile up at him, cheering him on, coaxing him to be nice.

– Go on, head over with the lads. I'll walk over with her if she wants to go.

– I'll head over in a bit.

– Deano, love …

– I said I'll head over in a bit, yeah?

She hits him with that look. That, d'yeh-think-I'm-scared-of-you-yeh-prick look. He's never seen anyone, from the junkie who tried to rob her phone off her outside Lidl, to the fishmonger who tried to short-change her, do anything once she'd given them the look.

– Yeah, I mean I'll just wait here a bit. Just need a break before it.

Her face softens.

– You'll regret it if you don't go to the rest of it. Follow us on when you're ready. It'll be a while getting over there at this rate.

The crowd is getting sparse now at the end. People heading back to their cars. It'll be all the hardcore flats who'll walk the whole way with Titch.

Sadie's shop is closed. As is the butcher's. The boxing club has a black ribbon on the door. A clatter of people are still milling around at the front of the flats, organizing lifts, giving each other lights. Wino, in his good coat, stands shaking hands with various people. People looking genuinely pleased to see him. Deano pulls an empty skins packet from his jeans, and fuck it, what's he supposed to do now?

He turns to head towards the Spar and there's the big woolah head of the guard moving through the entrails of the funeral crowd, staring at him or maybe someone behind him with any luck. Fuck off. Fuck off. Fuck off. But no, he's heading straight for Deano. Here, out in the open, in front of everyone and fucken Wino.

As he gets closer, he can see that the guard's definitely shaping up to get chatty. Smiling a bit, determined. Does he want everyone in the place to get clipped? Everyone's head in a bag in the canal?

– Deano? says Chucklehead.

The guard blocks the path, impossible to avoid him. Mind you, he'd block any path with the bulk of him. Like a big lump of a house.

– Terrible scene, wasn't it? That young Carolan lad wasn't a bad young fella at all shure. You knew him, didn't yeh?

– Not really, Deano says, folding his arms across his chest.

– Yeh must have known him a wee bit?

– Not really, Garda.

– What's with the Garda business? I'm not interrogating yeh here, Deano. Just this must be a bit hard for you, yeh know? Hard for everyone, all the lads. But more … it's bigger for you.

– How? How is it?

Bit too loud there. Deano feels the eyes of the last of the funeral crowd on him. The end of the walkers rounds the bend and the jam of cars follows behind, moving out from all the side roads.

– She'll never be right again, the guard says. His mam. Shure how could any mother be?

– I've gotta go.

– There's supports there. You can come and talk to me anytime you like, yeh know? Just have an aul chat.

– About what, Garda? What would I have to talk to you about? Deano shouts.

He's aware that the opening and closing of car doors, the calls across the parking spaces outside the flats, the hum of craic around Wino have all stopped. Yeah, look, look. I'm setting this pox of a garda straight. He doesn't know if it's an echo in his head from earlier or what but he hears a slight hiss. But he isn't giving up, this culchie. The guard smiles a little, like he hadn't even noticed Deano's raised voice, and he lowers his own. All softly, softly, like he's someone's mammy.

– There's a meeting we're going to have in the community centre at the weekend. You could maybe come to that? Young fellas like you, it's important that ye come to these things. Stay involved.

– Involved in what? I'm not involved in nuttin.

He was smiling but now his face falls. Deano stalks off towards Cork Street but the fucker matches his pace. Deano speeds up. There's no way … yes, yes, there is a way. He's still alongside him. He can't lose him. Right by his shoulder. This is fucken mental. He's powerwalking with a garda with the whole fucking area watching behind. He's matching Deano stride for stride, panting a bit. Like the arsehole he is. Deano stops dead at the railings by the methadone clinic. The lads queueing up outside the portacabin nudge each other. Yeah, yeah, why not all watch the show.

– Stop it would yeh, yeh fucken *loser*!

The guard's chest is heaving but he's trying to keep breathing through his nose.

– Deano. Deano, he says, holding up his hand.

He has to give in. He bends forward and gasps, hands on his knees. The methadone boys start jeering. He straightens himself. Admirable recovery for a fat fuck.

– I know yeh don't want to talk to me. Shure why would yeh? But I don't want the likes of you ending up like that poor lad. Look at his mam there.

He looks over his shoulder as the jeering gets louder. Even Deano's feeling the heat now. He reduces his voice to a whisper.

– That woman is destroyed. I don't want to see another woman in that state round here. D'ya hear me?

Jaze, is he going to bawl?

– Are you bleedin cryin, Garda? Cos that's fucken bent.

Deano cracks a smile. Yeah, he *was* gonna bawl. He was! Oh yes, he was! Wait'll he tells the lads this one. Glad that pointing it out put a stop to it, but jaze, yeh can't have that. A fucking garda whinging on your shoulder. And Deano thinking about telling these dopes anything about Snitchy! They stand facing each other. Deano sticks his hands in his pockets and flips a coin over his knuckles, over and over and over.

– Yeh don't want to end up like that young fella, right? And June and yer mam ... the guard says.

His mam! This fella is relentless.

– And yer da ...

– You fucken serious? Deano says, and shapes up to him, sticking out his chest.

The guard's jaw clenches.

– I'm saying, I'm *saying*, no one wants that for you. You don't want that for yerself, Deano.

– Nah, yer joking. I'd a lovin that, Garda. I'd a fucken lovin to have bits of me all over the gaff.

The guard swallows.

– Yeh know, we lost me father when I was a bit younger than you.

– Ah yeah? Where'd yeh lose him? Down the back of the sofa? Yer da a pig too?

The guard says nothing. Moist eyes blink in the roundy head.

Why'd he say that? That's just a shit thing to say. There's that tightness in his chest and his throat hurts like something is forcing its way up and out of him. Get back down whatever the fuck yeh are. Turning into a cunt now. But he's a fucken garda. And a dopey one too. And they're watching, the lads at the clinic, the girls passing by. They'll all be watching.

– I've gotta head off ...

– He was just out one night at a do, me da. Fitzpatrick's Hotel in Bunratty. And he was there one minute and then he collapsed the next and that was it. Lights out. It's not easy to lose yer da, yeh know? Course yeh know. And he was a decent man. Yeh want ta have seen the amount of letters we got after, telling us about him. People from all over, telling us stories about stuff he'd done for them. Stories we didn't know, yeh know?

Deano stands there looking at him. What are yeh supposed to say to guards who start this shit?

– He coached the hurling. Like yer own da … but it's worse to lose a child.

He glances back at the church again.

– Words have been had with a certain party back there, Deano. We won't put up with pressure being put on young fellas like you.

Fucking fuck. He can't mean that. Is he trying to get people chopped up, the thick fuck?

Deano marches past him, staunches back down the road towards the church, towards the traffic jam, towards the boys, towards what looks like a hundred guards. And that's only the ones in uniforms. He turns around.

– Hey Garda, fuck you and yer da, he shouts, and gives him the finger.

The fat head crumples.

Why'd yeh say that? Why like? Coz he's a fucking guard! A pig! And his fucken friend now?! He was just trying to talk. About his da. Fuck. Fuck Fuck. Fuck them all. Fuck Wino. Fuck Jim Harrison. Fuck the lot of them into the sea.

The thing in his throat feels like it's going to tear its way out, and he swerves off down a side street. Because that's what he's gonna do. He's gonna keep on walking. Forever. He starts to skip along and then he's running. And they can all stay back there behind him.

Down past Sophia where the weavers stretched their linen. Down through the Tenters, past Oisín's house, the mad one's going back in her gate, probably at the funeral. Oh hello, she calls, but he's already past her. And now it's a blur, down into Blackpitts, stomping on the Black Death bodies and the knackers' tanning pits, up onto Clanbrassil and past St Patrick's with King William's chair and ragged Union Jacks and a man called Swift banging on about his modest proposal to eat the poor of Dublin, and Gulliver towering over the Lilliputians.

Past the park with the kids playing on the swings beside the junkies gathering in the corner passing deals out through the railings, Howya Deanooooh. Past Oisín's ma's café with its smells of bread and coffee and wholesome soups. Past the Iveagh Buildings, the best housing in Dublin that Guinness could build, up the hill to Christ Church with the tourists hola-ing each other outside and Strongbow at rest in the crypt.

Down Fishamble Street past Handel's first Messiah and alongside the bunkers of Dublin City Council that buried Viking ships and nit combs forever and ever, looking across at the Four Courts. Towards Heuston Station, take me the fuck anywhere outta here, St Patrick's madhouse on the left where the cutters and starvers and fruitloops get drugged until they act proper. Past the criminal courts where young fellas with one too many baggies get sent to join their brothers in the Joyful Home for the Flats.

Through the gates of the Phoenix Park, past the daffodils and tulips where Roma girls pick flowers to stick in their hair, before Dublin scalds pick them up for torture and bullets and shallow bog holes in the mountains. Past the spot where Brit lords get stabbed in the neck, past the front gate of Michael D's presidential white house, to the back wall and dry moat that nobody scales. Clawing and scrambling, he's up, and he's almost over, but he falls back panting in the leafy, muddy dirt.

His heart and breath settle and he sits up and gets the spins. Tall trees tower overhead, shading him. There's nothing for it, he has to go back. He clambers back up, pulling on brambles, spiking his hands. Over the top, he falls flat on his back again, watching the sky pass by. It's gonna be a scorcher this year, the summer. Forty degrees. He closes his eyes, inhales the earthy smell, soaks in the warmth of the April sun, until it's blocked out and there's a dull thump beside him and his eyelids snap back, ready for action.

– What ya doin, bro? Benit says.

– What the fuck are you doin?!

– Checking you out, fam. Coming back?

– Be over now.

Benit folds himself easily onto the ground beside Deano's head. The fucker is like a superhuman, hardly breathing hard.

– How'd yeh find me? This is mental.

– Behind you all the way, fam. Let's go back, yeah? Boys are waiting.

20
KARL

Meant to be rustling themselves to head out to meet some of Hamza's relations coming into the airport. Hamza or his da always goes to collect the relatives since the thing with the uncle off the ferry. But Oisín's got a tip-off in one of them secret groups he's in. Someone testing out a new edible product – samples hidden down by the basin. He hops on a Dublin Bike to go searching for the free-to-the-first-ten-people chocolate, leaving the rest of them stretched in the sunshine, by the canal.

– Why's it so much nicer down this end of the canal? Deano says, rolling over onto his belly on the grass in front of Patrick Kavanagh.

– There's more birds even down here. Look, grey wagtail, Benit says.

– That's not grey, it's all yellow on its belly, Hamza says, and he throws himself down beside Deano. Wanna be lovers, Deano?

– Haram bud, Deano says.

– The grey wagtail is really like the yellow wagtail but the yellow one has more yellow, innit?

– Great, Benit, thanks, Hamza says sarcastically.

But Karl can see over his shoulder that he's googling 'yellow wagtail'.

Beside them, the little park beside the building site – more offices by the look of it – with its deck chairs and its people walking miniature schnauzers, has a giant screen showing ads, big logos and fake laughing people an all.

– Time for a riot. Public space should be in the hands of the public, Hamza says.

– Like you're gonna riot, Hamza, Deano says. All this rioting and commie shite, you'll head off to UC fucken D and yeh'll get in with all the business heads and yeh'll get the big job and the fancy coat and that'll be the end of yeh. Cop the fuck on.

Hamza's only messing. Probably. It's Oisín who's been on about rioting and shit since he got in tow with the skateboarders. A form of meditation, he says it is. The skateboarding, not the rioting.

A flash of yellow catches his eye, a black girl in a swishy dress – Grecian, it's called – makes her way down from the Leeson Street Bridge. Denim jacket over her shoulders, scarlet Michael Kors maybe, can't tell at this distance, over her shoulder. A knock-off, prolly.

She keeps walking towards them. Deano sits up straight.

– Bring it, Benit says, still gazing at the canal.

Nice shades. She flicks her hair. She's tall, maybe as tall as Benit. And skinny, which isn't Benit's thing. Gotta have some bundha for Benit, but she's the best thing Karl's ever seen at the canal. Like a colourful parrot amongst the crows and seagulls. She lifts her head a little higher as she's nearly level with them.

– Hiya, Benit says, flashing his perfect teeth.

– Hi, she smiles back, a bit snobby.

That's what you want from girls: little bitta fuck you, you're not good enough for me. Tanya has it a bit.

And then she's gone, the parrot girl is gone, she just keeps on walking.

– Losing yer touch, Deano says.

– Never get the hop with that lack of swag, Hamza says.

Benit holds his head in his hands.

Karl pulls off his jacket. He's actually starting to sweat and the sparkles off the water are giving him a bit of a headache. He closes his eyes. His da hasn't mentioned the business studies course for a while but he will. He'll have to do the change-of-mind form in anyway. Only Oisín has fixed his up so far. Karl woulda liked to be a doctor, a bone doctor, he thinks. He's handy with a saw. 'Why aren't you doing art?' Oisín said to him. Bit late for that now. 'No, a portfolio course,' he said. But how can he do that? If things are shite enough now, what'd happen if he said he wanted to spend a year doing drawings to put in a folder? That'd go down well. His da's still bigging up his drawing, but not like it's a career path. 'I know it's just a hobby, but it'll keep yeh relaxed. Help yeh heal any wounds.' That craic has nearly gone too far with him now. Taoism or philosophy or some shit. He's all Men's Sheds and helping the junkies. Doing his law degree. What if yeh don't want to make bird houses or whittle things or become a lawyer?

– Ah here, boys. I'm only after getting this young one's number, Oisín's voice says, getting closer.

Karl smiles and keeps his closed eyes turned towards the sun.

– Did yiz see her? Black, yellow dress? Hot as.

Hamza's roaring laughing.

– Ah, what? Benit says. You just stopped her and asked her?

– I'd stopped to have a look at the brakes on this yoke. Lucia her name is. This is whopper, boys.

– Slimeball, Deano says. Perving on some poor girl walking along the canal on her own.

– Call the number, Karl says, eyes still shut.

– Can't call it straight away, she'll think I'm some simp.

– Here, call her from my phone, Karl says, finally looking at him.

Oisín doesn't want to, but everyone's waiting.

– Here, take a bit of this first, Oisín says and he pulls out a small, cellophane-wrapped bar.

He breaks it into small pieces, tells them Gaymie says that he's used a more balanced mix this time.

– Tastes like cooking chocolate mixed with Toilet Duck, but it's not too bad.

They're not letting him off but. They make him call the number and put it on speakerphone. Some physio's place. Benit thumps Oisín on the shoulder.

– Ha ha! Yeh thought yeh were in there, lad. The blondie head didn't impress her this time. She had a flat arse in anyway, Deano says. Don't worry about her.

Oisín hangs his head, looking at his phone and then starts to smile.

– 'Mon, we'd better start heading into town.

*

– This is trippy almost, Karl whispers, as he plonks down at the back of the bus, between Benit and an aul one with love heart glasses. She looks none too happy, as she nudges her shopping trolley further into the corner at the window.

A big, fit-looking guard appears at the top of the stairs.

– There, the one with the bag, he shouts, pointing down the back.

Suddenly, there's a swarm of them charging down the aisle. Karl's wondering what contraband the aul one's got in her trolley, when they grab Benit and reef him up and outta the seat.

Benit's shouting:

– What the fuck? What did I do? What did I do?

And Karl's left sitting there watching their backs disappear down the stairs. That was a bit strange, wasn't it? The aul one turns to him and says:

– Should you not be helping your coloured friend there?

He just lets that wash over him. He can't stop smiling though.

– He's coloured black. Where'd you get those class glasses?

– Never mind me glasses, you, yeh whelp. Get down them stairs and help yer friend, whatever he's done.

Whatever he's done? Whatever he's done. Hold on …

– Get off now and see what's happening him, the aul one says again, and gives him a little shove.

He gets the vibe. He's up and off, bouncing down the stairs. His feet are kinda dancing. Surges running up his spine, behind his puddins. He bursts past the driver and out onto the wide O'Connell Street pavement. People are giving the bundles on the ground a wide berth, rushing past, pretending they don't see. Others, young fellas mostly, are filming the scene, some jeering, most serious. Benit and Hamza are slammed on the ground, not even struggling. They've turned to face each other, laughing.

– I live chu, Benit says to Hamza, spit at the corners of his lips.

– I live chu chu, Hamza says back, and Karl thinks they might wet themselves.

– Shut it, you two, one of the guards says, as another reefs out receipts and tears apart Benit's mini first aid kit.

They've a thing about Benit's bag. That bag's bad luck. He got an exact replica of the first one they lifted that other time. His mam didn't notice a thing. And now here they're at it again.

He becomes aware of Oisín and Deano beside him. Deano's chomping Monster Munch loudly in his ear.

– Why are they on the floor? Deano says.

Yeah, why? Better ask. Feeling good about this. Feeling pretty good.

– Eh, Garda, Karl says. Why have you got these two young men on the ground? They have to get to the airport.

The guard, who seems a bit knackered with holding his knee on Hamza's back, looks like he wants to kill Karl. More and more people are gathering, phones held high.

– Ah, how are yeh, Benit, a gravelly voice says from over Karl's shoulder.

What's Johnny-Two-Cans doing on O'Connell Street? He's not supposed to be here.

– Garda, them's two good young men there, Johnny says, pushing closer. Get off them, would yeh?

Benit and Hamza turn their heads towards Johnny's voice.

– I've a bit of news for yeh, Benit, bit of a job for yeh, if yeh want it, he says, and takes a glug of his can. Sure I'll talk to yeh about it when you're not so busy.

Benit tries to mumble something up at him but his face is too squashed. Is Johnny-Two-Cans actually here?

– Karl, will yeh hold onto me can there, I've to go for a piss, Johnny says. And he leaves Karl holding an almost empty Druid's and shambles across towards the Gresham.

Must be real.

And then someone shouts, 'He's down there', and they're up, the knee guard reefs Hamza up onto his feet, and the whole lot of them, four, maybe five, charge though the crowd and down the street. Whoever the fuck *he* is, he's in deep.

Hamza's jacket has white feathers pouring out at the shoulder. A pity because it's the one bitta Hamza's gear that Karl has ever liked.

– I was a bit hot, actually, the footpath felt nice on me cheek, Benit's saying.

– Yeah, pretty warm today, Hamza says, as Deano hands him the rest of his bag of Monster Munch.

– Ah shit, he's closed the doors!

Hamza charges at the bus, and they cop it and rush after him. The bus driver's staring straight ahead, Hamza and Deano banging on the door. He turns to look at them with a face like thunder that melts into a wide grin as he presses the button to open up. Young fellas slap their hands and cheer. Women stare them down or look away. They tramp up the stairs and Karl drops in beside the old woman again.

– Yiz were gone a long time, she says, and stares out the window.

*

The display is still saying the flight's delayed, and no sign of by how much anymore. Karl's belly is rumbling. He can't hold out for much longer. Hamza's directing operations as usual.

They start heading back up to the food hall and there she is, walking towards them. Karl turns to search for Hamza but, from his face, he's already seen her. He's gone all squashy, smiling, shy even. Who's the bender now?

G-Star skinnies, Uggs, the real kind, gilet – could be Tommy, could be Sweaty Betty, but either way, good. Candy's not smiling though, not at all. She stares right through them, hard at Hamza, then turns, all showy, to look back behind her.

Marian, with a couple of pufferfish where the lips used to be, is walking along with two girls, Roma, on either side of her, dragging their cases. Wino and that Harrison fella who's always stretching tracksuits to their limits, staunching along behind, engrossed in their phones.

Hamza stops but Candy just sails past, stony-faced, unseeing. Marian doesn't even notice them and calls after her:

– Candy love, come back here and help this young one with her bag.

But Candy keeps on walking. Wino spots them, Hamza's just standing there, arms hanging.

– Well men.

Staring them out of it.

No one says anything.

– Going back home, is it? Nice time for it. Come on ladies, he says, rounding his arms around the girls' backs.

He turns as he goes to walk away and gives Hamza a long look up and down, and then they're gone.

Hamza's frowning, silent, looking at the ground. That crowd looked like they were well tight. On family business or sum. And she seemed so decent about Hamo, even if she was acting weird, the night of the Strictly thing.

– What the fuck was that? Oisín says.

– A lucky escape, Deano says, as he walks away. I'm going jacks.

He looks like he's gonna puke. And Hamza looks like someone's died.

Ghosted in front of them all. And his mot hanging with a crowd of knackbas. It hurts a bit. Hamza's trying to pull his manhood back together. Gotta do something.

– Don't think she saw, yeh, Hamo. She was off in a dream world. Are we getting that scran or wha? Karl says.

Hamza looks up at Karl and half smiles.

– Yeah, sure fuck it, let's go and eat.

*

Benit and Karl load up the trays with as much food as the five of them could afford once they'd pooled their money. Karl wants falafel and plenty of it. Falafel has become the thing at home since his da insisted the year before last that they should have a Middle Eastern feast for the Crimbo instead of turkey and ham. Jesus was from there, he said. And so they had a tajine and Oisín's mam supplied the hummus for the starter but his da made his own falafel. His mam was morto and decided that they couldn't have any family over because of it, and everyone looked at them with pity when they arrived out at the uncle's place in the evening and offered them all 'a bit to eat' that included the whole lot, turkey, ham, stuffing, gravy.

Great, it was. Doubler. His mam said that she'd be leaving if his dad pulled that shit ever again. His da just smiled, but he messes with her Christmas like that again …

No one's asking, but it's pretty weird that Wino didn't even look at Deano. Maybe all that business wasn't true at all. Oisín's stopped giving Deano grief about it. Everyone laying low in anyway. Even the cousin's less of a head-fuck. Who knew that's all it took? Titchy's head in the canal.

Only the likes of Russians would do that to a young fella, some of the flats are saying. Normal shams'd give yeh a bullet in the back of the head. Merciful, like. There's been near total silence from Deano and Oisín about Titchy. Karl kinda prefers it that way. They don't wanna be talking about young fellas' heads.

They went to see the bog bodies in Transition Year. That was good, everyone agreed. One of them was only a bit of a person. Head all squashed, long hair, dreaded up. Decorations in it. Pretty cool really. But cut into a third or even a quarter of himself. Looked like a person handbag, quality leather.

Years before, in primary, they'd gone on a school tour to a bog down the country. Full of holes it was and you got to jump into them and come out covered in black water. Bog swimming was great but after seeing the bog men, Karl got the chills thinking about it. What if a person handbag floated up beside yeh in one of them bog holes? He'd dreamt about it recently. The head bobbing up beside yeh like that seal out at Dalkey.

Karl's no sissy at swimming, but that time, the seal just appearing beside him in deep water, in a swell out there? Nah. The others could laugh, up on the steps. Only he was out floating in the swell, looking up at the grey skies, the Sorrento villas on one side and the Sugar Loaf on the other. Seals are bigger and far better swimmers than you. Karl's not fooled by their big brown eyes either.

– 'Member the day with the seal out at Dalkey? Karl says.

– Never saw you move as fast. Like a fish. Or a Beluga whale. A dwarf Beluga whale! Benit says, delighted with his crap slag.

– You'd never have made it outta the water if it was you, Benit, Deano says. It'd have eaten yeh.

This is true. Benit can't swim for shite. Black people: good at running, shite at swimming. Least that's the way it seemed at primary school swimming.

– Yeah, why can't black people swim proper? Karl says.

– I'm sure in the whole continent of Africa there's lads who can swim, Oisín says.

– The lakes and rivers there are full of things that crawl into your eyes or up your cock, lay eggs then burst out of you, like testicle-stuffed caterpillars, Hamza says. No point in learning to swim in those circumstances.

Acting like the Candy thing never happened.

– Yup. And Mokele-mbembe, Benit says. Big monster who stops rivers altogether. Gotta avoid him.

– Yeah, see, you're built to work with your environment, Oisín says. Look at Deano: built for no sunshine. Benit: built for lots of sunshine.

– Also hurling, Benit says.

True too. Benit's built for hurling.

– You've evolved to be good at that game, Hamza says. You're an example of high-speed evolution. With climate change, you'll be perfect for here. Me too. These whities are fucked. Shit, flight's landed, let's bounce.

Summer

21
DEANO

At Portobello Bridge, Deano stands in the shadows, holding his and Hamza's bikes, while Hamza gets the papers. Neither of them remembered to bring a lock. There's always advantages to having Benit around for this kind of thing. He'd normally have a couple of locks.

Robocop, wide and blond, appears down the lane.

– What are we doing here?

Deano sighs. The third time in the past week – beyond a joke. If some journalist bothered to report on this shite, the Garda'd be in front of the UN or a taskforce or the Nuremberg thing in no time.

– Nuttin. Just standing here, Garda.

– Move on now, away outta here now.

– I'm waiting for a friend.

– Move on before I arrest you.

Arrest him. Great. Benit's sister got mugged along here. A homeless fella was half rotted before anyone found him down here. Anything's possible. In fairness to Deano's local guards, they leave him alone. Garda Gerry's an annoying cunt, but they don't search him or give him any shit. Here in Dublin 2, it's Wild West territory. They're all the sheriff.

– Where'd you get those bikes? Both yours, are they? he sneers.

Fucksake.

– Alright Deano?

A girl's voice coming from the dark.

– Dharma, it's Dharma, she says.

Like magic, outta the blackness, it's her. And that smile.

– What's up, Garda? she says, all sweet, rubbing the back of her head. Everything alright, Deano?

She's still hanging onto that freak hairdo.

– Both of you, move along, Robocop says.

– Why, are we doing something wrong? Dharma says.

– You're loitering.

And he makes to usher them down the lane towards the light.

– I've only just arrived, and no, I'm standing here talking to my friend.

– And I'm waiting for my mate to come outta the shop, Deano says.

– Turn out your pockets.

– What? Dharma says, eyes popping.

Just give up. Get it over with. He lifts his jacket.

– Do not, Deano! Dharma says. What law are we breaking? We're standing here having a chat, Dharma says.

It's no good getting lairy with them. That's the worst thing to do. The gardaí don't give a fuck what yeh say or do, as long as yeh do whatever they tell yeh. Sometimes that's not even true either, sometimes they'll just beat the shit out of yeh even when yeh have done whatever it is they've told you to do. Dharma's flats, she knows this.

– Just come on, Deano says to her. Sick listening to this lad in anyway.

– No! This is a free country, she says, folding her arms. What law have we broken, Guard? What law?

– You're loitering.

– We'd have to be loitering with intent. My intent is to talk to my friend here. I'll remind you that not long ago a murdered boy was found in this canal and this is what you're busy doing, harassing this young man?

In all honesty, if Deano was the guard, he'd want to give her a slap at this stage.

The guard coughs, looks away from her and says:

– Name and address? to Deano, who lets out another big sigh.

– Simon.

– Simon what? That's not what she called you.

– Yak.

– Simon Yak?

– Yeah.

– Address?

– 245, Ballymun Road.

– Ballymun, yeah? What are you doing over here?

– Loitering.

– I'm making a complaint about you, she says. I'm a law student.

– Open your bags.

– You must be joking! You've no right, Dharma says.

– You, Madam, can stop your squawking.

Hamza turns the corner, freezes for a second, catching Deano's eye, ducks back round and, hopefully, legs it as fast as he can as far away as he can.

– Come on Dharma, let's just go.

Why waste yer time on this bollix?

Deano starts to move off. He feels her follow him after a bit of hesitation. They turn the corner onto Richmond Street, the guard close behind, and there's no sign of Hamza, thanks be to the baby Jesus, because Hamza has an eighth on him. Dharma slows and moves back.

– Where are you? Rathmines station is it?

She starts jumping up to see his badge number and the guard covers both of them with his hands and walks along with his hands on his shoulders like some kind of faggot. Deano's laughing now but Dharma's raging, wants to follow him down to make the complaint like a mad thing. But when he refuses to go with her she hesitates and follows Deano instead.

– You really a law student?

– Yeah, well, doing a Level 7 but I'm gonna go on, just working the café part-time.

– Thought you were into music?

– I am but there's more money in law, she says with a laugh. And it's interesting enough. I want to be able to stop fuckers like them, yeh know?

– The guards? You can't stop them. You got away with it there. If that hadda been me on me own chattin shit, I woulda ended up in the cells for the night.

– He was messing with us. They're not above us. They work for us.

Deano laughs and shakes his head, wrangling the two bikes. Thinks she's going to save the world or change it, or whatever. A lot of people think that. He glances at her as they walk along. Those black eyes.

Hamza texts to say he's gone Benit's house to lay low.

– Wanna come to me mate's house for a while? Gotta give Hamza, me other mate, his bike back.

She's bouncing along beside him, swinging her arms.

– Hamza who? Hamza Hussein? she says.

– Yeah, you know him?

Why is he surprised? Course she knows Hamo. Everyone does. He looks at her sideways again. She's maybe a ten, if it wasn't for that dirt hairdo. Weird clothes, some Indiany patterned trousers. Karlo would know.

– Where is it yiz moved to when yiz left the flats? Naas, I heard.

– Yeah, Naas first, then Walkinstown. Mam and me stepdad bought a house. It's only small.

– Is it still just you?

– One brother, one sister. Axel, he's seven, he's a cutie. He's learning difficulties, so he's a bit more like a younger kid, but he's great. Aoife's eight and she's a little bitch. But I love her, yeh know?

– Axel?

– Yeah, their dad's Swedish. We go over to Stockholm and all.

– How do you know Hamo? Like I know everyone knows him, but ...?

– That thing, you know up in DCU? The thing for ...

And she stops and turns to him, pulling a face and doing the inverted commas thing with her fingers.

– ... *bright* kids?

Deano laughs.

– No way! Clever camp? You're a swot too?

– Was, but I kinda got a life there for a while, yeh know? But anyway, anyway, let's go to your friend's house then. Will his parents be cool with that? With me arriving?

Benit's mam and Owen *are* cool, and Fenella would be ecstatic to see a girl, any girl, arriving. And a law student! To go with Benit the soon-to-be doctoring student. They walk on up the road, she's blathering away, keeps offering to take one of the bikes but he won't let her. Easier for him to walk both of them, plus he looks cooler this way. What's she even on about? She keeps waving her hands and saying 'anyway, anyway' a lot. Sometimes she goes back to giving out about the guards, and what she's going to do to them tomorrow, and then she says maybe not tomorrow, maybe she'll wait until she's got a load of examples of police brutality. She's mental, thinks she can *do* something.

She starts on about the trees along the road. He tries to remember what she was like years ago. What was her mam like? Blonde, he thinks, like everyone else's ma in the flats, but maybe not. Her being a hippy and all. He pretends to look at the chain of the bike to take a better look at the trousers and her arse. They're too loose and billowy so you can't get a proper feel for the shape of it but she's not too skinny, not too fat. The arse is probably alright too.

– And what kind of lawyer is that, that yer going to be? he says.

Pretty sure that was a good moment for that question. Show an interest, keep eye contact, don't look at her tits whatever yeh do. Make out that yer keen on their brains.

She goes off on one again. When she says things, she waves her hands about. She takes big steps for such a small person. And she's smiling nearly every time he takes a sneaky glance at her. Except when she's talking about 'that fucking guard'. She turns to him every now and then to say something like, 'yeh know?' and her eyes are a bit sparkly. He catches another glimpse of the back of her head.

– Did you do your hair yerself? he asks.

She stops, mid-flow. Stops walking and everything. Obviously the wrong thing to ask. Fuck it. He leans the bikes against his body and pulls out his Amber Leaf. A smoke saves every situation.

Hamza's da comes out of the Polski Sklep carrying a bottle of keffir. Loves it, he does. Hamza says he can't get enough of the stuff and Ami is disgraced with him buying stuff like that when she makes all the good food he could ever need. Feeding his biome, Hamo's da told Deano last time he was in the flat. The da stops to shake Deano's hand and ask how he is, and to warn about getting the studying going, and laughs. The happiest and stonedest Muslim in town. Deano and Dharma watch him jog up the steps of the house, looking left and right as he turns the key in the door.

– That's Hamza's da, Deano says.

– Looks a bit like my da, she says.

She's looking for him to ask about her da. Dharma only ever had a mystery da.

– Ah right, so your da's here?

– Nah, she says. He lives in this kinda commune, ashram sorta thing, you know? Hamza Hussein is Pakistani, right?

– Yeah, Pakistani Dub.

– They're the same people really, Pakistanis and Indians. I'm thinking of going over to see me da. Don't think me mam wants me to but. Keeps suggesting other things I should do instead. Putting me off. She was lying to me all the time, saying she had no photos, didn't remember him hardly. I found loads of photos of him hidden in a box. His address and all. I'm not talking to me mam.

This is kinda uncomfortable but he'll go with it.

– She kept them but. She coulda fucked them in the bin, he says.

That's stopped her in her tracks. That was good. And it's true.

– Do you look like him?

– Nah, he has a moustache. He just lives there in this big place, people come from all over and stay, you know, meditating and all.

Ah yeah, that fella's gonna be real happy if Dharma Baldy-Head turns up on his doorstep while he's eating his lentils.

– On yer own?

– Yeah, why not?

– Cos they rape girls and pull their guts out through their fannies on the buses.

Oisín showed them that. Pulled bits outta some young one and her fella cos she was on a bus at night. Say what yeh like about Dublin.

– Wanna smoke? he says, offering the pouch. Better not to roll one for her. That'd be sexist or some shit.

– I'll have one if you'll roll it for me. I'm crap at rolling. I'm trying to not smoke, at the moment. Me mam got me a voucher

319

for this yoga place for me birthday. And I've been going every day for the past week and it's really, really good. Like, I feel great and you sweat loads and then you feel a-mazing, I swear ... I'll have a smoke if you roll it. Anyway, anyway, so I didn't work at all for the Leaving but I got like a *loada* points and stuff cos of the dyslexia and also, a few I think, cos of yeh know, where we live.

– Walkinstown, you get points for Walkinstown? he says, but alls he's thinking about is Dharma sweating at yoga.

He wants to ask how bendy she is. She's probably hella bendy with the walk of her.

He rolls a small one for each of them on a gate pillar and pauses to admire how good they look side by side.

She walks along flicking ash on the ground and the hair outta her eyes. This might not be the best idea – bringing her into the middle of the boys. At Leonard's Corner he turns left to go down by the canal. Buying time with her.

– Anyway, anyway. How's your mam? I do see her the odd time in the café since yiz were in. She's looking much better, isn't she?

– We're nearly there. I'll just text Benit.

She stays silent as he pretends to send him a message. Nearly no point in heading over there now, it being so late. And she's only gonna wonder why he took her this way when Benit's over by Meath Street. Now he's fucked it up. And she's trying to chat about his mam. The phone rings while he's typing and he can't stop it fast enough. Hamza. She's looking out over the canal, one foot on the low wall, still pulling on the rollie. She can hear Hamza, he knows. Telling him to get down there, they're starting a game of poker. Yeah, yeah. Be there in a minute. Got someone with me. Shoulda said nah, he was tired, he was sick, anything.

– I play. Texas Hold 'Em, is it? she says, when he gets rid of Hamza. What's the buy-in? I don't have any cash on me.

He should not be bringing her down to these boys at all. There's no chance once she sees Oisín or even Benit. They're gonna be all over her.

– I won a tournament. It was only a charity thing like, out in the community centre. But still, sixty-three people in it. There was a loada Romanians, card sharks like.

His balls are gonna burst.

– Come on, we'll walk down this way in anyway, and turn down at Dolphin's Barn. He lives up by Gray Street.

She smiles, does a little frown, but nothing else.

– The scenic route. I like the canal, yeh know, he says. There's all yellow wagtails an all along here. Did yeh know that?

Fenella answers the door, her arms covered in flour. Her eyebrows shoot up and she's all over Dharma. And Dharma's all over her. All chat about what she's making, and does she mind her being there, and all polite. All the lads are there, already playing in the back room, sitting on the floor at a low table, with his stack ready for him.

– You'd better deal her in. This is Dharma, yeah? Used to be a neighbour.

They play it cool, say hiya, but it's all for show. They're all, even Karl, giving her the once-over.

– Aren't you the one Deano squashed the 99 into the back of yer head? Karlo asks.

Dick move. Karl's gonna suffer for that after.

– Is that what happened yer …

– Sherrup Karl! Deano says.

– Yeah, that's me. Had me bawling for ages, she says, as she pulls off her jumper revealing a Repeal T-shirt underneath.

– Do you ever see those beardy pricks going round still with the Repeal sweatshirts on? Hamza says. That's the only way they get the hop from the Trinity girls. Everyone knows that's why they're wearing them. *I'm a feminist.* Yeah, right you are, bro.

His latest thing. And he's right, bunch a cunts. Now's not the time though. Dharma just laughs her head off but.

– That's so true, she says. I never thought about it that way.

She's like, perfect. Oisín's pretending he hasn't even noticed how good she is, but that's his game – make out you're not into it, that you wanna be friends.

By 3:30, they're all too knackered. Karl, Hamza and Benit are out, and Hamza's not happy about it. Not happy at all. But then he hasn't been happy since the airport, but that's what happens when your missus ghosts you right there in front of everyone like a fucken skank, strutting along with the scumbag Kardashians.

Karl and Hamza decide to head off. They've been sitting there bitching at each other for the past hour, and Karl's nodded off more than once. Deano's short-stacked but itching for a comeback. Dharma's killing it and has nearly as much as Oisín but she looks jaded and Oisín offers a three-way split. Pretty generous given Deano's situation, but probably not actually generous at all. Just trying to impress Dharma.

She says she's staying in her auntie's gaff on James's Street, and the three of them walk out the door together. So, it'll be himself and Oisín walking her up the road and Oisín will expect him to bow out and leave him to it, and maybe that's what she wants too. Oisín's a good-looking lad. He just is. But no, Deano's not standing aside this time.

– Ah wait, I'm after leaving me phone back there. Fuck it! Oisín says, fumbling in his jeans and patting his jacket.

– Fuck, we'll wait here for yeh, Deano says.

He's gone down the street when he shouts back:

– Nah, go on, youse head on, I'll just head home.

Deano shrugs at Dharma who doesn't seem that unhappy about it. Not that she's showing, in anyway.

– Anyway, this is weird, isn't it? After all this time, and then we bump into each other twice all of a sudden?

– Yeah, and Dublin's really small like. Yeh meet everyone all the time, he says.

What the fuck's he on about? Acting like a gobshite.

– So your mam and me, we do have the chats. Getting herself sorted, seems to be.

It's this weird feeling. He's not even pissed off with her for saying this.

– Yeah.

Yeah? Yeah? What the fuck does he say? Make the words come out, the right words.

– She's always all talk about you. About you going to college and about the watch you got her. Says you're doing really well. What are you going to do after the Leaving?

– Ah, dunno. Sum, spose.

This is not the direction he'd like this conversation to go in. Deflect.

– Me and the boys applied for medicine.

– What? All of yiz? she says, laughing. Are yiz any good at that kind of thing? No offence but …

– Only for the mess. Gonna change it. Dunno what. Nuttin I wanna do, know what I mean?

– College isn't for everyone. Loads of people don't go and they're grand. Yeh don't have to decide on your whole life now.

– Yeah, that's what I think.

– Bill Gates dropped outta college, yeh know? And loads of other people and it didn't do them any harm. Anyway, anyway, wanna go up the back way? It's shorter.

She's just being nice. Making out that he's not a big flaker. And no, he doesn't want to go up the back way, past that door and all its locks, and Piotr behind it. But he can't say that because he'll sound like a weirdo. It'd be just his luck to run straight into someone that recognizes him or even the man himself up this way. And he doesn't want any of that near him when he's got this one here beside him.

Nearing the gateway and no one's around. He'll get away with this if they just get past it quick but a car, a big green Merc, edges its nose out through the pillars. The driver's acting as if they're making his life impossible on this dead-end side street with not a sinner about, never mind a loada traffic.

– Will yeh come on, buddy? Deano says, being all cheerful and relaxed about it.

She'll like that.

The car finally pulls out and they walk on past. They're a good thirty seconds down the street when Dharma says:

– That was kinda strange. What was he waiting for? That's not the gaff they're using as a brothel, is it? Me auntie was telling me she heard there's a place round by here. That Wino Nestor.

– No idea. Sure there's them places everywhere, I'd say. Yeh wouldn't know.

– Here we are. She's gonna kill me in the morning for staying out this late. I've to get up and babysit my little cousin for her while she goes into work.

– You'll be knackered.

– Be grand. Anyway, anyway, I can stay in town tomorrow afternoon. You around?

And she's pulling out her phone and he's giving her his number, and she'll message him tomorrow. And it's pretty warm so maybe she'll be going with some mates to the beach or sum, and maybe he'd like to come and maybe, maybe, and she's gone and he's alone on James's Street, as an ambulance, lights flashing but siren off, nearly does a two-wheeler round the corner and into the hospital.

22
HAMZA

Probably his favourite month, May. Here anyway. A big fat month, in his mind. You can start to feel a bit of warmth. Not shorts-wearing warmth – leave that up to the white boys – but still, enough that you can wear your light jacket.

He might even treat himself to a late afternoon ice cream. Take advantage before Ramadan.

He bypasses Spar and heads to Sadie's. Whatever about being in the flats, she has the best 99s. He skirts down Washington Street and hopes he doesn't run into any of the boys. A bit of peace is all he needs.

– It's warm isn't it, love? You'd need this, Sadie says, slowly piling the cone. Syrup? You're for the Leaving, aren't yeh?

Obsessed, all of them. Like there's nothing else in this world. It's a numbers game, that's all. Balance your natural ability with effort to achieve a projected number. Leave yourself a bit of extra leeway, just in case everyone suddenly decides to apply for what you want to do. Take all the freebies you can get for mentalness, sickness, postcode. The principle of right effort. He's got that perfected. No more, no less than you need to achieve your aims.

– Nah, not doing it.

– Aren't you a friend of Deano's? I thought yiz were all for the Leaving.

– Nah, Ramadan's coming up.

– And what's that got to do with your Leaving Cert?

Ignoring her, he shades his eyes to peer at the framed drawing on a shelf behind the counter. A big woman's head on a tiny body in a Marie Antoinette dress. A caricature nearly, except, yep, just a very lifelike Sadie head on it.

– Who did that drawing there?

Sadie follows his gaze.

– Ah yeah, he's your friend too, isn't he? Karl? The pet did that for me for my birthday. Course my Derek's gay too. Happily married to Greg, lovely fella, lawyer. In Florida they are.

– Great.

Doreen walks in with that rotten little dog that always seems to have a cold, looks him up and down, and asks for one a them 99s, she's melting, Sadie.

– This fella here is telling me he's not doing the Leaving cos of his *religion*, Doreen. Would you believe that?

Ramadan ends two days before they start but no reason not to mess with the ladies' heads a bit.

– He's only codding but, Sadie says. And I know he's only playing the smart lad because I went with a Muslim man for a while, didn't I Doreen? And he worked away all through Ramadan. Starving he was.

– She did, Doreen says, and gives him another once over. Big fella he was too.

– *Very* big, Sadie says.

And she raises her eyebrows and gives Hamza a look that he thinks is supposed to make him feel uncomfortable. It's working slightly too. Women. They think they're very clever or funny. But they're really not.

– Ah leave him, he's going all red, the poor fella, Doreen says, and she sticks the dog onto a little cushion that Sadie's pulled from under the counter and starts talking in the dog's face.

– Didn't I see you out in Blanch with Wino's young one, holding hands yiz were.

Sadie jumps back from the counter.

– Who're yeh talking to, Doreen?

It'd better be that manky dog. The Doreen one keeps talking into the dog's face.

– Oh it was, wasn't it, Bimbo? It was him we saw. Wino won't like that.

– Stop with that talk, Doreen. Leave the young fella alone.

Sadie's looking at Hamza with, what is that, pity or fear?

– You talking to me? Because I have *no* idea what you're talking about.

– That's right, pet. Don't mind Doreen, she sees things that aren't there. That right, *Doreen*? Sadie says through gritted teeth.

Doreen laughs and turns away from the mutt to look at Hamza.

– Ah yeah, she says. Come to think of it, it was probably some other young fella. Definitely her though, good-looking girl that she is. I do be mistaken sometimes. Whoever that young fella was'd want to be careful, am I right, Sadie?

– Leave him alone, Doreen.

Now she's looking him hard in the eyes. Like some kinda witch. Her face softens and she reaches for his arm.

– Wino wouldn't be happy with young fellas like that courting his young one. He'd want to mind himself.

The fan on the counter is blasting Sadie's helmet hair away off her face and she looks like an orange football with a big unhappy face drawn on it.

– There love, I'm gonna give yeh a double flake because I know yer working hard, whatever messin yer at, because yer mammy tells me all about yeh and yer studying, when she's in. Don't be minding Doreen.

The circumstances that would lead to Ami ever being in Sadie's shop – war, famine, alien invasion – haven't happened yet, so she's lying. Like they all do.

– UCD, Business, Doreen. That's where this fella's going, his mammy says. He wouldn't be out in Blanch.

Doreen turns down her lips in that shocked-approval kind of way that women do.

Lucky break. She's guessing about the course. He pays Sadie and tells her to keep the change as he walks out. He can feel it. His face is red. The last time he remembers his face going that kind of red was in second class, in PE when the cord on his tracksuit bottoms snapped and they dropped around his knees.

– I'll put it in the poor box, love. Good luck with the studying, she calls after him.

He heads for the canal, licking the ice cream off his hand. Just a nice sit down on the steps. Time out. Before she arrives. Meet you under the bridge. He's hankering after the chilled out, lazy days with his cousins back in the village. Nothing to bother anyone bar maybe getting drinks in the afternoon. You don't get the girl but you don't even need drugs in Jhelum. What the fuck were those aul ones on about?

By the time he gets to the traffic lights on the South Circular, both flakes and almost all the ice cream have disappeared and he finds himself switching off his phone – fuck her – and turning left, heading for home. Except it's not for home, and before he knows what he's doing, his hand is being shaken by smiling men who couldn't look happier to see him, and call him brother, and he's taking his shoes off, and he's padding across the thick turquoise carpet, staring straight ahead. Dhuhr prayer will be starting soon. He doesn't need to meet anyone else. He sits down, back against the wall.

Some kids come in with a ball and start to have a kickabout just inside the door. Maybe he should join them. Forget about it all. Just mess about like the old days.

'For your sake,' she had said, looking through her bag like there was nothing going on. 'Thought you were with your cousins,' she said. But he wasn't with his cousins. He was with the boys, she could see that. She fucken knows them all, no point pretending. Just standing there in the airport. When she'd passed, she could have turned back, come and said something to him but she didn't. Looked right through him, as if she's never seen him in her life.

'I love you,' she said. She said that a good bit now. But that time she said it while she was looking in her bag. Because she knew the cousins weren't there with them.

But he hadn't asked her directly. Hadn't articulated it, because what's the point? They're winning, beating you, as soon as you start asking questions. Needy is not something he is. 'Are we okay then?' she asked. Yeah, we're okay, he said. But no, it's not okay at all because she ghosted him in front of everyone. And she's making out like it was nothing and she's not saying why.

Haroon from fifth year walks in and smiles and waves at him. He should have started praying. Now here he comes.

– You okay? Haroon says. Haven't seen you in here in a long time. I'm carb-loading.

Hamza laughs despite himself. Haroon is the fat kid turned gym freak since he got into boxing. Looks like a bodybuilder now, except smiley.

– Wanna kickabout outside? Too warm in here, Haroon says, glancing at the rowdies fighting over the ball.

– Nah, just gonna sit here for a bit.

Haroon nods and gets up. Message received.

– You need anything, bro, just shout, yeah?

He grabs a Quran from the shelf, sits back down, and stares blankly at the opened pages. No one will bother him now.

An old man moves nearby. He can't remember the last time he came for Jummah even. And that's the best craic ever, Jummah sesh.

Once, for maybe five seconds. That's it. Once ever. It was the heat of the moment. After coming out of the hotel. He knew it was bad luck breaking into the Ami Garden fund. He knew it and he still did it. For one night out in that hotel in Blanch where no one knew them. And they were so careful. Him booking in on his own in the suit Ronnie lent him. Her arriving later. Meeting in the bar and sneaking her upstairs.

Maybe it was the sunny day next morning or maybe it was the two brekkies he'd ordered to the room for himself. And the way the girl who brought them looked at him and laughed. Whatever it was, he grabbed her hand. Fuck it. Why should anyone tell them what to do? But it was her who'd pulled away and said, better not, in case you're seen.

She's lying. Not lying, but not saying something important. And he's not saying something important too. And not saying things out is shite, wrecks your head. He should have just asked her straight out why she ghosted him at the airport. Shouldn't have made out that it wasn't that important, didn't matter all that much. It did matter.

He lifts his head just a little at the sound of someone quietly walking in front of him and the old man. Someone's going to be in deep shit. Socks and jeans, a young fella, walking straight towards the mimber. The old man sits up. The football kids pipe down a bit. Fair play, this takes some balls. The young fella grabs the mic and starts mumbling. The mic's not on, and Hamza strains to hear. He might be rapping. He doesn't recognize him but he's well enough dressed, not a full scald.

– Give us this day our daily bread ...

Oh fuck! Hamza holds in the laughter, but this one's going to be tough. The old man starts to rise, unsteady on his feet. Hamza reaches for him and holds his elbow. The young fella starts shouting out the words, loses his train of thought and starts shouting about Jesus being the only god, and everyone needing to bow down. Gotta hand it to him, whoever he is, this is a solid brave move. Two men walk past to join the old man who's nearly there. They smile and nod at the young fella but he's preaching to the unconverted and he holds the mic with one hand and raises the other, pointing at the ceiling. Probably saw that on some video.

– You've really got to go, one of the younger men says.

– This isn't good, the old man says over and over, shaking his head and fumbling his subha beads.

They've got it covered but it's probably best if Hamza shows a bit of brotherhood here, so he goes towards them and walks alongside, still trying not to laugh, as they usher the young fella out. He's gone quiet, all pink in the face as they block the doorway while he puts his shoes back on. And then they move him out all the way to the road with the boy kids open-mouthed but ready to laugh, and the girl kids copying their mothers' shocked and appalled faces as they come around the corner from the women's entrance.

Fuck it, he'll go. He'll go and see if she's still there, under the bridge. Thirty minutes late but it'll be like a test.

She's walking up and down in the cool dampness, tapping her phone, half panicked, half raging. She rushes at him when she sees him, waving the phone in the air, green eyes flashing, like she's been crying in temper.

– What the fuck, Hamza! What the fuck?! Where were you? Why didn't you answer your phone? I was freaking out.

– Mosque. Had it switched off.

She stops short of hugging him, takes a step back to look at him. Seeing through him. Weirdo. His weirdo.

– What's the flex about, Hamo? Feeling moody? I was seri-ously freaking out. Guess who I just saw?

– Your da?

She does her almost unnoticeable frown.

– You high? she says, half starting to laugh.

She runs her fingers through her hair.

– Right you're on some mosque buzz or something, I get it. Snitchy.

– Snitchy what?

– That lad Snitchy, the one who's missing. The one at the party with the poor Titch fella.

– I know who Snitchy is, everyone knows who Snitchy is.

He's trying to be cool with her, whatever mad shit she's on about.

– OK smartarse. Snitchy. I saw him just now. Well just now a half an hour ago when you should have been here.

– Not a hope that Snitchy would be round here. He's long gone one way or another.

– I'm not mental, Hamo. Swear to God, it was him.

– Where?

She hesitates.

– Round by Cork Street.

– Snitchy would never be seen around Cork Street. Why were you on Cork Street?

She's never round their way. Since her mum and her moved out to the fancy mansion in Rathfarnham, the only time he sees her is when she manages to get the keys of some of the gaffs her mum is looking after. Property management always seemed an unlikely career for Marian but he wasn't gonna query things when it provided free gaffs in the afternoons.

– Coming here.

– To under the bridge. Again.

– Yeah, and you left me here on my own and it's creepy after Titch.

– He was under the bridge in Inchicore. Some one just said something weird to me. Before I went to mosque. About you. About your family. You talk about your mum, and about Jack. You never talk about your da.

You'd expect her to flinch but no, quick as a flash:

– He's long gone. You know this shit, why are you being weird? He went to England before we did.

It is far-fetched. Deano's even talked about her da – a fat fuck whose famous trick was squeezing himself onto kids' tricycles. Those mad bitches in the shop have it arseways.

– Why are we meeting up anyway?

She looks relieved and smiles.

– Wanted to give you this, for the exams. Protection.

She pulls a small piece of fabric out of her pocket.

– A miraculous medal, she says. Me nanny gave it to me when I was born.

– Ah yeah, great for a fella like me.

– That's why I wrapped it up, so it won't burn your Muslamic skin, she says.

And she can't help starting to smile.

– Protects you from monsters.

– Exam monsters? he says, smiling and pulling at the front of her top to draw her closer.

– All monsters, Hamo, she says, pulling her head back just as he was diving in. People say things to protect themselves. Or other people. They mightn't always be true though. How's Deano doing?

He looks at her, confused.

– Deano's grand. What the hell? What mightn't be true?

What's all this cryptic shite? You're better getting things out in the open. Risk it. Be like the young fella in the mosque. A man. Ask her. Ask her and destroy everything now? After the exams. She leans in and long and slow, she tastes and smells and feels like she always does and there it is, straight away, the heat and throb. He grabs her shoulders, holding her away, ready. Hamza's not afraid of anything. Fucking ask. But there it is. In her eyes: don't.

When we saw the wounds of our country
appear on our skins,
we believed each word of the healers.
Besides, we remembered so many cures,
it seemed at any moment
all troubles would end, each wound heal completely.
That didn't happen: our ailments
were so many, so deep within us
that all diagnoses proved false, each remedy useless.
Now do whatever, follow each clue,
accuse whomever, as much as you will,
our bodies are still the same,
our wounds still open.
Now tell us what we should do,
you tell us how to heal these wounds.

23
KARL

There's nearly nothing left of school. And when you leave, that's it, no going back. Yeah, he'll be happy leaving. It's a hole. But still. Karl leans back against the wall, half shiny paint, half matt. Framed photos of hurling winners and science winners and bits of art from the actual art students line the corridor.

– What are you doing? one of the teachers, eyes popping, asks Deano as he comes out of the staff jacks.

– Taking a fat shite, Miss, Deano says. Haven't been able to take a shite during the day here for the past six years. Just leaving a part of myself for posterity now.

They don't even bother arguing, these days. What are they gonna do, suspend him?

They ramble out the way and Deano laughs that he's heading off to study. Karl heads for Portobello because he can't fucken face going home in case the cousin's there, lying around like a wanker. Oisín's already in the square, doing what he counts as skateboarding with some other fellas, but he stops and comes over and sits on the lock gate beside the swans with Karl, looking out at the water. The language school students, all sorts, stand around in groups, stop-start chatting to each other.

Oisín's quiet. Probably worried about the Leaving or sum.

– Guards came to the door last night, he says.

– Your door? What for?

– Just going door-to-door again, you know? About Titch and shit. But ...

He rubs at his nose.

– They came in. I asked them in.

And then he tells it, tells the whole thing. Snitchy in his mam's kitchen! But he didn't tell the guards that. Just said about seeing the shams on the street. But fuck the lot of them.

– So, yiz all knew this, even Benit, who can't keep his gob shut about anything? But not me, I didn't know?

– Telling you now. Fuck, Karlo, I'm wrecked here.

How can his mam be okay with this? Her and all her yoga and fancy bread shite.

– Anyone who knows could be in deep shit.

That's right. And now Karl knows.

– But no one else saw them, right? Only you.

– Yeah, Oisín says, hanging his head.

– And you've told them what they look like now? And you really didn't know them from around?

– Nope, never seen them before.

– Wait a minute, does Hamza know?

– You joking? Candy? With her ma all over Wino Nestor? Yeah, Karl, that'd be right.

Yeah and not just her ma either, by the looks of things at the airport that day. All cosied up, like a family business, importing Roma girls.

– I'm sick with it, Karlo. Know what I mean? I *was* sick with it. Now it's gone.

– Wait, was yer mam there when the guards arrived?

– Nah. Out at yoga with June.

That'd be right. Mindfulness of ignoring maybe dead young fellas.

– A carriage full of people went into the canal here, yeh know? Full of people. It's haunted, this lock.

Obsessed with hauntings, he is.

– A tour of all the places where people have drowned in the canal. Or died, or had bits of them dropped in, Oisín suggests.

Karl looks at him. He looks alright. Maybe even a bit better than he has been doing since Titch, since Boston.

– Ruairí didn't visit last night. First time in ages. Every night, it's been.

– It's you, you know? It's not Ruairí, Karl says. The púca-djinn.

Oisín says nothing but gets up and steps along the algae-covered walkway. He hops off the end and then he turns and smiles at Karl.

– Gotta get back to studying. This board won't skate itself.

He's got it in the bag. Music college, even though he coulda done almost anything else. And his mam doesn't mind as long as he's happy, she says. Easy to say when she knows he'll always have back up if things don't work out.

– Wanna go, Karl, come on, Oisín shouts over.

But Karl just smiles. Not likely. Ever. Although it'd help the snowboarding. He's changed the choices, secretly. Applied for the portfolio courses. Fuck it, how hard can his da come down on him?

Hamza appears, popping down to provide his services. Likely the last time. Proper shady for some fully grown adult to be feeding pills to school kids. Karl heaves himself off the lock and strolls back down the road with him.

– So, you and Candy okay then? Karl says, when Hamza finishes a grunty call that was obviously with her.

Seems seriously weird why anyone, but definitely Hamza, would put up with that crap. He gets it, Candy's special but come on.

– Yeah, all grand.

There's to be no more of this talk, by the looks of Hamza's face. If there's one thing Karl knows, it's when to shut up.

Strolling up ahead on Martin Street, Anto from fifth year is tunnelling in his nose and wiping the snot on the bricks of each house as he passes. Hamza and Karl look at each other.

– Ah jaze, that's rotten, Karlo says. Scumbag.

– Leaving his mark, Hamza says. He's only a kid.

– He's seventeen and Simone from the top landing is having a baby for him next month.

– You gonna study and shit? Karl says as they get to the gate at Hamza's gaff.

– You gonna lie around picking your hole, Karl? Hamza says.

Maybe that's exactly what Karl'll be doing. But something he definitely won't be doing is being a simp and getting himself dragged into all sorts.

– Yeh know the way Candy's mam and Wino? They're friendly like?

– Karl, fuck off now.

– Nah. Think you should just look out for yourself, yeh know? You and Candy. And her ma and Wino. I'm only saying, yeah? Looking out for yeh, bro.

Hamza's hands are in his pockets and he's staring hard at the ground. Karl takes a step away from him. Better safe than sorry an all.

– Remember the other week, I was away in my uncle's? We were in Blanch. In a hotel.

– Is your uncle into Blanch?

– Me and Candy.

– You didn't get married!

– Fucksake Karl.

– Sorry, yeah. What happened in anyway?

He's looking down, kicking the bottom of the railings.

– Nothing, just saying. She says she thinks she saw Snitchy. She's saying weird shit.

He never talks like this. Not about her. His best kept secret.

– Like Ois's djinn?

– No, in the flesh.

Hamza takes a few breaths. And when he looks up, he looks like he wants to talk more.

– Heading in, wanna come up, Karlo?

– Serious?

– Need a break from the studying, Hamza shouts back over his shoulder as he's staunching down the path. Wanna come up or what?

24
DEANO

They're alright. No one passed any remarks when himself and Dharma rocked up at the door of the house. Georgian and falling down.

Some lad has decks. They've got a load of empty drink bottles displayed on a shelf and a blue poster for some French film with a woman with huge lips and a smoke in her mouth. What is it with students and traffic cones? There's a keg, and someone passing out cups of beer. They've buckets with ice but he's not too sure about dumping his four cans of Karpackie in with all these students here. Everyone knows about students. Rob yeh blind, they will.

This crowd looks like they're up for a laugh in anyway. Someone's passing bumbles to a couple of mates in the corner. A skinny lad in a red Ché T-shirt has a word in Dharma's ear and she laughs and then asks Deano would he like some shrooms. Where's this fella getting shrooms this time of year? Must be a culchie. Culchies know all the spots.

– He freezes them, she says, reading his confused look.

June runs the freezer section like some big corporation. He'd never get away with tucking a few in the back. Good for him, the culchie lad, that he manages to store them up and not wallop into them himself. If Deano had a store of shrooms they wouldn't last too long. Yer man doesn't even want any money for them and he passes a little package to Dharma, and gives him a look that says he was thinking maybe of some payback at some point from Dharma but at this stage he needs to give Deano some too, to make sure that's in the bag. Yeh have to be wide to these fellas.

*

They're playing Oisín's type of music – guitars, bit shouty, then quiet and whingey.

Someone lights a joint and passes him a cup of beer. The green flame dances in the air, separate from the lighter itself, and he's saying, Oh, and the other four people standing around are saying Oh and Wow, and Dharma's going, Oooh, and they're still all watching the flame and the fella says:

– I need to stop this now. It's gotta go off, back with the fairies.

And he lets go of the lighter button and the flame just stays for a while, dancing there in the air and the four of them smile at each other, and when they look back it's starting to fade off into the ether but it doesn't just disappear.

He starts laughing and he can't stop.

There's holes in the walls and layers of whirly and flowery wallpaper, some of it stripped. One room upstairs is painted a dark blue. That's how yeh know the place is fancy, dark blue. They borrow a couple of bikes from the heap in the hallway and head off up O'Connell Street.

They race down the street the wrong way. People beep at them but it's fine, they can see everything, totally, everything.

And it's all so fucking funny. They pull in at the Spire and slump down.

– Do this, Dharma says sticking her face into her chest, giving herself a load of Jabba the Hutt chins.

– Ah here, he says. How's that even possible? Where'd you get all them chins? I want some.

And he sits down beside her, their heads against the cool metal.

– It's a phallus, yeh know. They'd Anna Livia here before, a woman, a river, Dublin's a woman. A cock I mean.

– I know what a phallus is, 'member we used to look up all the dirty words in your ma's dictionary? In Benit's place, there's a monster lizard yoke that stops rivers flowing.

– In the Poddle? I heard there's frogs that come up out of the drains. Didn't know there's a monster.

His lungs feel like they're going to burst through the sides of his ribcage, they're shaking so much with the laughter.

– Congo.

– Ah, right. Now we've got this huge shiny metal cock in the middle of the city anyway.

– Don't remember anything other than this being here. When was that here, olden times?

– Don't remember it either. It's gone ages. I've seen pictures of it, loadsa rubbish in the water. The hoor in the sewer she was called.

– What was it?

– A statue of a woman with stringy hair lying down in a fountain.

– That's cool, the hoor in the sewer. Was it better than this? I like this yoke.

He strains to look up at the top of the spike that's puncturing the sky.

– Wait, is that not down along the quays?

– What?

– The hoor?

– Oh yeah, they didn't kill her. Yeh can't kill Dublin.

*

They arrive back into the party, happier, laughier and start in on the Karpackie – miracle it's still there. The mushrooms have faded to a warm glow. Sitting along the river on the boardwalk with the dealers and the tourists and the homeless, and the sparkles on the water, it was perfect. And further down when they went looking for Anna Livia, the best thing ever: otters, playing at the base of the bridge. Universal consciousness, she said. They came out for us. Jumping in and climbing out and jumping in again. Like young fellas.

There's more than students here now. Tracksuits and a couple of swaglords.

A few of the students are doing hot knives in what counts as a kitchen and two of the lads give each other a blowback and then actually start wearing the faces off each other.

– They're not even gay I don't think, Dharma says. Sami and Johnny. They'd ride anything.

They offer some to himself and Dharma, and he's a bit reluctant cos there's no way he's getting tongued by these lads. Worse again if they expect to tongue Dharma. But maybe she's okay with that, and maybe what's okay by Dharma has to be okay by him. But no. No, he doesn't want that shite. They take turns drawing on the bottle but he stands between the two lads and Dharma. He feels her hand on the middle of his back, the heat. The lads don't make a dive for him. He must be giving the right vibes. If they start, what's he gonna do? He can't give them a dig in front of her. But the two of them walk off, the Sami fella ruffles Deano's hair as he passes, just for the craic. They head for two blue-drink-holding girls and they start on them. Maybe being a student'd be grand. If yeh didn't have to do what yeh were told all the time. It's not like school, Dharma'd said to him when they were looking at the otters.

Turns out none of them except Dharma and one other girl and one other fella are law students, the rest are architects or go to NCAD. Which explains a lot about the state of the place. That's where Karl needs to go, NCAD.

Dharma kinda disappears, and he sees her off in the corner, and then he sees her dancing. Fly paper strips hang from the ceiling with Caro smokes stuck to them. Some smart cunt had called and got sponsorship for a students' union event, someone told him, and they got money for the keg and there'd been wine and cheese earlier. The smokes weren't bad.

Dunno how long she's gone. Chats in the hallway. Bullshitting about some philosophy or some shit and she's nowhere to be seen until he pulls open the front door and finds her outside on the steps.

The icy air catches under his T-shirt as he pulls off his jacket to put it round her shivering shoulders. She sits, legs apart, head hanging between her thighs. She'll have to sober up a bit, because he's fucked if he's carrying her to James's Street.

– This ariss making me pissed. I sping like an angel. Love Enya, d'yew?

And she starts a high-pitched whine.

– Yep, that sounds like it's from heaven alright.

She lies down on the step and curls up into her fluffy brown coat. She looks like a teddy. A minute later she springs back to the legs-apart sit and hurls puke down between her feet and all over the steps, making sounds like an animal being crushed in a vice. So she's not perfect after all. It's not just the baldy back of her head.

And then they're walking along through Pimlico and she's weaving a bit still. There's running behind them, and two lads come racing down the street with shoe-boxes piled high in their arms. When they've passed he bends down and picks up a black lace-up leather shoe, size eleven, and hands it to her.

– I love it, she says, as she looks up at him with tears in her eyes, hugging the shoe to her chest.

She's looking rough. Her hair's sticking out everywhere and her eyeliner's smudged all over her face, but she's the greatest, standing there hugging her shoe.

And she is. Projectile puke or no projectile puke. She *is* perfect.

He realizes they've been looking at each other for ages, and next thing they're kissing. Slow and soft and warm.

*

The noise of traffic and kids squealing wakes him. He's surrounded by cement. The tubes in the playground. Head to toe in the tube. She doesn't like being squashed up to someone's face when she's sleeping, she'd said. It's gross. She needs space to breathe.

She's a sight, make-up and God knows what other kinds of crumby stuff all over her face. She spit washes her face with the sleeve of her jumper.

– Don't wanna worry yeh, she says, but there's a big shoe in here.

25
BENIT

Benit walks slowly out through the back archway onto Mill Street. A man with a career path. Feels good. Working on the Viking Splash, fixing up old gear, doing real stuff – like a dream. All those games of Operation are gonna pay off.

He'd got the handshake on the way out the door. 'First black fella we've had here,' the boss man said. The place was overrun with Chinesers and Filipino fellas in overalls, tinkering with bits of engines, going at the one big yellow Duck that was still in the shed. 'Great workers them fellas, the lot of them,' he said. 'When you walk out that door after the few years here, you'll be a proper mechanic, not like them boys down the road. Do you know why? Because you'll know how to fix things. Not replace, fix. The lost art of repair. See these Ducks? Reduce, reuse, recycle. Used in the war, now in Dublin, filled up with happy campers bobbing around in the Basin.'

Him and the boys went on the tour one time for the laugh. And it really was a laugh, slowly moving through the streets, roaring at people walking along, being a Viking.

He knocks in to Marty, who's flustered.

– Little bastards in the park stuck chewing gum in me hair, he says.

The perpetual war of Weaver Park.

– Can you show them to me? I'll sort them, Benit says.

– And make it worse? Pups, with no one to look after them.

He persuades Marty to go back across the road to the park, just for a walkthrough. The place is mobbed with skaters and kids who should be in school at this hour. Kyron and Truman are hammering and sawing away at one of the bigger trees that's managed to survive this long, and some of the skaters are having words.

– So you got the job? Have you told the Two-Cans fella yet? Marty says.

– Sent him a message but he hasn't read it.

– Fair play Johnny for putting you onto it. What you need now, Benit, is a nice girl. Best thing I ever did was lay down on the side of a hill with a girl from the Liberties. We all need a good woman.

– You're telling *me* this? Course I need a girl.

– And we all need men. A brotherhood. Yeh get that in the army, Benit. But it should be grand for men to love their pals without having to be killing other men while they're doing it. D'yeh get me, Benit? A brotherhood.

A brotherhood. Fair enough. Maybe not right here, right now though.

– No seats here, Marty says. That's the problem. No aul lads the likes of me about the place. Have yeh ever been to Spain, Benit? Old people, gather themselves on benches, take in the day. And keep order.

– The weather's better there.

– True enough but the weather's not so bad here. A lot of the rain's up here, Marty says, tapping his temple.

Oisín arrives, skateboard in hand.

– Well?

– Got it, fam. You're looking at a working man.

– Fucking class, Oisín says.

He tells the rest of the skaters, and they all come over and have the bants and offer him a smoke. Now he's gotta break the news to Fenella that he's not going to college at all. Fixing things, keeping things going, old things, that's what he's ready for. He can go anywhere with that training, Marty says. This could be anywhere. He turns his face up to the sun.

– There's no sign of them here at all, Marty says. But sure, isn't this grand? Help me down onto the grass there.

– Something happen, Marty? Oisín says.

– Little bollixes is what happened.

– Some scalds stuck chewing gum in his hair. They're not here though.

– I'm alive and sure, that's all yeh can ask for, Marty says.

Kyron sidles over.

– Sorry bout the gum, Benit.

And just like that, Oisín has him reefed away by the back of his jumper and is standing over him sticking his finger in his face. Then he's dragged back and forced to stand in front of Marty who's sitting with his legs at an awkward angle, trying to hold himself upright with no back support.

– Sorry Mister, Kyron says reluctantly.

– Never saw yeh in me life before, son, Marty says.

– You're a cunt Oisín, Kyron shouts back, as he's running away. Gonna get yeh.

– Yeah, yeh'll do nothing Kyron. Fuck off, Oisín says.

*

Hamza didn't want to rock down to Weaver, said he wanted to go Kimmage. Sundrive Park, Benit's second favourite running spot after the Phoenix Park.

The back of the bench is digging into his arse as he's waiting for him. He's home and dry, nothing to worry about, not a care in the world, job to go to no matter what happens with these stupid exams. He catches the top of his thumb with the knife blade as he's whittling a twig, and pulls out his first aid kit.

Hamza needs to take a break from studying, his message said, and to take his mind off the fact that he's starving. Two days to Eid. Never, ever, has he seen Hamza so strict. Wouldn't even go for the fry the other morning in June's and that was one not to be missed. That woman can cook a sausage like no one else. Man needs a time out.

– Candy's on her way down, Hamza says, as he approaches.

– Why did you ask me to come down if Candy's on her way?

– Cos you're bro, bro. What did you do to your hand?

– Blade slipped when I was making a spear. Looks worse than it is. Not deep. Just trying to find a plaster in here.

Benit smiles. So Candy's still in fashion. Hamza's let it go, the airport, obviously. Benit would have let it go too. The others are still chatting shit about it, apart from Karl, but you only get one chance at this life and Candy's Hamza's dream girl. That much is obvious. If a girl like Candy ghosted Benit, he'd be back in the saddle as soon as she called too.

A whole schoolful of parents and kids are spread out on the grass by the playground, on picnic blankets, passing around Tupperware. Some of the kids puck balls at each other and he wishes he'd brought his own hurl. A few parents are cracking open boxes of wine.

– If that was women from the flats with a slab of Dutch Gold … Hamza says.

They look happy, the families. After-school knacker-drinking though, dunno. There's no way Fenella'd ever go for that. But hey, Dublin in the sunshine, fam.

Benit's and Hamza's phones beep at the same time. In the group, wishing them luck for the Leaving:

Whacker:
doesnt matter how you do its what in your hearts warriors men finn macool soldiers and keep on hurling

Candy walks up slowly, looking fly, smiling. Benit's pleased to see that she's pleased to see Benit. Still has all the lashes and stuff but she's better. And she fist-bumps Benit.

– How's the studying going, Candy?
– Alright. Fecked for physics though.
– Me too, Benit laughs.
– Yeah, she's doing honours, fam, Hamza says.

Candy stretches out on the grass.

– How'd English go, Candy? Benit says. Hear you wanna be a writer.

She sits up and beams at Hamza.

– Aw, Hamo, you telling your friends about me?
– Yeah, and what? Hamo says, but he's smirking and looking at the ground like a sap.

He reaches down to hold her hand.

– Best place in the world, if you get the weather, Kimmage.

He's a new man. The place is filling up. A crowd of Arabs arrive and they stop at the gate to admire the young fellas stuffing a pony through the stop-start gate, some of them shoving its arse and others pulling on its reins. Never knew they could be so flexible. Mohammed's there. Benit hasn't seen him since the night of the party. Hamo hasn't either, as far as he knows. Although, Hamza's a bit of a snake when it comes to sloping off with these particular Arabs. Over the other side of the cycle track, what the hell?

– Hamo, here, is that Snitchy over there with that lad in the red tracksuits?

– Give up, Hamo says, keeping his eyes on Mo.

– Hi Mo, Candy says, but she's looking in the direction Benit's looking.

But no, must have been the sun in his eyes.

Mohammed flips up his glasses, sidles over to Candy.

– Hey sweetheart, he says, in that weird deep voice he puts on like a porn king, as he bends down to kiss her on both cheeks.

Hamza pretends he doesn't even notice or care.

– Hamo, Mohammed says, as he nods, then walks on to the next bench, his phone to his ear.

His crew hangs around between the two benches. They move a little bit away but not far enough. Candy knows some of the rest of them. Hamza gets up and goes over to them. Plaster on, Benit picks up his stick and gets on with his work. No harm being occupied when these lads are around.

Christina messages him:

Sista:
Fen is going mental here, says come home now to study.

Easy knowing Christina's got no exams. He leaves down his knife and the spear and writes back that he'll be home soon. Then she gets into slagging him about being thick and having to go to some kind of rehab thing after he finishes. Rich! He calls his mum and walks away over to a tree so they don't hear him as he softens her up. She yells down the phone at him but he tells her to listen, woman, it's all in hand. Relax.

Shouts behind him and he turns to find a full-on brawl. He can hear Candy screaming to stop, over and over. And Hamo's nowhere to be seen. Benit drops the phone and the bag at his feet and he's running. Candy screams:

– Benit! Benit! Help him.

He's aware of kids scattering and gawping from the playground and picnicking parents straining to see what's happening as he wades in, taking blows from all sides. Hamza's holding his own in the middle of it. The mass moves sideways and back, people break off and dive back in. Where did they all even come from? He catches an elbow in the nose and is stunned for a moment.

Someone's shouting, Knife! Knife! They stumble down the slope, crash into the fence of the cycle track, Benit losing his breath from the impact. The ball sheds more, and Benit's dragging fellas off, throwing them out. Hamza lands on Benit, who tries to prop him back up onto his feet. But he crumples, holding his belly.

Blood! Lots of it. Fellas scatter, Arabs, white fellas, up onto the hill, out the gates. Mohammed stumbles back towards them:

– What the fuck, fam? What the fuck, Hamo?

And then he's off and running.

Candy rushes to where Hamza's collapsed, cradles his head, rocking to and fro like a maniac. Benit reaches around for his bag, it's not here. He sees the Swiss Army knife on the ground, covered in blood, grabs it and is frozen for a moment, Candy rocking and staring at him with the knife in his hand. What the fuck! Stuck to the spot, blood on his hands, blood on his T-shirt. Blood, just blood. Sticky, sweet-smelling.

He charges across to the tree where he left the bag, throws the knife straight in. Bandages. Magic water. Bandages. Magic water.

Black tears pour down Candy's face and onto Hamza's beard. Two guards, a woman and man, drop beside them, ask their names, pull up Hamza's sticky T-shirt, revealing the small, dark holes.

– Right, Benny, Candy, the woman guard says, looking them in the eyes. What we're gonna do here is, we're gonna block these holes, right? Can you do that? Candy? Are you okay to do that?

Candy's nodding and sobbing. She's white as paper. Benit says:

– I'll block two. Big hands. I have water.

– Right, we'll leave the water for now. I'll keep pressure on this one, like this, look. Hard, press down. You hold his head, Candy, keep talking to him, yeah. Hamza, Hamza, you with us? It's a lovely day, isn't it? I'm Breege, this is Donal.

– Can you tell us what happened here, Benny? the Donal fella says. We'll get Hamza here sorted. He's a friend of yours?

– Yeah, the best, the best.

Hamza groans.

– That's a good sign, right? Right?

– Yes, it's great. Keep talking to him, Candy, Breege says.

Candy's leaning over, covering half his face with her hair, whispering all the time. Urdu, it sounds like.

And then there's guards everywhere, blocking the gates, hauling fellas back from all corners. People all around. Guards pushing them back.

And then Candy's hesitating before climbing into the ambulance, and she's got Benit's bag slung over her shoulder.

*

Over and over and over, telling the story in the squad car, back at the house, making a statement, telling his mother, telling Owen, telling Christina, Christina hugging him, Roman and Alex hugging him, sitting on his knee.

He's not allowed near him, not allowed in, and Sumera keeps texting. The boys arrive round and he tells and tells and tells until everyone's silent and waiting.

Breege and Donal, the guards, arrive at the door and are taken in, and offered all sorts. They're not even on duty, and they sit at the table with him and the boys. They've been with the family down at the hospital, and after they've left, Oisín says:

– They're not cunts.

Everyone says yeah, because they're not and they don't seem like the types to even search you.

– Did they take the bag as evidence? Karl says.

– What bag? Oisín says.

– His bag, his bird bag that the guards are always after. The bag.

– It's gone. Candy had it. She took it, Benit says.

The others look confused. Or wary.

– Has anyone talked to Candy in anyway? Deano says.

No one's talked to Candy. How would anyone talk to Candy? But yeah, someone should talk to Candy. No one has her number, and when they search the socials, she's gone. Nowhere to be seen. They haul in Christina, who's started on the vodka in her room and leaves the bottle down in the middle of the table as an offering. If ever there was a time when Fenella might tolerate this, it's now.

Of course, she has her number, and of course, she texts her, and she answers, but no, she's not at the hospital, and yes, she's desperate for news, the guards haven't told her much. She says to tell Benit to call her.

When he does, from the backyard, whispering, she tells him straight off that she has his bag. First thing she says. She's cool and calm, but her voice breaks when he tells her that Hamo's out of surgery and his dad says he's out of serious danger for now. By the time he gets back into the kitchen, the mood has changed.

– It was the Arabs. Fucken Mohammed and his crew, fucking yitnas. We should get a few boys together and go and sort them out. I fucking swear, Oisín says.

– Yeah, we can't just leave it. There's word it was over a scooter or sum, Karl says.

She has the bag. We need to meet asap, know what I mean? she said. Not really, not really but, yes.

Messages fly around in groups. Facebook and Insta posts crop up. Everyone who wasn't there knows what happened. A 'Justice for Hamza' group has already been set up. By who, no one knows. Word is, Mohammed and the rest are still being questioned. Oisín refuses to even look at the socials or even any news about it, but Karl does the necessary and shouts out the best bits.

– Blackrock College students being questioned, is Mo at Blackrock?

– No, Oisín says. Get off that yoke, it's all gonna be bullshit.

Thinking it over and it doesn't seem right to Benit.

– Mo came over when he saw him on the ground, he says. He was losing it.

– Oh wait here, Sultan's son, someone's saying here.

– Who's that supposed to be? Hamza or Mohammed? Deano says.

– Would you fucking quit, Karl? Oisín says, and jumps up and slaps the phone out of his hand.

*

Oisín's bedroom smells of soup. Benit's stomach's queasy.

– There's something I've gotta tell you, Benit says.

He claps his hands on top of his head as he paces up and down.

– What? About Hamza? Oisín says.

– I couldn't see. I don't know. But I had the knife.

Oisín just looks at him.

– What knife?

– It was in my hand. There was blood.

– Bro, what knife?

– My Swiss Army yoke, the one I got off Snitchy. I was messing with it down the park. Found it on the ground. After. And it was all bloody.

– You're going mental, bro, Oisín says. It's not like you stabbed Hamo. Come on.

Oisín seems so sure, sitting there on the bedroom floor but his body tightens, he pulls his legs close. There's fear in his eyes.

– Fucken shake yourself, Benit. It's not your fault for fuck's sake.

That's not good enough. Not good enough at all. It's not Oisín with the knife in his bag that Candy has. It's not Oisín with the blood on his hands and his fingers on the holes in Hamza.

– Speaking of Snitchy, I think I saw him there, Benit says. In the park, before Hamo.

– Come on Benit, he's hardly going to make an appearance round here, even if he isn't in a bin or a boghole somewhere. Mirage. You wouldn't be used to the hot weather.

*

The text comes in from Hamza's mum. Benit's allowed down to see him. Only him. Because he was there.

To see him lying there with tubes and bags and beeping things attached. It's not the same as Operation. Hamo looks like a hairy baby in the bed. Things taped to him. Nurses smile and squeeze his arm. Hamza's mum holds his hand and says:

– Fine, fine, he's going to be fine.

It's like a nursery rhyme, over and over, and he smiles and says yes, and Hamza's dad looks out the window with one hand in his pocket and the other holding prayer beads.

Sumera follows him out into the corridor and stalls him in the empty stairwell.

– I took the money. I've it hidden but you'll need to take it.

She looks a bit wild-eyed and mental but that's just the jihadi in her.

– Dunno what you're on about. Are you okay?

– Shut up, Benit. The box under his bed. There was four grand in it. I took it before they searched the place but they'll be back, and anyway Ami will find it in my room. I need you to take it.

– Thought he put it in the Credit Union?

356

– It's the Ritalin money, Benit. Don't be thick. Take the money and keep it safe. If they find the money, they won't even try to find who did this.

He's never in his life heard this many words out of her. He always assumed she was a bit of a nerd and a dope at the same time. And here she is, all Peaky.

*

– There were others there, Oisín, Candy says. White fellas, a couple of them in the middle of it.

– Who though? What were they doing with Mohammed's crew? Oisín says, looking at Benit who's pouring everyone a mug of Dubonnet on Karl's desk.

– Why'd you get mugs and not the glasses? I told you where they were, Karl says.

– Your cousin's kipping on the sofa, blocking the door to your mam's glass cabinet. I didn't want to wake him up.

Candy's edgy, perched on the edge of the bed, surrounded by the rest of them. Almost like the Candy in the church at Jack's funeral, a bit mental.

– Dunno who they were. Don't think they were with Mo. Thought it looked like Mo was trying to reef one of them out of it. I just saw they were white. There was a lot going on, yeh know? I know I saw them. And then he was bleeding and someone was shouting about the knife.

Her breathing's going funny. And she's always so cool.

– OK maybe. Remember you saw Snitchy that day, Benit? I saw Snitchy before that. I maybe know why they were there. Who sent them.

Benit doesn't know what kind of women's intuition shit this is. He'd convinced himself that he'd only imagined Snitchy. The sun in his eyes.

Deano's staring hard at Candy like she's mental.

– Fucken Snitchy?!

Benit looks at Oisín, who knocks back the Dubonnet.

– I can't be around. I've gotta go, she says.

– What do you mean you've got to go? Oisín says. Hamza's lying in intensive care, Candy.

– Do you think I don't know that? she says, with her bottom lip wobbling. It'll only be worse for him if I'm here. Karl settles down beside her.

– Be grand, Candy, he says, handing her a full mug. Are you going back home or what?

– Not home, no.

She stares straight at Deano and Deano stares straight at her. She does an almost unnoticeable nod at him and says:

– I only came to tell yiz that I'll be heading off and to give this to Hamza.

She holds out an envelope and Deano takes it off her.

Candy stays looking at him. This shit's getting too weird.

– Can we all just relax here, fam? Benit says.

– Candy says she needs to go, she needs to go, Deano says.

– She can't go anywhere, Oisín says. Have you told the guards about the fellas you saw in the middle of it, Candy?

She looks at the ground and says:

– Yeah, I have, right?

Deano gives Oisín a look.

– Need us to get you back outta here? Deano says.

– Yeah, Candy says. Maybe.

She doesn't get up though and Deano doesn't move. Some seriously awkward shit this.

– Give us more of that Dubonnet, Oisín, Benit says.

There's a thirst on him like he's never had. And he's been off drink altogether these days, apart from the odd glass with the Sunday dinner.

– I've to get down to Connolly.

– We'll get yeh a taxi.

Benit shifts on the floor.

– Got no money, fam.

She says she has money. Her mam sorted her out. But she's worried about getting in a cab. Never know who you'll get. Bit sketch.

– She's not getting a taxi. Is your fuckwit cousin's car here Karlo? Deano says. You drive?

Karl chokes on his drink.

– How the fuck am I meant to take his car. I haven't been driving this years.

Karl was pretty legendary back in the day, but this is outta nowhere.

– Sure you're like Lewis Hamilton, Deano says.

– 'Cept paler, Benit says.

– And fatter, Oisín says.

Karl's suddenly all energy.

– It's a banger. We won't need the keys. If we can slope out past him, he's probably stoned in anyway, he'll have it downstairs.

– Karlo's the best hotwirer the Liberties has ever seen, wait'll yeh see, Candy. He'll have us there in no time.

Immobilizers killed that career path.

– You're a hero, bro, Deano says, clapping him on the back. 'Mon, we'll get the car sorted. Youse follow us down.

– Will you two check outside for me, Oisín? Candy whispers to Benit and Oisín. See if there's anyone on the street or in cars or anything?

Right so, she looks proper scared now.

– Are you sure it wasn't Mohammed's lads? Oisín says.

– I'm telling you, it wasn't. Here Benit, before I forget.

She pulls the bird bag out of her holdall.

– I washed it and everything.

Outside, there's kids everywhere, shouts and roars and laughing from the green. Traffic moving and no sign of anyone weird. But then anyone around could be a problem. Benit wouldn't know.

– You gonna check your bag? Oisín says.

He hesitates, afraid to look. Knows that Candy wanted him to look straight away.

– Check the bag, Benit! You need to know if the knife's still in there, and if it's not, you need to know what she's done with it.

There's a waft of sweet fabric conditioner as he pulls the string, loosens the top and sticks his hand in, feels around. The condoms, the bandages, the water bottle even, all there. And then he finds it at the very bottom and pulls it out.

And it's black, folded up, clean. And he turns it over, holds it out, flat on his hand. And he feels sick.

Oisín leans closer, doesn't touch it.

– That's not your blade, bro. That's not fucking yours! Oisín says. How the fuck did you pick up his knife?

He stares at the knife. Not his at all. He's looking straight at Oisín but it's hard to understand what he's saying.

– See the holes? The little diamonds are missing … look, it's a love-heart.

Oisín grabs his other hand and runs Benit's index finger over the bumps and holes in the plastic on the blade. And he leans in and whispers:

– Snitchy. It's his.

– Blood, there was blood all over it. Just picked it up.

Benit dives back into his bag, feels everywhere. No other knife.

The cousin's shitty black Vauxhall Nova with the go-faster stripes down the side screeches to a halt down below them. No way has he insurance for that yoke.

– Go grab Candy, Benit.

Karl's reversing up and back when they arrive downstairs. Must be like riding a bike.

– That yer bird bag back, Benit? Karl says. C'mere, can yer ma not help yeh head off, Candy?

Candy, now squashed between Benit and Oisín in the back, gripping the holdall on her knees says:

– She is Karl. She just can't do … this is her helping.

– Drive, will yeh, Karl. Let's just get this done, Deano says.

It's the longest wait of Benit's life trying to turn onto Meath Street. What happened *his* knife? Why's she got Snitchy's knife? Now she's given it to him. Candy sinks low in the car and Karl takes it easy. He stalls only once. On O'Connell Bridge. He was nicknamed The Stig at thirteen.

People everywhere. Tourists and Dub Dubs, students and hippies, hipsters and nerds, blue hairs and Chinesers, Pakis and brothers. The air is thick, muggy. Karl's getting into his stride, elbow out the window. What beef did Snitchy have with Hamza? None.

They pull in on Amiens Street on double yellow lines.

– Here yeh go, Candy. Where's it yer getting the train to? Karl says, taxi driver style.

– Don't ask her that, Deano says. Jaze!

Benit feels his chest tighten and she grips his hand as she starts to move toward the door. If she's done something, she's not acting like she's done something bad. He climbs out to let her pass and she stands on the footpath for a moment beside him. The rest of them, the others, bar Karl, start to haul themselves out of the car awkwardly but she tells them not to bother, she's got to head now. She's got runners on and her hair tied back. No make-up. She looks like a different person. Younger than he ever remembers her looking. The holdall dwarfs her.

Deano's outta the car. He throws his arms around her and grunts:

– See yeh, Candy. Mind yerself, yeah? and jumps back into the passenger seat.

She turns, reaches up and gives Benit an awkward hug.

– Will you be alright? Know where you're going? he says, but he's not sure he really wants to know. He just wants her gone.

She pulls back and looks at him.

– Away.

– Right, yeah. See you soon then, Benit says.

– You won't, she says with a wave of her hand.

Back in the car, he turns to watch her as she crosses the road and heads into the train station.

They sit in silence for a moment. Then Oisín, rubbing his thighs, says:

– She had Benit's bag. There's a blade in it. Snitchy's knife. The one he had at Hamza's birthday. The one he blinged to give to his mam. The sparkles are gone but ...

– What the fuck are you on about? Deano says.

This is too much for Benit right now. His head needs to be got straight. Not some heavy shit.

– Candy gave Benit back the knife he picked up. Not his knife.

– Ah here, Karl says. You picked up a knife? *The* knife? What the fuck Benit? Yeh don't pick up the knife.

Really? Really, don't you? He rubs and rubs at his scalp.

– Next time his best mate is being stabbed, he'll check in with you, Karlo, yeah? Oisín says. He thought it was his fucking knife, Karl!

– So ..., Karl says. Snitchy's mam has a blinged-up knife ...

– Fucking hell! Snitchy was there, in the park, Benit saw him. Whatever shit he got himself into, Snitchy shanked Hamo.

There's silence again in the car as a screaming squad car and ambulance fly past.

– Get that fucken yoke outta this car, Deano says, quietly.

Karl drops his head onto the steering wheel then suddenly lifts up, pulls out into the traffic and puts the foot down. When the street widens, he pulls a U-ey, throwing Oisín on top of Benit in the back.

– Take it easy there, bro, Deano says. Where are you going?

– The Basin, we're fucking that yoke in.

26
KARL

– Lying there almost dead on that drip in the bed, Karl says.

– Fuck off. The drip's only fluids now.

Karl squeaks himself into the pink plastic-covered armchair.

– What else would be in a drip only fluids, Hamza, yeah? See they've called off the guards. You no longer at risk of being murdered?

– Seems not, Hamza grins, and then grimaces as he pulls himself up in the bed.

The smell's woegeous in here. Three other beds are occupied by aul fellas. All with tellies. None with headphones.

– Jaze Hamo, what's the story? A hospital shouldn't stink like this.

– Gangrene.

– What the fuck? This the North Pole explorers' ward or sum?

– Talk up, Hamza says, I can't hear you with the tellies.

All the windows are shut, the sweat's pouring down the back of his Fred Perry and sticking him to the seat. He drops to a complete whisper up close to Hamza's ear.

– Are they any further on with who, yeh know …

– Knifed me in the guts?

Karl's stomach lurches.

– Dunno. We won't talk about that here, right? Think we all know now though, yeah?

He still looks small in the bed. Skinny and sad when Karl woulda expected him to be a bit raging by now.

– Gonna say 'I told you so', Karl? Here's your opportunity.

– Not my style, buddy.

Karl's not in the business of being a prick, for a start. But in fairness, Karl had no idea that this kinda shit was gonna happen. He just has a personal policy of staying the fuck away from anyone and anything to do with shams like Wino. Getting yer hole, and even love and shit, is grand but come on.

– We gave her a hand out, Karl says.

– Yeah, I got the letter. So she's gone.

He smiles, but looks like he's in pain.

– So the guards know nuttin bout the actual stabbing like? Bout yeh know, Snitchy.

– Nothing they've told me.

– Might be best if it stays that way, Karl says.

– They'll be getting nothing from me.

– Is she really his, yeh know, *daughter*?

– Fucked if I know. Maybe. Maybe her mum just protecting her. Dunno if Candy even knows.

The Corrie theme tune blares out from opposite corners of the ward.

– How long more will yeh be in?

– Not long, I don't think. I've been moving about. They try to get you out as quick as possible.

He's pale, propped up on the pillows, a book of that poetry open on his legs.

Hamza says:
– Pull that curtain round a bit more, bro.

He stays kinda sideways to Hamza while he closes the curtain the whole way round. Trying to keep an eye on him. He's not himself at all. Missed all the major bits, wounds not that deep but it's like something's leaked outta him. When he turns to face him, Hamza's leaning back, head tilted, eyes closed. Jaze! His long black lashes look wet. Karl clears his throat and sits back down.

– Thanks, fam. Thanks for helping her.

– Yeah, grand yeah, no bother like. It was Deano really who was stepping up to help her.

– Yeah. He owes her.

– Does he?

– She got him left alone. Never mind, Hamza says and shuts his eyes.

That's that conversation over.

– Has she messaged yeh?

Hamza just turns his head from side to side. If the room wasn't so noisy with Mancs roaring the heads offa themselves from one direction, and some kinda lions or hippos riding or sum from the other, the silence would be deafening.

– Food still shite?

– Yeah, Ami brings in stuff. She was just bringing in shite lasagne and sambos. Didn't want to be too Paki, you know? I'd had enough by the tenth plastic cheese sambo. Now she's bringing in bits for the aul lads as well.

Ami. He never calls her Ami in front of them.

– Oh yeah, got anything on yeh now? Karl asks.

– Yeah, Hamza says, gesturing towards the locker. There's chapatis in foil and some biryani in that box on the bottom shelf, have some of that. But do not, do you hear me, Karlo, I'm serious, do not touch the box on the top shelf. That's saag for later.

What the hell is he doing with so much grub in here?

– This is gonna go off, bro, in the heat.

Hamza's lying back again, eyes closed.

– No it's not, Karlo. Spices.

– Ah yeah, it is. Yeh need a fridge.

– Touch that saag and you are a dead man, I swear.

– Yer ma have anything to say about Candy an all? How'd yeh explain all that?

– Keep your voice down. No, Karlo. I wouldn't still be here, like, if they knew about her. Said she was Benit's girl. Got in the ambulance by mistake. I was out of it. There were enough questions about that, being in the ambulance with her. Aunties and all.

– Fuck yeah. Course. Bet yer da has suspicions but.

–Yeah, he seems all relaxed but he'd have me on the first flight to Punjab if that ever got out. Can we not talk about this shit?

He's definitely getting better.

– You're done now then, innit? All of them done. The exams.

– Yep.

– Benit says you all left early.

– Nuttin left ta write.

A smile spreads across Hamza's face.

– Oisín?

– Nah, don't think so. Nah, he didn't leave any early, I don't think.

– You'll still get into that PLC anyway. You'll be fine. How about Deano? He says it's no problem. Think he passed?

Karl looks at him. His voice definitely went funny there.

– You OK?

For fucksake! The evening sunshine from the high window sneaks over the curtain and hits his face, and Karl sees them. Both sides. Like little diamonds at the corners of his eyes.

– Wanna see something? Hamza says.

He whips back the covers and pulls down his pyjamas.

366

– Have you ever seen the likes of that, Karlo? he says, looking down at his huge black-purple balls.

No, Karl has never seen the likes. He didn't know that balls could get that big without them actually bursting, and he starts to laugh.

– Nah, bro, never saw sum like that before. Will they stay that big? Not sayin anything but that's a lot of growth. That one on the left there looks like Benit's fist. Have yeh shown him these?

– Nah, don't wanna make him feel inferior, Hamza says. It was something they did during the surgery. Post-op balls. That one looks like a baldy purple baby's head, I think.

The tears look to be gone and he's covering his nads and his dressings back up.

– Seen Tanya recently?

– Nah, but seeing her later. Been busy with the Leaving, she has.

– You should stick with her. She's decent, Tanya. Dunno what she sees in you but she's decent, Hamza says, and he looks towards the window.

– She might be back, yeh know, your missus. She maybe needed a break from all that stuff.

Better hope she never comes back.

– She won't be back, Karlo. It's okay though. We don't need bitches, amirite? I am. Here, will you head off now? I'm knackered.

Karl rubs his head, ruffles his shiny blacks curls as he's leaving. Hamza's eyes stay closed but he murmurs:

– Fuck off, paedo.

*

The breeze is wrecking his hair. Brylcreem was not made for Irish weather. You think it's all smooth and slick-looking. And it is, it is all smooth and slick-looking. Neat on top, skinned

367

around the sides. Shiny and thick. But then you go out and it gets tossed about, and it just looks filthy and like you haven't washed it in years.

He shifts over on the rock. She's late as usual, but yeh don't mind when you can sit and watch the seals over on Dalkey Island, shiny in the sun. He could have died. You could have died, that's what he wants to say every time he sees Hamza. You could have died but you didn't. You're still here. You're still with us. With the boys. But he never says it and it hurts his throat not to say it. Right in the centre, a dull ache that clamps his teeth shut and gives him a headache between his eyebrows. And it's doing it now.

Titch in the water and in the fire. And Snitchy, fucking Snitchy. That's the worst bit. Karl's had good laughs with Snitchy. They all have. At Hamza's gaff even. And no one's gonna say anything because that's just the way it is. Because no one wants to end up like Hamza. Or worse.

– Boo, scumbag! she says, covering his eyes.

How the hell does she manage it every time, sneaking up on him?

– Are we getting in? Did you bring your gear?

Don't think so. Maybe he's not ready for Tanya viewing him just yet.

– Me bikini body's not up to scratch yet. Mid-July I'll be cooked and ready for eating. Didn't bring me stuff in anyway. You get in but.

There's a froth on every wave though and he wouldn't be getting in at the slipway where it's all churned up and throwing foam up into the park.

– Why we meeting out here then, if you're not swimming? Tanya says.

– Nice, innit?

– Yeah, nice, Tanya says, as she settles down beside him and throws her arm around his back and her head on his shoulder.

– All of that, Karlo. All of that for a few hours scribbling and now it's over. Six years gone in a few hours. All over until the results. And then it won't matter anymore. It's weird if you think about it.

– Yup.

Tanya coming to this late isn't her fault, but he could have told her this shite years ago.

– You still heading to Ibiza at the weekend then? Karl says.

– Yep. Wish you could come, Karlo.

He could have come, but what would he be doing over there with Tanya and all her friends?

– But I know, with Hamza and all that. I heard it was a racist thing. Some guys in Gonzaga said it was some complete Nazis. They were lying in wait, a whole gang of them. Some guys are organizing a vigil thing or a protest, I think.

– What are they protesting?

– Like racism or something. White supremacists.

– Ah right, fair enough.

– Yeah, I'll go if it's on. They're gonna march to the Dáil. You or Benit or someone could read out a message from Hamza, if he's still in a bad way by then. Imagine if he was able to do the speech himself! The guys mentioned a video link to the hospital and like, Hamza could have a BLM thing behind him or something …

– Not so sure …

– But like, I don't think there's the money for that but one of the Gonzaga guys' dads is a big doctor in that hospital, so it could be done some way, maybe. You should ask Hamza.

She's looking out at the sea and she's smiling and her eyes are sparkling. But oh fuck, Hamza would love this. He'd piss himself.

– I'll message him now about it. He'd a lovin to be involved in this, Karl says.

– Do you think he would? He'd do a speech or something?

– Oh yeah, no bother. Hamo would definitely be up for that.

– You laughing at me, Flats?

– Nope. Just texting Hamo here about it. Black Lives Matter, isn't it?

– Yeah, you're laughing at me. Racists can't get away with attacking and stabbing people because of the colour of their skin, you know? That's just wrong.

– Ah yeah, totally with you there. Might have been the colour of his dick was the problem though, more than anything else but yeh know … yeah, see here, Hamza's well up for it.

He shows her his phone where Hamza's said GET FUCKED.

She puts a sarky face on and says:

– Well, I think it's a good idea and the thing will happen anyway. Like a vigil for him but against racism generally.

– How many brown and black people do you know, Princess?

She doesn't even look at him but the corners of her mouth are quivering because she can't help but laugh at herself and this is what he likes most about her. She's not like the other yuppies. She knows this is funny.

– Lots.

– Hamza and Benit, is it? How many brown and black girls in your class?

He knows the answer to this and she knows he knows, so she just laughs.

– But you're down with the homies, am I right, Karlo?

Yeah, yeah, she is right. Because Karl is down with the homies and the brothers and the Pakis and the dealers and the losers and the fellas lying in pools of their own vomit. He's down with all a them and he's down with her too.

– I'm gonna go on that skiing trip with yeh this year, Tan. I've started saving again.

She claps her hands.

– Yay! For sure now? This coming winter?

– Yep.

– You won't be able to be working so much by then though, because you'll be working on your portfolio.

– Me da's been talking about me maybe going away. Maybe go do art somewhere else. Says there's more to life than Dublin. Thought he was all about the business studies.

– My friend Karlo, the international artist. She thumps his shoulder.

She's only messin, but yeah, it feels good to hear her say it. The friend bit and the artist bit. Imagine him an artist. From the flats an all. People will be expecting a street artist but he doesn't have time for that, although his tags were always the best. That spray-painting thing is just not his gig. His da brought home three big art books, left them on the coffee table, said nothing. They just appeared. He thought it was his mam who'd done it, and he thanked her for it when she was still in bed that morning, and his da said nothing and just finished up his tea and said he was heading out to work. Not a word. Picasso, Van Gogh and a big fat one, all in French about everything in the Musée d'Orsay, which is in Paris, he now knows.

– Maybe you could do fashion design. Imagine that!

– Gonna be a proper artist first. Gonna learn to paint properly. You know Banksy?

She rolls her eyes.

– Nah, Karlo, I've *never* heard of Banksy. Who is he? One of your artiste friends, is it?

– Yeah, he's me mate, lives on the downstairs landing. Anyway, he says something like, so many artists say they would die for their work but so few of them can be bothered to learn to draw for it. Something like that. *Wall and Piece*, the book, it's in that.

– I know, I got you that book for your birthday, asshole. I hear Candy's gone.

– So you did! Soz, buddy.

He lies back, stretches and draws in the blue sky with deep gulps of air.

– Ah, so you don't wanna talk about Candy. She was alright you know, I talked to her a few times at different gaffs. She was smart too.

– She's not dead. What's with the was?

– I know she's not dead. Or wait, actually, I don't know that. But I hope she's not, but with all the shit going on round your way, she could be. She's not, is she?

Well, he hopes to fuck not. And he wants this convo to stop right now because what's the point in coming all the way out here, miles away from everything and everyone, to start chatting shit about Candy and deaths and shit.

– Right, let's not talk about this. Do you think we could swim to the island?

She, medal-winning swimmer, probably could, but he's all about the floating, nothing about the action unless he's got a seal motivating him.

– Hold on, I'll look up the boat times. Why don't we do that, Karlo? Let's get off this island altogether, go to another one.

And yeah, that'd be nice. That'd be very nice. To get away from it all. Anywhere. To look back at the coast and the city and to be apart from it.

– I love you, Karlo, you know that, don't you?

– Yep, he says. Me too. You're a sap.

*

It's late when he gets back, but the sky's still light in one patch. Hamza says he loves autumn best, but what kind of a retard loves autumn more than this? Weaver is alive when he gets there. Masses of skaters are standing around the bowl and Oisín is sitting to the side with a group passing a huge joint around. He's already gone brown on his face and arms. Annoying fucker. The whir of the Garda helicopter is partially drowning out the roars of kids.

– Saw a load of squad cars and the armed fellas down the road there, Karl says, as he settles himself into a spot between Oisín and Marlon the rapper.

– The brothel, they're at that gaff, raiding it, Marlon says.

Marlon knows this shit cos Marlon is of the streets. Oisín says he's very good, but Karl can't understand a word he's saying when he's rapping until he does some slow bits.

– All over the news, Karlo, CAB hit some of Wino's gaffs. His sister's, I think, and other ones. Cars and shit. This morning. Where've you been? Oisín says.

– Far away. Did they lift Wino? Karl says.

– Nah, don't think so. Deano says he's not around, as far as he's heard.

– Spain, that's where they all are, says some long-haired hippy fella with a droopy moustache and mental bell bottoms.

You don't say, fella. Spain, is it? The posh lads coming here telling him the suss on Wino.

He didn't notice the scald arriving – Tech Fleece, hair stuck to one side of his head – but now that he's aware of him, he's pretty sure he's been sitting there on the low wall for a while. He spits into his hand.

– Fucker, look at me tooth, the fella says.

– Fuck, are you alright, bro, one of the skaters says, and they all seem to get up as one and go over to the man.

When Karl gets closer, he sees that the scald's hair is stuck with blood.

– You're pretty busted up, what happened? Karl says.

He's poking at a can of Karpackie, but it won't open.

– Me ex-bird called me over to the gaff in Sophia there. Her new fella was giving her gyp. She wanted me to come and take the kids in case things kicked off. Here, can one a youse open this, me fingers aren't working.

– Looks like they kicked off alright, Oisín says. You're fucked up, bro.

– Yeeeaah, he says. Fuck, the bastard was there when I arrived, and then she started having a go as well. He pulled a fucken knoife. A fucken knoife like. I gev him a few digs, but the two a them started on me. No joke, so it isn't.

He wobbles to a stand and looks down at his leg, rubbing the dark patch on his thigh.

– That his blood? Karl says.

– Nah, I think … he says. I think, hold on …

And he struggles with his belt and fly.

– He did! The cunt stabbed me!

Karl's seen stab wounds before, but the hole in this thigh, oozing dark liquid, is just too much to look at, and he turns away. Maybe it's the day away, out in the sun among the lovely gaffs, with a clean person with white, white teeth, that has him acting like a sap. Maybe there's just one too many horrible things. Maybe you have a quota and maybe Hamza's balls were Karl's final thing. Maybe he's maxed out.

When he turns back, the hippy is tying his T-shirt around the fella's thigh and all of the skaters are trying to give the fella money to get to the hospital, but he's having none of it. T-shirt bandaged, trousers back in place, he sits back down.

– Nah, jaze, be grand. Just open this tinny, yeah? Be grand.

He won't listen to any talk of needing to clean it and it needing stitches, so Oisín heads over to the Centra, and they all make him lie down while they hold his arms and pour the naggin of vodka over the hole. But the fella didn't flinch at all, just lay back smiling up at the stars that are just starting to show.

– Yeh can't see many stars with the city lights but they're out there, he says. Shooting stars tonight. A meteor storm. Wish upon a star, follow where you are …

He's singing now.

– Love that shong.

No matter how much persuading they do, this lad's not on for budging. Karl tells him that it'll get infected and that he could lose his leg, and the fella laughs, and says:

– Great, shure I'd get the disability then. Can't believe the cunt stabbed me an I didn't even notice.

He heads off eventually, telling them that he needs to sleep, and he'll look in the morning to see if it needs looking at.

– This is the Weaver life, am I right Karlo? Oisín says.

This is the way it is. Mickey, who's about twelve or so passes through the park at about midnight, a look of deep concentration on his face. Oisín bounces outta the bowl, flips his board into his hand and blocks the young fella's path.

– Where you going Mickey?

The young fella's got swag, North Face, looks like a fake.

– Oim sellin rock for Tommo.

Fucksake.

– Show us it, Oisín says.

Like an eejit, he pulls out the brown nugget. Oisín slaps it outta his hand and starts on at him about how he's gonna end up dead by the time he's sixteen, or locked up, and all of this is true, but Karlo pipes up:

– He can't just dump it. He's gotta deliver it now. Who's Tommo, in anyway?

– Scumquat who has the chungfellas selling for him, Oisín says.

But he relaxes and shakes his head.

– Go on then, Oisín says, and he picks up the rock and hands it back to Mickey. But I'm warning you Mickey, you've gotta quit this shit. Tommo doesn't give a shite about you. D'yeh hear me?

He sends him on his way.

Karl's a pragmatist – Hamza told him that. A pragmatist. There's nothing you can do when it's gone this far. His da was maybe right, maybe time to get away from this shit.

– Mickey's a good kid like, Oisin says, watching him run off down Cork Street.

– Apart from trying to stab Kenny with the screwdriver last week, one of the skaters says.

Oisín throws down his skateboard.

– Get up on that board, Karlo. You're dropping in.

27
DEANO

He pulls up and locks the bike to the railings, right beside the sign that tells him not to lock his bike to the railings, and steps back to eye the wheel again, as if it's suddenly going to get unbuckled. As a self-employed, yet somehow not quite self-employed person, he's responsible for his own equipment, apparently. That's in his contract. Not that he's seen his contract but whatever.

He drags the two bento boxes, one for himself, one for Oisín, out of his courier bag. It's rare enough that they get to go on a break at the same time, so this is a cause for sushi celebration. He was always dead set against eating raw shit, especially raw fish, but, turns out it's grand. And since he's living the productive life of a working man now that Oisín got him in there, he's gonna go full-on healthy. Reducing the smoking, nothing too chemical. Wearing the sunscreen the odd time.

He stretches out on the steps of MoLI and unties his shoelaces. A screech of brakes and the man himself has arrived.

– You parking up here? They'll take the bike off the rails if we're in the Green. I'll sit down here for a minute. Just nearly had a knock with some cunt in an Audi. I was almost fucking killed and he's out mouthing about his cunty car. Went over the handle bars …

Deano sits up, opens his eyes. Fuck, his hands are a mess and the back of his jacket is ripped. Oisín pulls up the jacket.

– Feels like my back is wrecked, is it wrecked?

The purple and blue is already starting to come up and a scaldy scarlet scrape runs from his shoulder blade down to the waistband of his tracksuits that he wears under his cargo shorts.

– It's a fucken mess, bro. You need to get that cleaned up.

– Guess how many people asked if I was alright? Guess. I'm there flat on my back, between a parked car and yer man's Audi, he nearly drove over my head like, and guess how many.

– Zero. None. Got yeh a bento box, yeah, sit down.

–You fucking genius. Can you believe that though? No one came near me. Coulda been dead.

Yeah, he can believe it, and Oisín can believe it too because he was at this craic weeks before he got Deano into the game.

– Was in Mackey and Simon's up there by the Black Church, Deano says.

– That mad fuck of a one, yeah? Snobby cunt. Thinks she's better than everyone.

– Yeah, her. Had a big list of drops and pick-ups come through while I was there. There's a new girl …

– Cutie? Oisín says, stuffing sushi into his gob with blackened and bloody fingers.

– Yeah. She's alright like. Tits a bit big for my liking.

– How can tits be too big, bro?

His voice is muffled from all the fish in his mouth.

– Like them a bit smaller than that. Any more than a handful is a waste.

– Any more than a mouthful.

– Yeah, spose. She's blondie too and …

– You like the darker version these days, yeah? Oisín says.

– I do, buddy. I do.

– A changed man, Oisín says, smiling. You're smashing that, right?

– What do you think?

This line of questioning is not Deano's kinda thing anymore. No, he doesn't wanna talk about smashing anyone anymore. And definitely not Dharma.

– It's great, I like it. This new you. You're like a family man or something. I was thinking about this idea …

– I'm telling me story yeah? So, I dropped and picked up from them, and yeh know the sofa over in the corner? Well, I go and sit down with the list to work out me route. I'm only sitting, maybe, max thirty seconds before I'm seeing the aul snobby bitch one having a word with the new girl, and then the new girl is standing in front of me, all nervous like. And then she asked me was I alright and could she help me. So I says, nah, yeh know, I'm just looking at me next route. And she stands there and she's getting awkward. So I says, aw wait, are you telling me to *leave*? And she just looks at me, and she looks like she wants to fucken die. So I says, it's alright, I'll leave then. I was only gonna be a few seconds but it's alright. No bother.

– Where was the cunt of a one?

– Standing behind the desk pretending she wasn't watching.

– Getting the new girl to do her dirty work for her. Shoulda taken a dirty shite on that fancy glass desk. That's what I woulda done.

– Nah bro, yeh woulden a shitein on the desk.

– Would.

– Nah.

Always with the bullshit about all the great standing up to dickheads he woulda done, Oisín. But yeah, he probably woulda said something to yer one. He never knows his place. But he woulden a shitein anywhere.

– What is it about the Black Church? If yeh walk around it three times ...

– Walk around it backwards, Deano says.

– Ah yeah, walk around it three times backwards, the devil appears and tries to take your soul isn't it?

– Same at Usher's Island, if yeh walk around the petrol station three times, a scald will appear and try to sell you rock, Deano says.

A knackbag bombs down the pavement, roaring out of him. A dark-haired young one has taken his begging place. She stands up, hands on hips. He'd only gone for piss, he says. He flings her bag across the street.

– Ah here, Oisín says. Yeh can't be doing that, man.

And up he gets and starts gathering her stuff for her. She accuses the knackbag of being a junkie. He accuses her of being a hoor. What looks like yer one's ma arrives and she joins in. Oisín holds them apart and Deano can't hear what he's saying quietly to them but the two women head off, shaking their heads.

– They gonna take turns? Deano says, when Oisín arrives back.

– Looks like. Or they'll arrive back with their fellas.

– Best thing I've ever done, this courier thing, Deano says. Out and about with the shams and scumbags and yuppies. Yesterday evening, I was sitting outside near Busáras, yeh know that green bit? Hadn't got a run to go to, counting down the minutes, and this full-on business-type woman comes out of the IFSC, sits down on a bench, pulls out a huge joint and lights up. Just sitting there in the middle of all this rush-hour traffic, runners, suit, everything.

Not long to go now to the results and then Oisín'll be off to college and that'll be the end of all this. Everything'll be over just when it's getting started. June's expecting an offer of a house down in Drimnagh and nearly all the flats have been cleared and they've even started work on the new road and the new houses.

– I'm thinking about keeping going. Not stopping, Oisín says.

Deano's phone rings. Can only be the one person left in the world who calls people. Fucked out her smart phone, got herself a burner. Driving me mad, she said. Totally addicted, she said. Yep, it's her.

– Take that, you know you want to.

– Nah, chillin with me homie, amn't I?

– Bitches blingin up yer trap phone?

Fuck he wants to answer it.

– Answer the fucken poor girl, will yeh?

Fuck, she's gone.

– I'll catch her after. You gone all romantic, yeh sap?

He is a big sap at the best of times in anyway. No lie.

– You're only sayin that cos you're all embarrassed cos you've got a girlfriend.

– She's not my girlfriend.

She is his girlfriend. But they haven't said she's his girl-friend. But she is his girlfriend. She better be. The phone starts beeping.

Dharma:
Fayrouz tonight, can we do a bit earlier?

Dharma:
Your mam has a thing.

Dharma:
Deano!!

Got it in her head it'd be a great idea for them to have dinner. Fayrouz is just round the corner, Deano. And they've no drink. And it's well cheap. And it'll be great. And yer mam's real into it, if you are.

Me:
K

– I tell you what, Oisín says, if I were you with the head on yeh, and a young one like Dharma showed any kinda interest in me, I'd be making sure that she was my girlfriend. But since she's not your girlfriend, you won't mind if I make some moves, right? Oisín says, straightening himself. Myself and Dharma, nice.

Deano looks around him. Anywhere but at Oisín. Change the subject. Act like you don't care at all. This is the man's way.

– What do yeh mean about keeping on going?

– Ah so, totally OK with you if I give it a lash with Dharma? Grand so.

– Yeh go near Dharma and I'll fuck yeh up, bro.

And that's all he wanted to hear. A little bit of hard man.

– Nice bitta road rage there. We should go, Oisín says.

Deano pops the last bit of fish in his mouth and lies back.

– What do you mean keep on going?

– Cycling. Just keep on. You and me, on the road.

– I'm not going down the country or shit.

– Nah, keep on working. On the road. Like warriors of the road. Cowboys or something.

– Yeh'd hardly get part-time when you're at college.

– Nah, I'm not sure that college thing's for me. Might defer or something. Dunno. I love it, yeh know. Just out here, like the Wild West.

– Will that not be a waste? Like just cycling around when you could be studying some brainy shit, Deano says, but he doesn't believe it.

Why would anyone not want to keep on doing this? Hanging with the Brazilians after work, playing minors at the weekends, Dharma in her shitty flat. If this was it for the rest of his life, he'd be a very happy man.

– I'm just thinking of it, Oisín says. Haven't decided. I'll see when the results come out.

– Better than what Hamza will be doing in anyway. Poor cunt. Had the chance of repeating in the Institute but decided no way, principles or some shite. Another year in Colmcille's would kill a lesser man but Hamza's made of tough stuff. No one should be that determined at eighteen. Proletariat this, equality that. Fucken eejit. Anything to stay off the subject of *her*. Not that Deano wants to talk or even think about her. Now that Hamo's not getting the ride, he's worse than ever. Got himself a commie hat an all.

– Deano, Oisín! a voice calls from a wheelchair rattling past being dragged by a pitbull.

One-legged Terry Groarke. That man's no skinny-minny either.

– Saw that dog take him up St Patrick's hill a couple of weeks ago, Oisín says. Where do you even get a dog like that? Its shoulders are as wide as mine.

– Mongolia or somewhere. Terry could be a courier with that yoke pulling him.

– The dog'd probably get a better contract. Laters, Oisín says, as he pushes off.

And he's gone back to base to pick up. And Deano heads towards the quays. There's that dark-haired cutie on reception in Donaldson's and she even gave him a smile last time he was in. He's spoken for but there's no harm looking. The cuties always go for you more if you've got a missus. Fact. Wino told him that one night, out of the blue, for no reason. Told him that's why he wore a wedding ring. Fanny magnet, Dean, he said. Fanny magnet.

Fucken dick.

*

383

– See lads? I can't get him to get up, June says, shaking her head. This is a disgrace, Deano. You've taken the day off work to head out for the day and now you're just lying in the bed. I'd be waiting meself until I got the results tomorrow before I'd be celebrating but sure, it's your choice. Sit down there and I'll bring yiz in a pot a tea. Deano!

As she bustles out into the tiny kitchen, Deano rolls his face into the pillow and Hamza kicks the end of the sofa and winces, holding his belly. Deano hisses at Hamza:

– Do not stay for food. I'll meet yiz down the end of the road in half an hour.

June sticks her head out into the main room.

– Hope yiz haven't eaten, I've a pile of grub here.

Hamza bites his lip and says:

– Nah June, parents are away. Got up late and there's nothing in the house.

– Oh OK, grand. Well, I've got some veggie sausages for you.

Hamza looks like he's gonna chuck up and Karl pipes up:

– June, if you've a good few of them sausages, I'll have some. Not the veggie ones, I mean.

He does a sorry face at Deano's one visible eye.

– Yeh can't resist the sausage can yeh? Deano says absent-mindedly, as he stumbles over to the bathroom, squeezing past the rest of them sitting around the table with his duvet wrapped around him.

He tries to hang the duvet up on the hook outside the door but after four attempts he gives up and leaves it in a heap at his feet.

– So what are yiz doing for the day then lads? June says, as she lays down oven trays of rashers, sausages, puddings and eggs, a plate of buttered sliced pan balancing on top.

– Ketchup?

– Do you have any hot sauce, June? Benit says.

– Course I do Benit, yiz got us all on the hot sauce. The twins are practically drinking it. Put hot sauce in the coddle when I had me back turned last night. Didn't they, Deano?

– Yeah, he says, reluctantly sitting back down on the sofa, watching the lads milling into the scran.

– Are you not having some, Deano? Karl says, spraying ketchup-covered crumbs all over the oilcloth.

– Ah, fuck yiz, alright, he says, as he gets up and grabs a fistful of sausages and slaps them onto a round of bread.

– Ah lads, he's in! Hamza says as he sticks a pile of pig and pretend pig onto a hot sauce-soaked slice of bread.

– Ramadan's well and truly over, bro, amirite? Oisín says, laughing.

– And Lent, Karl says.

– Lent? Lent's nothing, Hamza says. Lent's gay Ramadan.

– Oh shite, June, my mam gave me soda farls to bring. Oisin says. Will I get them out now for with this?

He starts rooting at the rucksack he left sitting on top of a pile of packed boxes stacked by the door, with 'Bed' and 'Toys' scrawled across them.

– None of that Nordie shite at my table, June says. Only messin. Keep them for the day if yiz are hungry. But tell her I said that, in anyway.

The whole place shakes and vibrates every now and again with the trucks and knocking equipment clearing the rubble of the last block they knocked.

– Might be the last brekkie we have here, June, Karl says.

– It will surely be the last one. Moving in in a week, hopefully. And I can't afford to be feeding yiz again in between. Yiz may go off down to Helen's for that.

*

They ramble down the road to Oisín's to pick up their bikes and head back up Donore Avenue on foot. Karl runs into the shop for supplies and the others wait, leaning on their saddles further up the road. A cement truck comes rumbling past the church behind a hoodied young fella with shades on, who's cycling slowly in the middle of the road ahead of it. Karl's Frankie.

He blocks the road like a tool. The driver bows the horn at him. Frankie, roaring all the fucks and threats out of him, picks up the bike and fires it at the front of the truck.

– Yer wrecking yer bike, Deano shouts over.

– Not his, probably, Benit says.

Karl danders up the road towards them, shoving bags of crisps and drinks into his backpack.

– What the fuck are yeh doing, Frankie, yeh lil bollix? he shouts. Get away from that truck.

– See you? I'm gonna fucken find you and I'm gonna fucken kill yeh, d'yeh hear me? Frankie shouts at the driver, and tears off down the road.

The big fella in the cab's laughing his head off. He winks at the rest of the lads as he's passing them and turns into the demolition site where the blocks used to be.

– Yeh need to have a man-to-man with that chungfella later, Karlo, Deano says. Let's go, it's getting late.

– I'm not in the mood for this at all boys, Karl says, throwing his leg over the bar of the bike.

– Yer such a lazy cunt, Karlo.

– Nice. Coulda got the DART but whatever.

*

– Hole in the Wall or Lion's Head? Hamza shouts forward to the others, as they pass by walkers and joggers and women pushing buggies along the front, the breeze cooling them.

Hamza will wanna go Hole in the Wall. Loves the place, hidden away, says it's like an island in the Indian Ocean.

– Sure we're out here to go Lion's Head, Karl says.

– I just wanna lie down on a beach, Hamza says. I'm not that fit, you know? The climb down?

– Here he goes, poor me, stab victim, Oisín shouts back from the front of the convoy.

Bit harsh.

– OK, yeah, I'll give it a go, Hamza says.

– One of us will go tight behind you, one in front, yeah? Deano says.

Leafy gardens, with high walls. You can't see them but you know they're nice, buried in there somewhere. Some woman got her head battered with a brick in one of these, June told him.

They pass through the forest of pines on the side of the slope, climb over the metal gate and head towards the cliff's edge. Ireland's Eye sits like an emerald in the sparkling blue, sheep grazing on it. Some Yanks are ahead of them, half-scrambling, half-slipping down the almost sheer rockface towards the concrete platform built with gelignite and sweat by some mad bastard poshie.

– She's gonna fall, the stupid fuck. Deano says, looking down at the group, gripping the rope that's pinned into the rock.

– Not in the mood for this, dealing with someone splattered on the rocks, Hamza mutters as he reverses into position to follow Deano.

– Oi, Missus, hold onto the bleedin rope, for fuck's sake, Deano shouts.

– There's no dope like a Yank dope, Hamza mutters.

The woman nods, gestures that she's heard Deano and grins.

– Don't bleedin run yer hands down it. Are you fucken stupah? Deano says to himself, shaking his head.

She's only gone and burned the fuck outta her hands when the five of them reach the bottom.

– Will I go over and see if her hands are alright? Benit says, rubbing his forehead in exasperation. I'd better.

Everyone knows he's loving this. Hasn't had the opportunity to play doctors in ages.

– Hope you've got the magic water with you, Deano calls after him.

Here it is in all its faded glory. Bits of seats are still dotted around and the coloured tiled outdoor jacks is still there. Pretty gross if you use it, but in fairness, if you're out here for any length of time, you're going to need to piss. Hopefully no one's shat in it. Jack brought them, their first time here. It was sunny that day too and they lay about, diving in and climbing out and drying off, until it got dark nearly. Just six Dub fellas, mates. And then they all went home and Jack went wherever.

They all strip off down to their trunks and lie on the hot concrete. All except Hamza, who keeps his T-shirt on.

– It's like being at the coast in the Punjab. Astola Island. Except freezing. Like Achill, remember? Bad idea, leaving twenty-five young fellas in that dorm. What did they think was going to happen?

Karl set the alarm off twice. They almost got kicked out. That's what happened.

Silence apart from the sound of a ship's horn, and then Benit says:

– You alright, fam?

– Yeah, why? Hamza says.

– Bit outta the blue is all, Karl says.

– Just thinking about other times. Before, Hamza says, rubbing his hands over his closed eyes. The last time we were here.

– Fuck them, Hamo, Oisín says. Fuck Snitchy and the rest of them. You're alright. Like, that's the main thing.

– Am I? Am I alright? I've got holes in me and my hand is gammy. And Jack's not here at all.

– The holes are closed up, Benit says. You're gonna be grand, fam.

– 'Mon, Hamo, let's dive in.

– Nah, I'm not getting in.

– Leave him, Deano says.

One by one, they get up and go to the platforms where the diving boards used to be. Hamza stays lying in the sun.

– He's not right, Oisín says to Deano, as they stand at the edge looking down at the crashing waves. It's all getting to him now because of the rest of us getting the results tomorrow.

– Yeh don't say, Doctor Oisín. You a shrink now, cos yeh went to Miss Hutchings a few times?

Oisín looks hurt.

– I'm only saying, we need to get him in the water.

– We saved him. If we hadn't saved Snitchy, Deano says.

– Yeah.

Karl comes bombing down the concrete platform, all his holy medals swinging, and floats past them out into the blue, gripping his legs, opening out into a sharp line just before hitting the water.

– Yeh fat fuck! Deano shouts after him.

– All that jiggling and then he can still do that, dunno how he does it, Oisín says as he and Deano look over the edge, waiting for Karl to surface.

– Cowardy shites, come on, Karl shouts.

Benit sails past them, lands out past Karl, and surfaces screaming at the cold.

– Probably boiling in there. Will we hold hands when we jump? Oisín says, and while Deano's telling him to get fucked, he backflips off, leaving him last, teetering on the edge.

The four of them tread water, letting their chattering teeth calm down. They push themselves away from the rocks and float on their backs, looking up at the clear sky.

– We're missing a soldier, Benit says.

Just as he says it, Deano points up.

– Look!

And there he is on the highest diving spot, the T-shirt still on, arms outstretched.

He swan dives into the dark water.

*

Hours pass, lost in this world away. The sound of wind and waves, gulls and goats in the distance is trancy. A waking dream. Deano doesn't know if he'll ever be able to peel himself off this warm concrete.

– Will I roll up? Oisín says. I've the end of the good American stuff from Elmond. I'm going straight edge but I'll roll for youse.

There's a chorus of nahs.

– You seeing Dharma tonight? Hamza asks Deano. She's sound. Doesn't even look like an Indian, doesn't have the head.

– What the fuck, Hamza? Doesn't have the head? Her da's Punjabi, same as yours, Oisín says.

– Indian Punjabi, you can always tell.

– Fucksake, Hamo. Bit racist, Oisín says.

Hamza yawns and stretches his arms above his head.

– You can tell just by looking. Same way any of you can tell the difference between a Dub and a culchie just by looking. Anyway, you seeing Dharma, Deano? Get fucked, Oisín.

– Nah, she's working, but she's coming out tomorrow night for a while. After youse all get yizzer results.

The round of protests from the rest of them is met with:

– I've told yiz I'm not and I'm not! Why would I wanna get them results?

– I should be getting mine, Hamza says.

Silence and Deano just stares out at the sea.

– I've got cuties on the continent, out there, waiting for me, Oisín says, after a while.

– Nah you don't, bro. Keep it real, Hamza says.

– Yeah I have. On Tinder, switched location. Tell you what, once yeh go on French Tinder you'll never go back. That's quality right there.

He's been getting the ride on Dub Tinder in anyway, recently. Benit said that's why he's not seeing the púca-djinn this past while, nothing like some sweet peng ting to sort the head out.

– A bird in the hand, but. Tinder's for scalds, Deano says.

– Marketing yourself. Purest capitalism, Hamza says.

– Why won't you go to the Institute, Hamo? It'd be more like college. You wouldn't have to wear a uniform or anything, Deano says, getting him off the most boring shite subject in the world.

– Ami was on to me about it last time I was round, Benit says. Telling me to talk to you.

– I'm not going to be in with a bunch of knobs.

– But you woulda been in UCD probably anyway, Oisín says. I wouldn't be going back to Colmcille's.

– I'm not going to the Institute because I won't take money from her.

The rest of them look at each other.

– Marian.

– Candy's ma Marian? No way! *That's* where the Institute money was coming from?

– Yeah, she arrived at the hospital. Said she was representing the community, they'd had a collection, wanted to pay the fees. Had to sit there listening to her bullshitting with my parents getting all excited.

Never mentioned a word about this before. Deano thought it was some government scheme for shanked young fellas.

– I'm not taking hush money from that slag, Hamza says.

Oisín lowers his voice:

– Maybe she just feels bad, Hamza. Wants to make amends and shit?

But there's no talking to him now and he doesn't even bother answering, he just rolls over and closes his eyes.

*

Winding their way back to the Liberties takes forever, sometimes cycling five abreast, sometimes in pairs, sometimes in a long string. The streets still giving off heat as the city winds down for the night.

When they come to a halt outside Weaver, he can't even be arsed suggesting going in for a smoke.

Benit's taking the long way home. Down the street, the lights turn on outside Sheedy's. The new hanging baskets have recently been watered and heavy drips rain down on the smokers outside, who hold out their hands every now and then, looking up at the sky. A car glides to a stop outside and an enormous gold tracksuit lumbers out of the driver's side. A much smaller man with black hair that lies over the collar of his camel-hair coat climbs out of the back of it. They shake hands and have words with a couple of the smokers. No one says anything. The moment seems to go on forever and then they're swallowed up by Sheedy's.

– What the actual fuck? How can he be back? Oisín says. You OK, Deano?

He shoulda been clipped or hiding forever.

– Course I'm OK. Why woulden I be? It's Hamo. You OK?

– Not my problem anymore, is he? Hamo says.

And he doesn't look scared but then he never looks scared. But he does look knackered and he does look sad.

– How can he keep getting away with it? Keeping coming back here? After Titch, Benit says.

Hamza, slumped over his handlebars, says:

– Because there's plenty who love him. Because he looks after his own.

He suddenly straightens himself and throws his arms around Deano's shoulders.

Hamza sighs, then grins.

– Don't give up on your dreams, Deano. You make sure you get the results, yeah? No messing, fam. I'll kill you if you don't.

– Sure, yeah, maybe, he calls after Hamza as he disappears down Donore Avenue.

Benit hops on his bike, thumps his heart three times and points at Deano, and then sails back down Cork Street. Karl leaves them with a fist-bump and turns up Marrowbone Lane.

The lights are on in June's flat when he and Oisín get there, showing the boxes piled up against the window, tipping the white lady statue on her side.

– Seriously, Deano, you not worried at all about him being back?

– Nope. Sure, he's nothing to do with me.

– I can't fucking believe he's just swaggering round town again.

– He's not, he's just in the Liberties.

– But they took all his cars and shit. And his Samurai swords.

– And his Elvis guitar.

– His Elvis guitar? Come on, Deano! Def Leppard or something.

He was laughing, but now he's frowning and he says:

– After Titch, yeh know?

Exhaustion's weighing him down, stinging his eyes.

– Doesn't matter, if it's not him, it'll be some other sham. Always someone. I'm wrecked, heading in.

– You coming in the morning? Seriously.

– I'll consider it. Knock in for me.

Acknowledgments

It took a city to raise this book, and I want to thank everyone as fully as possible but space is at a premium and everyone will get fed up. So thanks to … The Technical Team, the group of young fellas and girls who answered questions, recounted incidents, checked details with their Imam dads and their hard-pressed mams and let me bore them to death with my reading. Some of them just answered one or two questions. Some of them were in it for the long haul, around my table on the regular, plied with curry, coddle and bland white people's food. And the rest. Eventually, a few of them became the book's sensitivity readers. The Technical Team were: Mohammed Eraghubi, Moazam Ali, Sean Agbaje, Seán Cunningham, Tuán Birdy-Henrick, Christian Kazadi, Rado Dimitrov, Tommy Garland, Henna Redmond, Annaig Birdy, Ruairi Darcy, Odhran Darcy, Skye Atkinson, Dave Georgio, Alma Christmann, Finn Connolly, Haroon Hussain.

All of the staff on the creative writing team and my class-mates at UCD. Special thanks to those who had an extra influence: Anne Enright, Sebastian Barry, Lucy Collins, Gavin Corbett, Sinéad Gleeson, Justine Carberry and last but not least, the man who kicked my arse and shaped the very start of this book, the very brilliant and sound Declan Hughes. The biggest gift of the UCD Master's in Creative Writing – Liz Houchin.

The team at the Irish Writers Centre who took care of me and *Ravelling* since late 2019 when I got the fateful IWC Novel Fair call. Special thanks to Casia for all the coffee and chocolate Kimberleys and to Betty for being Betty.

The IWC led to The Lilliput Press. Lilliputians Antony, Sean, Bridget, Ruth, Dana, Enejda and Stephen – for their endless patience, endless care for books and their writers, end-less focus on doing the work of publishing mindfully, ethically and with love. There's one person without whose contribution there simply wouldn't be a book – a gift from Lilliput – editor Colm Farren. Thanks to him for every edit, every pretend argument, every bird photo, every story. He stitched the book together, took it apart and stitched it back better each time. I am proud and grateful to call him a friend. Niamh Dunphy – for her meticulous proofreading. Cover designer Graham Thew – for taking the boiling mass of my notions, for which I had only words, and turning them into something beautiful and perfect. All the wonderful authors who took the time to read and comment on my little book. Marianne Gunn O'Connor and Peter O'Connell – for always doing their best by me and *Ravelling*. Mia Mullarkey and Emmet and Rory at Sleeper Films – for all being cool AF.

Catherine Ann Cullen, Harry Browne, Ferdia Mac Anna, The3Percenters, Richard McAleavey, John Green, a load of teachers including Jim Darcy ('the baldy-headed goldfish') and Martin Kierans (the finest English teacher this country has ever known) – for leading me to believe I could write a bit. The Arts Council of Ireland – for consistently supporting my work throughout the past few years. Madeleine Keane – for always supporting me and other writers and books in so many ways. Martin Doyle, Nadine O'Regan, and Sarah Binchy – for helping me stay working in the world of books and writing.

My family, Annaig, Tuán, Lúmí and Mara. Swear to God, you are *all* my favourite! My dad who played cars with me every evening and took me to the library every Saturday for years in Dundalk. My mom who died in 2017 and who taught me at the earliest age to read and write and who never failed to stop on the way home in London to sit on a low wall to read the book she'd just got me because I couldn't wait. My sister, Emma, and brother-in-law Aaron – for everything. My cousins on the Birdy side: Fionula, Julie and Sandra and my cousins on the Purcell side: Siobhán and Sé – you all know why.

My various other cousins, aunties and uncles who always cheer me on, say the prayers and do the voodoo.

Annmarie McKenna, Lisa Shiels, Benie McGuinness, Kerry Whyte – for 40-odd years of craic and kindness. In various ways – listening, walking, Fibber's, carousing, politicking, organising, caking, culturing, eating, hugging, supporting, arguing – the following people have pulled me and *Ravelling* through the past few years: Helen Redmond, Judith Williams, Anne Hession, Rita Garland, Margaret Roddy, Katherine Duffy, Noel Collins, Claire Hennessy, Mark Corcoran, Frankie Gaffney, Alicia Beiro, Magi Gibson, Irene Coveney, Nathalie Cazaux, Paula Lonergan, Caroline Moreau, Sandrine Lacaule, Oonagh O'Toole, Jorinde Rolsma, Lauren Mackenzie, Karita Saar Cullen, Irene Kavanagh, Niamh McGarry, Geraldine Halpin, Ais Considine, Jacky McGrath, Sarah Anderson, Miriam Cotton, Bev Cotton, Helen Duignan, Petra Kindler, Jill Nesbitt, Deirdre Nuttall, Sinéad Fulcher, Colette Colfer, Tracy Dempsey, Stella O'Malley, Annaïg Riou, Xavier Louboutin, Jimmy Phillips, Mary Phillips, Paula Cregg, Ann Dempsey, Orla McAlinden, Ailish Faragher, Dave next door, Sinéad Hughes, Kevin Higgins, Sue Flamm, Anne Tannam, Jenny Jackson, Fearal Ó Glaisne, Ciara Byrne, Kirsten Farrelly, and Michelle Madden.

All the women in all the groups – the OG KCers, the Ladies' Soiréers, the Ladies' Luncheoners, the Culture Clubbers, the Nordies, the Women's Spacers. Everyone, past and present, in yoga. Everyone at Sophia. Everyone at Marlowe & Co. All at Casadh and Donore Community Drugs & Alcohol Team. And finally, from a long time ago, everyone in the cold store in Santry and the meatpackers in Ballymun.